THE SOUTHERN SORORITY OF SUPERSTITIOUS WITCHES

THE SOUTHERN SORORITY OF SUPERSTITIOUS WITCHES

A Novel

KATIE ORTIZ

alcove press

Published in the United States by Alcove Press, an imprint of The Quick Brown Fox & Company LLC.

Alcove Press and its logo are trademarks of The Quick Brown Fox & Company LLC.

Library of Congress Catalog-in-Publication data available upon request.

ISBN (hardcover): 979-8-89242-642-8
ISBN (paperback): 979-8-89242-643-5
ISBN (ebook): 979-8-89242-644-2

Cover design by Olivia Hintz

Printed in the United States.

www.alcovepress.com

Alcove Press
34 West 27th St., 10th Floor
New York, NY 10001

First Edition: October 2026

The authorized representative in the EU for product safety and compliance is eucomply OÜPärnu mnt 139b-14, 11317 Tallinn, Estonia, hello@eucompliancepartner.com, +33757690241

10 9 8 7 6 5 4 3 2 1

To all the women whose rights are debated
like theory and fears are treated like weakness.
Let your fear fuel you, and fight like hell.

Southern women are known for their
hospitality and honey-laced words.
Southern witches are not.
Down in the South, where the temperature
is closer to that of hell, one would expect the
witchcraft to be just as sinister.

Chapter One
Lucille

If a rat runs across your path,
you will be prosperous soon.

1870

Witchcraft didn't always require such a sacrifice. I usually only pricked my finger to get a few drops of blood. But, after months of the craft not working for me, I was willing to try anything. I touched the metal blade to the flesh of my palm and stretched my fingers wide. The sharp tip sliced into the taut skin as I dragged it across. My breath caught at the burning trail of pain it left behind.

Blood bubbled up and spilled over, staining the surrounding skin. I extended my shaking palm over the mixture of turpentine, herbs, and the severed rat's tail on the ground before me. Blood trickled from the wound as I squeezed my sweaty fingers. It dripped onto the small pile and ran through the crevices between ingredients, making a dark, almost black puddle in the dirt.

An unusual wind cut through the humidity of the Alabama summer heat. The corn stalks swayed around me and bent at such an angle I worried they might break. The cicadas' and bullfrogs' screams screeched louder, then went silent altogether. Eerily silent.

I sucked in a breath. This was it. This *had* to be it. The craft would work for me again. I had gathered everything it required: The Spirit, The Sacrifice, and The Superstition.

Without my permission, an image flashed in my mind. A lifeless body lying in my arms, caused by my own hands. By my own craft. My chest constricted, squeezing and twisting until no air remained. And just like that, the strange wind ceased. The wildlife resumed their usual cacophony of sounds. Stifling humidity returned with a vengeance and suffocated any excitement, and fear, that stirred in my belly.

I couldn't stay out here any longer lest someone notice my absence. Disassembling the pile before me, I wiped my blood-caked hands on my britches and threw the rat tail into the maze of corn stalks. With my boot, I rubbed the rest into the dirt, leaving no trace of what I'd done—or at least what I used to be able to do before that night. This had been the third time since then that I had tried to use the craft. Each time had been the same. What if it was gone for good?

My stomach sank as bells rang in the distance, and the faint sound of my name floated through the thick air.

"Shit." I scrambled to my feet. If Ma were here, she would've washed my mouth out, even now as an adult, to hear me use such language—though she'd whispered it under her breath plenty of times.

Sharp leaves scraped my skin, making small, bloody cuts as I ran through rows of corn. I barely felt them against my flesh, toughened over the years, like the hard shell of a boll weevil. As I burst through the last of the stalks my body collided with another. We both toppled to the ground. The sweet smell of the hay Marlow had been carrying filled the air. It floated like golden snow around us before scattering across the ground. If remnants of nature hadn't already covered my britches, they surely did now.

"Sorry, Miss Rockwell. I didn't see ya comin'," Marlow said as she collected as much of the fallen hay as possible.

"It was my fault. And I've told you, call me Lucille." I helped her gather hay as I got to my feet. "You need to bundle it tighter. It won't come loose as easily that way."

Marlow nodded as her posture went rigid. "I'm sorry, Ma'am. I'll be sure to do that next time."

"You've only been here for a few weeks." I shrugged. "It took me years to get the hang of it."

Marlow slumped, relaxing, but only slightly. "I'm not sure Mr. Rockwell feels the same." She squinted at the sun as she balanced the bundle of hay against her hip like a child.

Whether from having her own or raising a mistress's, I wasn't sure.

I snorted. "Pa doesn't feel many things."

Many things aside from dissatisfaction and anger.

He'd scoured the town and papers for months, searching for a more "suitable" worker to replace our last farmhand, whose name I could not force myself to even think anymore. I wasn't sure what had outraged him more: my actions that had led to needing a new farmhand or that the only one available within our budget was a woman.

"If you say so, Miss Ro—Lucille." Marlow wiped sweat from her forehead with her free hand and fanned herself. "You feel that wind earlier? Somethin' wasn't right about it. It's the middle of September. Ain't no wind ever do like that in the middle of September around here." She looked at the sky with scrunched eyebrows, bringing her free hand up to block the sun from her face.

I glanced around, acting as if I didn't know what she was talking about. I didn't need any more attention on my wrongdoings than what I'd already caused. "Must be a breeze coming from up north."

The bells repeated, as did the call of my name, louder this time.

Marlow looked toward the call. "There's a carriage out front. A suitor for ya, Miss?"

I wrinkled my nose. "I should hope not."

Marlow's thick, black eyebrows shot up into her hairline. "No men in town good enough for ya?"

I shook my head, then spat on the ground. The wet mucus beaded, refusing to mix with the red dirt around it. Its efforts were useless. The scorching heat would soon force it to evaporate into the thick, humid air either way.

"None I'd trust to pour piss out of a boot with the instructions written on the heel." I didn't mention I had once trusted a man, trusted him with much more than piss and a boot.

"Well, you're gonna have to trust a man some time or other. That's the only way this world works." Marlow adjusted the bundle of hay on her hip. Then, as if realizing she might have spoken out of turn, she nodded quickly. "Good day to ya, Miss Lucille."

She spun. The back of her neck glistened with sweat in the harsh sun as she returned to her tasks.

"Not in my world. Not anymore," I retorted.

Marlow was already gone, though. I frowned, but I couldn't be angry at the young farmhand. She'd surely experienced such a world in which men were the barrier we had to work through to accomplish even the smallest of feats. Or they were the force that plowed through us like a scythe during harvest season. Which is why I was determined not to let that world be my own.

I ran at the sound of my name again, heavier, angrier, demanding my presence. I sprinted around the old barn and through the cow pasture. The rancid scent hung thick in the air, made worse by roasting in the scorching sun. I didn't wrinkle my nose or hold my breath. I'd smelled it my whole life.

Roosters and hens crowed as I passed their coops, either asking for food or begging not to be food; I couldn't tell which.

Over the hill, a horse-drawn carriage gleamed in the sunlight. Its shiny, new exterior looked out of place beside our small farmhouse. Chipped paint, missing shingles, and half-fallen shutters appeared even more improper when reflected off the carriage's spotless black paint.

I slowed my pace as I neared our front porch, wiping dirt from my attire. I wrapped the cut on my palm with a hair ribbon. It helped me more that way than for its intended purpose, especially since I'd chopped my wheat-colored hair to my ears. Pa hadn't taken well to that either.

The wooden steps groaned beneath me as I bounded toward the front door. It burst open before I got to it, swinging hard and banging against the siding. The unfamiliar scent of musky cologne hit my nose. It certainly wasn't Pa's. He only wore the scents of manure, sweat, and alcohol. The latter more frequent since he returned from war.

"Lucille." Pa's dull blue eyes met mine with disapproval.

I wish I didn't see so much of myself in them; wished my eyes weren't almost identical.

"Where were you? What have you been doing?" He scanned the yard as if it showcased my latest transgression.

"Nothing. I was busy with my chores."

He squinted, no doubt wondering if he could trust anything that came out of my mouth. But what other choice did he have?

"You have a visitor," he grunted.

A visitor for me and not Pa? That must've ruffled his feathers. Even with that pleasant thought, it was still a surprise. Had I done something wrong that someone came to complain about? It wouldn't be the first time. And certainly not the last.

He opened the door wider before I could ask questions. A rather high-cotton-looking gentleman stood in the middle of our parlor, making the small space even smaller. Clearly, he wasn't from around here. Or if he was, he must have been able to afford more food than most from the strained look of his buttons barely hanging on by their gold thread.

Pa cleared his throat, and I jerked my head up. My lack of manners would earn me a scolding later, though the man had been staring at me, too, no doubt not used to seeing a woman in britches. I crossed my ankles in front of me and attempted my best curtsy, like a newborn calf stumbling to gain footing.

"Lucille Rockwell . . . Sir." I forced a smile.

"Pleased to meet you, Miss Rockwell. I'm Headmaster Sullivan from Brimham University." He reached forward with his meaty hand and snatched mine up. He pulled it in for a kiss, but grimaced at the sweat and dirt that layered my skin and opted for a pat instead.

"From Brimham University?" I slid my hand out of his grip.

Someone from the university was here to see *me*?

He repeated the university's name, more slowly this time, clearly misinterpreting my question as a lack of understanding. "I have an important opportunity I would like to discuss with you." He wiped his hands on his gold-threaded handkerchief as if he were wiping away the scarlet fever.

"Headmaster Sullivan, can I offer you a glass of iced sweet tea? Our maid makes the finest in the South," Pa interjected, never able to go too long without the conversation revolving around him.

I fought back a sigh.

He always drew attention to our maid, wanting everyone to know that the Rockwells could afford such luxuries. However, he wasn't wrong about Nina's talent for brewing the best beverages. She made tea so sweet one could practically taste the Southern hospitality infused within it. We could barely afford her, but we'd be damned if we didn't have Nina here to make tea when the weather outside felt like that of hell. No matter what it cost us.

Headmaster Sullivan accepted the offer. We all sat around the small parlor while glasses clinked in the kitchen. The space was modest, with exposed wood and forced ornamentation. Ma had always said the front of the house was meant for entertaining, but these rooms had rarely been used for it.

Unable to hold in my curiosity any longer, I blurted, "What's the nature of this opportunity?"

"Lucille, don't hasten the gentleman," Pa reprimanded, leaning forward in his armchair across from us. He still wore his mud-covered gaiters and, from the smell wafting from them, manure.

I bit my tongue, tasting copper.

Headmaster Sullivan cleared his throat. "Well, young . . ." His eyes roamed over my britches once more. ". . . lady, this opportunity is a once-in-a-lifetime endeavor. I thought it could never be done, but it seems the board of trustees thought otherwise."

His eyes grazed over Nina as she reached across to set his sweet tea on the small table in front of us. Before it could connect with the dark mahogany wood, the headmaster grabbed the already sweating beverage, lingering when their skin touched. Nina yanked her hand away from his as soon as the glass was in his beefy grip. He chugged half its contents in one gulp and wiped condensation from his thick upper lip.

Patience had never been a virtue of mine. My mind raced through the possibilities of his alleged "once-in-a-lifetime opportunity." I had sent applications to attend Brimham on a whim many times. Nothing had ever come from it before. I certainly didn't expect the headmaster himself to show up on our farm because of it now.

If it wasn't about the applications, it had better not be an invitation to some society ball they were hosting for women to meet eligible bachelors. That thought alone made me want to crow my head off like a hen being taken to the slaughterhouse. I might even throw my drink on him if it weren't such an atrocious waste of sweet tea.

The headmaster finally spoke. "Now, this is just a trial period of sorts, but for the first time in the state of Alabama, the university would like to offer women admission into Brimham University. Your application was chosen as one of only ten women selected. We wouldn't normally choose an applicant with such few prior academic credits. However, this is a rather unique situation and, thus, requires rather different criteria."

His voice droned on, fading to a dull hum. They accepted my application? Blood pounded in my ears from my fluttering heart. I could get a legitimate higher education, not just the podunk education I'd gotten at the schoolhouse when I was a girl. Though, I'd hardly even gotten that, since Pa's farm became a priority over anything else years ago, even before the war. I wouldn't know how to read if it weren't for . . . the previous farmhand. But I had dreamed of such a thing my whole life. Ma always said knowledge meant power, and power meant freedom, though she had never gotten either and had paid the price for it. I wouldn't end up like her. I had to get out of this memory-infested farm.

"You're inviting me to get a degree?" My voice dripped with disbelief.

Pa grunted before Headmaster Sullivan could respond. I hadn't told him I'd applied. He wouldn't have approved, and, from his squinted eyes burning holes in me now, he still didn't. My heart faltered like a moth with a broken wing.

"Lucille works here on the farm. Even though we Rockwells have plenty of servants—" Pa puffed out his chest, "—her help is still required."

The headmaster rubbed his fingers over his peach fuzz mustache beaded with sweat. I looked from one man to the other, hating how my future hung between them—an invisible tug-of-war with the fragile thread of my fate.

I readied myself to argue my case, but Headmaster Sullivan spoke up first. "Many of our students are from quite prestigious families. If your daughter were to marry one of them, I'd imagine that would inject a good amount of new monetary flow into your farm."

I clenched my fist. Of course, that would be the headmaster's selling point. Not my education. No, that wasn't nearly as important as money.

Pa's unimpressed expression didn't falter. He only grunted once more.

I opened my mouth to speak, but the headmaster beat me to it again.

"Not to mention their union would more than likely lead to an offspring, possibly an heir for your land." Headmaster Sullivan picked lint off his shoulder that I was sure wasn't there, as if he weren't talking about me as one would about breeding cattle.

Pa's eyebrows raised. Of course, he only cared about the possibility of what I could give him. What my *body* could give him. Pa looked me over like he was trying to tell a pile of fertilizer from plain ole shit. The corners of his mouth turned down. He undoubtedly remembered my last chance of procuring a spouse and its unfortunate demise.

"No man of prestige would marry her. This endeavor would be pointless."

I jumped up from the couch like a spring coiled tight with tension. "That's not—"

Headmaster Sullivan raised his hand, stopping me. I snapped my jaw shut, clenching hard enough to rattle my teeth.

"Well, I can see when my company is no longer welcome. I'll take my leave." He made a show of pushing himself off the couch.

My heart dropped into the pit of my stomach as he picked up his gold-tipped cane from the floor.

"I must hurry off to the Hamiltons' farm. I need to finalize my roster before sundown to secure a spot in the next newspaper print." Headmaster Sullivan straightened his hat, eyeing Pa.

"Newspaper print?" Pa shot from his seat. "For the Hamiltons?"

The headmaster continued to gather his things as if unaware of the interest he piqued or of the rivalry the two farms had. "Yes. Didn't I mention earlier that the paper would publish the candidates for this program? As well as their families and family businesses?" His lips curled upward around his words. He knew the meat he was dangling in front of the coyote's face.

"I don't believe you mentioned it," Pa said, no doubt picturing his farm on the pages of the newspaper instead of the Hamiltons', the attention it would gain. "On second thought, I think my Lucille would love to attend your university."

My mouth went dry as it fell open. If only the headmaster had mentioned the newsprint and the Hamiltons earlier.

Recovering, I asked again, "I'll get a degree?"

"Well, now, like I said, it's just a trial run for one semester and only the most general courses. We wouldn't want to overwhelm your mind too quickly." The headmaster smirked at Pa.

They both laughed.

Hilarious.

I clenched the sweating glass in my hand more tightly. My fingertips ached to be ripped open and spill blood for the craft. As I drank my sweet tea, I imagined the delight at watching their hands burn or the blood drain from their faces as they lost consciousness. Though, if my earlier failed attempt was any indicator, I doubted my crafting would work anyway, even if I could get away with it. Instead the two men sealed the deal of my future with a handshake, greedy smiles wrinkling their cheeks.

The cold beverage couldn't possibly extinguish the familiar rage from their belittlement and all-too-common view of women's incapable minds. Along with the last drops of the gold liquid, I swallowed down the words that threatened to spill over my tongue. They would only get me in trouble and result in another beating.

Or another death.

I certainly didn't need either. Thankfully, the cool liquid combined with my excitement for what was to come and coated my rage with honey and ice.

Chapter Two
Catherine

If your left ear is ringing, someone is talking ill of you.

The carriage jolted. My head nearly hit the ceiling.

"These damn potholes," Daddy grumbled. He straightened his top hat. "As much money as I pay this town, you would think they'd use some of it to fill the roads."

I stared out the window at the never-ending light of the scorching Alabama sun, not caring much about his money or how it was being spent unless I was the one it was being spent on.

"I've also paid a great deal of money to this university, and I expect you to uphold our fine reputation while there and get exceptional grades in your courses. Are you listening to me, Catherine?"

Daddy's mustache twisted upward at the ends, even though his lips nearly always twisted downward in a permanent state of discontent.

"I'm listening."

Mama's powdered makeup mixed with her sweat and ran down her chin as she fanned herself. "Grades are fine and dandy, but they won't get you what you *really* need."

I held my breath.

Oh, no. Here it comes. *Again.*

"This is the perfect opportunity for you to meet a respectable young man to marry. There are thirty-some-odd men and only ten women. They'll practically be lining up at y'all's doorstep."

Mama could hardly contain her excitement. Daddy grumbled, only worried about the dowry he'd have to pay. He'd already spent two for my sisters, and now that my younger sister was out in society, her dowry would surely present itself before mine.

Not for love, though. Never for love.

Memories tickled my mind at that thought, demanding my attention: the caress of soft skin and kisses stolen from one another. Kisses not entirely made of love, but certainly the closest we could come to love at such a young age. I squeezed my eyes shut and pushed them back into the deepest depths of my thoughts.

"This is perfect. These men won't even care that you're so . . ." Mama looked me up and down. "Healthy."

I winced. *Healthy.*

I knew what that meant in Southern hospitality-speak. Mama had never liked how I looked. I was bigger than my sisters from the day I was born, and now, as a woman, I certainly didn't lack curves. Add my bright copper-colored hair and freckles she'd tried to rub off with lemon juice until my skin was raw and blistered and I might as well have carved the frown lines into Mama's face with my own two hands.

"Just remember, Catherine Elizabeth . . ." When Mama used my full name, she was serious. Not that she was ever anything else. ". . . if this whole university thing doesn't work out—"

"Which it *should*," Daddy interjected. He checked his pocket watch and shifted his weight on the velvet cushions that lined the carriage's interior.

That fabric chafed the skin worse than my chemise.

Mama waved him off. "But if it *doesn't*, your third cousin, Frederick Baker, agreed to take your hand for necessity's sake. He's a very well-to-do gentleman."

I recoiled, scrunching my nose. Cousin Frederick was the furthest from what I would consider a gentleman. I'd heard the rumors and talk of the brothels he frequented and the servants who had mysteriously fallen pregnant while working for him, then promptly shipped far away. Between that and his ancient age, I couldn't be less willing to be his bride.

"Mama, he's old! I can't—"

"You can and you *will*, young lady." Mama squinted at me with her eyebrows raised and her lips pursed. A warning.

We came to an abrupt stop and lurched forward. I thrust my hand out in front of me to keep my face from connecting with the opposing wall then rushed out into the suffocating heat before the coachman could set down the carriage block. Our arrival couldn't have come at a better time.

"Miss Stanley, be careful now. I'd hate to have to sew up a tear in that new dress." Natalie stepped down from the coach box. The scent of carbolic soap followed her movements like a phantom wind of sanitation. Mama always said that's how you knew a good maid from a bad one.

"Nat, be a dear and fetch Catherine's luggage," Mama commanded with a flick of her wrist.

Natalie wiped her forehead and went to the back of the carriage. She let out a sigh as she looked at the pile of luggage. One would think I was here to stay for the rest of my life from the amount Mama packed for me. She had insisted on bringing all my finest dresses and prayed one of them would catch a man's attention.

The building before me was one of a dozen that made up Brimham University. It towered above us, with three arches plastered in different shades of red brick worn by weather and age. One of them housed an angry nest of wasps. They swarmed in and out of their makeshift home like soldiers guarding their own war-torn territory against enemy invasion.

I gulped. The building remained dark and ominous even with the sun's constant shining. The two windows at the top of the building were carved into the frame with stunning designs, but that did nothing to stop them from looking like eyes. Rust stains seeped down from them like tears. My legs stiffened, not wanting to carry me into the forlorn building, but Mama nudged me forward, regardless.

Inside, the air cooled slightly, but the humidity was thick, like trudging through fog. My chemise clung to my damp skin as we walked down the dark hall. Each mahogany wall housed a different portrait encased in gold-filigree frames. The portraits showcased one man after another. Each had different builds, hair colors, and eye colors, but they were all white and all men.

As we made our way into a spacious room at the back of the building, Headmaster Sullivan stood with another gangly man in front of a wall of shelves. Old books and encyclopedias filled each of its rows. Large, dark crown molding lined the top of the shelves and the rest of the olive-colored walls, one of which had three windows, spanning from floor to ceiling. Midday light poured through, bringing in the heat with it. Our bodies cast black shadows across the carpeted floor in its wake.

Chairs lined the center of the room, creating makeshift rows. Women had already filled most of the seats. It appeared that some of them were with their families and others were alone. I hadn't met the other women who would be attending the university, but it looked as if it were an interesting mix of attendees. There were a couple of high-cotton women, like myself, with tailored dresses and feathered hats. But there were also some who couldn't look more different. Regardless, the headmaster and the other man at the front of the room greeted us all as we came in.

"Reverend Ward." The man in robes introduced himself with a small bow. "Blessed to meet you." His eyes were sunken, and his long, sparse beard hung almost all the way to his belly.

I wasn't surprised to see a reverend here. Church and state weren't nearly as separate in the South as in our northern counterparts. It was merely two sides of the same coin, a coin that could be tossed in any direction and hit a steeple. Here, phrases like "God bless your heart" were used more often than not, though when said with a certain twang, meant entirely the opposite.

Daddy, Mama, and I found empty chairs in the middle of the room and sat down. I couldn't help shifting around on the uncomfortable seat as I lifted the back of my crinoline. The chair nearly didn't fit both my thighs and didn't even compete with the width of my rear. A rather loud groan echoed from the seat. Mama quickly shushed me and turned several shades of red as she forced a smile to stay on her face. The others snickered from behind me. My skin burned, no doubt turning crimson. With so many already staring, I didn't dare look to see who it was. My left ear didn't need to ring for me to surmise their words weren't of the friendly sort.

The headmaster cleared his throat, and all the chatter in the room died down to an unsettling silence. "Welcome all y'all to Brimham University. This fine establishment is our town's pride and joy. And thank you to Mr. Stanley—" he gestured to Daddy, "—for allowing his bank to generously donate to our academic funds."

Heads turned in our direction. I tried to sink deeper into my seat, but there wasn't any room.

Some of the men around us clapped. The same men I'd often seen in Daddy's cigar room before I'd gone with other ladies for our afternoon rest. The others only stared.

"Brimham University has been hosting fine young gentlemen in their pursuit of higher education since 1847, and now, 23 years later, we are opening our doors to women, thanks to our Board of Trustees." The corners of Headmaster Sullivan's lips turned down for only a second before springing back up. "Now, this is not a permanent arrangement just yet. This program is only a trial period before officially opening our doors to women. Consider it an experiment, so to speak."

Experiment? I didn't favor being compared to a test of science.

The others around the room didn't seem to feel as put off by the comparison. Most of them looked to be close to their twentieth year, like me, and were surrounded by parents or chaperones. Some of them, however, looked to be a few years my senior and were alone—without husbands. Mama would have a field day discussing them with her ladies' church league. Those ladies always disapproved of any woman older than myself who was unmarried. Even unmarried women of my age weren't looked upon particularly fondly.

And they didn't hesitate to let me know.

The reverend waved his hands while talking, making his black robe sway around his stick-figure body. "Though the Board has . . . persuaded us to this decision, I do not want you ladies to become overwhelmed during this endeavor. So, I will be on campus throughout this experiment to be your spiritual guide. Just as God pulled a rib from Adam's side to create Eve, so shall I take you under my wing to guard and protect your fragile minds from the temptations and trepidations of this world."

Fragile minds. The reverend sounded just like Daddy.

A snort came from a young woman in the row before mine. She had short, choppy, dark blonde hair, but that wasn't the only thing that made me gawk at the sight of her. She had on bloomers—actual bloomers—instead of a dress. Hadn't this woman heard of the ladies up north who had tried such foolish fashion? Hadn't she heard of the harassment and ridicule they'd received for such atrocious attire?

If the ladies' church league had a field day with the unmarried women, they would combust when they heard about this. I looked around to see if anyone else wore similar attire; no one did. A woman in the first row nodded vigorously and beamed brighter with every word the reverend spoke. She had the same sunken eyes and lanky figure as he. Her hair was in pin-tight curls underneath her bonnet, and she clutched a large Bible so tightly to her chest that her knuckles turned ghostly white.

The reverend's ivory square collar jostled with each of his movements as he continued to speak. The crucifix hung from it and sank into the hollow of his chest. "If at any point from now until the end of this semester at Christmas should you start to feel your mind is succumbing to hysteria or you cannot handle the weight of such knowledge being pushed on you, I beg of you to let me know, and we will stop the program immediately."

The headmaster's lips curled into a broader smile. "Oh yes, we certainly wouldn't want that to happen." He leaned back on his dark oak desk and crossed his arms over his chest.

The enthusiasm with which he said it made me wonder if that was precisely what he wanted. I pushed that thought aside as quickly as it had come, feeling silly I'd even considered it. He was a high-cotton gentleman like Daddy who only had our best interests at heart, of course.

A long, slender hand shot up in the air. It belonged to the bloomer-clad woman.

Headmaster Sullivan inhaled a long breath. "Yes, Miss Rockwell?"

"What do you mean by 'stop the program'? When would it start back up once stopped?" The woman's southern drawl was thick, even more so than mine or Mama's, her words were unrefined. More country than twang.

"Should you ladies need the program to stop, whether because of mental overload or behavioral demerits, there will be no starting it again." The headmaster's enthusiastic smile remained despite the negative connotation of his words. "If it fails, there is no second chance."

Miss Rockwell's hand shot up again. Headmaster Sullivan rolled his eyes, as if he had dealt with the woman before. "Yes?"

"What do you mean, behavioral demerits?"

"You may not be aware, Miss Rockwell, but on this campus and in society, certain rules and standards must be abided by. And if you cannot follow these rules, there are consequences."

"So, by breaking these rules," she stressed the last word, "we would no longer be allowed an education? Do the men of the campus never break such rules?"

That was a decent question. Though, I would have never asked such a thing out loud, especially with so many around to hear.

The headmaster coughed and sputtered on his spit for a few moments before regaining his composure. Another hand shot up in the crowd before he could answer the last question, though the person did not wait to be called on this time.

"What about other universities in Alabama? Will they allow this same opportunity for their town's female residents?" This voice didn't have as thick of a twang as Miss Rockwell's, but as with every southern woman, it was still there, dripping from her words like honey.

The headmaster wiped the thick layer of perspiration from his forehead with his handkerchief.

"That all depends on the success or failure of this program here at Brimham. We are testing it out for the entire state. If our program's attendees dwindle to half of its original participants, whether by choice or by expulsion, it will be canceled. For everyone. Statewide."

The room went silent, his words needing time to sink in.

Or down to the bottom of my stomach like lead.

"You mean, if we fail, no other woman in the entire state will be allowed a higher education?" I didn't have to look to know Miss Rockwell was speaking again.

"Well, there are always seminaries and women's colleges," Reverend Ward said.

Even I knew those weren't the same as a university. The programs were limited and didn't award degrees.

The weight of the journey we were all about to embark on weighed heavy in the air, heavier than the heat and humidity. We would take sole responsibility for the education and rights of every woman in our entire state. I may not have been one for education, even with all the tutors Daddy afforded me, but I wasn't sure if I wanted to be the deciding factor for the rest of the female population of Alabama. That was more responsibility than I'd ever had. An unfamiliar discomfort weighed on my shoulders and twisted in my stomach, but not as much discomfort as the thought of marrying old cousin Frederick, so I stayed put.

Anything would be better than the imprisonment of marriage to him.

THE BRIMHAM TRIBUNE (an excerpt)

Vol. 23—No. 1.

BRIMHAM UNIVERSITY TO BEGIN COEDUCATION TRIAL—FIRST OF ITS KIND IN ALABAMA

Brimham University has announced the launch of a trial coeducation program. It's the first in the state of Alabama. Until now, every college in the state has admitted only men. Should this effort prove successful, other institutions will follow.

The fall term will welcome ten young women, whose scholarship and conduct will determine the program's future. Headmaster Sullivan will oversee the trial alongside Reverend Ward.

The inaugural class includes Miss Josephine Ward; Miss Mary Ann Michelson; Miss Penelope Roberts; Miss Lucille Rockwell of Rockwell Farms; Miss Catherine Stanley, whose father has generously allowed Stanley Banking to support the college; Miss Victoria Woodhall; Miss Susan St. Clair; Miss Alice Paul; Miss Rebecca Ledbetter; and Miss Isabelle Keaton, whose father is also among the University's benefactors.

Separate accommodations and strict codes of conduct have been established to ensure propriety. All eyes now rest upon Brimham, as the success of this experiment may open Alabama's college doors to women for the first time.

Chapter Three

Victoria

Covering a mirror after a death will keep the spirit of the dead from haunting you.

The dormitories were much larger than the flophouse I had been living in. There, only the most essential living amenities had been stacked into one large room full of beds, if I was lucky—or mats on the floor if I wasn't. It hadn't been hard to fill my single luggage bag with my only belongings and lug them across town. In the dormitory, cobwebs filled the corners and dust covered every surface, but that didn't alter its magnitude in comparison to where I was before.

It must've been an office building in its prime before they had replaced the desks in each office with beds. The walls were discolored. Ghosts of framed certificates, corkboards, or timetables left lightened rectangles and nail holes scattered across them. Narrow squares indented the floorboards where desks had once sat. Now, beds took their places, with four posts and a thick, fluffy mattress stuffed with cornhusks and feathers. Most of the rooms had only two beds—not dozens, crammed together row by row. I walked down the dim hallway, looking at each one in awe. My eyes grew heavy at the sight of such comfort and the exhaustion that constantly weighed on them.

A room smaller than the others stood at the end of the long hall. The metal plate adorning its door had my name etched into it. The room was barely the size of a closet and had only one bed with little space left around it for walking.

It was a dream.

I threw my bag on the mattress. It sank in the middle. The blanket gathered in ripples. An oval mirror hung from the faded, floral-patterned wall adjacent to the bed. Light from the window reflected off it and across the dark floor like a phantom glow in the otherwise darkened room. Wear and rust marred its gold filigree edges. The reflection that stared back at me looked more skeletal than human. Midnight-black curls had fallen and stuck to sunken cheeks. Dark eyes rimmed with even darker circles made the rest of my magnolia complexion ghostly and pale. Maybe in a different life, I would've been pretty, but pretty wasn't something I had the freedom to worry about while trying to survive in this world.

I looked away, yanked the mirror off the wall, and slid it under the bed, careful not to break it. I certainly didn't need any more bad luck. A small set of wooden drawers rested at the foot of the iron bed frame. I filled one of them with my belongings, not caring enough to fold or organize anything. I wouldn't be here for long, anyway.

When the headmaster had entered the flophouse with university applications, I jumped on the opportunity he'd advertised. The thought of free board and food made my mouth salivate like a starved bobcat staring at a trapped rabbit. Not because I wanted to be here with all the other high-cotton women trying to get a higher education. I had already accepted my fate in society as a single woman who would work my life away in a factory or mill until I died. I was here because I had to escape that *particular* mill and flophouse, escape the girls within it and the memories that remained like ghosts. Living here without paying rent would afford me the time and privilege to save up money for a one-way ticket out of here.

The thought of *saving* money was foreign to me. Not because I didn't have the good sense to do so, but because it wasn't part of the reality of anyone living at those workhouses. Money was something we worked ourselves to exhaustion all week for, only to hand it over to our landlord for rent and a single slice of bread.

A shrill shriek pulled me from my thoughts. It echoed through the walls of the room beside me, so loud even I could hear it. Similar sounds from many months before invaded my mind, threatening to make the measly contents of my stomach come back up as they always did. I swallowed them back down, along with the memory. Peeking my head out my door, the red-headed woman whose wealthy father had apparently donated money to the school stood in the hallway with piles of bags scattered around her. She stared into the room in front of her with a look of horror. Her freckled skin was a deep shade of crimson, nearly matching her hair.

"These are our rooms?" the woman yelled, making her words easy for me to hear.

Her folks must've already taken their leave, or I'm sure her father would have paid for a larger room for her.

"They can't possibly expect us to stay in these . . . these . . . closets!"

The thump of footsteps trudged through my barely there hearing and into my consciousness as a group of men approached. Most of them wore clothes tailored to their war-torn bodies, if they were of a certain social class. If they weren't, their shirts and pant legs were merely rolled and pinned up to accommodate the absence of limbs. The war had marked its territory on our bodies just as much as it had on our land. Though I didn't have any outward wounds of my own, my hearing and lungs had suffered from hours spent working a loud, powered loom, inhaling the remnants of cotton in the air to make thousands of garments for the front lines.

A tall, broad-shouldered man stopped in front of us. A jagged scar ran like lightning from his chin, across his lips, and onto his left cheek. The rest of the men followed suit, like soldiers coming to attention. I watched the movement of his lips as they formed words.

"We've come to introduce ourselves." He smiled, and for a moment, he almost looked genuine.

A few of the other women in the hallway started to primp and preen, using their fingers to poof out their hair and pinch their cheeks.

Then, the corners of his mouth slithered like snakes into a grin. "But it looks like one of you has already gone into hysteria." The rest of the men mirrored his smirk and their shoulders shook with snickers I couldn't hear. "And here I thought we would have to get you kicked out ourselves. It looks like you don't even need our help."

He and the rest of the pack stared at us as if we were a meal. Or playthings.

These men were in our cohort? The men we would sit beside during our courses and lectures? Suddenly, I wasn't sure if this was the escape I had been looking for and hoped none of the garments I'd made during the war went to any of them.

The woman who'd been making the fuss flushed impossibly cadmium. Even though I didn't care for the woman, or any of them for that matter, I still had the urge to jump in and save her. I always had that urge. But I couldn't. I knew what would happen if I helped, if I let myself get too close and attached.

It wouldn't end well.

"Come on, Thomas. That is no way to make a first impression." One man at the back of the crowd hobbled forward on a cane. He had thick, dark hair and a well-fitted suit that hung limp where a leg should be.

"Oh, Henry. Don't be such a bore. We're only picking fun." Thomas's lips moved slyly around his words.

Henry retreated before he became the next target.

Just as I was about to turn away and flee to my new room, a blonde woman with trousers jumped in front of the redhead.

In an awfully thick southern accent, loud enough to be heard even by my ears, she said, "You can take your help and shove it right where the sun doesn't shine, and considering the sun shines everywhere around here, you better shove it pretty far up there."

Some of the men's mouths fell open. A few in the back, including Henry, laughed. Thomas snarled. His scarred face wrinkled up to his slicked-back, ash-blonde hair.

The trouser-clad woman didn't back down. She puffed out her chest and snarled back.

It was then that Headmaster Sullivan and Reverend Ward scurried down the hallway, though I only knew to look in their direction when everyone else turned their head, no doubt hearing the footsteps that I couldn't. The light from the open front doors behind them cast shadows as they approached. The darkness reached out before them like grasping claws.

"Now, Thomas, you know you aren't supposed to be in the ladies' dormitories." The headmaster shook his head disapprovingly at Thomas, though he seemed more concerned with the time on his gold-chained pocket watch.

"God would not approve of such close private proximities between the sexes," Reverend Ward added, fidgeting with his crucifix.

"We would hate to break any rules, sir." Thomas's persona switched faster than the needle on a loom. "We just wanted to stop by and give a good, hospitable welcome to these fine women and offer our help with their heavy bags. They mustn't exert themselves on the first day." He put on an expert performance, pretending to pick up the redhead's bags and bow to her and the other ladies standing around.

The blonde woman and I let out a snort at the same time. Our eyes met, and she nodded in greeting. I didn't nod back. Covering my mouth to stifle a fit of coughs, I turned around and shut the door behind me, shielding myself from everyone in the hallway.

Or perhaps it was shielding them from me.

Chapter Four
Lucille

Plug fennel into the keyhole of a door to ward off evil spirits from entering a new home.

After that cad Thomas left, followed by his pack of equally displeasing friends, Headmaster Sullivan and Reverend Ward weren't far behind them.

The woman who had caused the whole commotion to begin with approached me. Her face remained seven shades of ruby—so red she was surely second in color only to the devil himself.

"Thank you for helping me." She eyed her small hands, made up of rounded knuckles and stubby fingers. "I do greatly appreciate it."

I shrugged. "It was nothing."

"I'm Catherine." She smiled, her emerald eyes met my blue-gray ones for the first time, and she curtsied.

"Lucille." I didn't attempt a curtsy. None of those women needed to be subjected to that atrocity. They had already been through enough for one afternoon.

Catherine examined the room in front of us. Her nose scrunched. "It looks like we are to be roommates." She nodded to the nameplates on the door.

Of course, the headmaster would pair us with the most unlikely roommates—a rich banker's daughter with a lowly farmer's daughter.

At least I didn't get paired with the Reverend's daughter, or I would've been saying a few choice words to the damn headmaster.

"Alright."

Her smile spread from cheek to freckled cheek, making her eyes crinkle. She skipped forward, dragging one of her many bags with her and dumping all her things out onto the bed to the right. The rest of the women followed suit, introducing themselves to their assigned roommates, whether they liked the match or not.

As the sky turned from cotton bright to blackberry dark we made our way into the hall. It started with Catherine and me, then two other girls followed, and two more, until everyone gathered together, wearing nightgowns and robes. We sat with our backs against the diamond-patterned walls, and our legs stretched across the green carpeted floor. To my surprise, after several minutes of chatting with one another, they began to open up and let their down their guards—built on societal expectations and manners—ever so slightly.

"I've been a laundress since I can remember." Susan chewed on her nails as she talked, her white-blonde hair falling over her face. Her words came out muffled around bleeding nail beds. "Of course, my brothers had jobs that paid much more. But two of them died in the war, and the other came back with only one arm and one leg intact. From then on, everyone in our house had to work for income. Even my little sister. She's only in her ninth year."

Everyone nodded with sympathetic eyes and sad-turned lips. Catherine hugged a pillow to her chest. I thought she had wiped a tear from her eye, but I couldn't be sure, with only candlelight flickering around us.

"Her ninth year," Rebecca repeated, staring at the wall across from her. Her black-haired head laid back against the wall. "It's the same with us. I laundered as well but for the west side of town. The working people there needed it more than the rest. Their clothes always need a double wash to get all the dirt and grime out of them from their long hours out in the fields, yet they get paid half as much. And that's for the men. The women get paid half of that."

Alice's black, tightly coiled ringlets fell in front of her chestnut eyes as she nodded. "Everyone knows the west-side residents don't get paid nearly as much as the rest."

"Is that why y'all came here?" Isabelle's pale cheeks turned red. She was a lot like Catherine, came from a wealthy family and never worked a day in her life.

"Well, of course, but it's more than that, too." Alice hugged her bronze knees to her chest.

I hummed as I tied a knot in the bottom of my nightgown, closing it off between my knees, and slung my legs up on the wall in front of me. I rested my back against the scratchy carpet. There certainly was more. My imagination conjured an image of my name under the title of the university newspaper.

Lucille Rockwell—head writer and reporter.

"What else is it about?" Catherine pressed her chin into her pillow.

Only her eyes shone above its embroidered fabric and beaded edges. The pillow alone no doubt cost more than all of my belongings combined.

Rebecca, Susan, Alice, and I all chimed in.

"Getting greater and more equal opportunities."

"Having better jobs and income."

"Gaining more knowledge and self-awareness."

"Broadening your horizons. Learning ideas that differ from your own. Meeting people from different places, different cultures, different backgrounds. I mean, look at us already." Alice gestured to everyone in the hallway. "When, out in the real world, would this group of women interact? Rich and poor. Black and white. Working class and high class. Women from different lifestyles who have different ideals and morals."

"Different morals, alright." Josephine scoffed. Her bible clutched to her chest where she stood. She had refused to sit down with the rest of us but had lingered silently until now. Mary Ann and Penelope stood by her side, peering down at us.

Josephine's silence until this point had surprised me. She'd expressed her opinions plenty while we'd been moving in.

"You women should be ashamed of yourselves. First, for exposing yourselves as you are." She gestured to our nightgowns, which she had also refused to comply with, still wearing her day dress and bonnet. The style had been out of fashion since the past decade, although the South seemed to always be behind the rest of the world in most things, fashion was no exception.

"And secondly, for talking so ill of our town. This is a holy town. My father, the reverend, has seen to that himself. Things are the way they are because that is what God sees fit. And God's will shall always be done." Josephine huffed.

Mary Ann and Penelope stood by her side, mimicked her sneer, like puppets with either of Josephine's hands shoved up their rears.

"Will be done," Rebecca repeated, then asked, "If you don't want the world to change or for women to have more opportunity, then why are you here, Josephine?"

"I'm here to support my father, the reverend, and spread the word of God to people like you."

Her two puppets nodded their heads beside her. They clutched identical bibles.

"Why don't you spread that somewhere the sun doesn't shine?" I rolled my head to the side to give her a good wink before staring back up at the ceiling, splotched with mold and water damage.

Josephine and her two puppets gasped. She spun around, and they followed as they marched back to their rooms.

They slammed their doors, rattling the walls. The raven-headed woman from earlier, Victoria, stood against the door frame of her lone room. Half of her frail body hid behind it. Her lips set in a smirk from my interaction with Josephine. As soon as her dark eyes drifted to mine, she inched back into her room. Her ivory skin disappeared into the darkness, and her door shut completely.

"Well, Josephine certainly isn't too pleasant." Susan grinned around her now almost-skinless fingertips. What did she chew on when those were bloody and bare?

"Yeah, and neither were those men earlier." Isabelle wrinkled her nose, her voice high-pitched but somehow small, too, like a rodent.

"I just don't understand why Thomas and the rest of the boys were so mean. They don't even know us," Catherine huffed. She rolled onto her side and rested her head on her fancy pillow.

Isabelle nodded vigorously. Her straight, brunette hair shimmied around her heart-shaped face. "Especially to ladies like us."

"Exactly. They're supposed to be gentlemen, are they not?" Catherine adjusted her weight. The floor creaked under her.

Alice, Rebecca, and I snorted at her question. The candles' flickering light danced on our faces, sinking our cheeks and darkening our eyes.

Creating a hallway of skeletons.

"Oh, please, have you ever been around a man?" Alice asked the distraught pair. She leaned forward, stretched her arms to her toes, then melted back against the wall.

"Your wealthy pa's don't count," I argued.

"Don't count." Rebecca repeated, then chimed, "Neither do your brothers or cousins or anyone else in your immediate families."

A copper curl escaped Catherine's braid and fell over her reddening cheeks. She didn't respond. Neither did Isabelle, but they didn't have to. We all knew what their answer would be if they had.

Shadows crept and crawled along the surrounding walls. They darkened our underbellies and contorted our features. Made corners a home for unseen creatures and the ground where we lay a chasm of midnight ink.

"That's what I thought," Alice said. "Thomas is just a glimpse of what men in the real world are like."

The shadow-filled hallway went silent. Distant, soft snores floated from Josephine's room. I stared into the gloomy depths of the hall. Victoria's door opened a crack once more. A pair of eyes watched us.

I opened my mouth to call out an invitation, not sure why anyone would want to be alone when there were so many people to be around, but as soon as the dark, beetle-like eyes set in ivory skin met mine, the crack disappeared again, and the door closed. This time, for good.

The next morning, I awoke with the sun. Hot, burning rays poured in between the branches of a magnolia tree and through the tiny window. The small room heated to an already intolerable temperature. I squinted and rolled over to face Catherine, who slept a few feet away. She had thrown her covers off during the night and left only her nightdress to cover her childlike sprawl, all rounded elbows, and dimpled knees. Only her short stature kept her from falling off the bed.

I rolled quietly out of mine. The morning sun opened my pores. Drops of sweat leaked from them like milk from a too-full udder. Catherine's steady breathing filled the thick air, so loud only a stampede of cows could have awakened her.

Our single beds were against opposite walls, yet one had only to reach out an arm to touch the other person. I slid between them and threw on my britches and blouse, not bothering to attend to my hair. The humidity would have its way with it, regardless.

Fennel fell from the keyhole as I turned the bedroom doorknob. Catherine had insisted on putting it there the night before, claiming it would ward against bad luck. If only she knew the craft hidden within her beloved superstitions. Of course, no witchcrafting would come of them without the other two main ingredients. But I admired her use nonetheless. She believed in them, in their power—she had The Spirit. If she had that, I knew we would get along just fine.

The bedroom door creaked open and closed as I made my way out and down the hall. Though the light spilled into our room as bright as the sunrise on a treeless pasture, the hallway was a different story. All the doors were closed, and the entranceway lacked windows. The scent of rotten wood and musk hung heavily in the air. Hints of cigar smoke and tobacco still lingered, presumably from the men who once worked in these offices before they were so graciously turned into makeshift bedrooms, like hammy-downs for the forgotten stepchild.

A sigh escaped my lips as I opened the large front door. The morning light spilled over me. I soaked it in eagerly.

The landscaping around the university wasn't as impressive as I'd imagined. Buildings surrounded the campus in a semicircular formation. In the middle lay an open area with grass and benches. Magnolia and red maple trees grew sporadically throughout. A few bushes lined the cobblestone walkway that rimmed the grass and led to each building. The overall effect was decidedly underwhelming. Back at home, lush greenery covered the farm. Healthy trees, plants, and vegetation sprouted everywhere I looked, adding freshness to the air—unlike here, where it screamed with suppression.

Further down the cobblestone path, I found a bench to sit on as the sun peeked over the horizon. I retrieved a notebook and fountain pen from my satchel. The hand-sewn leather notebook was a gift. What I'd thought was affection, I knew now, was bribery. I'd wanted to throw it away or burn it, but in the end, I couldn't bring myself to do either.

A few days had passed since I'd written a letter to Ma. It was as perfect a time as any to write, especially since it was the morning of the start of this new adventure. Ma had always loved receiving letters and writing them, though she hadn't had many to write to. She spent most of her time writing in her journal. Or at least what I had thought was a journal until I was old enough for her to share the craft with me.

After I flipped past many pages of unsent letters in my own journal, teardrops staining the first few, I found a blank spot and began writing.

Dearest Ma,

Today is the start of my classes at Brimham University. I wish you were here to see it, to live out the dream that I'm sure neither of us would have ever thought possible. Women being invited to cohabitate and coeducate at an actual university seems like something out of a fairy tale. But alas, Ma, I wonder if this fairy tale has a dark twist—that of the Grimm.

I am confident the headmaster is not sincere in his endeavors and does not wish us success. Neither do our academic counterparts. Their most ungracious welcome yesterday told me all I needed to know. Even without that, I knew not to trust them, or any man for that matter. You taught me that, and so did Pa and Reece. To this day, I shall never forget it.

I do hope you have found peace, Ma. Tell me, do our souls remain chained to the restriction of our sexes even after death? I know our bodies do. I remember the day that I stood watch over yours as mourners came to show their respect. You didn't look like yourself. Even in death, they make us look like dolls, objects to be played with and discarded when we're no longer shiny and new, no longer useful to them. I hope I am never reduced to such things. You wouldn't have been either, at least not so soon, if only my efforts to save you hadn't failed, hadn't been thwarted by those we trusted.

Life. Marriage. Death. Is it all just another way to bind us?

Rest in Peace,
Your Lulu

The bell tower tolled in the distance, the sound profound and foreboding. I jerked my head up. The sun crept above the buildings.

"Shit." I sprang from the bench and snatched up my belongings. I shoved them back into my satchel and rushed down the path I'd come from earlier, determined not to be late to the lecture hall.

Upon entering the classroom, two things immediately became apparent. One: I was most certainly not dressed as formally as everyone else. Two: I was the last person to arrive, which meant everyone's eyes flicked toward me as I strode in.

"Nice of you to make our acquaintance, Miss . . ." The professor looked down at the list of names in his hand. "Rockwell, I presume?"

"Yes." I swallowed and declared more loudly, "Yes, sir, I'm here to get my degree and write for the paper."

Men around the room snickered.

The professor choked on his saliva. "Well, that's very . . . ambitious of you. Take your seat so we can get started, and in the future, Miss Rockwell, please do exercise punctuality."

Men had taken up most of the back rows, forcing the women to sit up front, maybe in a polite gesture, but I doubted it, if yesterday's introduction told me anything. I took the only seat that remained—in the center of the first row. *Great.*

The classroom itself was quite dingy. Dust motes floated in the sunlight coming in through the windows and collected on the surfaces of the bookshelves that lined the walls. The professor stood at a wooden podium in front of a black chalkboard smeared with the remains of old words, written and forgotten.

Several men stared in my direction, specifically at my attire. Was it that unbelievable for a woman to wear britches? Didn't they strut around in them every day? How different is it for a woman?

I let my thoughts slip from my mind and focused on the professor. I wouldn't let them or anyone else stop me from taking in every drop of knowledge I could during this program.

"Welcome, gentlemen—and ladies. I'm Professor Compton, and this is Foundations of Classical Languages. On each of your desks I have provided the course syllabus. Please read over it carefully before our next meeting. There *will* be a quiz. If you are familiar with this course, take notice that the number of required readings and assignments has been reduced for this semester."

A commotion stirred behind me. Several of the male students snickered. I looked around at the other women in the class, who looked at me in turn. Their chairs creaked as they fidgeted.

Thomas spoke to someone beside him, not trying very hard to be quiet, "They had to make it more *accessible* for our guests."

"Our temporary guests." His friend whispered back.

They both laughed.

"Thomas, Derek, is there something you would like to share with the rest of the class?" Professor Compton asked, pushing his glasses down to the tip of his nose to peer over the rim.

"Professor, we were merely wondering if it were fair for our education to be impeded upon just so our new and simple-minded classmates can keep up."

I spun around to face Thomas, heat already rising to the surface of my chest, and looked between him and the professor.

No reprimands came.

I bit my tongue. I didn't need to draw any more negative attention to myself than I already had, but I sure wanted to.

Instead, Henry spoke up from farther back in the classroom where he sat with his prosthetic leg stretched out in front of him. "On the contrary, I find quality over quantity is better for learning. If we have less to go over, it'll give us more time to delve deeper into the topics at hand."

Was he purposefully taking up for us? Or just tired of hearing Thomas's voice, too? I wasn't sure, but I wasn't about to trust him because of a few decent comments. A few good words could equal just as many broken promises.

"Right you are, Mr. Lockhart. Now, let's begin today's lesson." Professor Compton spun to the board without any further comments.

Once the professor finished and gave us our first assignment, he declared the class finished for the day.

As I packed my things, he announced, "Miss Rockwell, may I have a moment of your time after class?"

I sighed. "Yes, sir."

Catherine walked by and slowed, a look in her eyes asking if I would be okay.

I nodded. I'd herded cows bigger than the professor. Catherine accepted my reassurance and turned her curvy body sideways to scoot between the rows of desks.

Once the room emptied, leaving only the old, gray-haired professor and me, I cleared my throat and moved to the desk where he sat. "You needed to see me, sir?" I forced the last word out; such pleasantries didn't come to me as naturally as someone who grew up in high-cotton society.

"Yes, certainly. I wanted to talk with you about that particular . . . suit of clothes you're wearing today." Professor Compton only bothered to glance up from his book once while he spoke to look over my britches and blouse.

"My clothes? What about them?" My words came out sharp. I added, "Sir," to avoid accusations of being rude.

"It is not fit for this environment. You must wear appropriate attire to class, or I'm afraid I will have to dismiss you from attending."

Speechless, I stared at the top of his balding head bent over a leather-bound book. He would restrict me from learning because of what I was wearing?

"Do you understand?" he asked, as if I didn't speak the same language as him.

"Yes . . . well, no, actually. What do you mean by appropriate?" I gestured to myself. "I am not showing any more skin than anyone else was in this lecture hall today. My britches cover my ankles, and my blouse covers my shoulders and collarbones. What could be more appropriate?"

I tried to breathe, tried to fight the tingle in my fingers and palms, the urge to spill a drop of blood and use the witchcraft that had come so easily to me before. Witchcraft that could make the old man in front of me retch out the contents of his stomach. Witchcraft that could do so much worse.

I shoved those thoughts into my mind's darkest, coldest crevices, and willed them to stay there. If my last attempt at witchcraft had told me anything, it wasn't willing to be used anymore. Or maybe I wasn't willing to bear the consequences now that I knew just how dire they might be. No. I wouldn't use the craft here. The thought of it alone made my stomach clench.

The professor went bug-eyed as a bullfrog. "Well . . . I'm not one to talk of such things, especially not alone in the company of *your* kind, but I believe the proper attire for a young lady to wear is a dress, corset, and petticoats. Now, have a good day, Miss Rockwell."

I stomped out of the classroom and into the sweltering day, though the southern summer heat wasn't what made my blood boil or my fists clench until my nails drew blood.

Chapter Five

Catherine

Throw clothes to the ground and stomp on them before dressing.
This will keep the wearer from falling into bad luck.

Sweat dripped between my bosoms, soaking through my chemise and into my corset as I waited for Lucille to emerge from the lecture hall. I fanned myself with the thick syllabus Professor Compton had given us. The building's large shadow loomed over me and the rest of the courtyard but did nothing to stifle the heat. Instead, it made everything dark and suffocating. It crawled farther and farther over the landscape as the sun fell behind the building, like a creature chasing its prey.

More sweat dripped down my neck. Had waiting been a bad idea? I was about to turn when Lucille emerged from the front entrance. Her face was redder than the ruby-colored jewels Mama loved to wear to church to make the other women jealous.

As Lucille descended the stone steps, Thomas and his posse of equally offensive friends, leaning against the railings, called out to her. They made crude and vulgar comments about her body.

What they would do to it.

How they would use it.

Their dislike of having us here faded into a primitive show of attraction. Not the flattering sort, but in the same way animals mark their territory and show dominance. They hadn't done such catcalling when I'd exited the building. The bigger your size, the more invisible you seem to become. Lucille snarled at the men on the stairs, flashing a filthy gesture.

"What did the professor want?" I backed away as she approached so I wouldn't get run over by her irate march, like a freight train barreling down its tracks.

Lucille's nostrils flared. "He told me I wouldn't be able to stay in class if I wore this again." She gestured to her attire. "He said I need to wear something more appropriate."

That didn't surprise me. Mama would've had a heart attack if I ever wore what Lucille was wearing. But I knew better than to say that to the raging woman before me.

Lucille crossed her arms. "Apparently, our appearance is more important than our education."

I humphed, taken aback. When she put it like that, it did seem a bit absurd. Isn't that precisely the way Mama thought? Hadn't she always put my appearance over the value of my mind?

"I suppose that does seem unfair," I said as we started a slow trudge along the sidewalk.

Midafternoon heat radiated from the pavement. It made our movements slow and arduous, like wading through knee-high mud.

"I must say, I am shocked with how we've been treated thus far. First with those men and now with the professor. Why must they be that way?"

Until now, I'd been surrounded by my sisters, private tutors, and servants. Even though I was one of the youngest women here, surely I hadn't been *that* shielded from the world. This had to be an outlier, an anomaly.

Lucille snorted as she rifled through her bag. "You should—" her words halted, hanging in the humid air. "My journal. It's not here." She frantically searched, coming up empty-handed. "I must've left it on that bench."

She spun and sprinted away.

"Wait! I should what?" I called, confusion and frustration mingled in my voice, the perfect waltz of disorientation.

Lucille barely turned to look over her shoulder. "Do something about it!"

She swatted at a swarm of gnats as she went and left me to my own thoughts and new wonderings.

A day later, the lecture hall still smelled of chalk dust and cold wood polish just as it had during our first class. The sunlight slanting through tall windows made the shadows deeper along the desks. The scratch of quills on paper filled the air, punctuated by the occasional cough or rustle of gowns.

I barely noticed the questions on the paper in front of me. My attention drifted to Alice at my side. Her pen moved steadily as she sat with a straight back and her jaw set with a calm I envied. We had known each other for only a few days, and yet something about her drew my gaze.

Then Derek stood, and the air seemed to crack.

"Sir," he said, his voice cutting cleanly across the room. The silence shattering like glass dropped on the hard floor. "There has been misconduct."

George immediately followed. "I can attest to his claim. Those two women up front are sharing answers."

There were more than a couple of women up front, including myself, Lucille, Susan, Alice, and Rebecca. I hadn't sat there by choice, I had arrived too late to get a better seat in the back. It had taken longer than anticipated to get my hair into the intricate updo I now wore underneath my favorite feathered hat.

Without explanation of who the two men referred to, the professor turned toward Alice and Rebecca. I saw the accusatory look in his eyes, the barely hidden disgust. It was the same look Mama gave the maids when she claimed one of them had stolen a piece of china, even before I could tell her my youngest sister had taken it to play tea with. Judgment based purely on the color of their skin.

Alice looked up, calm and poised, though I could see the faintest flicker of tension around her eyes.

"That's not true," Alice said, her voice steady but quiet, as if saying it louder would only worsen the situation.

"They sat close together," Derek continued, as though proximity alone could condemn them. "And they were whispering to each other." His lips curved in a small, self-satisfied smirk—the sort that only someone secure in his entitlement could wear. It reminded me of Daddy.

The air thickened, but not from the ever-present humidity. The room had become smaller somehow, the walls pressing in. Rebecca's hand tightened on her paper, knuckles lightening. The men were not subtle. Their whispers and glances carried the weight of accusation, the casual cruelty of those who expect to dominate.

I cursed myself for feeling so surprised by their behavior, especially after the past couple of days listening to the other women swap stories and experiences in the dormitory. They certainly had plenty to share, and my own lack thereof was becoming increasingly clear.

Henry stood from just behind the two accused women, his stance off-kilter. "I've been behind them the entire time," he said, voice firm. "They haven't whispered. If they had, we all would've been able to hear it."

Christopher rose beside him. A smaller man, who had stayed quiet during our first class and seemed to always stay close to Henry. "Nor did I see any signs of cheating."

Professor Compton adjusted his spectacles, but his eyes lingered on Alice and Rebecca with a measured coolness that made my stomach twist. His patience felt like indifference, as if the world itself had already judged the women guilty.

"You must understand," he said finally, "standards have to be preserved."

Alice's back straightened even further, becoming impossibly rigid. "Sir, you may examine our work."

Rebecca added softly, almost a whisper, "Our answers won't be the same."

My pulse thrummed in my throat, making it hard to swallow. I wanted to speak, to say how awful these men have been and how they must be lying, but my hands were clenched tight. I was angry, yes, but also scared, though I wouldn't want to admit such, especially not to my roommate, who seemed to never be scared to do or say anything. This was nothing like the quiet classrooms on the estate. There, my tutors had deferred, smiled through mistakes, never dared raise an accusation. Especially not with the wages Daddy was paying them.

It was comfortable there. It was comfortable to stay silent. I hadn't spoken up when Mama had accused the maids, hadn't spoken up when they were fired, one after another, taking away their livelihood without so much as a second thought. I swallowed and straightened my shoulders.

Lucille's words echoed in my head. *Do something about it.*

Comfort be damned.

"I was the one whispering, Professor. It was me." My voice cracked around the words.

Everyone in the classroom turned to me, including the professor. His eyes softened slightly as they landed on me. I knew what he saw, a wealthy, *white* woman.

"Would you care to explain why you were whispering during an exam, Miss Stanley?" His tone wasn't as sharp, as accusatory, as it had been when he spoke to Alice.

I cleared my throat, desperately grasping for something to say. Heat rose to my chest.

"It was actually my fault." Lucille's twang suddenly filled the space, as it always did with any space she was in.

She stood as she spoke. I hadn't.

She was brave. I wasn't.

"I'd forgotten to bring extra ink for my pen, and I'd run out." Lucille held her chin high, as if daring the Professor to say she was lying. "I only asked Catherine if she had any ink I could use. That's all."

Professor Compton spoke again. "Well, if that's the case."

Alice and Rebecca nodded, but the professor didn't look toward them to notice.

"There will be no formal charge today. However, this accusation will be recorded. Should such concerns arise in the future, the consequences will be far less forgiving. For everyone involved." He eyed Lucille and me. "Three demerits result in expulsion. Govern yourselves accordingly."

As if we needed reminding.

"And in the future, you two," Professor Compton looked between Alice and Rebecca, "need to sit separate from one another. Lower the risk of distraction or temptation."

Alice opened her mouth, possibly to protest, but the clock tower bell rang across campus, loud enough to be heard through the windows.

"Turn in your exams before leaving and be sure to complete the required reading and essay before Monday." Professor Compton announced to the class. "You are dismissed for today." He turned to his desk, pushing his glasses back up his nose, not caring to give us any further attention.

Chairs scraped back against the worn floorboards. A sigh of relief escaped me. Derek laughed under his breath, and George's elbow nudged him. This was all fun and games to them. All a joke.

Their amusement hung like a dark cloud over the room.

I gathered my papers, hands trembling. My heart ached at the sight of Alice standing there, calm and dignified, even while the room seemed to conspire against her. A flush of something else, something I could never let myself feel, tightened in my chest. Something foolish. Dangerous, even.

A hard shoulder bumped against mine, sending the books I'd been gathering sprawling across the floor, and a gasp from my lips.

"My apologies," George smirked. "I would say I hadn't seen you there, but how could I not?" His eyes scanned over me, and his nose scrunched as he walked past.

My mouth hung open as I watched him go. These men were outrageous.

"Thank y'all for your help," Alice said as she bent, picking up my books and handing them back to me.

We reached for the same book. Our hands brushed. A shiver ran up my arm. I yanked it back, cursing myself.

Lucille came to my side, and Rebecca to Alice's. Susan came over as well, and Victoria, with her raven hair in an updo atop her head, stayed farther back, to herself, as she often did.

"We know y'all were innocent. Anyone sitting in this room would've known that. It was quiet enough to hear a pen drop. We would've all heard it if anyone was whispering. Those damn liars . . ." Lucille ranted on and on.

I was too distracted by the sudden feelings in my chest. Not just the ones I was trying to ignore from my brush with Alice, but the pride in myself. The rush speaking up had given me. The feeling of making a difference. Like I was doing something Mama would reprimand me for. Something slightly dangerous.

It felt good.

Powerful.

Chapter Six
Victoria

Crossing your fingers will bring good luck
and make wishes come true.

Since there were no classes today, I planned to search for work. However, after stopping by several of the large office buildings and lecture halls scattered around the impressive campus greenery, I had little to no success. Several professors turned me away from assisting them, and the high-cotton businessmen said an office was no place for a woman. Though, I imagined none of them shied away from entertaining their nightly escorts in such offices, where their wives were blissfully unaware. It was only a woman's place if said woman was offering their body instead of their mind.

At my third stop, in the registrar's office, it didn't seem my luck would change anytime soon.

"I could organize your files or keep the office tidy. I have plenty of experience in sanitation—"

The small man in front of me, with a shining bald head, slick with sweat, and a necktie so tight that he had to be close to suffocating, raised his hand to stop me. His mouth formed words I couldn't hear.

"Excuse me?" I cupped my hand around my ear so he would know to speak up. I hated drawing attention to myself by needing others to yell when conversing with me. Thus was the life—and curse—of a mill girl.

The man's face contorted in annoyance. "I said—" he yelled, and others in his office turned toward the commotion. My neck and cheeks heated at the attention.

"Your help isn't wanted here. This is no place for a woman."

I fought the urge to groan at the all-too-familiar words and hated the pleading that came from me. "Please, sir." I crossed my fingers. "I can mend your garments, or polish your shoes, or—"

"This is why women should never be allowed here," the man grumbled. "Perhaps you should ask if the servants need help emptying the chamber pots. Good day." He turned away from me, back to the papers at his desk.

My shoulders slumped. I heaved a sigh that caused the tightness in my lungs to rattle, like the tail of a cottonmouth, and exhaled a wheeze punctuated by a fit of coughs. I couldn't go into town for work lest I run into any of the other mill girls. They were surely out for my head. I also couldn't bear to see any reminders of . . .

I squeezed my eyes shut and blocked the memory of Maggie's screams out of my mind. I sighed. Maybe the chamber pots were to be my only hope.

"Excuse me. Ma'am?" A voice broke through my thoughts of human feces and self-pity. A short man with gray hair and wrinkled skin approached me. Round spectacles perched on the end of his nose and a scarf was wrapped around his neck, though I didn't know why, with the heat already torturously hot.

"Yes?"

"I don't mean to pry, but did I hear you're in need of work? You're part of the new women's program, yes?" He pushed his spectacles further up his curved nose.

"Yes, I am," I answered to both, thankful his words were easy to read on his thin lips.

He smiled. "I'm the librarian, Mr. Edmonton." He held his hand out to me before I could curtsy.

No one had ever held a hand out to me. Handshakes were reserved for men, their own personal gesture of respect for one another, never to be shared with us. And here this man was offering this gesture to me as if I was his equal.

Stunned, I tried to shake his hand without trembling, but failed.

"I've been needing help in the library. An old man like myself can't carry stacks of books or reach the higher shelves anymore. My back won't allow such extraneous work these days."

"The library?" My mouth dropped open. He couldn't be serious. He wanted me to help him with books? My luck had certainly shifted.

He nodded and continued to ramble on as he guided me out of the registrar's office and across the sprawling campus. Though, with his head turned away from me as we walked, I couldn't read his lips. My mind had already begun dreaming of stories written in ink.

Rounding the cul-de-sac at the end of the stone path around the university courtyard, we came upon the most prominent building on campus. Its tall bell tower rang with an ominous gong and scared the crows from where they perched. A large wooden sign posted in front of it read BRIMHAM UNIVERSITY MEMORIAL LIBRARY.

Mr. Edmonton led me up the side of the stone stairs, avoiding the other students filing in and out of the building. When we entered, I nearly fell to the floor at the sight in front of me. Shelves as tall as the ceiling held rows and rows of books.

My feet moved as if having a mind of their own toward the closest mahogany shelf. The books' musky scent filled my nostrils and the cool, hushed environment calmed my soul.

I had always wanted my own books as a child. Growing up with a mother who worked in factories, and other less socially acceptable occupations, and a father too busy raising his family to spend time with his secret mistress and his bastard daughter made it difficult to afford such luxuries. I'd found some books in dumpsters and alleyways that I'd read cover to cover more times than I could count, but this was immaculate. It was a dream.

Mr. Edmonton followed closely behind me. "As you can see, there is quite the inventory, and I've found myself unable to keep up with it lately."

"I can imagine." I barely registered my own words, still mesmerized by it all. My gaze jumped around from one shelf to the other.

"You must be here after your classes daily to shelve and organize new or returned books. You will also need to help with upkeep, such as dusting and sweeping. I'll pay you $1.50 a day. Does that sound—"

"That's perfect." The words burst out of me.

Mr. Edmonton smiled. "Wonderful. Let me show you around, and you can start tomorrow."

"I can start today." I beamed.

"This way then." He gestured for me to follow him.

As he led me through the aisles of the enormous library, I stared in awe at the endless shelves of books we passed. It seemed as if there were thousands, if not millions, of them. Classics, fairy tales, mysteries, poetry, everything I could imagine. Maybe staying at this university for a little while wouldn't be nearly as intolerable as I had imagined.

I had the smell of dust and old paper still on my hands when I reached the steps of the women's dormitory, still reeling from such good luck. The library lamps had gone dark behind me, and the evening air was damp enough to cling to my skirts. A basin of water and my narrow bed floated through my mind like a good dream when I heard shouting.

It came from the yard in front of the building. Men's voices loud and careless, the way they spoke when they expected the world to step aside for them. I slowed. My gloved fingers, now dirtied with dust and ink, tightened around the strap of my satchel.

Thomas stood near the steps, his coat unbuttoned, his hat tipped back above his jagged scar as if this were a sort of entertainment laid on for him. George lounged against the railing, and Derek was pacing like a dog that had learned it could snap without being struck back, handed treats instead. There were trunks and baskets scattered across the grass, their lids yawning open. Dresses, chemises, and stockings lay strewn about, pale and helpless as shed skins.

Mary Ann, one of Josephine's posse, stood at the center of it all, her face bloodless. She held a shawl clutched to her corseted chest, though it was not her own. I recognized the blue stitching along the edge. Without meaning to, my mind quickly cataloged exactly what type of thread and stitch was used. It belonged to Susan.

"What in the heavens is going on?" Josephine asked. She had come up behind me without my noticing, her spine straight as a church pew, her Bible pressed flat against her ribs.

George laughed. "We're doing the Lord's work, Miss Ward. Just like your daddy."

Derek nudged a trunk with his boot, tipping it so the last of its contents spilled across the dirt. "Can't have young ladies dressing above their station. Or tempting good godly men."

Something in me went very still. I had seen that look before. Not in a college yard, but in the mill, when a foreman decided a woman's labor or dignity was his to scatter if the mood struck him. The same careless authority. The same pleasure in the mess.

Mary Ann made a small sound, half breath, half sob. "That was all I had," she said. "My grandmother made these before she—"

Thomas cut her off. "Then your grandmother should have taught you how to dress modestly."

Modestly? Mary Ann was just like Josephine, dressed like she was a pilgrim from a different time. She must've just been the only one here when they came looking to cause trouble.

Wrong place at the wrong time. Just as Maggie had been.

I stepped forward before I had time to think better of it. My voice came out quiet, but it didn't shake. "You have no right to treat us this way."

Three heads turned toward me, surprised, as if I had spoken out of turn at a table where I hadn't been invited.

Derek looked me over, his eyes narrowed to slits. "And who are you to say so?"

"I am someone who knows what it is to have her work and her things treated as if they're nothing." I gestured to the dresses ground into the grass. At the mill, when a loom broke, they docked our pay. When a girl collapsed, they stepped over her. This was the same sort of cruelty, only dressed up in scripture and smiles.

Josephine drew in a sharp breath, whether at my words or my boldness, I couldn't tell. "Scripture doesn't permit theft," she said stiffly. "My father, *the reverend*, will hear of this." As if any of us needed reminding who her father was.

That gave Thomas pause. The reverend's shadow loomed large over this place.

Others had started to gather, some coming from the library, the study hall, or the cafeteria. Lucille, with her jaw set and her sleeves rolled, Catherine standing close beside her, fanning herself with an expensive-looking silk fan, Alice and Rebecca whispering furiously to one another as they bent to rescue what garments they could. Susan had already knelt in the grass, brushing dirt from Mary Ann's skirts with a tenderness that made my throat ache, reminding me of Maggie's gentle presence. Even though we all had been patronized by Josephine and her two followers, Mary Ann and Penelope, we wouldn't stand by and watch the mistreatment of any woman.

The men's eyes scanned over the small crowd now gathered. They were outnumbered, but not frightened. No, they had merely lost interest in their little game.

"This isn't over," George muttered, but he stepped back. Thomas had already spun, walking away as if this were nothing, as if we were nothing. Derek followed more slowly, his eyes lingering on those who had spoken against them, who would be their next targets.

"Damn right this isn't over!" Lucille picked up a stray garment and chunked it at the back of Thomas's head.

He spun, a snarl written like venom on his face. He eyed her, and then the garment, stomping it into the ground and twisting his boot on it. An ugly sound ripped from his throat as he hacked up a wad of mucus and spit it on the muddied fabric.

Mary Ann whimpered. Lucille growled.

When they finally moved on, their laughter faded down the path like wolves slinking back to their lair. For a moment, none of us spoke. Our shadows deepened as the last bit of light and color faded from the sky, leaving only darkness in its absence.

Lucille broke the silence. "We'll wash what can be washed," she said. "And mend what can be mended."

"I have thread," Susan added immediately. "And soap."

Alice lifted a bodice from the ground. "Some of it is ruined, but not all of it."

Mary Ann sank onto the steps, her composure finally giving way as tears slipped down her cheeks. Penelope sat beside her, one arm firm around Mary Ann's shoulders, repeating words of solace over and over.

Josephine hovered, uncertain. She laid her Bible aside and picked up a mud-stained sleeve. "Cleanliness is next to godliness," she said, almost to herself. "This is why we shouldn't be here, shouldn't try to be something God didn't intend us to be."

I ignored her comment and set my satchel down, joining them. As I worked dirt from cloth, my hands moved with the steady surety they had learned in the mill. Around me, the women formed a circle without anyone naming it, a small ward of our own making.

Chapter Seven
Lucille

Tie a knot eight centimeters across to find things that are at a loss.

It had been several days since I'd forgotten my journal on the courtyard bench.

After I'd left Catherine in the middle of our conversation, which I only felt bad about later, when I wasn't so worried all of my secrets were in the wrong hands, I practically ran back to the bench. If someone had gotten a hold of my journal, they would've had plenty of information to use to blackmail me. They could've kicked me out of the program, or worse.

The relief of finding it on the ground under the bench had been overwhelming; however, I'd been entirely too busy between classes, assignments, and dealing with unruly men to write in my journal until now.

As I got to my self-proclaimed writing bench, the sun barely peeking over the horizon, I took the leather notebook from my satchel and flipped through the pages of unsent letters to Ma. Stopping at the last written page, my eyebrows rose to my hairline at the sight of handwriting that wasn't mine.

Dear Lulu,

(Though I'm sure you'd much prefer me to call you Miss Rockwell.)

I didn't intend to read, much less write, in your notebook. I merely found it sitting on the bench and picked it up to take to the lost and found inside the registrar's office. However, my intention changed when the pages fell open to your last entry. Your words were far too intriguing for me not to respond. So here we are.

First and foremost, I convey my sincerest apologies and condolences for your mother. I am quite close with my mother and could not imagine losing her. But I am familiar with the amount of strength it takes to live through such a loss.

Secondly, I would like to answer the question you ended with. It was what caught my attention the most. You asked if life, marriage, and death are all ways to bind us, and though I am certain you were speaking of women, I would like to offer my own thoughts on the matter. Or at least the matter of marriage. I am unsure if I'm at a point yet where I could comment on life or death.

I cannot speak for the rest of the male population, nor would I want to, but for myself, I believe marriage is as imperfect as the people involved are and, thus, reflects their truest form. Therefore, if one intends to bind the other, they will. If one doesn't plan to, they won't.

Many men here think that a woman cannot be a successful wife and mother while exercising a profession, yet they have not let women disprove their hypothesis. For myself, I protest against this doctrine. At any rate, you should continue on your path of proving them wrong while rethinking your beliefs of marriage and men. We are not all what you think.

Sincerely,
Henry Lockhart

I couldn't believe this man's audacity, not only to look at my personal property but to vandalize it with his writing, acting as if we could be friends. As if he, a man, understood the world women lived in.

Though I didn't believe a word of his sympathy. Henry had seemed kind enough in classes, helping take up for some of the other women, but I wouldn't be tricked into trusting him that easily. I had learned my lesson on that.

As I walked back toward the lecture hall after writing another letter to Ma, letting her know of all the events of our first week on campus, the trees cast shadows in the early morning light. They reached across the path with patches of darkness.

A figure approached me on the path, shrouded in those same shadows. It loomed larger as it came closer. For a moment, chill bumps pricked my skin. A shiver ran down my spine despite the temperature. Then, in a blink, it was not a monster or a beast, but a person, which could be just as scary.

The tight curls under her bonnet gave away her identity before I could make out Josephine's face. Within minutes of meeting her the first night, I knew we were quite different, which wasn't necessarily a bad thing. Differing from others kept life interesting. The world would be boring if we were all the same, inside or out.

"Hello, Miss Rockwell. How are you this fine morning?" Josephine refused to call any of us by our first names—ever the proper lady. She clutched her Bible along with her other books in her hand and must've been coming from the chapel.

"I'm fine, thank you." I took a step forward. I had no desire to make conversation, nor did I want to be late for class.

She lifted her hand. "Wait, just a moment! I would like to speak with you."

There went my hope. "What would you like to speak about?"

"Word has spread of what the professor said to you after the first class." Her nose scrunched.

Oh, hell.

"I would like to offer my help and prayers for you. I know transitioning from how you grew up in such a heathen way to high society must be difficult. If you need any appropriate attire, you are more than welcome to borrow some of my dresses and bonnets. I have more than enough for myself, and I always love a good opportunity to be charitable to those who have strayed from Christ's flock." She smiled, and though her words dripped with Southern charm, her eyes showed more judgment than a priest in a brothel.

After everything that had already happened, even witnessing one of her own friends be terrorized by the very men she thought belonged here over us, her judgments and opinions on the matter had not changed.

Maybe the heat was finally getting to me. Between the professor's words on our first day of classes, Henry's letter, our male classmates' continuous mistreatment of us, and this exchange, I couldn't contain the anger that boiled inside me any longer. "Josephine, if I wanted to look like I'd just escaped a convent in a pilgrim village, I would've already come to you and asked. Good day."

I walked away without saying anything else. Her gasp felt better than I would've liked to admit.

The anger that had been building up over the past few days threatened to take over. It tingled in my chest, all the way to my fingertips, wanting to be released through The Spirit, The Sacrifice, and The Superstition. Just the thought of those three joining together, made my heart race in excitement, but fear quickly followed, cold and unyielding. Memories threatened to flash in my mind, making my hands tremble.

I shook my head at myself. No, my anger toward Thomas and his friends' harassment, toward Josephine for not seeing the world that was right in front of her, and toward Henry for thinking he has the right to take liberties upon something that is not his, would have to be released in another manner.

Maybe after class I would write back to Henry and tell him *exactly* what I thought instead.

As I entered the classroom, I thought of every word I wanted to say to Henry. I almost told him off right then and there, until I noticed nearly every bench at the front of the room meant for women sat empty. No whispering skirts, no hurried apologies, no rustle of books being set down too hard. Just the men, sprawled and smirking as if they'd been let in on a joke I hadn't heard yet. Off to the side, slightly separated from the others, Henry and Christopher's eyebrows scrunched, looking at me as if questioning the absences as well.

I checked the clock. Right on time, if anything. Class would begin any minute now.

"Where is everyone?" I muttered, more to myself than anyone else.

Thomas didn't even bother hiding his grin. "The ladies must've needed their beauty sleep." He mockingly tsked his tongue. George and Derek snickered.

They had done something. My heart sped to a pound.

No, no, no.

Anger lit in my chest, hot and fast, and I spun on my heel before the professor could arrive. I took the steps back to the dormitory two at a time, ridiculous skirts hitched in my fists, not caring who saw. By the time the building came into view, my suspicions had hardened into sharp certainty.

There, nailed dead center into the front door, was a sheet of paper.

I tore it down without reading it first, the nail scraping my knuckle, drawing blood. I harshly turned it over in my fists, nearly tearing it altogether, and read what was written there.

NOTICE: Women's classes canceled for the day by order of the administration.

I laughed without humor. "Lying bastard."

The handwriting was clumsy, the seal poorly drawn, but I could already hear the echo of laughter it must have earned Thomas and his friends.

The door opened in front of me, Catherine gasped, pulling on her shawl as if she'd just finished getting ready for the day. "Don't worry, I let the others know about the cancellation." Her words came up short, as if just taking in my alarmed expression. "What's wrong?"

"They tricked everyone," I said, thrusting the paper at her. "This notice is forged. They wanted us to miss class to get us in trouble. We have to get the others up. Now! Quick, before the professor notices we're not there!"

I pushed past Catherine, her eyes still scanning the paper in her hands, and ran down the hall, banging on each door and yelling for everyone to get up.

They spilled out of their rooms behind me as I went, rubbing the sleep from their eyes and pulling on their robes. I explained what had happened in one breath. Susan paled with worry, Alice reddened with fury, Rebecca and Penelope blinked as the truth settled in. Victoria stood a little apart, quiet as always, but her jaw was set in a way I recognized. Mary Ann looked as though she hadn't slept at all, a sewing needle and thread in her hands.

Susan said. "We thought—"

"Y'all get ready." I snapped, then softened my voice. "We can't be any later than we already are. Now! Hurry!"

Everyone rushed in a blurry storm of movement. Dresses were thrown on, hair pulled up into messy updos, and corset strings tied as we went. We stayed together, skirts brushing, anger knitting us into something solid and unmistakable. By the time we reached the classroom again, Professor Compton was already behind his podium, spectacles perched low, lecture notes open.

His mouth tightened the moment he saw us. "You're all late."

"Yes, sir," I said, stepping forward before anyone else had to. "There was a notice posted announcing the cancellation of women's classes. We believed it came from the administration."

His brow furrowed. "There was no such notice."

"We know that now," I said, trying to keep the edge from being too sharp in my voice. Disrespect would only dig us deeper into a hole. "It was nailed to our door. Now we realize it was placed there maliciously."

A ripple of sound moved through the room. Not surprise, but amusement. I turned my head just enough to see them. Thomas leaned back in his seat, arms crossed, his smile wrinkling his pale white scar. George covered his mouth as if stifling laughter. Derek didn't bother hiding anything. He smiled at us openly, like a child pleased with a prank that had gone exactly as planned. Other male students laughed along with them, elbowing one another in amusement, eagerly joining their vicious game.

The professor followed my gaze, then looked back down at his lecture notes. "Regardless of the cause, lateness is lateness. Each of you will receive a demerit on your record."

For a moment, I couldn't speak. My anger had nowhere to go, pressing against my ribs like a held breath.

"Sir," Alice said quietly, stepping beside me. Rebecca tried grabbing her, pulling her back, but Alice persisted. She was certainly brave. "They intended for us to miss instruction. They interfered with our education."

Josephine sat, stiff-backed and pale, in her seat, having already been there. She'd missed the notice altogether while at the chapel and had no doubt made it to class right on time. She didn't say anything.

The professor took a step back, as if Alice's mere proximity was offensive to him. "This institution cannot adjudicate every dispute between students. Take your seats. All of you."

The men laughed softly, but not softly enough.

I took my place, hands clenched so tightly my nails cut into skin. The demerit sat in my mind like a brand, unfair and burning. I thought of the way they'd scattered Mary Ann's things the night before, the way they'd looked at us then, measuring how much harm they could do and still be forgiven for it.

As the lecture droned on, I watched Thomas lean toward George and whisper something that made him snort. I memorized their faces, the easy cruelty of them. So much like Pa's. Like Reece's.

They thought this was a victory. They thought embarrassment and a mark in a ledger would send us back where we belonged.

They were wrong.

When the bell finally rang, I stood with the others, our shoulders nearly touching. I didn't look at the men as we passed them, but I felt their eyes all the same.

Outside, the sun was too bright for my mood. Catherine reached for my hand, squeezing once.

"They won today," she said quietly.

I answered, just as quiet, just as certain, "Only the battle, not the war."

And I had never been one to forget a slight, or to let it stand unanswered. That sentiment rang in my head as we made our way back to the dorm. I hadn't come up with a plan to get back at Thomas and his gang just yet, but I knew writing to someone, *anyone*, and getting my anger out, even in the smallest way, could help for now, at least until I came up with a better plan.

I scattered my things across the room, yanked my notebook from my satchel, and began to write. Ink blotches landed haphazardly all over the page in my haste and determination to say what was on my mind.

Henry,

I cannot bring myself to care about what you do or don't call me. In fact, I'd rather you not call me anything at all, as calling me something would signify that you're addressing me, and I'd rather that not be the case.

You seem to be under the misconception that we are alike or have experienced similar circumstances in life, and I am only writing back to inform you of your error. We are not, and never will be, alike. Furthermore, you will never understand the entirety of a woman's circumstances. The great soul of womanhood has been crushed and degraded.

Even a legitimate child born of a marriage belongs to the father in preference to the mother, even though the mother did all of the creating and birthing of the child. It is a simple fact that a legal marriage degrades every such mother and every such woman. It is meant only to further control our lives and our souls. Perhaps, as you say, the majority of men are not intentionally unjust to women, or perhaps that is exactly what they are, intentionally unjust, seeking only to have control.

I see no possibility of changing my opinion regarding this subject, and I warn you not to have any further interest in trying to change it for me. It will only result in disappointment.

Un-sincerely,
Miss Rockwell

It wasn't my best writing. Lyrical prose and thoughtful comparisons be damned. This was a declaration of retort, not meant to be swoon-worthy. If Henry expected some sort of reciprocity of affection, or thanks for standing up for us once or twice, he would be thoroughly disappointed. I knew my anger wasn't entirely because of him, nor was he to be blamed for our arduous morning, but it sure did feel good to let some of it out, even if it wouldn't solve our growing pile of problems.

Chapter Eight
Catherine

Throw a pinch of salt over your left shoulder
to ward off evil spirits.

Even though I had officially moved out of the Stanley estate and into Brimham University over two weeks ago, Mama insisted I come home on the days her ladies' church league met. According to her, "Devotion to the Lord doesn't come to a halt just because you've gone off on your own."

Which was ironic, considering they spent most of their meetings gossiping about other women around town. To them, "spreading the word" had nothing to do with the word of God.

We each held dainty, white umbrellas above our heads as we sat around the tea table in the backyard of Mrs. Flanagin's estate. Though, the umbrellas did nothing to block the sun's heat. My sister sat next to me. Three years my junior, she already looked like a woman. Mama had had her hems lowered last spring after she came out in society at the season's most grand debutante ball and couldn't be happier.

I leaned closer to her and held my umbrella at an angle to block the sun from my already-damp face. "Where are Elsabeth and Quenley?"

Felicity let out a small huff. A strand of her auburn hair caught in her breath and flew from her face. "Mama doesn't make them come now that they're married. She says they're too busy taking care of their households, and of course, Elsabeth has a child to care for. Maybe she'll stop dragging me along once I'm betrothed."

I hummed in agreement, then frowned. "I'm not sure I'll have any such fate unless it's to old cousin Frederick." I scrunched my nose.

Felicity mimicked my expression of distaste. "He was here just this past week. I heard him talking to Daddy."

That certainly couldn't be good. "What were they discussing?" I asked, and prayed it wasn't about marrying me.

"He was asking Daddy for money again. It seems he has . . ." Felicity glanced around, making sure none of the church ladies were listening before she continued. "Produced another bastard. He was hoping Daddy could loan him the funds to have the problem . . . taken care of." Felicity looked down into her glass of sweet tea, avoiding eye contact.

I stifled a gasp, not wanting to draw attention to us. "I thought Daddy and Mama were against such things. They're good churchgoing people."

"So is Cousin Frederick, apparently. It's only a sin unless it's helping *them*." Felicity took a gulp of the golden liquid and sucked her teeth. "That man is vile."

My stomach twisted into a knot. That man could be my husband one day if the women's program didn't succeed. I swallowed, needing to change the subject before I lost my composure. "Have you painted anything new lately?" I grabbed a slice of cornbread from a dainty plate on the table. Eating always helped when I felt like life wasn't in my control.

Felicity set her sweaty glass down. A smile spread across her face. "I have! Just this week, I painted a landscape scene of the estate. I figured I should do it before everything withers for winter. It'll look far too barren and sad to paint it after that."

I always adored how my sister's eyes lit up when she discussed her paintings. Though Mama only allowed such frivolous hobbies because she thought it made Felicity more desirable to suitors. She allowed me none, not after what she had walked in on all those moons ago. The only thing she allowed me to do before my escape to the university was find a suitor. A *male* suitor.

"What about you, Miss University Goer? How are your classes going? They started the week before last, right?" She smiled at me, her eyes big and round and innocent.

"Yes, they did." I was unsure how to tell her about my experience thus far.

If I told her of the less-than-ideal attitudes of our cohorts, and how, in just a week, they had already accused two women of cheating, caused the "loss" of another's entire wardrobe, and nailed a fake announcement to our dormitory door announcing the cancellation of classes for the day she would tell Mama. Mama would have me moved back to the estate and engaged to my lecherous cousin quick as a whip. And, though our counterparts' treatment of us didn't thrill me, I didn't want to marry greasy-faced, old Cousin Frederick.

"I've learned a great deal so far, much more than I could've imagined." That wasn't a lie.

I dusted the salt from my last slice of cornbread over my shoulder and reached for another, but Mama's hand blocked mine.

"You've had enough for one sitting, dear," she said, only loud enough for me to hear.

I retracted my hand, cradling it against me as if it had been slapped. It might as well have been.

"Have y'all heard of what the Yanks up north are doing lately?" Mrs. Flanagin preened, no doubt having held this gossip in for half the luncheon, waiting for the perfect moment to disperse it.

Gasps from around the table ensued.

"Do tell."

"Yes, do go on."

"One of those carpetbaggers that lives over by the slums told Mrs. Cullenton, and she told me . . ." Mrs. Flanagin drew out her story. "The women up north are . . ." She paused to ensure we were hanging onto her every word. ". . . giving public speeches! *Ladies* making actual speeches in front of crowds about their so-called right to the vote. Apparently, they think it is the thing to do if you want to make changes."

"The audacity!"

"Have they no shame?"

"Where are their manners?"

"Don't they know women are better seen and not heard?"

Mrs. Flanagin's smile couldn't have stretched any wider. Neither could my own.

Making changes. Being heard. Could I do that? Could I speak to the public so candidly about our mistreatment? Convince them of our equality? Speak up like I had in class for Alice?

"Well, aren't they pretentious? Lord, bless their little hearts." Mama fanned herself with her new hand-painted, silk-covered fan.

"Yes, indeed, Lord bless them." Mrs. Flanagin went on. Now that she had their attention, she would keep going well into the evening, as always.

I could no longer pay her any mind, with my head full of ideas and excitement. They were giving speeches up north, exercising their freedom of speech just like the gentlemen did?

How very pretentious, indeed.

So much so it had to be genius.

"This is outrageous," Lucille grunted as I pulled the last corset string into place and tied it. I'd borrowed the corset from Felicity before leaving the estate earlier. Her thin frame was much more similar to Lucille's than my short, curvy one.

It had taken me several days to convince Lucille to let me do this, and even now, I remained shocked she hadn't bolted at the sight of the skirts, laces, and corsets.

"You're telling me I must put on *all* these layers daily?"

"Absolutely." I came around to face her and looked over my handiwork. "They all have their uses and necessities."

"Both the crinoline *and* the petticoats are necessary? The corset cover *and* dress protectors? That's ridiculous." Lucille crossed her arms over her now heavily layered chest.

I inhaled before reciting, "The crinoline keeps the petticoats away from the legs and gives you a more desirable shape. And the dress protectors keep sweat from getting on your dresses and needing frequent laundering." Mama had repeatedly explained this to me as a child, though I had begged for my first corset from the time I could speak, desperately wanting to be like her and my older sisters.

Lucille rolled her eyes.

"Now for your hair." I patted the edge of my bed for her to sit and retrieved the necessary supplies from my dresser drawers.

"My hair? What's the matter with my hair?" Lucille inspected the ends of her short, choppy layers but sat on the edge of the bed.

When she did, her crinoline sprang up, effectively covering her head and exposing her underclothes.

"Argh!" A slew of curse words flew from her mouth. "If Professor Compton thought my britches were inappropriate, the full sight of these ridiculous split-crotch pantaloons will surely make him turn red six ways to Sunday. How the hell am I going to wear these things to class if they attack me when I sit down?"

As Lucille's eyes peeked over the top of her crinoline, her eyebrows in her hairline, I couldn't help but laugh. Even Lucille cracked as she got the crinoline back down to the floor. We laughed until tears ran down our cheeks, and our voices became hoarse. I wiped the tears from under my eyes. Lucille kept her hands on her skirts, holding down the caged structure.

"You'll have to relearn how to sit. It's easy, just remember to always lift the back of your skirt before sitting down. You can do it like this." I demonstrated flicking my hips to make the crinoline bounce upward right before I sat on the edge of the bed. Mama had made us girls practice this motion for hours every day when we got our first crinolines, lashing us with a hickory whenever we failed to sit without *making a show of ourselves*.

"But if that's too difficult, you can also reach back with your hand, grab the upper layer of the hoop, and lift it just a little." I demonstrated again. Using our hands wasn't an option for my sisters and me. It wasn't *ladylike*. But for Lucille, it would be just fine.

"Not only do I have to dress and do my hair differently, but I also have to sit differently? This is horse manure. I might as well be between the Devil and the deep blue sea." Lucille huffed, but managed to sit on the edge of the bed without exposing herself.

"See, you're already getting the hang of it. It took me weeks of lashings from Mama to get it right." I tried to laugh, but it came out like gravel. All hard edges and sharp points.

What would Mama think of my wanting to give a speech? I didn't have to think too hard to come to a conclusion. She would be absolutely appalled.

Lucille's hard gaze scanned over me. Her eyes softened. "You're not so bad at this whole teaching thing, ya know? I didn't need any lashings, and I'm already learning. My pa would give me one anyway and say I was trying to show off."

"Sounds like your pa and my mama would get along quite well." I tried to smile.

"Sounds like maybe we're not the ones who truly need the lashings." Lucille smirked and then cleared her throat. "Let's get this hair business over with. I'd like to not waste the rest of the day's sun."

She was right, our folks were the blameworthy ones. Maybe it didn't matter if Mama disapproved of my activities. Maybe that's precisely what I should strive for.

"Right." I turned to my dresser, blinking back the burn of tears in my eyes, unsure of where the sudden sting of emotion came from. I cleared my throat and pushed the intrusive feelings back down to whatever hidden inner crevice they came from.

"It's most fashionable for hair to be swept up and back, piled into a voluminous bun on the back of the head." I looked from my supplies to Lucille's short bob. "Though, I'm not entirely sure how we'll manage that with your style."

Lucille grinned, poking her chest out. "I chopped it off myself. You should've seen my pa's face afterward."

"I can't imagine." But I could.

Or at least I could imagine exactly how horrified Mama would be. Such an act would be the first gunshot signaling the start of another war. Or, at least, the equivalent of a war for Mama. Bad hair was practically a sin around here. Might as well carve it into the Ten Commandments and write it in the word of God.

Thou shalt not leave home with unstyled hair.

I grabbed the bottle of hair fixative Mama had made for me before I left for the university. Holy water's equivalent. I turned it upside down and let the thick slime slowly ooze out.

"What the hell is that?" Lucille eyed the goop suspiciously, her nose scrunched.

I tried not to flinch at her crude language. Only Daddy had ever used such words around ladies, and only ever under his breath or when Mama wasn't within hearing distance.

"Surely you've seen more grotesque substances working out on the farm." I grinned, enjoying the sight of Lucille, who never seemed deterred by any gross or scary thing. She looked at the hair fixative with a scrunched nose and pinched lips.

Lucille straightened her nose and lifted her chin. "Oh, I certainly have. In fact, that there has a mighty resemblance to the pig's placenta I pulled straight out from its—"

"I get it." I regretted trying to challenge her and held up my hand. "It's just a mixture of some sort of gum, tragacanth, and some other things. My mama knows the full recipe. It's a miracle worker. It'll make anything stick together and hold your hair up all day!"

"Great. Like I need another so-called miracle worker in my life." Lucille grumbled.

A pool of the slimy substance formed in my palm. It seeped between my fingers and under my nails, like a creature trying to hide in the nearest dark crevice or damp burrow. I laid the half-empty bottle on the dresser and used the gel to slick Lucille's hair back.

"We should give a speech," I blurted as my hands stuck to Lucille's hair with a squelch. It had been on my mind since Mama's luncheon and I couldn't hold it in any longer.

There was no reply for a moment, and I wished I weren't standing behind her, wished I could see her face, read it for any signs of what she may have been thinking.

Finally, as if it had taken a moment for my words to sink in, Lucille asked, "A what?"

"A speech. Where we talk in front of an audience—giving reasoning and facts to support our argument, to persuade a crowd? Mama's church league talked about women up north who've been giving speeches about suffrage. They're using their freedom of speech and whatnot." I rambled, my words spilling out before I could stop them.

Lucille seemed to weigh my words before replying, "Have you ever written a speech before?"

"Well, no. But how hard could it be? And you could help me. You write in your journal all the time. We could plan it out together, maybe make some flyers to pass out. I could go to the headmaster and see if maybe they would let us use the auditorium. It could be a whole event." Again, my words wouldn't stop.

"Yeah, I have a journal, but I'm not sure—"

My stomach dropped with her words. "Please help." I was practically begging now. "It doesn't have to be—"

The door to the dormitory slammed, interrupting my desperation. Footsteps padded against the carpeted floor, and small sniffles filled the dark hallway outside our open door.

Susan's short stature moped by, her pale skin sprinkled with red blotches.

"Susan, are you alright?" I called from where I still had my hands stuck in Lucille's hair. Literally, *stuck*. I might need to tell Mama to adjust her recipe next time.

Susan halted and she shook her head. A strand of her white-blonde hair fell into her narrow face. "This morning in class, I turned around to address Rebecca, and George *stole* my notebook."

"I'm so sorry." Though I wasn't sure why I apologized. I didn't steal her notebook. But that was just what women did. Apologized.

"That bastard." Lucille spat, pure venom and unfettered rage—as if her anger sat just under the surface, always nearby, always ready to emerge into the open at any given low tide or rip current.

"When I reported his theft to the professor, he accused me of lying to cover up my mistake of not bringing all my required materials to class. The professor marked a demerit on my record. He said if I got one more demerit, I would have to leave the university!" She sobbed. Each cry racked her body and shook her shoulders.

"Oh, honey." I yanked my hands from Lucille's goo-covered hair and left her on the bed. I tried to hug Susan without getting the goop on her but ended up giving her an awkward side pat with my elbows.

Someone needed to do something about those men. But could I be the one to do it? Could a speech help. Susan wasn't the only one of us who was close to getting expelled. If five of us left, that would be the end of this program entirely. The program couldn't end like that, because of those outrageous men. I certainly couldn't go back home to get married off to cousin Frederick.

Lucile kept her hands on her skirts as she stood, like she was afraid the crinoline would fly up and attack her again. "You're not the only one." She growled. "I've heard Rebecca and Alice received demerits because of Thomas and his friends, too."

"That's horrible," I gasped. Cousin Frederick's wiry mustache and slimy smile filled my mind. I couldn't live with him. The thought alone made me want to gag.

Susan cried harder. Her head dropped to her hands.

Why did these men think they had the right to treat us in such a vile way? If they were actively working to get us in trouble, then we women should actively be working against them.

Chapter Nine
Victoria

Bad luck will follow those who listen to conversations unwanted and unaware by the ones speaking.

For a week, I worked at the library daily. While I completed my duties, I chatted with Mr. Edmonton more than with other library staff and patrons. The quiet nature of the library made it that much harder for me to hear anyone, anyway. The old librarian was quiet, too, but his lips moved slowly and easily around his words, which made them easier for me to comprehend. And I read many books to make up for years of lost time. I read during my breaks, between classes, and even at night instead of sleeping.

Mr. Edmonton gave me a list of tasks as we moved through the library, including cleaning the older rooms in the back. However, when I got to the room Mr. Edmonton had directed me toward, a large old book lay on the table. I turned to ask about it, but the bustling librarian disappeared before I could.

I held the lantern up to the book, careful not to cause a spark. Dust covered its surface, all but five fingerprints, as if it had recently been handled. No title marked the leather cover and age had worn and yellowed its edges.

Did someone leave their diary here? Perhaps I should turn it in to Mr. Edmonton lest the owner return to retrieve it.

I picked it up and strolled toward the main area of the library as I searched for a name or address of return among the pages. Inked handwriting covered every surface, some in cursive and others in fine print, as if there weren't any one person who wrote in it, but several authors. Dates labeled the tops of the entries, but no names.

As I scanned over the scrawled words, my steps halted. One word sent a shiver through my bones and into my deepest being.

Witchcraft.

I sucked in a sharp breath. It rattled in my chest and an inevitable fit of coughs followed.

I slammed the book shut and searched my surroundings for any witnesses. No one was in sight or paid me any mind. I backpedaled to the small room until I reached the depths of the archives, as far from prying eyes as I could be.

My hands shook as I took a deep breath. I opened the leather cover once again and read the first entry.

Then another.

And another.

My heart raced with each one.

The authors wrote the pages like recipes, as if it were merely a cookbook. They described superstitions followed by lists of herbs, crystals, or—most interestingly—blood. The bottom of each page recounted the outcome of each "recipe."

Or, I supposed—as little as my brain wanted to comprehend it—they weren't recipes at all.

They were spells.

Incantations.

Witchcraft.

Though southern history wasn't known for witch trials quite like our northern counterparts in Massachusetts, Connecticut, or Virginia were, we still had our own tall tales and passed-down stories of witches—and what happened to them.

My mother's mother witnessed a witch hanging not far from here, in Russell County. They called her Abigail Abercrombie, though no one ever asked whether the name had been hers to begin with.

She arrived at Claymore Plantation with a single trunk and married the overseer, because that was the only way a woman without land, father, or history was permitted to stay. When the overseer died in his sleep, the plantation whispered. Mr. Claymore questioned neighbors and counted coincidences.

They called that witchcraft. They hanged her for hours while the men watched and the women learned what the weight of that word meant.

I'm sure the newspapers of the time and any man you ask about it, would have a very different way of telling it. But one thing was for certain, women accused of witchcraft, even without basis, were as good as dead. I couldn't even begin to imagine what they would do if they actually had written evidence like this journal.

I made sure to glance around while I explored the pages to make sure no one had spotted me. The pound of my heart in my ears would further limit my hearing if any footsteps approached. Dust wafted from the pages. I sneezed and went into another fit of coughs.

My thoughts drifted to the girls I had worked with in the mill. Mistreated and dying. Maggie had only been past her fifteenth year when she'd been beaten and left for dead by men who wouldn't use their last drop of piss to put out a woman on fire. Society ostracized my own mother for falling in love with a man who never cared for her. And in the end, she died of diseases that no doctor would treat because of her poverty.

If these journal entries were real—if this witchcraft was real—it could do so much to help them.

My own internal battle of morals ensued. Should I give it to Mr. Edmonton? Or the headmaster? Should I burn it? Hide it?

Steal it?

In the end, I stashed it behind a pile of books meant for the furnace, too moth-infested or mold-eaten to be good anymore—thankful they only ran it on Tuesdays—and went about my work. I tried not to think about the handwritten pages or the forbidden words they housed. I wouldn't—couldn't—go back to it. Or read any more of it. Though, with each passing thought, my mind slowly changed and morphed into a series of conflicting opinions. I tried to stop, or at least push, the metamorphosis deeper into the recesses of my mind. But my fingertips continued to tingle with the phantom feel of the old leather against them. My chest rattled with more than its usual cotton-laced cough.

It rattled with the will to fight.

By late afternoon, I couldn't take it anymore. My whole body felt lit with flames, unable to be extinguished until I had the book in my hands again. I refrained from sprinting through the shelves to get to it faster, lest someone notice me. I forced myself to make sure no one saw where I went or the wild anticipation that no doubt reflected in my eyes. My zigzagged steps led me through the shelves; anyone who saw me or tried to follow me through the maze of archives would lose sight of me.

When my fingers finally made contact with the old leather again, I gripped it so hard my knuckles turned white and bloodless. My shoulders fell slack with relief.

My body had been a drought-ridden desert.

The book was water.

I needed this. I could use it or sell it. I wasn't sure what I would do with it, but deep down, in the hollows of my brittle bones, I knew without a doubt I couldn't go back to not knowing. Not having it. Or at least, that's what I told myself as I hugged it to my chest with all the might of a child to their mother. A sinner to their savior.

As I crept back through the library, I peeked around each shelf before I stepped behind the next. I tried to convince myself that this was somehow rational. That I wasn't completely delusional or demented. Yes, I was stealing. But it was for the greater good. This could help so many.

It could have helped Maggie, saved her when I couldn't. Before I could stop the memories from coming, small, too-still limbs flashed in my mind. Her eyes—open and glazed. Not seeing. Not feeling. Not breathing.

I gulped down the sick that threatened to rise and spun on my heels.

The journey through the enormous library felt longer than usual. I normally relished any time among the rows of books, but not at that moment. It was an endless maze of dark corners that housed wondering eyes. Anyone could jump out of them at any time and snatch me up to take me straight to the headmaster.

Or the gallows.

Finally, I made it to the last row of shelves. I lifted my foot to step into the open. A loud voice halted me.

"Mr. Edmonton!" Thomas's booming voice echoed through the vast space.

My foot hung in the air.

I would've groaned if it weren't for needing to stay unseen and unheard. I clutched the book tighter to me.

Was I protecting myself? Or was I protecting *it*?

I peeked ever so slowly around the sharp corner of the mahogany shelf. Mr. Edmonton stood on the small stepladder with books clutched in his wrinkled grip. He turned and squinted at Thomas.

I sneered. If Thomas so much as whispered a rude word to the feeble man, I would . . .

I would what? Use the witchcraft I stealthily attempted to smuggle out of the library? I wasn't sure I would *use* it at all. Surely, I wouldn't consider it so soon. The thought both horrified and excited me.

"Mr. Edmonton," Thomas repeated.

I held my breath.

"Please, let me get that for you, sir."

Mr. Edmonton's lips spread in a warm smile. He slowly descended the steps. Thomas offered his hand to help guide him and even braced the old librarian's back when he stumbled on the last step.

I watched the exchange in stunned silence. Thomas could be *nice*?

I had seen Thomas interact with many, but never in such a . . . generous manner. I supposed it was daft of me to think he was all bad. But seeing the good in him didn't make the bitter taste of his untoward behavior any easier to swallow.

While contemplating this, I hadn't realized I had leaned too heavily on the shelf before me until a book slid from the edge. I watched in what seemed like slow motion as it fell through the air and hit the floor. The thud echoed beyond me. Mr. Edmonton's and Thomas's gazes snapped toward my direction.

I sucked in a breath and dropped down to the floor as far behind the stacked books as I could.

They scanned the area. I waited to be discovered. The end to this foolish escapade.

After a moment, Mr. Edmonton seemed to lose interest and returned to Thomas.

I sighed, my breath shaky.

"Thank you, dear boy." He smiled. "I quite appreciate it."

"No thanks needed, sir." Thomas took the books from Mr. Edmonton's hands and climbed the stepladder.

As the librarian told him where to place each book, I spun and sprinted from behind the shelf on the other side. I slipped through the library door and down the stone steps. My heart pounded a steady rhythm of hot blood in my ears. The leather-bound pages burned a reminder of my transgressions into my arms.

Chapter Ten
Lucille

Knock on wood to prevent bad luck.

The lamp burned low on Catherine's bed, its flame turned down until the glass chimney breathed more shadow than light. Outside, the campus had gone quiet in the way it only ever did after midnight, when even the crickets seemed to know better than to draw attention to themselves.

I sat on my bed with my boots off and my sleeves rolled up, rubbing at a smear of ink on my thumb. I still wasn't sure why Catherine wanted to give a speech, or how she had talked me into helping her plan for it. Her friendship must've grown on me, as unlikely as it may have been.

My roommate paced in the small space between the bed and the window, careful even in her nervousness, as though she'd been trained not to take up too much space.

"What if it isn't really about rights?" she said after thinking for a long while. "What if that's not the heart of it at all?"

I looked up at her, scrunching my eyebrows. "Everything we're fighting for, everything we're here for, is about equal rights."

She stopped pacing. The lamplight caught her just right. She was soft, thoughtful, unmarked by the kind of hard living that carved lines into a woman early. "I know. But if I say that outright, they'll stop listening before I finish my first sentence."

I let out a short laugh. "They'll stop listening anyway."

She frowned. Catherine still believed attention could be earned if you chose the correct words. That was the difference between us. Men had always listened to her. Tutors leaned in because her pa paid them to. Ministers smiled because her family filled pews and coffers alike. When Catherine spoke, the world had been taught to hush.

"I've tried to get them to listen," I said, more tired than angry. "I've explained. I've argued. I've yelled until my throat burned raw. Men don't ignore you because you're unclear. They ignore you because they have no intention of hearing what you have to say at all."

She sat on the edge of the bed across from me, folding her hands in her lap. "I don't want to stand up there and demand anything. I want to make it so they can't pretend not to see us anymore. See our struggles. See our worth."

"You've never been shouted down," I said quietly. Or betrayed and made to watch the one you love most die because of it.

"No," she admitted. "I know I've been protected. I know I've been listened to because of who my daddy is. But that's exactly why I should speak. They can dismiss you as troublesome. They can't dismiss me without revealing themselves."

The lamp flickered. Somewhere down the hall, a door creaked, then stilled.

"And what do you hope comes of it?" I asked, this time in a whisper. "Really."

She thought for a long moment. "I hope the men feel uncomfortable enough to hesitate next time. I hope the faculty can't claim ignorance anymore and pretend they don't see what Thomas and his horrid friends are doing to us."

I shook my head slowly but didn't protest.

"I know it won't fix everything," she said. "But silence has never fixed anything at all."

I lay back on my bed and stared at the ceiling. I thought about all the times I'd been ignored by Pa, and then Reece. How Ma did the same and ended up dead because of their ignorance. I'd learned the hard way, that noise didn't equal power.

But I also thought about Susan crying. About Mary Ann clutching borrowed clothes. About Catherine, who had lived her life cushioned and still chose to step forward.

"Fine," I said at last with a heavy sigh punctuating the word. "If you're going to do this, then you don't make it about freedom or law or God-given rights. And when you go to the Headmaster, make it about patterns. About proof. About how often this happens and how quietly."

She nodded eagerly. "Yes. Exactly."

"And you make them see that what they call isolated incidents is a system," I added. "One that only works because people pretend not to notice."

Catherine exhaled, like she'd been holding her breath for hours. "That's it. That's what the speech should be about."

I rolled onto my side and looked at her. "I still don't think they'll listen."

She met my gaze, steady as ever. "Some of them will."

I shook my head, blew out my lantern, and rolled away from her as the room filled with darkness.

The next day, I marched across campus with the letter I'd written days prior in hand. I hadn't meant to wait so long before delivering my reply to Henry, but Catherine's insistence on my unfortunate makeover and her incessant planning for her speech had halted my own plans. And I didn't intend to leave this letter lying somewhere to be found and read by its intended audience, as he had. No, I would hand it to him myself. See the look on his face as he realized what he'd gotten into and *who* he'd gotten involved with.

The men's dormitories were much larger and newer than the one the women resided in—no surprise there. There were two, one for the lowerclassmen and one for the upperclassmen. They designed them for comfort, whereas the women's building was barely considered living quarters at all.

As I marched through the front door and down the halls of the dormitory meant for the lowerclassmen, I expected to be met by someone to keep me out. Actually, I had hoped for it, if only to have someone to fight with, but there was nary a soul in sight. All the doors had the names of the residents posted on them.

I searched door to door for Henry's name. The longer it took, the more my annoyance flared. Of course, he *would* be the furthest down this damn well-to-do hallway.

Just as I was about to get to the final door, a voice carried out from the room before it. The voice was, of course, deep and male, but not one I initially recognized, though there were only so many men it could be. It wouldn't take me long to guess.

But it wasn't the pitch of the voice that interested me. It was the topic.

"Of course, Thomas dislikes their presence here. Wouldn't you, after what that poor chap went through?"

Was it George? Or maybe Derek?

"I mean, sure. If I'd been engaged to a woman when I went off to war and returned scarred and beaten only to find her shacked up with another man, I'd be torn up about it, too. But you don't think he seems a bit extreme?"

No, that was definitely George. The first one must be Derek.

"Extreme?" Derek huffed. "Nah, I think it's perfectly reasonable. I don't want those women here taking up our seats in the lecture halls, either. Besides, if they stay, the Headmaster might start giving away our scholarships to them."

"I suppose." George's voice faded.

So, Thomas's hate for us was merely revenge for a broken heart? How pathetic.

However, a little voice in the back of my head argued that I, too, hated men because of a heartbreak. But that was different. My heartbreak was far worse. Ma's death was a result of it.

I strangled the small voice of reason until I silenced it permanently and swung open the door with Henry's name on it. I didn't bother knocking, which, in hindsight, might not have been the best decision, but I had never been one to think before acting. I stomped into a much larger room than we women had been afforded and came up short. My eyes widened.

"Uh . . . I was looking for . . ." I stumbled over my words as I stared at the person in front of me.

They weren't Henry.

At first, I thought they were a woman, maybe here on some rendezvous. The longer I gaped, the more I realized they weren't a woman but a man in women's clothing.

His cheeks turned bright red, the same shade as the dress he modeled. "Please shut the door," he whispered.

As I yanked the door shut behind me, I glanced at the name posted beneath Henry's. *Christopher Nems.* I'd seen him in class, but certainly not dressed in that attire.

I wasn't sure what to say or do. I had never seen a man in women's clothing before. I had seen a man taking off a woman's clothing, my own. The memories of rough, callused skin against mine and the sound of our heavy breathing flashed through my mind. Memories that were now tainted by what had followed shortly after. Christopher cleared his throat before the memories could consume me.

"Please don't tell anyone. They would kill me." His words spewed out like vomit.

He meant them, too. If someone around here saw a man dressed like that, the whole town would turn against him. He'd wind up cold as a wagon tire.

No one could be too different in the South.

"I won't." I looked anywhere but at him. The room had two beds, a dresser, and a desk—much more spacious than Catherine's and mine.

"Swear it?" Christopher asked. Sweat collected above his brow, and the skirt of his dress shimmied with tremors. Why would anyone ever choose to wear such a thing? I was born a woman, yet I despised having to wear such atrocious attire.

"I swear," I spat as I reached over and handed him the letter. "As long as you don't read this. It's for Henry."

"I won't read it." His gaze scanned over his attire and then back at me with raised eyebrows as if to emphasize all the reasons he would do as I asked.

I turned around to leave but stopped. "Does he know about . . ." I knew he would understand what I referred to—the elephant, or rather, the dress and heels, in the room.

"Yes. He's a good friend and would never tell anyone. He knows how dangerous the consequences would be." Christopher's gaze dropped to the floor. His long lashes created spider leg shadows over his blood-red cheeks.

"Then why risk it?" Being a woman was already an arduous ordeal. Why would someone choose such a fate when they didn't have to?

"Because dressing like this makes me feel like myself. It feels right."

I nodded without giving a response and made sure not to open the door too wide while leaving, just in case anyone was in the hallway. I didn't need another death on my hands.

Chapter Eleven

Catherine

Crossed knives signify a quarrel soon to come.

After planning it for several days with Lucille, I was even more determined to give a speech and exercise my rights, as the women up north had. And even more so given how despicable the male students acted toward us the whole third week of classes—worse than the first.

I repeated this in my head as I walked to the headmaster's office and rehearsed what I would say to him. I reminded myself that Headmaster Sullivan and Reverend Ward were intelligent, well-educated gentlemen. They would understand my qualms and admire my bravery. My tutors had always listened, Daddy had, too, when he wasn't smoking in his cigar room or monitoring his bank's performance. Even Mama had listened, if it were always accompanied with a snide remark or degrading comment.

As I pulled open the large, double doors that led into his office, I briefly admired the intricacies of the carved wooden panels sculpted into a scene from the Bible, a relief of Adam and Eve. She held a half-eaten apple in her hand, and Adam glowered at her in disappointment and rage.

Headmaster Sullivan and Reverend Ward were both hunched over a large oak desk, examining papers strewn across its surface. As I entered, their heads snapped up, and identical frowns appeared on their faces.

"How can we help you today, young lady?" Headmaster Sullivan wiped the sweat from his forehead with a handkerchief.

I looked between the two men. They would understand my reason and logic.

They had to.

Reverend Ward straightened up and placed his hands in front of his chest. His sunken eyes roamed over me. My skin prickled with chill bumps.

"Are you in need of spiritual guidance?" He reached for the Bible resting on the edge of the desk. Did he take it everywhere with him? Ready to crack it open for any woman who might need a push back to the right path.

Reverend Ward's path, that is.

"No, I want to propose something to the headmaster." I tried to speak loudly and calmly so they would think of me as confident, as Lucille had advised, but the quiver in my voice betrayed me.

"Whatever you have to propose to me, you can express in the presence of the reverend as well." The headmaster tilted his head. His double chin squished to the side.

The walls displayed crossed swords and stuffed heads of dead animals—a circle of death. Their beady, lifeless eyes stared down at me. The words I had rehearsed escaped my mind. With open mouths, the men and the stuffed heads waited for me to speak. I cleared my throat and wiped my palms on my skirt.

"Well . . ." I cleared my throat again for the words to come out without a squeak. "I want to propose a speech."

They continued to stare as sweat rolled down my spine.

I went on, "A speech to give to our cohorts in the university auditorium about the right women have to be here and get the same chance at a higher education as men."

"Do you not already have that? Is that not the whole reason you're here?" Headmaster Sullivan asked pointedly.

"Well, yes, but . . . I . . . I'm asking to speak about what is happening within these walls, to speak about punishment that falls upon us women when it's not deserved and patterns of intimidation by our male counterparts. They're making it rather difficult." My voice faltered, and I stuttered. I'd felt so much more confident when discussing this with Lucille, my words and ideas had flowed easily, now everything jumbled under their stares.

"Difficult? Obtaining all the best things in life is difficult. That's what makes it so rewarding once achieved. But if you and the other young ladies can't handle difficult things, then this may not be the place for y'all to be." The headmaster's eyebrows thrust upward with each word, making his forehead have as many rolls as his chin.

"That's not what I—"

"Besides, women shouldn't be giving speeches. It says in the Bible, 'I permit no woman to teach or to have authority over men; she is to keep silent.'" Reverend Ward's hand lowered as he spoke. He caressed the crucifix that hung from his thin neck below his long beard. "You should strive to be meek and mild. Do we need to meet for some private sermons?" He lifted a too-thin brow.

I sucked in a gulp of air. This was not the reaction I had been expecting.

"No." My gaze dropped to the floor.

I couldn't believe this. Had Lucille been correct? Would they really not listen to reason and logic?

"Well, I'm glad this is resolved. You are dismissed." Headmaster Sullivan nodded to the exit and resumed his examination of the papers on his desk.

Defeated, I trudged to the door and pulled it open with the large, wooden handles.

Just before the doors latched shut, Reverend Ward called out, "God bless your soul."

Eve, holding the apple, looked submissively at the ground as Adam scolded her, and stared down at me. Did the headmaster choose this scene to remind him of how weak he thought women were? How little space we should take up in this world? Meek. Mild. Quiet. Small. Out of sight. Out of mind.

I wouldn't be like Eve. I wouldn't hold my head down and shrink under the angry gaze of a man. I would stand up before him and state my piece.

I would do this. I had to. With or without their permission.

Chapter Twelve

Victoria

The number thirteen is an ill omen.

Over the past few days of reading the old handwritten pages of the book, or grimoire rather, I'd been captivated. Witchcraft hidden in old southern superstitions passed down from one generation to the next filled its pages. The surviving witches who fled the north appeared to have come here seeking refuge. By then, they had learned to better disguise what they could do, using stories that were passed off as silly little wives' tales and superstitions. Witchcraft, as told by the unknown authors of this grimoire, required only three things: The Spirit, The Sacrifice, and The Superstition.

The Spirit was the willpower needed to wield the craft. It sounded like an easy endeavor, but if that were true, women might've won the vote by now.

The Sacrifice was by far the one that scared me the most. According to the grimoire, crafters had to give something, usually part of themselves, to get something. An equal trade.

The Superstition was the easiest part, choosing the right one to get the job done.

One page in the grimoire was titled "Bad Luck for Enemies." I'd heard The Superstition said among the girls at the mill, "*Walk under a ladder, and you'll have seven years of bad luck.*" I'd always thought it nonsense, but hidden within the words was a curse. All you needed was a piece of wood broken off from a ladder, some herbs, and a sacrifice.

I daydreamed about these things as the morning turned into afternoon and the classroom heated to a near-unbearable temperature, it seemed like class would never end. I tried to suppress the growls from my stomach, but they only grew louder. They were always there and always loud before I came here. Hunger remained ever present in the stomachs of mill girls and slum dwellers. A way of life. It lived in us, deep and comfortable, gnawing at us through every moment of every day.

Professor Compton finally brought his lecture on the history of the English language to an end. "Remember, students, every word, no matter how big or small, has immense meaning. Powerful meaning. Spanning across cultures, territories, and beyond."

The professor asked us to submit our reports, then we were free to go. I sprang from my desk, all too eager to get out of this hell. I gathered all my things and bent to grab my paper. I spent the last week working on it. My movements came to a startling halt when I realized my paper wasn't there in my bag where I'd put it.

I searched frantically, but it was nowhere to be seen.

I gestured to Catherine a row over from me. "Have you seen my paper?"

She looked around, only half awake from the long lecture, and then shook her head. "I don't see it."

"I can't find it anywhere." I turned in circles like a spool of thread coming undone, but I wasn't leaving until I found my paper.

The professor let out a loud gasp, so loud that even I had no trouble hearing it. "Mr. Black, this paper is marvelous."

My head snapped up at the commotion. I squinted. The professor held *my* paper in his hand. I immediately recognized my cursive scrawl and the brown ink, which was cheaper than the black and the only one I could afford. Thomas stole my paper.

Red flashed in my vision.

"That's my paper." I hoisted up my skirts and rushed to the professor's desk. "I wrote that paper. He stole it."

The professor squinted at me, then scanned over the paper. His lips trudged through his words with down-turned corners. "Is this true, Mr. Black?"

Thomas never broke eye contact with the professor or bothered to look in my direction and made it that much harder for me to hear him. I strained to listen as best as I could. "No, sir. I would never do such a dishonor to a lady."

The professor flipped the pages over in his hand and turned back to me. "Did you sign your name to these pages, Miss Woodhall?"

"I . . ." I clamped my mouth shut.

I hadn't signed my name.

"Well, as there is no name to these papers, and Mr. Black was the first to claim them, I will take them as his."

"But I spent the entire week working on it. My hands were ink-stained for days." I held out my hands and then cursed myself for scrubbing them clean that morning before class.

"I will let you have until tomorrow morning, Miss Woodhall. A moment later, and I'll chalk it up as another demerit in your file." He raised one eyebrow and looked at me as if I were a common thief.

I nodded solemnly and cursed under my breath as I turned away. The others watched. Lucille, with her choppy hair and tall, rigid posture, observed the scene with narrowed eyes. I wasn't normally one to cause a scene or pick fights, but something itched in me today. Something I imagined was like the sinister burn of witchcraft tingled my fingertips and palms.

I walked into the courtyard and waited for Thomas to emerge from the building. As he did, he laughed with his friends about what he'd just gotten away with. I bent down and retrieved a sharp rock from the ground. My fingertips began to throb with an unfamiliar burn, as if all the blood from my hands pooled into them, turning feverish and ready.

"Thomas, may I speak with you for a moment?" I feigned my most alluring voice and hoped to separate him from his pack.

That's how you took down a wolf, wasn't it?

He waved for his friends to continue on as if to say, *I can handle this.*

"You wanna write more papers for me, honey?" His lips slithered up in mockery.

"I won't do anything for you. And you won't steal any of my papers again," I said, with a calm that surprised even me.

"Oh, really? And what's going to stop me?" He sneered.

I squeezed the sharp rock into my palm as hard as I could, as hard and tight as my chest always felt between fits of coughing, until hot liquid dripped from it. I thought of one passage I'd read in the old grimoire.

The number thirteen is an ill omen.

Write a thirteen in blood on your hand and touch it to your enemy; wherever you touch will become ill or with pain. The illusion will expire when the blood is washed away.

Behind my back, I drew the number thirteen on both of my palms with my blood and brought my hands in front of me. I closed my fingers over them to keep the marks hidden. The burn in my fingertips spread to my palms and up my arms. The burn of witchcraft, I realized.

"Your hands might stop you." I tried to rein in the grin that threatened to spread across my face.

Thomas's eyebrows scrunched together. He brought his hands forward to assess them. I flattened my palms against his and held my breath.

A strange wind blew the moment his skin touched mine. Thomas doubled over, screaming. He yanked his hands away. His face darkened with screams of pain, making his pale white scar stand out—a phantom in a sea of red.

My thoughts of revenge vanished, and my heartbeat became as frantic as his reaction. *Was that supposed to happen?* I had read the witchcraft would be instant and intense, but those were only words. Now, it happened in front of me. A course set into motion that I no longer controlled. A train derailed. Heading for disaster.

I couldn't afford more casualties.

"My hands! My hands are on fire!" Thomas screamed and waved them around like he was trying to put out flames, though none were visible.

Passersby stared at him, not knowing why he yelled or how to help. Someone suggested sending for the campus physician. Thomas's face showed equal parts pain and mortification.

I took a step back, and then another, and nearly stumbled into the bushes. Thomas's screams dulled and muffled under the pounding of blood in my ears.

While everyone else watched Thomas's hysterics, Lucille stood down the path and stared with squinted eyes once again. This time, though, a smirk pulled at the corners of her thin, cracked lips. Her stare roamed over Thomas, his hands as he frantically waved them around, and then to me. To my hands, still covered in blood. The corners of her mouth lifted to a sly grin, as if she knew something—knew a secret.

A dark secret.

I yanked a layer of my skirts up and scrubbed the remaining evidence from my palms. Surely, she didn't know what I had done. She couldn't. I jerked up and spun around. I couldn't be found at the scene of a crime I caused.

Again.

The next day, every bump or thump I heard throughout the dorm made me jump. I had already made the mistake once of not locking my door and had to shove the book under my covers when Josephine barged in to rant about some nonsensical thing. I wouldn't make that mistake again. It was too dangerous. This time I had bolted the door behind me.

But even with the risk that hung over my head, opening the age-colored pages felt like coming back home after a long day. They continued to captivate me more and more, even with the scare with Thomas the day before. This book could provide someone with anything they wanted in life, it may be exactly what I needed to get out of this town, get as far away from the memory of Maggie, from the rest of the mill girls who blamed me for her death, rightfully so. But I couldn't stop myself from thinking about all the ways it could help those very same girls, even if they did want to condemn me.

I wasn't naive, though. It would be dangerous if someone found out I practiced witchcraft. Abigail Abercombie's story ran through my mind again. She hung for hours. She was buried vertically, so as not to pass on to the afterlife. Even in death she would not find peace or refuge from the cruelties of this world.

A scream reverberated down the hall and through my door. I nearly jumped out of my skin and shoved the book under my pillow.

My heart hammered in my ears, I took a deep breath and listened for a moment. It was probably some silly commotion, many of the women had a flair for the dramatics. Isabelle probably found another spider in her room. The spider she swore was a brown recluse last time ended up being a Granddaddy Long Legs. Everybody knew those wouldn't hurt anybody.

More screams followed the first and I jumped from my bed and crept to the door. With a gulp, I hoped whatever I found wouldn't be deadly—or dying. Maggie's too small and too cold body flashed before my eyes. Her hand still gripping mine, even as the rest of her went limp.

Cold metal met my hand as I gripped the handle and pulled. Its unoiled hinges creaked loud enough for even my ears to hear, but it was nothing compared to the chaos ensuing on the other side.

A large rattlesnake slithered in the middle of the hallway. Its tail vibrating a warning. Its mouth was open, ready to strike. From the screams that came from some of the bedrooms, it must not be the only one either.

I wanted to retreat back to my room, but another snake had slithered out from where Catherine ran from and into my own room while I'd watched the pandemonium before me. I jumped away and ran into the hallway, narrowly avoided stepping on the snake. It had begun to coil itself tightly and spring out at anyone too close for its liking. It was scared, and I didn't blame it.

"Where is Lucille?" Alice shouted from on top of her bed. She used a broom to bat a snake that had taken too much interest in climbing her bedpost. "She can get them out!"

"Who let them *in*?" I nearly had to play hopscotch to jump from one safe square of carpet to another.

"Who do you think?!" Alice swatted a bird out of her bedroom window. "We had our windows open to let in the breeze. Thomas and the others threw them in and ran off!"

I sucked in a breath. This was because of me, because of what I'd done to Thomas the day before, after class. The wound I'd caused to his ego.

"One of them almost landed on my head!" Catherine screamed. "Shouldn't we get out of here?"

"And leave the snakes in here to hide? Then we'll never be able to find them and get them out!" Alice abandoned her broom as the snake she'd been batting latched on to it with its venomous fangs.

It was hard to hear either of them. Isabelle stood on top of a small stool by her bed, screaming at the top of her lungs. The snake that'd been in the hallway had retreated to her room and was now scaling the side of the stool. Before I could do anything, as if in slow motion, the already angry snake got to the top of the stool, coiled its scaly body, and sprang. Sinking its teeth deep into Isabelle's flesh.

Everything fell silent. Everything, reptile and human, went still. Then her shriek pierced the air.

Chapter Fourteen
Lucille

Never speak while a clock is chiming; evil spirits will be attracted, and death will follow.

An earsplitting scream met me at the door of our dormitory. It flew open before I could grab it. Alice grabbed my arm hard enough to bruise. "Lucille! Thank God!"

"Snakes!" Catherine gasped from behind her. "They threw snakes through the windows!" Victoria was behind Catherine, her pale skin even paler.

For half a heartbeat, I thought they meant garter snakes, the harmless sort that slipped through fields and barns like stray cats. I'd caught and played with them plenty out on the farm.

Then I saw the thick-bodied coil on the floor in the hallway. Its tail was nothing more than a blur; it vibrated so violently. Its mouth opened wide, showing us its fangs, like a soldier on the battlefield, waving a loaded gun at their enemy—a warning. My stomach dropped.

I crept around it, checking the other rooms, trying to form a plan. As I made my way to an open bedroom door, the never-ending scream rang louder, splitting the air and my ears. Isabelle stood on a chair, trembling, skirts gathered to her knees, her face pale and her eyes wide. Her ankle dripped blood like melted wax from a candle. I caught a glimpse of the perpetrator as it slithered away and under Isabelle's bed upon my arrival.

"She's been bitten," Catherine called from where she remained by the front door, voice tight with terror. "Lucille, please do something."

They all looked at me then. Not just as friends, but as people who had already decided I was their only hope. For good reason. I knew snakes the way other people knew hymns. I'd pulled them from henhouses and wells, learned which ones struck fast and which only bluffed.

"Everyone, stay calm," I commanded, my voice steadier than I felt. "Move slowly and don't scream."

Another snake slid from mine and Catherine's room, angry and rattling. Poisonous. I counted them off in my head. There were three that I could see, probably more hiding.

"Thomas, George, and Derek, maybe some others with them," Alice whispered. "They were laughing as they threw them in and ran."

Of course, they ran. Cowards. Though I couldn't help but wonder how they had caught so many. If I hadn't disliked them so much, I might have admired their efforts.

"Catherine, Victoria, get Isabelle out of here and tie one of those ridiculous stockings around her ankle, just above the bite. Tight. Alice, go check the other rooms, make sure there aren't any others." I barked commands and cringed at how similar I sounded to Pa.

Once everyone left Isabelle's bedroom, I crouched next to her bed, which her attacker had slithered under to hide. Its rattle still echoed from the dark shadows.

I took a deep breath and closed my eyes, like I had more than a dozen times before, the way Ma had taught me, and her ma had taught her. The Spirit burned through me in rapid succession, without much effort. It tingled, not just in my fingers and toes, but everywhere in between.

I snatched a sewing needle from Isabelle's dresser and quickly shoved it into the tip of my finger without a flinch. Blood for The Sacrifice bubbled up. Drops of ruby red fell to the floor like tears, blending with the dark stain from Isabelle's wound.

The words of The Superstition came to the forefront of my mind with ease, but as I opened my mouth to chant them, they caught in my throat.

The room tilted, and suddenly I was back there again. Back to that night with Reece. Mud. Blood. Fear. The burning tingle in my body too strong, too hot, too angry. The screams that followed me into sleep, even now.

My chest seized. My vision tunneled.

And before a strange wind could begin, the burning in my chest disappeared altogether. My blood stopped dripping. The wound on my finger crusted over.

No witchcraft came.

My hands shook so badly I had to press them into the floor to steady myself. The words wouldn't come. Whatever I'd once had access to was locked behind the memory, and terror, of that night.

"Shit," I cursed myself, cursed Reece, cursed Pa, for taking the one thing that made me feel a sense of control in a world that forced submission. For taking what Ma taught me, what held her close to my heart, along with a long line of women before us who used the craft.

"Isabelle? Isabelle!" Catherine's voice rose from our room and then rose higher. "She's unconscious!"

I pushed myself from the floor, hands still shaking, and sprinted down the hall. Isabelle's body was slack, eyes rolled back. Her breath came shallow and wrong. Blood stained the side of my bedsheets where she lay.

"Go get the Headmaster! Get the doctor from the infirmary! Get the reverend!" I threw out the words in Alice and Victoria's direction.

As their footsteps pounded down the hall and the front door slammed behind them, I sat down on the bed next to Isabelle and took hold of her hands. I didn't bother praying. Venom spread faster than prayer ever had.

My eyes darted to the shadows, to the space beneath the furniture, to the places snakes loved best. We hadn't caught a single one. They had all hidden by now, somewhere in the rooms, rattlers still rattling, reminding us that even if we survived this, the danger hadn't left.

And neither had the men who put them there.

My dreams were filled with screams. First Reece's, his body limp and sweaty in my arms.

Then the world spun.

The body in my arms morphed into Isabelle's. She trembled, looking up at me with desperation in her eyes. Silently asking why I hadn't saved her.

Why I had failed.

I jolted from sleep, bleary-eyed and discombobulated. At first, not recognizing where I was. Cots were lined in two rows of five in the middle of the empty auditorium. Our makeshift home for the past couple of days while campus security searched for and captured the snakes from our dorm. Thankfully, this would be our last morning to wake up here. Headmaster Sullivan informed us that the snake-removal efforts were complete as of yesterday afternoon, and we could move our things back to the dormitory today.

Catherine's hands gripped my shoulders from where she shook me.

"What is it? What's the matter?" I searched for any signs of trouble.

The others stretched their aching backs as they rose from their own cots. The open space filled with grunts and frustrated sighs. We were all ready to be back in the dormitory, even that was better than this arrangement.

"I'm nervous about my speech today. I couldn't sleep." Catherine swept a piece of her fiery hair behind her ear. "Besides, you were making an awful lot of noise. What were you dreaming of?"

"Nothing," I replied, a bit too quickly.

Catherine raised her eyebrows. Her freckled cheeks squished against her eyes. "Were you having a naughty dream about someone?"

She wasn't far from the truth.

"No, of course not. Why are you nervous?" I swung the covers off and stretched my arms above my head, my back cracked in more places than one. I patted down my tangled mess of hay-like hair.

Catherine's cot gave way to a loud squeak as she sat on it and looked down at her hands. "Well, I've never really given a speech before. My sister Elsabeth is magnificent at singing in church. I've never been as talented as her or any of my other sisters, though."

Being an only child, I couldn't imagine having as many sisters as Catherine, though living in the dorm and now in this auditorium, I was certainly getting a feel for it. Ma had gotten pregnant plenty of other times, but each time had never amounted to much more than blood and pain. Pa wanted a boy, consequences be damned. She swore it would kill her, and so did the doctor.

They were right.

"I doubt your sisters can teach someone how to sit with a crinoline or wrestle down my wild hair like you can," I offered instead, pushing my thoughts of my folks down as if pressing down soil in a freshly tilled garden. Or over a hole dug for a dead body.

"You know, if you came and stood beside me, I'm sure I would feel much more confident." Catherine's emerald eyes pleaded.

I shook my head for the dozenth time at this suggestion. "You know how I feel about this. No speech is going to do a damn thing." Catherine's frown made me add, "We've rehearsed plenty. Your speech is going to be great whether they listen or not."

A speech wouldn't work, it wouldn't change the direction of the tide, but witchcraft would.

Just the thought alone made my fingers itch to be pricked. But it also made my heart race, and my mind flash with those awful memories. I quickly shifted my thoughts, not wanting the nightmare to resurface, instead my mind moved onto the last person I had seen do witchcraft besides myself: Victoria.

As I pulled on my chemise, dress protectors, and drawers. I recalled when I had seen days prior, before the events that had ensued and landed us here in this stupid auditorium. At first, I thought I had to be mistaken. I'd never seen anyone besides myself or my Ma practice the craft before. But, alas, I had not been mistaken. Somehow, Victoria had used the craft. Gave that scoundrel, Thomas, a good scare, no doubt.

As Catherine and I left the auditorium, I gave her an encouraging "good luck!" as we went our separate ways on the cobblestone path. I went to my regular writing bench, my mind circled around Victoria. How had she gained knowledge of the craft?

I resolved to find out more later and took Henry's latest letter from my bag. He'd slipped it under my dormitory door before the event of the snakes. I was thankful I'd gotten back to the room before Catherine. I couldn't imagine how many questions she'd have had if she'd found it.

I'd considered throwing away the letter without reading it, but admittedly, my curiosity had gotten the better of me. As I unfolded the crisp piece of parchment, I couldn't help but admire his elegant penmanship. He repeatedly cross-wrote just to fit more on the page, seeming to never run out of words.

How truly typical of a man.

Dear Miss Rockwell,

I believe there has been a miscommunication between us. It is not and never will be my intention to pretend to know the extent of women's, or anyone else's, experiences in this world. One can't possibly know those things unless they have lived in the person's heart and mind for some time.

I believe this situation can be rectified by getting to know one another. Perhaps if you knew me, and I you, we could more clearly see the perspectives we both come from and understand our differences, even if we can't come to agree.

Normally, I would insist a lady goes first on such occasions, but since this situation is of a peculiar type, I shall start.

My name is Henry Alexander Lockhart. I am six years past my twentieth and have a sister three years my senior and a mother twice my senior. My father died at the beginning of the war. I, too, fought in the war. After losing my leg and returning home, I attained a position in business.

I feel it necessary to say that my idea of a relationship involves no sacrifice of individuality. I would like to have perfect equality in a relationship, but it should be the equality of progress, not of decay. If both parties cannot think more, feel more, talk more, and work more than they could alone, I will remain an old bachelor and adopt a dog as an object of my affection instead.

Now, may I have the privilege of getting to know you? I shall write to you again either way. You can burn the letters if you like or answer them as you feel inclined.

Your friend (if you'll have me),
Henry Lockhart

I snorted. Privilege of getting to know me? *How ridiculous.*

The bell tower scared a flock of birds from their perch. It was time for Catherine's speech. Guilt rose in my chest. Maybe I should've gone to support her, even if I didn't think her speech would do any good. We had become friends, hadn't we? I had hoped that this friendship wouldn't end in heartbreak and betrayal. And I had worked tirelessly to help her plan this whole damn thing, might as well be there to see it through to the end.

I gathered up my things and made my way to where Catherine's speech would be given.

For the first time in days, maybe weeks, clouds gathered in the sky and blocked the sun. Shadows crawled across the ground. They made the campus ghostly and unnatural. Sickness churned in my stomach.

I quickened my pace and tried to sidestep a group of men gathered on the path.

"Oh yeah, she won't see it coming." They spoke loudly, not caring about being heard by others, not raised to be meek and quiet.

"Serves her right for trying to preach to us."

I halted. Were they talking about . . .

"About women's rights of all things."

"She'll never try to preach to us again after what we have in store for her."

Catherine. I ran toward where she was giving her speech.

Chapter Fifteen
Catherine

Burning cheeks are an indication evil influences are working against you.

The large wooden box I'd struggled to carry across campus became my impromptu stage. Men gathered with their hands covering sly grins and whispered to one another.

I cleared my throat and smiled at those before me. I hoped I looked confident despite my burning cheeks. I tried to remember to keep my back straight and my stomach sucked in like Mama always nagged me to.

"Good morning, y'all," I began, then stopped to swallow. "Thank you for taking the time to listen to what I have to say."

Everyone gawked at me. The whispers dissipated but didn't stop entirely. Thomas stood in the center of the small crowd, ready to make the lives of everyone around him much more difficult. He had a hand in his overstuffed satchel and a grin on his scarred face.

"I wanted to talk to all y'all about something dear to me that should be dear to all y'all as well. Everyone has a woman in their lives; a mother, sister, aunt, or grandmother that I'm sure you care deeply about." I had imagined someone would clap at this when I'd written it with Lucille. But no one did, so I continued.

"I stand here to make something clear. There is a habit, long practiced and rarely questioned, of declaring women intellectually lacking. Not openly, not always aloud, but through lowered expectations, through the careful way opportunity is rationed and explained away. We are told, again and again, that men are superior in mind, and that women's failures merely confirm a natural order.

"But superiority cannot be claimed until equality has been attempted. You cannot deny women the same education, the same encouragement, the same latitude to err and grow and then point to the outcome as proof of deficiency. That is not assessment. It's design. It's a test administered with one hand tied behind the back and then cited as evidence that the subject could never have succeeded."

"I know some will say these are isolated incidents. That each slight, each failure, each punishment exists alone, unconnected to the last. But isolation is a convenient fiction. When the same outcomes repeat themsel—"

Something wet and solid hit the side of my face, an inch from my mouth. Then, another, before I had time to process the first one. It squelched as it pelted my stomach and fell to the ground with a soggy thud. I lifted my hands to protect my face. A sticky substance met my fingers. My mouth hung open and shock froze me in place. It was warm and runny to the touch. I yanked my fingers away and stared at them. My muddled mind stalled, then slowly processed what I saw.

Blood.

I searched the ground. Two small, glistening lumps lay there.

No. Not just lumps.

Bodies. Dead rats.

Their fur glistened crimson in the scorching sun. The day's heat melted the blood on my skin. It ran down my cheek and dripped onto my dress. My stomach churned and bile rose in my throat.

Another smack against my body, then a dull thud on the ground. And then again. Small bodies pelted against mine and fell to the ground in thumps. Before long, it was as if the sky had opened up and was raining dead rats. One after another, they kept coming.

Shock turned to adrenaline. Throwing my arms over my face, I jumped off the wooden box—my stage turned execution block.

Laughter and shouting ensued. I ran, and part of the crowd followed. They continued to barrage me with rat bodies. I recognized a few of my assailants from class.

How did they have so many dead rats? Splotches of blood caked all over my skin.

"Serves you right!" someone yelled. "You'll learn your lesson!"

Others joined in, whooping and hollering as if this were a pleasant evening out on the game field for them.

I tripped over a hole and tumbled to the ground. My dress ripped. Then there were hands on me. I fought them off, thinking they must belong to my attackers. They were out for *my* blood now.

"Catherine, it's me! It's me!" Lucille's eyes were wild, her face slick with sweat, and her hands bloody as she tried to help me up. I couldn't speak but could only hold on to her with all my strength as we raced through campus, trying to distance ourselves from the hell we were in.

Once we reached our dormitory, Lucille yanked the doors open and dragged me into the building. She slammed the doors and shoved a broom into the door handles behind us. I had never been happier to be in this undersized and underwhelming hallway.

Chapter Sixteen
Victoria

Never bring an old broom into a new home lest you bring negative energy with you.

In my dark, closet-like room, I tucked the old grimoire underneath my mattress as I finished unpacking the few things I had bothered bringing with me to stay in the auditorium the past few nights. The experience had been far too similar to packed flophouses, and I was more than happy to be back in the privacy of my small room. My need to go to work outweighed my desire to stay here and bask in the quiet solitude it offered. The bed creaked as I arose and opened the door with a squeal of protest.

I froze.

Lucille and Catherine lay sprawled against the front door. A broom shoved into the handles of the doors behind them effectively barricaded them in—or someone else out.

Their chests heaved with each gulp of air. Their hair disheveled, and their dresses torn. But the most shocking of all was the substance that covered them. A bright red liquid coated them completely. The stench of copper and rust hit my nose.

Blood. Blood covered them.

I gagged, then held my breath.

Bits of fur and other parts stuck to the blood-like paste. It was all over their skin and clothes and matted into their hair, like two soldiers who just emerged from war, lives hanging on by a thread and a will.

Lucille and Catherine turned to me with frantic, wide eyes. Their mouths hung open. The desperation in their faces reminded me of Maggie, but for her, it had already been too late. I had failed to protect her, failed to stop the men that came for her for what we had been doing, who attacked her instead of me because I hadn't been there. And the other girls at the mill hated me for what I had done—what I let happen, what I hadn't been there to stop.

It wasn't too late now, not for Catherine and Lucille, not for the rest of the women at the university. That thought made my feet move further down the hallway. The helpless and wild panic on their faces made me sling an arm under Catherine and help Lucille hoist her up. We carried her down the hallway to their room. I slammed the door behind us. We needed privacy.

I spun around and stared at them.

Catherine began explaining without me asking. It started as a mumble and then became frantic. Her words spilled out of her like cotton pouring from a gin. I only picked up about half of her words, but that was enough to piece together the nightmarish events.

I wished I hadn't panicked the day I had used witchcraft on Thomas—wished I would've done more to the vile man. He and his friends were getting out of control. If no one stopped them, they would end up doing more than just hurting one of us. And it wouldn't be just a snake bite or rat's blood that would cover us.

I pulled towels from their dressers and handed them to the two blood-soaked women. Lucille had less blood and entrails on her than Catherine. They covered her completely. The blood acted as glue. Rat fur stuck to her, like being tarred and feathered.

Lucille and I plucked the entrails from her skin and hair. Both women had to remove their outer dresses. They stood in their underclothes, exposed and shaking. We threw the dresses into a heap on the floor instead of the hamper. There would be no use trying to launder them; they'd need to be thrown away.

Or burned. The memory of such mistreatment permanently scorched from the earth forever. If only I could scorch it from my mind, too.

Catherine sobbed. Afraid her wailing would reach across campus and alert those deviants to their victory; I patted her back.

"Sh. Sh, it's okay. It'll be okay," Lucille soothed Catherine. She did it better than I could, so I kept quiet.

"No, it won't. They're never going to give up. They're just going to keep torturing us." Spittle and tears dripped onto her chin as Catherine talked through her sobs. "We might as well all leave now. That's how it will end for us, anyway. Why go through being mistreated like this?"

Lucille stopped wiping Catherine's skin and sat straight up. She looked from Catherine to me.

"That won't happen," she stated with a tone of finality, as if something had just clicked into place. She'd made a decision.

"You mean we're going home?" Catherine's eyes lit up.

Lucille shook her head. "No. We're not. We can't. If we leave now, every woman in this state will have to abandon their aspirations for a higher education. If we give that away, we might as well give everything else up, too. Our freedom. Our right to vote. Our right to own property. We need to stand our ground and fight for our right to be here now."

Lucille's eyes blazed. I wished I could be like her, brave and fearless instead of always running.

"But how? They always win." Catherine's voice broke. She sat so hunched that her chin touched the tops of her breasts.

"Witchcraft," Lucille replied simply, as if it were the most ordinary thing in the world.

Catherine gasped but I didn't even flinch.

The word that could get us all killed almost seemed normal after reading about it, and even practicing it, over the past few days.

"My ma taught me before she passed. Not much of it, but enough that we can turn the tables on this war against us." Lucille bent down, lifted her mattress, and grabbed a journal similar to the one she was always walking around with, but this one was older, tattered around the edges.

"This is what she taught me." She flipped through the pages. It was thin, made even thinner by missing or torn-out pages. It looked similar to the grimoire I kept hidden under my mattress, only smaller.

Before I'd made my decision, my legs moved of their own accord. I marched out of the room. Their stares burned into my back as I went. They probably thought I was off to tell the headmaster about this discussion or refuse to be part of it. Either of those options would've been smart, better than the one I was about to take. I grabbed the overstuffed grimoire from under my mattress and went back to their room. I slammed my grimoire down on Lucille's bed before I could change my mind. They both sucked in surprised gasps.

Selling it for a train ticket was officially out of the question.

"I found this in the cellar of the library."

"I knew it!" Lucille grinned. She snatched it up and flipped through the pages. Her eyes grew wider with each page. "Holy hell! This is at least three times the size of mine. It's got witchcraft for everything."

"Wait." Catherine held up her hand.

I expected her to go into hysterics again at any moment. Maybe this was it. She had come to her senses and might report us herself.

"Are we a coven now?" Catherine asked simply. She was untroubled, especially given her tendency to be rather naive. Or, perhaps, her naivete was exactly what made her so agreeable.

Lucille snorted. "Well, we can't just go around calling ourselves a coven unless we want to be put to death by hanging."

"What about a sorority?" Catherine asked. Mucus and tears dried and crusted on her face.

"A what?" Lucille and I asked simultaneously.

"It's a society of women. It says so in our entomology textbooks Professor Compton gave us for language studies."

I doubted the professor had imagined his textbook would be used in such extracurricular activities as this.

Lucille sat silent for a minute. She seemed to turn the word over in her mind. "A sorority, you say?" she asked as if testing out the word on her tongue. "I like it. Sorority it is." She smiled.

Catherine and Lucille looked at me expectantly. I returned their gaze, but could only see the girls forced to work in the mills and factories, most of the time dying there, too. I saw my mother, who died as an outcast in her own town. It could have changed all their lives if they'd had the opportunity to have an education. Their deaths could have been prevented.

It might have prevented Maggie's . . . I couldn't finish the thought. Instead, I blurted, "Fine. I'm in," before I could change my mind.

Both of their smiles spread to their gleaming eyes.

"We'll be just like Mama's church league, but even better," Catherine giggled, then added, "But we'll need to recruit more members."

Lucille nodded.

I couldn't help but think we were the farthest thing from a ladies' church league as one could get.

The corridors in the infirmary were narrow and overheated, the air thick with camphor that reminded me so much of the tinctures Maggie and I had made many times before, probably using many of the same ingredients.

Lucille swept in ahead of us like she owned the place, skirts snapping at her boot-clad heels, already demanding that the infirmary attendants tell her where Isabelle was. Catherine followed more carefully, gloved hands folded, her expression schooled into a calm concern she must've learned from years of practice in high society.

Coming here had been their idea, to check on Isabelle, invite her to be a part of our newly formed so-called sorority, our secret coven. I trailed behind them, quiet as ever, counting my steps and the way my chest rattled like the tail of the snake that had put Isabelle in here.

They had placed Isabelle near the back, away from the windows. She looked small. Her dark hair unpinned and braided loosely over one shoulder, her skin pale against the white of the sheets. One leg lay uncovered with her ankle wrapped thickly in linen, blotched faintly with rust-colored stains. I couldn't see the wound itself, and I was grateful for that. It would only bring up blood-soaked memories of Maggie.

Lucille was the first to speak when we got to Isabelle's bed. "You look like hell," she said, honest as ever, but then she added in a brighter tone, "Which means you survived. That's all that matters."

Isabelle turned her head slowly. Her eyes hazy with the laudanum that must be swimming through her veins. "You shouldn't be here."

Catherine smiled a soft, polished smile. "Of course we should. How are you feeling?"

"I feel," Isabelle said, "as though Thomas and his friends tried to kill me."

The words landed heavy and plain. No one contradicted her.

Lucille tightened her jaw and crossed her arms. I stood at the foot of the bed, my hands clasped so tightly together that my fingers tingled. Not the same tingle as when I had used the craft. Not nearly as intense.

"They said it was a prank. Said they didn't know the snakes were venomous," Lucille spat. "The headmaster and reverend barely batted an eye. '*Boys will be boys,*' they said."

Isabelle laughed then, a short, bitter sound that ended in a cough. Not her usual childish windchime giggle. She turned her face toward the plain, empty wall. "They'll call it whatever keeps them safe. All of them. The headmaster and reverend, too."

Silence pooled between us. This wasn't the same naive, doe-eyed girl that we'd met the first night here.

Somewhere down the hall, a man groaned, long and low. I focused on the rhythm of my breathing, careful not to draw too deeply, lest I cause a coughing fit.

Lucille cleared her throat. "Listen. That's not all we came for. This isn't just about them."

Isabelle's gaze flicked back, her eyes squinted. "Isn't it?"

"No," Lucille said, and barreled on before anyone could stop her. Her bravery was admirable, and dangerous. "It's about us. About staying. About not letting them win, not letting them take this opportunity away from us and everyone else in the state."

Lucille nudged Catherine with her elbow. We'd discussed this on the way here. Catherine held the same social status as Isabelle, was from the same societal rank. If Isabelle was going to say yes to anyone, it was Catherine.

Catherine looked at Lucille, who nodded encouragingly. The redhead inhaled, steadying herself. "We've been talking," she said. "About forming something. A society, of sorts. We're calling it a sorority. You know, a group of women united for a purpose. And, well, our purpose is . . . Well, it's to support each other and protect each other. A way to look after one another."

Lucille elbowed her again. Catherine's rambling ceased. Her mouth snapped closed.

Isabelle eyed us. "A sorority."

"We'll call it a sorority." Lucille leaned in eagerly, no longer able to stay silent. "Underneath the title, it'll be something stronger."

I watched Isabelle's fingers curl into the sheet. "You think a sorority will save you?"

"I think women together are harder to pick off," Lucille said matter-of-factly. "But we'll *really* be a—"

Coven. That's the word she was about to use. Say out loud. Admit openly. But Isabelle beat her to the punch.

"No," Isabelle said flatly.

My heart dropped. I knew this wouldn't work, but I hadn't been able to stop myself from having a little bit of hope. Hope that was now crushed.

Catherine blinked. "No?"

"I'm leaving," Isabelle said. "As soon as I can walk without help."

Lucille stiffened, jutting her chest out and her chin up. "You can't mean that."

"I very much do."

Lucille's voice sharpened. "You can't just walk away. Not now. You know what that means for everyone else."

Isabelle's gaze glistened as tears collected before spilling down her cheeks. "I nearly died."

"If you leave," Lucille pressed, "you're only making it easier for them to win."

Isabelle yanked her chin away from us. "That's not my responsibility."

I almost wanted to laugh at that, at the absurdity of it. Of course it wasn't. It wasn't anyone's responsibility as long as they had enough privilege for it not to affect them. But regardless of privilege or class, silence only supported oppressors.

Catherine reached for Isabelle's hand, stopping just short of touching it. "If five women leave," she said quietly, "they'll cancel the program. If you go, that leaves only four more women until they shut it all down. They're looking for any excuse."

Isabelle shook her head, but she remained looking away from us, not making eye contact. "Then let them."

Lucille's temper flared. "Do you know what that means? For the girls who come after us, their futures?"

Isabelle's voice cracked around her words, "I know what it means to wake up in a hospital bed, being told you barely survived, and realizing no one will be punished for it."

The room tilted with hopelessness. They kept talking. Voices rose and fell. I caught fragments: duty, fear, precedent. But I could see it then, clear as day. Isabelle was already gone. Her body lay before us, but her mind had packed its bags and was on its way out.

I swallowed and stepped back.

"I have work." My voice came out thin. I cleared my throat. "If you'll excuse me."

They turned toward me, surprised, as though they had forgotten I was there. Something I was used to.

Catherine nodded first. "Of course, Victoria. Thank you for coming with us."

Lucille nodded, already turning back to Isabelle. I slipped out quietly, the argument continuing behind me like a storm I couldn't stop.

I made my way back down the dim corridor, quickly asking the attendant where the doctor's office was. My steps were quick and quiet as I followed their directions, not wanting Lucille and Catherine to catch me in my lie.

The doctor's office was cramped and dim. A large desk took up most of the space. Bookshelves lined the walls on either side. Papers covered its surface. The doctor was an older man, stooped, with ink-stained fingers and tired eyes. His head jerked up as I entered. A frown turned the corners of his lips down.

I wasted no time getting to the point of my visit. He listened while I spoke of my concerns, though I kept it brief. I always did.

"You worked in a mill," he said, not unkindly, "for quite some time?"

"Yes, sir."

He examined me with brisk efficiency, listening to my chest, asking about the ringing in my ears, and the way voices blurred when I was tired.

"Cotton dust has collected in your lungs," he said finally. "And the noise from the powered looms damaged your eardrums. You're not the only one. This kind of thing . . . happens often to girls like you."

Girls like me. I thought of the girls I'd left behind. Prim with her perpetual cough. Beth, who had gone half-deaf before sixteen. The way the air in the mill would glow with lint, thick enough to taste.

"There's nothing to be done?" I asked, though I hadn't put much stock into having hope for a cure.

He hesitated, and his brow furrowed. "Plenty of rest. Clean air. Avoiding strain or overwork."

I nodded. Rest was a luxury I could afford now, but the other girls, the girls still at the mill, were broke for it. Clean air, even more so.

As I left his office, being sure to look both ways before exiting, not to run into Lucille or Catherine, the weight of it all settled heavy in my chest. Not just my own breath, and the rest of the mill girls', but Isabelle's choice, and the fragile thread holding the rest of us here.

Five girls. That was all it would take.

Four if she left.

I thought of the mill. Of the women who would never even have the chance to choose to leave it, especially if this program failed. And I knew, with a quiet certainty that did not ring or waver, that I could not afford to walk away. I had to stay. I had to be part of this movement, this purpose, this coven.

And if noise was not power, then perhaps endurance was.

Chapter Seventeen
Lucille

Always cover your mouth whilst yawning lest you invite evil spirits to enter your body.

This would either be our beginning or our unfortunate end. Only the women who showed up for the first sorority meeting could determine which.

Our dormitory had two floors, the first floor contained our make-shift hammy-down bedrooms. The second housed an open space with vaulted ceilings that exposed the wood beams holding up the pointed structure. Its patterned walls were an odd shade of dark green with sconces lining every few feet. They were the only light source, causing dark shadows to encompass much of the room, especially the corners. Heat rose from below and filled the space like a furnace. Sheets covered old furniture, desks, and chairs scattered about the room like ghosts. We speculated it had served as a meeting room or storage area at some point; in either case, it perfectly suited our sorority's needs.

Since Catherine, Victoria, and I established the sorority a few days ago, our goal was to recruit more members. Only ten women, including ourselves, were in our university program, so we didn't have many candidates to choose from. But we had to be extra careful with who we invited. We only asked those whom we felt we could trust and who could handle such an enormous secret.

Even if we could only get one or two women to join our cause, our secret coven hidden under the guise of a sorority, it would be better than just the three of us. However, the talk of adding more members made Victoria uneasy, all fidgeting fingers and darting eyes.

To my surprise, she was the next to arrive on the second floor. Though she came alone, I was relieved to see her come at all. To no one's surprise, Catherine brought in the most new recruits out of all of us, Alice and Rebecca. Her exuberant personality always had a way of attracting others into her circle. I brought Susan.

"Did you check on Isabelle again? See if she would change her mind?" I asked Catherine. She'd be the only person who'd be able to convince Isabelle she needed to be here.

Catherine shook her head. "Tried, but she was set on her decision."

For a few minutes, we stood around the large room in silence, fanning ourselves with stray leaflets and parchment. I could only stand the silence for so long. I pushed a thick strand of short hair behind my ear and cleared my throat.

"We're glad y'all came." I smiled and tried to remember what Ma had taught me about hospitality and proper greetings.

Catherine added, "Yes, we are!"

She used her elbow to nudge Victoria, who jumped and looked at Catherine with scrunched eyebrows before she realized what she wanted.

"Yeah . . . me too." She clearly didn't enjoy the spotlight.

I took her out of her misery. "Let's get down to business. As I'm sure y'all know, you're here because you want to be part of our sorority." I paused, unsure how to go on.

The women were told upon invitation that we would do something about the way we were treated. They knew it was a secret and even dangerous, but they didn't know the risk it entailed. They didn't know the extent of what we were here for, but sensitivity had never been my virtue and wouldn't be now, either.

"Also known as our secret coven."

The women around the room gasped. Eyes grew as wide as hay bales.

I went on. "Victoria and I have each been practicing the craft hidden in our ancestors' superstitions, and now are teaching Catherine, too, to help combat the discrimination shown to us by the men on campus. It has helped, but the three of us can only do so much on our own. If we all join together, we can make a greater impact."

Some more gasps sounded across the room, and a few worried whispers spread thick in the air like the scent of cow patties in an open pasture. Alice lifted her hand above her head as if she were asking a question in class.

"Yes?" I asked.

"Isn't witchcraft dangerous? Couldn't we get in a lot of trouble? Or worse, if we're found out for using it?" Alice held her chin up. "Especially for us." She motioned between her and Rebecca.

"This *will* be dangerous, but we have to do things we wouldn't normally do to get results we wouldn't normally get." My words floated in the air for a few seconds. I gave everyone time to absorb them. "And clearly, it's already dangerous just being here. As we saw with Isabelle. But it's dangerous anywhere in this world as a woman."

Susan chewed on her nails like she was trying to grind them down to nothing and Rebecca's lips moved silently as she repeated every few words Alice and I said. Their eyes darted toward the door. But they didn't turn and run. That had to be a good sign.

Alice nodded.

Rebecca spoke up, "Are the results worth such a huge risk? We'll just be winning the right to study here for a few more years until we graduate."

Another voice cut through the tension-filled air. A voice I certainly didn't expect.

"This may just be a brief part of your lives, but if we complete this program, it opens the door to higher education for the rest of the women in this state. A door like that being opened could be the difference between life in the slums and an early death or a life of more opportunities and a way out of poverty. Education is the key to our freedom; with that key, we can open even more doors down the road." Though Victoria's voice was quiet, it didn't lack strength. "Do this for yourselves, but more importantly, do this for all the women who will come after you. Your friends, your sisters, your daughters."

I gaped for a moment before nodding in an encouraging manner. Victoria didn't back out. She stayed, and even more so, helped our cause.

The light from the wall sconces and the candles we'd laid out around us lit the room in a wild dance of luminescence and shadow. They fought to win over each other on the patterned walls and faded carpeted floors. The battle of darkness and light. Good and evil. How very fitting as our environment for such a meeting.

Alice's head bobbed. She and Rebecca seemed to be out of questions. Susan mimicked her gesture of agreement, too, a little less wide-eyed. They were all so close to agreeing to this. I could see it in their eyes. They just needed a little extra push.

"Don't y'all want revenge for the way those bastards have been treating you? Don't y'all want to give them a taste of their own medicine?" I knew from experience nothing sealed the deal—like wax melted on an envelope holding our fate—quite like revenge.

Everyone nodded more enthusiastically now.

"Okay. I'm in," Alice announced. She stood close to Catherine. Their shoulders brushed and their puffy sleeves wrinkled. Catherine's body shook with a small shiver. "But I'm not doing this for me. I'm doing it for my sister and all the women to come after us. For women whose skin doesn't allow them to pass between communities, who don't get the same privileges."

"Me too," Susan agreed. "For my community. For the girls who don't get choices."

Rebecca looked at each of us. We stared back. She shifted from foot to foot, ready to take off.

Please. Please. Please.

I knew we were asking a lot, especially of her and Alice, their risk greater than any of ours. I mentally begged her not to turn on us. Not to be our demise. I hadn't even gotten to see my writing published yet.

Her foot twitched toward the door. I imagined our unfortunate ending. Would it be by rope? Or fire? Maybe they would allow me to write the inscription for my tombstone. Or would I even get a stone? Maybe an unmarked grave would be our fate.

My heart raced, pounding blood in my ears.

Rebecca let out a long breath. "Alright. Me too."

"Yay!" Catherine clapped. "We should sign some sort of contract or pledge."

"That's a great idea." I pulled out my journal and flipped to the last page. I tapped the pen against my chin as I thought. Then I began to write, allowing enough room at the bottom for us all to sign.

When I finished, everyone leaned in to see it. Catherine read aloud:

"We, the Southern Sorority of Superstitious Witches,
will use the craft to help pave the path
for the women of the future,
and the retribution of women past."

Catherine smiled and her eyes almost disappeared behind her cheeks. "Short but effective. I like it."

"It's perfect," Victoria said.

"Shall we sign it?" Catherine gestured for me to hand her the pen.

I started to pass it but paused and shook my head. Mama always said our blood was part of us, part of our soul. What you spilled your blood for remained one with your soul forever. Bound you eternally, a promise never to be broken, a sacrifice never to be given back.

"This isn't something we should sign with normal ol' ink. We need to bind ourselves to this. Make it into witchcraft of its own. It'll protect us. Whoever signs it in blood, gives themselves to it, will be bound to this coven, bound to protect it. May I borrow a hatpin?" I asked Catherine.

She pulled one out and gave it to me. A stray copper-colored curl fell from underneath her dainty, feathered hat. I jabbed the sharp tip of the hatpin into the soft pad of my finger. Blood bubbled and dripped as I pressed it against the bottom of the page. It left behind a dark ruby smudge. A piece of myself left there forever.

I brought my finger to my mouth and sucked the small wound. Salt and copper met my tongue like an old friend. After I wiped the edge of the hat pin on my handkerchief, I passed it to Victoria. She didn't hesitate to mimic my actions and stab the sharp point into her flesh without wincing. Her bloody fingerprint sat beside mine, which was now turning brown with oxidation. Catherine went next. She winced and let out a sharp gasp as she pricked her finger.

Alice followed, and so did the rest. Eventually, every woman in the room had pierced their skin and marked the pledge with their own blood. A piece of them, forever on the parchment. A piece of their soul permanently left behind.

"What should we do now?" Susan asked around her bleeding nails. She'd been quiet through most of the meeting.

"We get revenge." Catherine responded without hesitation, as if this thought had been at the forefront of her mind all afternoon.

Victoria and I didn't need to question who or what she was referred to, with the memory of Catherine and I covered in rat's blood imprinted permanently on our minds.

"What will be our first big act as a sorority?" Alice cupped her bleeding finger to her white bodice. It left behind a red stain.

I'd been thinking about this since that hellish day. I'd imagined many dark and twisted ways we could exact our revenge on them.

"They didn't seem to have any problem getting their hands bloody, did they?" I asked. A devilish grin spread on my face. "But, before we do anything too big as a group, we'll need some time to practice and to gather a few supplies."

Everyone nodded and leaned in. They seemed to feel the excited energy that came off me as I described the different things we would need and how we might practice before we exacted our big revenge.

I woke up early the next day, leaving our dormitory before the sun rose, while darkness and silence still shrouded the campus. It was not yet on fire from the sun's heat and the war, much like the war that had ended less than a decade ago. At least in this one, we were no longer just helpless victims.

I took a deep breath and let the dewy morning air fill my chest. Then I started writing. I wasn't sure yet why I kept writing to Henry. Maybe I liked to argue with him. Maybe I just liked having someone to talk to. Maybe it was the distance we kept, not saying any of these words to his face, but rather on paper. Not in the same way I had spat things in anger, which I did quite often, but rather the vulnerable, defensive bits hidden behind those words.

Henry,

You must be sick in the mind or delusional if you think I would waste my time, time which I have far more important things to do with than participating in this little game of yours. Experience has taught me that it is far better to be alone and true to oneself than to procure companionship by being false. One can well afford to purchase loneliness if the price is a life rendered full and intense by a worthy purpose. And if it is the case of lacking funds, I regard moral independence far more needful than monetary independence.

Though, if I were going to spend my time becoming familiarized with someone, I might start with the facts. That is, I have worked on a farm my whole life. I have seen life and death and everything in between, repeated over and over again. I have raised animals only to slaughter them.

I have bred animals, which is no different at times, I should think, than women reproducing. So much like pigs or cows. Bred for an offspring and then forgotten, left to the slaughterhouse. And the offspring, too, are looked over and forgotten. If it is the runt, that is, not meeting society's standards in any way, then it too is taken to the slaughterhouse. And the cycle, a deadly one, repeats.

How soon the character of gender and race would change if pure and equal, real and kind marriages took the place of the horrible relations that now bear that sacred name? I must admit, some of your views on the topic have surprised me. However, I'm not surprised that the only authors you named as your favorites are male. Until you use your monetary gains to support women professionals, I suspect you will not see any signs of change or achievement for them in society. I know the objectives I seek to accomplish will not be attained until long after my body has gone to ashes, but I shall not falter in my opinions or beliefs. No man shall make me yield. My words may come off as angry, but anger is far more desirable than quiet indifference. Are you angry on behalf of us women, Henry, or just quietly indifferent?

Un-sincerely,
Miss Lucille Rockwell

A weight lifted from my shoulders when the first bell tolled through the campus. Other people began their hustle and bustle between buildings. Writing had always organized my jumbled mess of thoughts and turned them into something tangible. It took me out of the present, if only temporarily.

Though when I lived at home on the farm, there didn't always seem to be as much worry. Or at least there hadn't been at first. Being young and naive, falling in love with one of the farmhands almost seemed a rite of passage. Losing my virginity to him did, too. But the heartbreak that came afterward, and his dead, lifeless body in my arms, was not part of that passage.

Before he was dead, though, he was my love; before that, he was my friend. Reece—even the echo of his name in the recesses of my mind was startling—he had worked on our farm since he was a boy. I had only begun to notice how his muscles flexed as he lifted hay bales over his head or the hard curve of his jawline when he chewed on a strand of hay.

After Pa had taken me out of school on account of needing more help around the farm, even though Ma disapproved, I had come apart. I didn't usually cry, but this had been important to me. More important than anything else ever had been. School was my way off the farm and out of this town.

On my second day working, Reece took notice.

"What's the matter, darling?" He'd asked, shovel in one hand and bucket in the other.

I'd wiped my tears away, sniffed, and stood tall as I'd told him, even then not wanting to seem like I couldn't handle myself. Couldn't handle the world.

A lopsided grin graced his suntanned face. "Well, that ain't no problem. I can teach ya."

And he did.

He had gone to school before working on the farm and had learned the rest from his older brothers who went to college. We spent our evenings hiding out in the fields surrounded by stalks of corn or rows of tomatoes. He wrote letters on parchment, teaching me the sound they made. Once I'd gotten the hang of that, he'd brought books and helped me sound out words until I could read whole sentences and then whole pages. We'd stayed out in the fields until it was too dark to see the words anymore. Even then, we'd forget the books and chase lightning bugs. Catching them in our hands, laughing when they tickled our palms with their fluttering wings.

The transition from friends to lovers was without friction, as smooth as freshly churned butter. Our evenings spent over words and books melted into time spent staring into each other's eyes and planting gentle kisses onto each other's lips.

Pa didn't seem to mind our infatuation, as he'd grown just as close with Reece, no doubt seeing him as the son he'd never had. And Reece took on that role with pride, glad to have someone to replace his own deadbeat father. But that didn't stop Pa from wanting to try for his *own* son. He needed a blood relative, a boy, to pass the farm down to. Someone to be his heir. His successor.

Several months of easy love went by as fast as a Southern winter. Here and gone in a blink.

And then the heat came, bringing our demise along with it.

Chapter Eighteen
Catherine

Biting one's tongue is a sign of negative words said or curses provoked.

I pulled my corset as tight as I could around my waist. It hugged against my curves, forcing my back straighter and my breasts higher. Like a caterpillar in its cocoon, morphing into something beautiful and strong, ready to spread my wings and take flight. However, I did not have the same affection for the sharp hatpins that pushed through my hat and scraped bloody trails across my scalp.

I applied powder to my cheeks and hoped I wouldn't sweat it off before I got to class. The walk, though not long, always did that. I wished Daddy's money would've been used to hire chauffeurs to take us to class. Surely, carriages weren't too expensive. Even riding horseback would be better than walking.

I carried myself tall and proud to the lecture hall—as tall as my short stature would allow. My emerald-green dress and matching green hat, complete with a peacock feather sticking out of it, made up one of my favorite outfits. My lucky charms. My own suit of armor. It was the only attire Mama had ever permitted herself to compliment me on. When she purchased it for me, she said it made the red hue of my hair more tolerable. I wanted it to be that way today.

In class, I turned sideways to scoot down the aisle between the desks and chairs. The width of my skirts didn't help. They snagged the corner of a desk. It screeched, as loud as the wrong key on a violin, against the floor.

As I set my belongings down and sat, stares burned holes into my back.

Good. Let them look.

Let them all see that I didn't give up and I'm ready to fight. I'd memorized everything Lucille and Victoria had taught us and studied harder than I ever had for any of my tutors. Who knew what all I could learn when I actually applied myself.

I memorized The Superstitions and their hidden meanings, loaded my pockets with the herbs and tokens I'd borrowed from Lucille, and mentally prepared myself for The Sacrifice.

Just as I got as comfortable as possible in the hard wooden lecture hall seats, Derek sat behind me.

"Excuse me, Miss." He made a show of getting my attention. Others turned their heads, too. "That is a mighty fine dress you have on today."

I raised my eyebrows. My cheeks heated. "Why, thank you." I smiled hesitantly and added, "It's my favorite."

He smiled, too, then his eyes narrowed to slits. "I can imagine it is. I'm only surprised you could buy it."

I squinted back at him. Where was he going with this?

"Would any dressmaker in town have that much fabric? You must have needed a whole mill's worth just to get it wrapped around your circumference."

My smile disappeared. Gasps and snickers erupted around the room.

Lucille, Victoria, and the others spun in their seats. Lucille opened her mouth. Her nostrils flared. She was no doubt ready to chew the bastard out.

I held my hand up.

A smirk grew on her lips. She nodded. Something gleamed in her eyes, something like . . . pride.

A warmth I'm not used to spread in my chest. Under my desk, I found the extra hatpin I had hidden in my dress layers and nicked the tip of my finger. I winced and sucked in a breath. The Superstitious words ran through my mind, along with the witchcraft hidden within.

Biting one's tongue is a sign of negative words said or curses provoked.

Draw blood and smear on a mint leaf to clear the negative words or curse away from you, sending it back to the person whom it originated from."

The Spirit. The Sacrifice. The Superstition.

I pressed my bloody finger to the mint leaves I had brought, along with other necessities I'd collected.

Nothing happened.

I rubbed it again—still, nothing.

Derek continued to laugh with his friends and spew more ego-driven words of hate.

I glanced back at Lucille. My cheeks heated. *What had I done wrong?*

Lucille mouthed *more blood* and nodded for me to try again.

I held my breath and brought the hatpin back to my fingertip. I plunged it in much deeper than I had the first time. My head spun with the sudden burn of pain, but blood instantly bubbled up and dribbled down my finger. And along with the blood, something else bubbled up, something burning, like fire. Something like power. I repeated my actions from before.

I didn't have to wait to know if it had worked this time. Derek immediately stopped his ramblings and jerked his head back, yelping. His hand flew up to his mouth.

"My tongue!" he squealed.

It came out muffled and distorted as if he'd bitten his tongue, and it swelled, jumbling his words. He continued to squeal and hold his mouth as he leaped from his seat and ran for the exit.

My frown from the earlier mishap spread into a satisfied smile. Lucille and Victoria beamed with the same satisfaction and the other thing from earlier . . . They were *proud* of me. Proud of something I had done, all on my own.

And so was I.

"Derek's oversized tongue must've gotten in the way of his own teeth." Alice joked. Everyone snickered and laughed.

Professor Compton cleared his throat behind me.

I jumped and spun around as the room suddenly fell silent.

"What do you have there?" The professor eyed me.

"Umm. Pardon?" I gulped. Sweat beaded on my forehead.

"Have you hurt yourself? Shall I send you to the infirmary?" He gestured to my still bleeding finger. His eyes squinted, crow's feet appearing even more pronounced than usual in their corners.

I jerked my hand under the desk. "No. No, sir. I merely scraped my finger against a stray hatpin. It's nothing serious."

"I should hope not." He stared at me a moment longer before he turned and announced the start of class.

I let out a huge breath and slumped in my chair. I thought I had been caught red-handed doing witchcraft and had condemned myself for good.

And my new friends.

My heart raced as I noticed Alice staring at me. She smiled and nodded approvingly, her black curls bounced with the movement. Her dark eyes stared into mine so intently I thought I could melt. For a moment, I wondered if her smooth, light brown skin would be as soft under my touch as it looked. Then the professor dropped his books on the podium with a bang. I jerked from my thoughts and pushed them down as far as I could. Besides, I told myself those thoughts and feelings were just innocent, like ones for a friend.

Nothing more.

It could never be more.

A voice deeper down noted that I had never thought about Lucille or Victoria like that. I quickly shushed that voice and told it to be quiet.

I knew what would happen if it didn't. My skin prickled with the memory of it. Her skin had been much lighter than Alice's. Buttery soft. That velvety skin had caressed me. Made me feel things I had only ever imagined. I needed those feelings to stay deep inside of me.

I couldn't put anyone else or myself at risk like that again.

It was too dangerous.

I was glad to be away from campus for a bit, even if it was for Mama's church league meeting. I'd avoided Alice's fleeting glances for the rest of the week, and when I couldn't, I maintained as much indifference as I could without being downright cold.

While the church league members prattled on about who was baking what for the next fundraiser or how the pastor should use the raised money on new pews or stained-glass windows, my sister and I maintained our own conversation.

"Oh, he's so handsome, Catherine. I wish you could see him. He's an absolute dream," Felicity gushed about her newest suitor. "I think he's *it* this time. He's even invited me to come to his family's estate and meet his mama. You know what *that* means."

I squinted against the sun. Our dainty umbrellas barely shaded us. The women around the small table fanned themselves, but it didn't stop the sweat that dripped from underneath their hats. At least this meeting was on our own estate, with our own familiar views and regular servants.

"What does *it* mean?" I knew it would satisfy her to explain it to me.

She scoffed and threw a hand up. "It means he's serious. If he wants me to meet his folks, then it won't be long until he asks for my hand in marriage." She smiled from ear to ear.

"Congratulations!" I returned her smile and hoped she couldn't see the disappointment hidden behind the mask of happiness. "Have you painted anything new lately?"

Her smile faded, but only for a moment. "I started a new landscape the other day but haven't had much time to work on it. This courtship has taken all of my attention."

I could feel the slow downturn as my smile melted into a frown. I tried to do my best to imitate Lucille's confidence and authority. "Don't let a man stop you from your passion."

Felicity waved me off. "Don't fret, it's merely a lack of time, not of passion. I'm sure I'll get back to painting once we're betrothed."

I doubted that but didn't say as much. Once married, her household duties and child-rearing would take up all of her time as expected of a good subservient wife.

"Now, ladies, have you heard of the latest scandal?" Mrs. Flanagin was back at it with her dramatized gossip.

Everyone around the table leaned in close.

"Go on," Mrs. Cunningham urged. She was a wrinkled old lady, used to getting what she wanted with a snap of her perfectly manicured fingers. Her patience was as thin as her sun-spotted skin. Her blue veins popped out so strikingly that it looked like they would break through the surface.

"Well, I heard from Ms. Martha at the market that she heard from her cousin, and they had heard from someone else that a few of the factory girls had taken up rummaging through the garbage. And when they'd dug through all that, they'd even started . . ."

Everyone leaned in closer. Her lips curved up in a menacing grin.

". . . stealing! They've stolen from Mr. Richard at the grocery store and the dressmaker in town. Who knows where they'll steal from next?"

Everyone gasped. I snuck another cornbread muffin from the table while Mama was distracted, lest she catch me and give me a scolding. If they thought stealing was so terrible, I couldn't imagine what they would think of my friends and my latest activities at Brimham.

And certainly, about what we were planning on doing.

"Lord Almighty, they've gone mad!"

"I've heard that happens to those types. They lose their minds."

"I declare! Lord bless them!"

The ladies all chimed in at once.

"They should be arrested," Mama said. "May the Lord have mercy on their souls!"

They all nodded in agreement.

"Shouldn't we try to help them? Bring them food and some of our old clothes we no longer need?" I asked and earned a sharp look from Mama. I couldn't help but picture some of the women in the program who came from less fortunate families, alone and hungry. "They're only stealing because they can't afford those things, right? They're just trying to survive."

Mrs. Flanagin replied, "Dear, you can't possibly believe that!"

"You want us to spend our own hard-earned money on people who can't even help themselves?" Mrs. Cunningham interjected. This was quite ironic since she'd never earned anything by herself in her entire life. Neither had her husband. Their money was old money, passed down from one generation to the next.

"But why not?" I looked at each of them adorned in their expensive hats and hand-sewn dresses. Jewels hung from their necks and wrists. Servants were at their beck and call. They never lifted a finger or had to fight for anything in their lives.

Was this what the other women at the university saw when they looked at me? Spoiled? Privileged? I suddenly wanted to yank the pearls from my neck, rip the hat from my head, and strip the satin garments from my body. The expense of them weighed on me and drowned me in a sea of privilege and entitlement.

"Because if you give them everything now," Mrs. Flanagin went on, "how will they ever learn to acquire things on their own? They won't. They will only become more reliant on the hand that feeds them. We are doing them a favor by not helping. You'll see one day and come to understand."

Would I end up like them? Like Mama? The price of my materials more important than that of my actions? No empathy? No kindness?

She patted my hand as if reassuring me. I jerked my hand away and hoped she was wrong.

"Excuse me," I said suddenly, my voice sharper than I intended. "I have a headache."

Mama frowned, but I was already standing. No one stopped me. A woman's discomfort was a small price for decorum.

I ran up the stairs and only slowed to a walk when I made it to the hallway, blessedly cool and dim. I exhaled, pressing my fingertips briefly to my temple as I walked, trying to shake the sound of their voices from my ears.

Footsteps tapped against the marble floor behind me. Must be Felicity or Mama coming to check on me.

"I'm alright, I just need—"

"Catherine."

My stomach dropped.

I turned just as Cousin Frederick stepped out from a side corridor, his smile slithered, more dangerous than the snakes Thomas had tortured us with. He had always been too generous with his smiles, too fond, too close. Tall and narrow as a switchblade, he carried himself with the confidence of a man who had never been denied anything.

"Frederick," I said, angling my body to pass him. "Mama hadn't mentioned you were visiting."

"And miss the chance to see you while you're home from that university?" he spit the last word. Warm wet drops landed on my cheek.

I tried to step past him, but he moved faster.

His hand struck the wall beside my head with a sharp crack, the sound echoing down the corridor. I prayed Mama or Felicity would hear it. The other hand came to rest on my hip, heavy and possessive. He leaned in, musk wafted from his sweaty body, thick with an onion scent, and his breath was sour with bourbon, though it was barely noon.

My back hit the hard paneling. The boning of my corset dug into my skin.

"Don't," I said, my voice steady despite the panic flooding my veins. I tried to sound as calm as Victoria, but just as stern as Lucille.

He chuckled. "You always have been too proud for your own good."

"Move," I said. "Please."

His eyes dragged over me, slow and obscene. "You've changed," he murmured. "Makes a man wonder what you've been learning while you're away."

My skin crawled. "Get away from me."

I wanted nothing more than to prick my finger, use the craft, make him bleed. But he had me pinned so tightly against the wall, I could barely move.

"You know," he went on, as if I hadn't spoken, "a woman with your name ought to remember her place. Your parents certainly do."

Something hot and reckless flared in my chest. "My place," I said coldly, "is nowhere near a man who needs to corner women in hallways to feel powerful." Lucille would be proud of that line.

His smile twitched. I thought maybe I had gotten to him, wounded him. Then his smile widened, showing all of his teeth, yellow and decaying, like those rattlesnakes showing their fangs in warning.

"Well," he said softly, "that mouth of yours certainly needs taming."

He lifted his hand. For a moment, I thought he might strike me. Instead, he ran it through his grease-slicked hair, then placed it back against the wall by my head. The other hand tightened painfully on my hip.

"I *will* marry you," he said, voice low and vicious. "Not because I want you." His cold gaze raked down my body, before meeting mine again. His nose scrunched as if he hated what he saw. "But because I can. Because claiming you will be a victory. Because breaking you will be a conquest."

"I'll refuse. I won't marry you." I swallowed hard, forcing myself not to look away.

He leaned closer, his breath brushing my ear, wet and hot. "You won't have a choice."

Footsteps sounded somewhere in the distance, servants or one of the ladies needing to empty their bladder of all the sweet tea they'd drunk. Frederick straightened at once, his hand dropping as if it had never touched me. A polite smile slid back into place like a mask.

"Family should stick together," he said loud and cheerful, stepping aside.

I didn't run. No, that would only have given him satisfaction. I forced myself to walk, legs trembling, heart hammering so loud I was certain the house could hear it.

But as I went, one thought burned clear and steady beneath the fear: If this was the world I was expected to submit to, then I would burn every rule that upheld it.

And I would never let that man, or any man, own me.

Chapter Nineteen
Victoria

If you ever want to see a friend again,
never part ways on a bridge.

A final moan escaped my lips. Sweat dripped off my skin and onto theirs. For once, the never-ending heat and suffocating humidity did not cause it.

I untangled myself and crawled from the bed with the man and woman I had met only hours before. I had needed a break from classes and from the sorority's newfound "crafting" lessons, needed to get off of the campus for just a little while. Old habits came back.

The couple didn't bother asking me to stay, still too enthralled by one another's presence, and I didn't want to, anyway. That's how I liked it. No attachments. Just pleasure. Just to quiet my mind and clear my thoughts, even if it was brief. Only the feel of their body and reactions under my touch—under my mouth.

I yanked on my underclothes without bothering to put on my corset, my skin sticky with sweat and other bodily fluids. I pulled my dress over my head and straightened it hastily before I grabbed my corset, and left. I needed to head back to the university before it got too late.

My walk through town was familiar. In fact, I would've enjoyed walking alone if it weren't for constantly looking over my shoulder.

Constantly being on guard, ready to flee at the sight of any man on the street whose eyes lingered too long on me, changed the experience entirely. Men had the luxury to walk alone without worry, no matter how dark the night. Women only dreamed of such things. The peace and bliss one must feel while doing so made me burn to my core with jealousy.

A branch snapped somewhere in the distance. I spun, my heart racing. Black silhouettes from trees and broken limbs surrounded me. Their branches clawed at the sky and tore through the bloated summer air. I wasn't far from the campus. If I sprinted, I could get there in only a few minutes.

I strained to listen, hearing more snaps and rattles. My muscles went taut, ready to run. My mind conjured the path from here, across the bridge, and to the university as a figure appeared from the trees. Their dark shadow crawled across the ground in front of them. I sucked in a breath. It rattled in my already tight chest.

"Victoria?" The female voice sliced through the silent air.

Chill bumps scattered across my damp skin.

I squinted my eyes. "Prim?" Though I already knew it was her. I could recognize her pin-straight brown hair and tall stature anywhere. Her thin, malnourished figure was a trademark of all mill and factory girls. But, I used to recognize Maggie's features in the same way—until they were too still and too cold.

Nighttime shadows danced across Prim's face, angry and unsettled. She hated me. Of course she hated me for what I had done and then what I had run from. And now, I ran again, just like I had after the night Maggie died, unable to confront the despair I left behind.

My feet carried me faster as Prim yelled my name. It echoed off the trees, across the bridge, and through the thick air. It taunted me with a cacophony of her loathing.

I only stopped running when the campus came into view. My breath came out in wheezing pants and then in a fit of coughs as I slowed to a walk. I had planned to go to my bedchamber upon arrival, but my desire for sleep evaded me, replaced by adrenaline and angst.

A new plan formed. I would rush into our dormitory to wipe myself off and change clothes before heading to the library to help Mr. Edmonton close and lock up for the night.

Of course, the plan was always easier than the execution. Lucille arrived at the front entrance to the dormitory nearly the same moment as me. She looked from my ruffled hair to the limp corset in my hand like a dead animal.

"Fraternizing with the enemy, I see." Though her words were harsh, the corners of her mouth curved up just enough to indicate she was all bark and no bite.

Well, in this instance, at least. Over the past few days of spending time with her and the rest of the sorority during our lessons on witchcraft, I'd learned that Lucille wasn't afraid to say what was on her mind but hardly ever meant harm by it.

Her tendency to say everything in a volume that competed with a powered loom was what I liked most about her, though. I never had to ask her to repeat herself or pretend like I knew what she said. Never had to second guess myself and what I heard—or didn't.

I knew she was referring to a tryst with a man from the campus, but I didn't bother correcting her or explaining myself. Adrenaline drained from me as quickly as blood drained from an open wound.

"We might as well take pleasure in them. They sure as hell don't hesitate to take pleasure in us," I said simply.

Lucille grunted in agreement, or at least understanding. She said her farewells and pulled the door handle to disappear down the cozy depths of the hallway.

After I freshened up, I made my way out into the night and down the path to the library. Its large brick walls and stained glass windows always fluttered my heart with excitement, maybe even more than the night's earlier escapades.

As soon as I entered the familiar building, I breathed in the combined smell of wood, ink, and parchment. I wished I could make that scent into an aromatic candle.

"Good evening, Miss Woodhall." Mr. Edmonton's voice carried a hint of surprise, but he smiled all the same. "I've told you before that you don't need to help close during the weekends. I'm sure you have plenty of studying that needs to be done during the evenings." He stood at his post in the front of the library. His glasses perched on the end of his nose, and a wool coat adorned his arms even though it was already plenty warm, if not hot, in here.

"Yes, sir. But I can never stay away from the library for long." I smiled.

Mr. Edmonton, the old librarian, and I had grown closer over the past few weeks. We bonded over our love of literature and old classics. He often talked of his wife, with both love and sadness, and pointed me in the direction of books she once loved. He claimed we had similar preferences. So far, all of his suggestions were spot-on.

Mr. Edmonton even talked of his wife being a suffragist and women's rights activist. I suspected that was precisely why her reading taste was so similar to my own.

I made to walk away from him but then spun back around before I could change my mind.

"Mr. Edmonton?"

"Hmm?" he replied as he looked through a magnifying glass he held over a writing scroll.

"Some of the other women and I . . . we've made a sort of group. A sorority, we're calling it. And well, it's mostly for women's rights and fighting on behalf of women, but if you ever wanted to join us, you're more than welcome to. We've just had our first meeting a few nights ago." I wasn't sure how the others would react to him attending our meetings, but that was a bridge I would cross when I got there.

He looked up at me, his expression unreadable for a moment. Then, a slow smile spread across his face, and his eyes welled with tears.

"That's awfully kind of you, dear. My Annie would have been delighted to hear such a thing." His hand, still adorned with his gold wedding band, drifted to linger over his heart. "But I'm sure you women don't want an old man like me lobbying in your midst."

"Well, the offer still stands if you change your mind."

He thanked me and returned to his work.

After I stacked books, organized papers, and swept floors, the night came to a head. Mr. Edmonton called out his farewell, and the library slipped into its evening stillness. I placed the last book back onto its shelf as carefully as I'd been taught and stepped away to survey the room. Tables straightened. Chairs aligned. Everything returned to its proper place, or as close as I could manage after only a few weeks of practice.

I lifted my lantern to make one final observation of the place. Another light, faint but unmistakable, burned deeper among the shelves.

My heart gave a startled jump. I hesitated only a moment before moving toward it. The library was old, full of nothing but cedar and parchment. The thought of an unattended flame in such an environment set me on edge.

"Hello?" I called. "The library is closing."

There was a rustle of movement. A chair scraped back. Then a familiar figure stepped into view, looking as though he'd been pulled reluctantly from his thoughts, hair tousled, eyes glazed. Christopher. Another student in my classes, one of the quiet ones. We had that in common. We often occupied the same corners and back rows of rooms, unnoticed but observant.

"I'm sorry," he said, running his hand through his auburn hair. "I didn't mean to stay so late."

"It happens," I said, shrugging my shoulders. "But I do need to put that lantern out."

He nodded and reached for it, dimming the flame himself. As he did, the book under his arm caught my eye.

"Little Women," I said before I could stop myself, raising my hand ever so slightly to point at it.

He looked down at the book, then back at me. His eyebrows raised. "You've read it?"

"Yes." I nodded. "Not recently, but . . . it stays with you."

"It does," he agreed. "I only meant to read a chapter. Jo has a way of refusing to let you stop."

I smiled. "She does. She wants too much, and somehow that makes her honest."

He studied me for a moment, then nodded. "That's exactly it. Everyone tells her to be smaller. Thankfully, she never quite manages."

We began walking toward the front desk, the conversation taking on a life of its own. He spoke of reading the book in secret the first time, of how rare it felt to find a story where women were allowed to be contradictory, allowed to be ambitious *and* kind, selfish *and* loyal.

"I like that none of them are punished for wanting more," I said. "At least, not in the way one expects."

"Alcott doesn't mock them," he said. "She listens to them."

I wondered if that statement made him feel as seen as it did for me. We reached the front desk, the lantern light low and steady between us, casting our faces in a warm glow. He adjusted his coat as if he weren't quite comfortable in it, still holding the book carefully. Outside, dusk had settled over the grounds, the windows reflecting a dark wash of blue.

"I'm glad you found me," he said with a sheepish smile. "I don't often get to talk about books with anyone."

"I'm glad I did too," I said, and before I could talk myself out of it, I added, "If you ever find yourself in dire need to discuss such things—books, and Alcott, and whatnot—I would be happy to oblige."

"I'll certainly keep that in mind," he said as he opened the big oak doors and made his way out. Giving a little wave just before he disappeared into the night entirely.

I extinguished the lantern and made my way deeper into the recesses of the library to find a book for my own pleasurable reading.

Once I'd gathered quite the pile of books, I took it to a nearby table, sat down, and pulled the last lit gas lamp close to me as I opened one.

I stared down at the pages but didn't see the words. The way Mr. Edmonton talked of his wife, and Christopher talked of Jo, made me think of Maggie. I had once been so close to her. I missed her so dearly. Some days, the thoughts of her made me want to fall to my knees and cry. On other days, they made me numb, like I could never feel any emotion again. But every day, the thoughts were there. Happy or sad, they never subsided. Never disappeared.

I often wondered if that was what kept our souls alive after our earthly bodies were buried and decomposing. If it was the memories people have of us that kept us from truly disappearing. Not some sanctuary of light and peace that only believers are granted access to, but rather the impression we left on others when we were alive. That has to be what we lived for. Not some selfish notion of where we went because of the good we did. Good done with only the desire to receive something in return wasn't really good at all.

Chapter Twenty
Lucille

It is bad luck to pass someone on the staircase.

The sky turned purple, then pink and orange as the sun slowly crawled its way up from behind the horizon like a rodent clawing out of its hiding place.

"Must we be out here before the day has properly begun?" Catherine covered her mouth as she yawned and stretched her short arms above her head.

Victoria and the other girls only smirked. As women who had also spent most of their lives working, I knew they hadn't a problem with waking before the sun.

"If I can relearn how to sit and wear all these layers you insist are *necessary*, then you can get out of bed at a decent hour." I flipped through the grimoire in my hands as we walked toward the dark woods surrounding the campus. "Besides, this isn't for promenading. This is official coven business."

Catherine perked up. "Ooh, are we about to mix a potion in a cauldron? Or learn to fly on a broom? Or—"

"No."

Victoria and Alice snorted.

Catherine's shoulder slumped. "Well, then what *are* we doing?"

"We're going to collect tokens needed for The Sacrifice."

Susan's eyes widened. "Sacrifice? Don't tell me we have to kill an animal."

"No animals. Just herbs and feathers and things," Victoria assured her.

"Someone has already been practicing." I grinned as I remembered Thomas's face the day he stole Victoria's paper and then acted as if she'd set his hands on fire.

"Witchcraft always needs exactly three things." I held up my hand and counted them out on my fingers. "The Spirit. The Sacrifice. The Superstition."

I explained what each of those meant, the same way Ma had explained it to me when I was younger. Flour covered her hands as she mixed the biscuit ingredients. That's how she had explained the craft, like making biscuits. You had to have all the right ingredients, so your biscuits turned out fluffy and moist. Too much of one ingredient or too little and they could end up hard as a rock or doughy as mud. Never too much. Never too little. When she'd said this, she had used her finger to smudge a bit of flour on my nose, making me giggle. I had exacted my revenge with my smudge of flour on her cheek. An all-out flour war had ensued.

I wished such a sweet memory wasn't tainted by those that came years later.

"How do you know how much of a sacrifice to make?" Alice lifted her skirts and stepped over a tree's corpse laid across the floor of the woods. It was dead, but not useless. Opossums made a home out of its carcass.

"It depends. Say you were making biscuits for just you; you wouldn't need as much of each ingredient." I repeated Ma's words, which were a song in the back of my mind. A singsong melody that never left. Always remained. Always haunted. "However, if you were making a batch of biscuits for a large group, then you would need much more of each ingredient. Y'all understand?"

They all nodded. Rebecca swatted at a swarm of skeeters that found themselves a meal out of her blood.

"What about the other items? Herbs and feathers and things?" Catherine smacked her hand down on her arm.

She had never once raised her hand in our classes with questions for the professors, but now it seemed her curiosity was endless. Maybe Professor Compton should take a few teaching lessons from me.

A crunch of leaves sounded from somewhere behind the crowd of trees. We all froze and dropped to the ground. I scanned the area. My heart pounded in my ears. What if someone had followed us? Heard our conversation?

We stayed crouched and silent for several minutes. When it seemed there was no other movement around us after a while, I sighed and straightened. A deer must've passed through. Or a coyote.

I cleared my throat and tried to recall the topic of our conversation.

"The Spirit, The Sacrifice, and The Superstition do most of the work. But the extra ingredients help, too. They guide the witchcraft in the direction it needs to go. Kind of like if I told you to shoot an arrow over there," I pointed to the woods in front of us, though I used a quieter voice this time, "you could do that, but it would be much better if I gave you a specific target and said to shoot at that tree. You may still hit the same spot either way, but you're much more likely to hit the exact spot I instructed you to hit if I gave a more specific target."

Victoria, Alice, and Rebecca nodded. They picked items from the brush-covered ground. They scared off any lingering creatures that crept around us, any creature that tried to glimpse who the invaders of their home were. Catherine and Susan blinked at me. Sweat beaded on their foreheads.

"Maybe shooting isn't the best analogy." I surveyed the overgrown woods and underbrush as I tried to think of something more relatable for someone of high society. Underneath my dastardly corset, I scratched the itch between my dress's fabrics. "Okay, how about this! It's like the difference between only wearing skirts and petticoats or wearing skirts and petticoats with a crinoline underneath. Both options cover your body the same. The skirt on top will still be of the same color and pattern, but the crinoline will get it that much closer to being the desired shape. They're essentially the same attire either way, but . . . one is *more* of what you wanted. Does that make sense?"

Catherine nodded this time. "So, we need to collect items to give our witchcraft the desired shape?"

"Yes!" I clapped my hands in front of me, killing a gnat with the impact.

Professor Compton should definitely take lessons from me.

"The other week, when I . . . used the craft on Thomas. He acted as if he were in severe pain. Is it always that intense?" Victoria eyed me.

"You were horribly angry, weren't you?" I grinned. "You wanted to hurt him, didn't you?"

Victoria gulped. "Well, yes, but not quite so bad. Or well, maybe that's what I wanted at first, but seeing it actually happen was entirely different."

"That's just it." I looked down at the leaves and broken twigs on the ground. My brain fought to dredge up the images of my own overly outraged witchcraft. "You have to have The Spirit to make it work, but if you have too much of any of the three ingredients, it might just come out too strong."

The women audibly gulped.

We spent the next hour collecting herbs, flowers, stray feathers, and bits of fur. Catherine narrated her every move and find. Her voice mixed with the sounds of nature around us, an intermingling of the wild and tamed. Victoria sometimes looked at Catherine as if she didn't quite understand what she said but nodded and hummed along anyway. She and Alice were meticulous with their collection. It took several minutes for them to pick the best petal from a flower or examine a feather for any flaws before they decided to put it in their baskets. Quite the opposite of Catherine and Susan, who flung anything and everything into theirs. Rebecca was somewhere in the middle. She inspected some things, but not others.

Catherine picked up several white magnolia petals that had fallen from the tree above her. "These are the same sort of petals my sisters adorned the chapel with during their weddings."

Alice hummed a response. I picked the wings off of a dead cicada.

"Do y'all think you'll ever get married?" Catherine stared at the petals in her rounded hands as if they were an ill omen.

"No." Victoria and I responded at the same time.

We looked at each other. I smiled. The corners of Victoria's mouth curved upward, ever so slightly before she turned back to the patch of wildflowers in front of her.

"Why not?" Catherine still hadn't lifted her eyes from the petals, as if in a trance.

"Men caused my ma's death. I'll never forgive them." I said, blunt and sharp like the edge of a knife.

"Like murder? You should report them to the authorities!" Catherine stared at me with wide eyes. Her mouth hung slightly ajar. Alice and Rebecca didn't even flinch, as if they too had been scorned by the injustice of a man's fury.

"Well, no, they didn't *physically* kill her, but their actions led to her death nonetheless."

"Surely it wasn't *all* men that caused her passing," Susan suggested.

Catherine let the petals drop from her hands. They drifted through the humid air, then lingered just above the ground before falling to their final resting place.

"If you were given a bag of snakes, and you knew only one out of the dozen was poisonous, but not *all* of them, would you still stick your hand in there?" I looked at her pointedly, even though I'd been dipping my own hand in that bag more often than I'd like to admit, but I just couldn't bring myself to stop writing to Henry. He seemed to be the one snake without fangs.

"Of course, not." Catherine shook her head, disgust written on her features.

"Exactly." I said.

"I'm sorry for your loss." Victoria turned to me. Her eyes stared into mine for a moment, just a moment, but she seemed to see into my deepest depths.

"What about you?" Catherine turned to Victoria. "Why wouldn't you get married?"

"I'm not one for relationships." She shrugged.

"But, why—"

"Alright. I think we've collected enough for today." I announced before Catherine could question her further.

Victoria gave me a small nod of gratitude as she lifted herself from the ground.

I winked back. "Let's make our way back to the dormitory for the day."

"Shouldn't you show us how to use them? How to do the witchcraft?" Alice held her basket on her arm and looked at me with wide brown eyes, excitement gleamed from them like lightning bugs in darkness.

"I suppose I could." Even as I said it, my hands began to tremble. The memory of Reece's lifeless body flashed in my mind before I could stop it, before I could squelch it out like a spark about to start a fire. I may have chosen this path of using witchcraft to get back at the men, but that didn't make the memories of the last time I'd used it any less fear-inducing.

"I'll be late for my shift at the library if we don't head back now. Let's practice next time," Victoria suggested.

Alice gave a little sigh but spun back toward the direction of campus nonetheless, followed closely by Catherine and the others.

It was my turn to give Victoria a grateful nod. The corner of her mouth lifted into a half smile before she turned, too, heading back in the direction we had come.

We would get along just fine.

We exited the line of woods with the others as we whispered back and forth about our upcoming plan of revenge and how we would use the things we'd collected. I came up short at the sight of Josephine, Mary Ann, and Penelope standing like gargoyles on the stairway to the dormitory's entrance.

Josephine looked toward the woods and back to me. "I don't think you're supposed to gallivant in the woods like that. What were y'all doing?" she asked with her nose turned up.

"It's none of your business, but we were picking flowers and berries as a sorority," I said, folding my arms.

"A sorority?" Penelope asked, excitement clear in her voice.

Josephine turned and gave her a stern look, before turning back to us, her nose scrunched. "Does the headmaster know about this?"

Penelope's face fell, and my heart began to race. *Shit.*

"Maybe I should go tell him—

"He already knows." I blurted. "He thought it would be a great way for us to bond." I held my breath and hoped she would take the bait and wouldn't ask to join.

She snorted, "That's ridiculous. Such things won't matter when our Lord and Savior returns, which I'm certain is going to happen soon, so you'd better prepare yourself."

Josephine prattled on, but my attention was drawn through the open door of our dormitory to the figure standing at mine and Catherine's door.

"If you'll excuse me." I ignored Josephine's protests and huffs of annoyance.

Henry stood in front of our door. He raised his hand, ready to knock, but then dropped it and lifted it back again as if unable to commit to the action.

"You couldn't get enough of my charming personality through my letters?" His head jerked in my direction at the sound of my voice.

He dropped his hand and cleared his throat as he met my gaze. A dimple appeared on his right cheek. "I have quite enjoyed our written correspondences. However, I've decided it would be best if I receive your blatant hatred in person now, instead." He bent forward to take my hand. "May I?"

My hand lifted to his without my approval. His lips gently pressed to my skin for only a second.

"Well, you may be many things, but a quitter most certainly isn't one of them." I said as I brought my hand back to my side. His smile grew as he straightened up. "But an ass most certainly is."

I expected his smile to falter or his complexion to redden. Instead, Henry's smile widened. "And here I thought your letters were outlandish only because we weren't facing one another. It's good to see that your charisma holds up in person."

"Well, you can take my *outlandish* letters and shove them right up your—"

"Lucille, aren't you going to introduce me to your fine suitor?" Catherine interrupted and curtsied for Henry as she approached.

I rolled my eyes. "You've seen Henry in class and around the university. And he's not my suitor."

"Well, it's still a pleasure to have a formal introduction, I should think."

"The pleasure is all mine, Miss." Henry bowed. He repeated his delicate kiss on Catherine's hand.

I pushed down the absurd burn that rose in my chest at the sight of his lips on her skin. Before I could get too worked up—not that I was really getting worked up at all, especially over a man—Catherine's attention diverted as Alice walked by.

"If you will both excuse me." Catherine yanked her hand from Henry's grip and sprinted down the hall after Alice.

I let out a small laugh to disguise my sigh of relief. "Looks like your charm doesn't work on everyone, as I'm sure you'd believed."

"I don't need it to work on everyone," he winked.

My knees wobbled. Being away from farm work for so long must've had that effect on them. I needed to take care of these frequent weaknesses before they caused me to do something ridiculous.

Like fall.

For Henry.

I never thought I would let that happen again after Reece's betrayal. Even if he were just trying to please Pa. It had started at the beginning of the summer. When Ma's courses didn't come, Pa was ecstatic with the possibility of finally having a son, until the doctor's visit.

"He said it will kill me." Ma's voice had floated out the window that I'd crouched under.

"He said it was a risk, not that it was certain." Pa's voice had growled.

"And you're okay with that risk?" Ma asked, her voice breaking. Though I'd known as well as she had that if he'd been guaranteed a son, he'd risk us both.

"You're going through with this pregnancy," Pa had said in finality, stomping out of their bed chamber.

I'd known what I needed to do. I couldn't let Pa risk her life. I couldn't watch her go through that again, losing a baby, along with buckets and buckets of blood. Or worse. After several days of letter correspondence with the unknown stranger rumored to help during these situations, I'd talked Reece into taking me to town, telling him I wanted to promenade with him. He'd been surprised, knowing that I wasn't normally the type for such things, but had obliged.

In town, we walked the square, going in and out of shops and stores. He'd asked me to wait for him while he ran into a store selling leather wears. It was my opportunity. As soon as he had turned away, I'd sprinted between shops and buildings. Knowing I hadn't much time, I made my way to the industrial park, where our secret meetup was arranged to take place. I'd waited in the dark alley for only a moment before the girl showed up, younger than I had imagined, and traded her the brooch I'd stolen from Ma's jewelry box for the tincture.

The exchange was quick and without pleasantries. Shoving the tincture far down into my bodice, I raced back across town, managing to get back to the square just as Reece emerged from the leather shop, notebook in hand. He'd custom ordered it weeks ago as a gift for me, that and a fountain pen. A new invention from up north that held its own ink. Even with sweat dripping down my back and the hidden tincture pressed against my skin, I'd stared in awe at the gifts.

Not noticing that Reece's eyes lingered in the direction I had just come. That his gaze traced the unusual lump under my dress.

When we'd gotten back to the farm, we'd parted ways. I hadn't known that as I told Ma of the tincture and how it could help her, Reece was telling Pa what I'd done at the same time. I didn't hear Pa's heavy footsteps until it was too late. I didn't hide the tincture fast enough. I should've gotten Ma to drink it right away, as soon as I'd gotten there.

Pa barged into their bed chamber with Reece on his heels. I didn't need an explanation to know what they were there for. He threw the tincture into the fire and me to the ground. Even after the beating, I went back to Reece. Asked him how he'd found out and why he'd told Pa. He claimed he'd done it all because he loved me and wanted to protect me. I tried to believe him, but condemning Ma to a fate filled with death didn't feel like love to me. Reece had said he would keep doing what needed to be done to protect me.

I hadn't been entirely certain what he'd meant by that until I followed him out that night. I followed him until he met up with other men, until they drank whiskey from glasses and shattered them on the ground, until they went like a mob to the same dark alley I'd been at only a couple of days prior. I followed them until I realized what they were there for. *Who* they were there for. The girl I had gotten the tincture from. The girl that had been rumored to help so many others in similar predicaments to mine. They were there for her. "To carry out God's will." One of them had claimed

By the time I gathered up The Spirit, The Sacrifice, and The Superstition, they'd already begun attacking her. Beating her with fists as much as they took advantage of her body with ugly, unnatural pleasure. So much rage had filled my Spirit and strengthened the craft, that when it took effect, it had done more than I'd intended. I'd meant to knock them out, knock Reece out, but instead, I'd sent them into a much deeper slumber.

I'd killed them. Just like that.

I'd held Reece's limp body in my arms for a moment, shocked. When the enormity of the situation caught up with my stunned brain, I ran. I ran all the way back to the farm. Pa was there waiting for me as if he already knew the trouble I was in. He'd thrown me in the cellar, locking me in there for days. I banged, scratched, and clawed, begging him to let me out. I thought I would die in there.

My trust in men, myself, and my craft had been marred for good.

Or so I had thought.

Chapter Twenty-One

Catherine

See a penny, pick it up; all day long, you'll have good luck.

I chased after Alice because that's what friends are for, right? A friend wouldn't let another friend walk across campus alone, especially where women were overwhelmingly in the minority. I was being friendly.

"Alice, wait a moment." I caught up to her as she made her way down the hallway and didn't care if I'd left the conversation with Henry and Lucille abruptly.

Alice slowed as she glanced over her shoulder. Her lips spread into a smile. Her black curls bounced lightly.

"Where are you off to?" I patted my head to make sure my hat was still in place. The feather tickled my palm.

"Y'all have inspired me. I hoped to go to the library to do research on the matter of women's rights and maybe even . . ." she looked around to check our surroundings for any listening ears and leaned in closer, "the craft." Her breath warmed my cheek and sent shivers down my spine.

"I shall join you. It's quite a walk to the library." I held the doors open for her to step out into the humid air.

"Why, thank you. Company is always nice, especially yours." Alice smiled. The skin around her eyes crinkled in a manner that was most endearing.

In an endearing *friend* way. Definitely not in the way that made butterflies swarm my stomach or made my heart race. No, those feelings would be unnatural and wrong.

"You are beautiful in that dress today, by the way." Alice's eyes roamed over me. My heart leaped into my throat. "Who is your seamstress?"

My heart sank.

Right. She was interested in the design. Not in me.

Of course.

"My mama hired Madame LaRouge from the shop in town. She says one needs to wear the best to be the best," I recited in a monotone and hated the taste of Mama's words on my tongue.

"Your mother must not be able to see you are already surpassing those expectations." Alice's eyes no longer scanned my attire but looked into mine. I almost stumbled on the uneven cobblestone path.

Her words muddled my mind. It was almost as if she meant for them to, for her words to make me feel things. Flirting words.

No, I was mistaken. It was only my perverse mind acting up. I shoved those thoughts and feelings down again and mentally locked them in a cage like wild animals that couldn't be tamed.

Alice cleared her throat. "I wanted to thank you for inviting me into the sorority. People like me rarely get such invites." Alice stopped walking, even though we hadn't reached the library.

I stumbled to stop with her. "Of course. I couldn't imagine a world in which you weren't here." I swallowed. "I mean, in the sorority."

Sunlight gleamed copper from the ground. I bent over and picked up the stray coin, head side up.

"For you." I handed the penny to Alice. "For good luck."

"Thank you." Our fingers brushed as she took it. Lightning jolted awareness up my arm.

Alice's smile was delicate and fierce. Her light, tawny skin wrinkled around her upturned lips. Perfectly exquisite.

The butterflies turned into wasps in my stomach and swarmed harder. They intended to sting. I cleared my throat this time as I searched for something to say to fill the empty space between us. I had to squelch the silence before I did something completely inappropriate.

Words exploded from my mouth like a teakettle reaching its boiling point. "I was friends with many of the girls who worked on our estate when I was younger. We were really close for a bit, even though Mama didn't like that much."

Alice's smile dropped. *Oh no.* I immediately regretted my words, wanted to shove them back in my mouth and swallow them back down.

She started walking again. I stayed stock-still for a moment and then picked up my pace beside her. Why did I say that? Why must I always say things that made me prefer biting my own tongue?

I hurried to match her pace. "I only meant—"

"I know what you meant." Her voice was calm but no longer warm. "You were kind to them."

"Yes."

"And after their work," she continued, "were they paid? Or had they been paid for?"

The question struck like cold water and was followed by shivers of shame.

She did not look at me as she spoke again. "Kindness does not undo ownership."

Heat climbed up my throat. "I was a child," I said weakly.

"Yes," she agreed. "And so were they."

We walked several paces in silence.

"Your mother is not unlike many in high-cotton society. My skin is only barely light enough to be accepted here. I can pass as something

I am not." Alice held her hands up in front of her as she spoke. She turned them over to inspect. "I have a sister born with a darker pigmentation than mine. Many act as if she were born unlucky, cursed. People say I'm fortunate." She turned her palms over. "*Fortunate* is an interesting word."

I wasn't sure what to say. I'd witnessed the mistreatment of black men and women. The risks were dangerously higher for them in every area of life. Things could turn for them in the blink of an eye.

"I didn't mean—"

"I know you didn't," she said again. This time more gently. "But intention and impact rarely keep company."

Alice stopped walking once more. This time, though, we'd made it to our destination.

"This fight your sorority wishes to wage, it's not simply about letting women read Latin and study law." Her eyes held mine. "For some of us, it is about being recognized as women at all."

The words landed heavily. I swallowed the lump forming in my throat and blinked back the burn in my eyes.

"If the doors open only for white women," she continued, "then they are not open. They are merely rearranged."

I felt suddenly small beneath the wide Southern sky, and the unfairness of the world loomed larger than ever.

"And I am not here because you saved me a seat," she added. "I am here because I intend to take one."

A flicker of something fierce passed through her expression, not anger, but certainty.

I nodded slowly. "Then I will stand beside you."

She studied me, weighing the statement. "Beside," she repeated. "Not in front. Not speaking for."

"No," I agreed, nodding my head fervently. "Beside."

A pregnant pause stretched bloated and full between us.

"Good," She nodded in farewell and then turned to ascend the steps of the library.

I stood there, mannequin still, and repeated her words in my head. She was right, of course. For the first time, I understood the battle we were stepping into would not simply be about education or sororities or even witchcraft. It would be about who was allowed to claim humanity without permission. And whether I was brave enough to loosen my grip on the privileges that had always cleared my path.

It was the fight for being equally human.

And, in turn, being treated as such.

Chapter Twenty-Two Victoria

A bird flying left to right will bring bad luck.

The university's chapel was small and old, which described most things in this town and the South. Its steeple, worn from weather, stood crooked. The point of the cross curved slightly to the left as if it, too, would rather be somewhere else. Most of the white paint had chipped off the walls and peeled down like nails curling to capture anything in their grasp. And though plenty of light flowed in through the windows, I couldn't help but feel trapped in a cage.

Mother and I had never been churchgoing types. We tried once but once was enough. I knew we'd made a mistake from the moment we walked in. It was resplendent in velvet carpet and ruby stained-glass windows that bathed everything in red light. It was more like hell than heaven. Whispers of judgment arose like demons from every corner.

I knew what they judged us for. I was young but not naive. Mother had an affair with a wealthy, *married* man. She was his dirty little secret until she got pregnant with me. Mother tried to support us by working in factories and mills, but word had spread around town about her transgressions. No one cared that he had also taken part.

After we'd nearly starved to death, she took to the street corners, selling the only thing the world convinced her she had left to give. That's what the women in the church whispered about. It didn't take long for us to make our leave, Mother with tears streaking her cheeks, and me with anger singing in my heart.

Until then, I hadn't been sure Mother believed in God, much less Heaven. After that, though, I knew she at least believed in Hell. Not the fiery pit that we went to after living a sinful life, but the hell that we lived in on Earth, the circumstances that we put ourselves in when we made bad choices.

Or when we were just too poor to afford the good ones.

In the hot, oppressive chapel now, though, I was even more sure that religion wasn't for me and was glad chapel attendance was only mandatory on communion Sunday.

Reverend Ward yelled his words of Christ's sacrifice in a crazed rage. Spit flew from his mouth, hitting us in his own baptism of condemnation.

Even God's son had been turned against and subsequently murdered for being different. He must have lived in a small town too.

Once he finished his sermon and spraying us with spit, it was time for communion. "Ladies first," he announced and gestured for us to stand and approach the altar. He instructed us on how we were to repeat words after him, then drink the wine representing Christ's blood and eat the bread representing his body. It sounded an awful lot like witchcraft to me, but I knew it was only labeled in such a way when women did it. For men, it was religion.

We each received a small chalice filled with a deep, red liquid and a square of hard, unleavened bread. Catherine stood on one side of me. Lucille on the other. We stood in two straight lines facing one another as we repeated the words Reverend Ward chanted.

"May the blood . . ."

May the blood.

"And the body of our Lord."

And the body of our Lord.

"Wash away our sins and evil ways."

Wash away our sins and evil ways.

"And keep us from eternal damnation."

And keep us from eternal damnation.

"Amen."

Amen.

The words echoed off the dilapidated walls.

Together, we brought our chalices up to our mouths. The cold glass against my lips sent a shiver down my spine. The bitter scent of fermentation seared my nostrils. I tilted my head back. Dark, red liquid flowed onto my tongue. Both sweet and bitter, it burned all the way down to my stomach, where it pooled, heavy and hot. The bread that came afterward was tasteless. Impossible to chew and almost more so to swallow. Somehow, we managed.

Then, it was the men's turn to receive communion. Having returned to the hard, wooden pews that dug into our backs and thighs, we all watched as they walked to the front and lined up in the same formation as we had.

As Christopher made his way out into the aisle, I cleared my throat. He glanced over at me and I gave a sharp shake of my head, nodding to the pew behind him. He looked between it and me, his eyebrows scrunched, but he sat back down nonetheless.

I exchanged glances with Lucille, Catherine, and the rest of the women. Lucille lifted an eyebrow at my actions. I just shook my head and mouthed, "He's on our side." Her expression didn't change but she nodded regardless.

Nerves showed on some of their faces; excitement on others. Lucille looked more nervous than the rest, fidgeting with her hands on her lap, which was rather out of character for her. Was there something she wasn't telling us?

But it was too late to second-guess our plan now, as the men passed their cups around. I held my hand underneath my fan. The others did the same under their own pamphlets or Bibles. We each slid needles from our dress linings and used them to pierce our fingers, drawing blood as ruby as the wine we'd just consumed.

I barely felt the needle break the surface of my skin. My fingers were used to it from accidentally pricking myself daily while working in the mill. Blood dripped from my finger. I pulled another hidden object from my clothes, a bird's feather.

A bird flying left to right will bring bad luck or transformation from good to bad.

Draw blood and smear onto the feather of a bird in a left-to-right pattern.

I swiped the bird feather in my blood. It smeared the hot liquid across my fingertips and stained them red.

The Spirit. The Sacrifice. The Superstition.

The men lifted the chalices to their lips. The ruby liquid that poured from the cup onto their tongues came out thicker and darker than the wine we drank minutes before.

I sucked in a breath. It worked.

Our crafting worked.

And this time, I wasn't even frightened. In fact, I felt quite the opposite. Weightless. Free.

Powerful.

Beside me, Lucille blew out a long breath. Her hands ceased their fidgeting, and her posture straightened.

Loud gags cut through the stifling air. Choking followed.

"Blood!" Thomas shrieked. He spewed a crimson mist into the air. It covered the pulpit. "That's blood!"

Reverend Ward's eyebrows scrunched together. "Well, yes, wine is a semblance of Christ's blood."

"No!" George choked out from beside Thomas, who had bent over and gagged. "It's *real* blood!"

All the men spat, coughed, and heaved up blood. Before long, it puddled on the ground, dripped from the walls, and stained their suits. The inside of the small chapel resembled the aftermath of a massacre, a murder scene.

A baptism of death.

I couldn't help the grin that wrinkled my cheeks.

Screams sliced like knives through the tension-filled chapel as people ran from the gory sight. Reverend Ward descended from his pulpit and tried to calm his congregation. He patted the men's backs who were still choking. "Demons leave them be! God help them!"

Lucille stifled her own giggle beside me, a quick one, but long enough to make me look over at her. She was practically glowing. I had seen her look confident before, but she looked more than just confident now. She looked powerful.

Witchcraft became her.

Henry came to stand beside us, having come in late. Lucky for him.

His eyebrows rose to his hairline as he took in the chaos ensuing. "Looks like this morning's sermon was much more exciting than usual."

Henry looked over at Christopher, still sitting innocently on his pew, not a speck of blood marring his church attire.

Christopher shrugged his shoulders. "I didn't feel up for communion today, my stomach's been in a fuss."

I smiled at Christopher's excuse, happy with the decision I had made to trust him.

Lucille watched the reverend's attempts to regain control among the screams of terror and expulsion of bodily fluids. "It seems someone must've confused the wine with something less appetizing."

Thomas, covered in blood, and the contents of his own stomach, stumbled toward us. "You—" he pointed his finger at us, "you did this!"

Christopher stood and Henry stepped in front of us. He seemed more interested in wiping invisible dust from his shoulder. "How could these fine women have anything to do with this, Thomas? There was clearly some sort of mix-up. That is all."

"Mix-up?" Thomas repeated incredulously and gestured to the horrors around us, "You call having to drink blood—"

"Rat blood," Catherine interrupted with a devious smirk.

"Why, you little . . ." Thomas sputtered and then bent forward. He gagged and dry heaved again.

"He seems to have quite a weak stomach, doesn't he?" Lucille grinned.

Thomas lifted his head to shoot one last infuriated look our way before he ran from the chapel with his hand clapped over his mouth.

The sorority followed suit not long after him, lest we stick around and bring attention to ourselves. Once we arrived safely back in our dormitory, out of the morning heat and away from prying eyes, I couldn't help the laugh that escaped my lips. Lucille laughed with me. And then we were all laughing—maniacal, gut-wrenching laughs.

Chapter Twenty-Three

Lucille

One crow for sadness, two crows for mirth;
Three crows for marriage, four crows for birth;
Five crows for laughing, six crows for crying;
Seven crows for sickness, eight crows for dying;
Nine crows for silver, ten crows for gold;
Eleven crows a secret that will never be told.

The week after the incident in the chapel came to me in pieces, gathered deliberately as I slunk from one place to another. I listened for accusations, our names being said, anything that might warn us of trouble.

On the stairs of the girl's dormitory hall, Mary Ann and Penelope descended just ahead of me, skirts lifted from the worn stone.

"They say it was just the wine," Mary Ann murmured. "It had gone bad."

"It couldn't have been blood," Penelope replied. "That's ridiculous."

I kept my pace even and my head down, fingers light on the banister. *Good*. Let it be ridiculous. Let it be wine. Let it be anything but what it had truly been, anything but proof that the witchcraft had finally worked for me again. Finally answered my call again. A small, almost giddy warmth sat in my chest, there since the chapel.

I thought back to that feeling. It was like having my first sip of water again after a long day in the fields. I had been plenty nervous, and plenty scared, but when the memories came, when the shaking started in my fingers, I looked to my sides. Saw all the faces of the women around me. Felt their warmth. I was not alone. I wasn't doing it just for me. It was for them.

And it had *worked*.

Eight crows flew in the sky as a group of students lingered near the chapel doors. They weren't part of our cohort. They took different courses, possibly the sciences or arithmetics. They spoke with the confidence of those who needed the world to make sense.

"My brother says this happens more often than people admit," one of them declared. "Especially in poor storage, under inadequate supervision."

"So they fired someone?" another asked.

"Demoted," came the reply, "the lowerclassman who prepared the communion. He's on chamber pot duty now."

They laughed. I passed them without looking over, my steps lighter.

The corridors nearer the lecture halls echoed with more speculation.

"Did you see it?"

"Not properly. My cousin did. Swears it was darker than wine."

"People see what they want to see."

I had seen it. I had *felt* it. The precise moment the witchcraft took hold, the way the air produced a strange breeze, the way the fear I'd carried since the last time loosened its grip. For months after Reece's death, after the pain, the blood, I'd wondered if something in me had broken for good.

But it hadn't.

It had worked.

I said nothing as I walked, the joy tucked safely beneath my composure.

Outside the classroom, students gathered in loose knots, waiting for the class before us to finish and vacate.

I leaned against the wall, half-shadowed by the tall window, and let the relief spread through me. The narrative was settling now, smoothing itself into something harmless. Spoiled wine. Carelessness. Overactive imaginations. No mention of us. No whisper of witchcraft or intent.

I was still savoring that quiet victory when Thomas approached. My small smile immediately dropped to a frown. He stopped short, clearly irritated to find me there, unharmed and unrepentant. His eyes held the same resentment they had since the chapel, but now it lacked its edge.

"You seem very calm," he sneered, then looked around at the small crowd. "Everyone's pretending nothing happened."

"They usually do," I said, trying to feign more interest in my nail beds and cuticles, which were both covered in dirt and grime, than him. "It's easier. Especially for halfwits like you."

He growled, his scarred face wrinkling into anger. "I know you were involved."

I met his eyes, steady and unafraid. He had no evidence, just suspicion.

"You would do well to put the matter behind you," I said, dropping my hand to my side and jutting my chin forward. "Much like you already have with any lick of intelligence your mama gave you."

"Why, you little—"

The classroom door swung open behind him. Students began to file out in one direction or the other. Whatever he might've said next dissolved under the weight of witnesses and routine. He snapped his mouth shut and stepped aside, jaw tight.

I passed him, not giving him the satisfaction of a glance back, and entered the room.

By the time I reached my seat and set my books down, my hands were steady. The fear that had haunted me since the chapel was gone, replaced by a careful, private joy.

It had worked.

And this time, nothing had gone wrong.

Professor Compton commenced class by informing us of an upcoming bonfire event and the opening of this year's *Brimham Tribune* writers' applications, the university's long-established newspaper whose popularity had spread beyond the university to the entire region. My heart raced at the announcement.

"The headmaster and I will take applications to fill the newly vacated positions for lowerclassman writers," Professor Compton declared. "We expect to see enthusiastic participation and maybe some friendly competition." He smirked toward the male students he'd obviously picked as his favorites.

Finally! My hand shot up in the air.

"Yes, Miss Rockwell?"

"What is required for this application?" I prepared to take notes. This was the moment I had been waiting for and had fought to get to.

Professor Compton replied hesitantly, "Miss Rockwell, you don't mean you intend to apply for *The Brimham Tribune,* do you?"

"Yes. Yes, sir, that's exactly what I intend." I had intended to from the day I stepped foot on the campus.

Professor Compton coughed into his hand, though I swore he covered a laugh. Thomas and George didn't attempt to stifle theirs.

"I'm sorry, Miss Rockwell, but it's only for our male students. I'm sure you understand."

He wasn't sorry. And I didn't understand.

My chest heated to molten lava. My fingertips ached to be ripped open and spill the blood that heated with rage in my veins. The words of The Superstition tingled on the tip of my tongue.

I swallowed them down. I couldn't let my anger put the other women at risk with such a public display against a professor.

Thomas spoke up from a few rows behind me. "We would hate for your feeble minds to become too perplexed by working at the *Tribune.*"

I spun around in my seat or as far as my outrageous skirts allowed. "Well, if you can do it, how difficult of a task must it be?"

Thomas's face turned beetroot-red, and his mouth opened to object, but Mr. Compton interrupted instead.

"Settle down. Miss Rockwell, if you have further comments, you can take them to Headmaster Sullivan. Now, let's get started on today's lecture." The professor turned to the blackboard, chalk in hand.

I sure as hell would!

Thomas squinted his beady eyes. I gave him a dirty look before I turned around in my seat and furiously wrote on my parchment, but I wasn't writing notes from the lecture on Greek and Latin root words. I was making plans.

If they wouldn't let me be a part of their newspaper, I would have to start my own. Or rather, we, the sorority, would start our own.

I spent the rest of class and much of the walk to my little writing spot thinking it through. However, my thoughts of newspapers and revenge came to a halt when a puddle glinted in the sun close to the walking path. But it wasn't any ol' puddle. It was dark red, made even darker from mixing with the dirt underneath it. Blood.

My breath caught in my throat. My stomach turned flips like a tumbleweed in a thunderstorm.

I followed the ruby droplets deeper into the gloomy woods lining the campus.

Eventually, I came to the source and gagged. I've seen plenty of dead animals in my time. I've even slaughtered some myself to put food on the table. That was just the way of life on a farm. You raise animals, feed them, care for them, and then when the time comes, they feed and care for you.

Someone didn't kill this animal for that purpose.

It was mutilated.

Chapter Twenty-Four Catherine

The corpse of a hare is a trickster; disguising bad luck as good.

The weather had just begun to have a slight chill in the mornings. However, by afternoon, the sun was back to its games of torture. It roasted everything and everyone its rays touched. Thank goodness layers had become all the rage in fashion.

I peeled off the short cape covering my arms and shoulders and folded it as I walked. I quickened my pace to keep up with the members of our sorority. Lucille had called an emergency sorority meeting and prompted us to follow her outside without any explanation, only that it was urgent.

"Why are you insisting we make haste in this heat?" My groan sounded more annoyed than I meant for it to.

"We live in Alabama. It's always hot. You should be used to it by now," Lucille called over her shoulder. Her short hair bobbed with the turn of her head. "There is something out here y'all need to see."

"What is it?" Alice's voice wavered with worry.

I wiped the sweat from my brow and hoped my curls were still intact under my hat as I quickened my pace to get closer to her.

"See for yourself." Lucille stopped farther from the cobblestones than I would've liked, not one to ever wander from the beaten path, but I followed just as the rest of the sorority did, only a step away from Alice.

I yanked my skirts up to keep them from getting tangled in the underbrush. Victoria, Susan, and Rebecca gasped beside Lucille. I hurried my steps. The women ahead of me huddled around something on the ground.

I was about to complain again between gulps of air burning my lungs when something red stained the bottom of my shoes. The object of their displeasure, no doubt. Among the swarm of flies and other insects that eat dead, decomposing things, fur was ripped from a body. Gashes leaked blood. It pooled around the corpse of the large hare, the same size as a small child. Unnatural cuts zigzagged this way and that, making shapes and symbols. They opened the body and exposed the wet, blood-soaked organs underneath. My stomach fought to reject the food I had eaten earlier.

I swallowed hard. I couldn't throw up in front of Alice. How mortifying.

"Who would do such a thing?" Susan spoke up for the first time since leaving the dormitory. Her eyes were wide, and her skin turned even paler than normal.

"I don't know, but whoever it was clearly meant to do some sort of witchcraft." Lucille turned in circles, inspecting the ground. "Dark witchcraft."

"Dark witchcraft," Rebecca repeated and asked, "That's not the witchcraft we do, is it?"

I watched Lucille search the ground to distract myself from looking at the grotesque sight before me.

"I don't recognize the symbols but I certainly know it's witchcraft, but not the kind my ma taught me. Not the kind we do." Lucille bent down and patted the ground with her hands. "I would guess whoever is doing it needs a large sacrifice, too large for them to give on their own. They need something to give the blood for them. And instead of using feathers or herbs to direct it, they're carving these symbols."

Lucille clawed at the dirt with her fingers. The underbelly of her nails turned black with soil.

"What are you doing?" I desperately tried to swallow the bile that threatened to rise in my throat.

"Digging a grave. We can't just leave the poor thing out like this." Lucille grabbed and tossed clumps of dirt to the side. Her hands became increasingly covered with the dark brown soil.

"Won't other animals just . . . eat it?" Victoria whispered. Unlike me, she hadn't taken her eyes off of the body since we arrived.

"Animals can feel things more than we can. Feel energies. They won't come close to something with those markings. And we can't just leave it where someone could find it. We'd surely be the first to get blamed."

Victoria's gaze finally left the mangled corpse as she bent beside Lucille and helped her dig. Alice and Rebecca followed suit. The bile in my throat finally won the tug-of-war battle with my mind. I sprinted a few steps away from the group and bent over a nearby bush. Sharp leaves scraped my cheeks as I heaved the contents of my stomach into the foliage. My esophagus lit on fire. Tears blurred my vision.

Though it wasn't entirely the sight of the animal's blood and gore that caused the sickening feeling. It was, in part, because of the memory the sight evoked. Another body surrounded by a puddle of blood. But an unknown person hadn't caused that gore.

I had.

I'd been the one to kiss her, to convince her we could get away with our secret affections, even though our love was forbidden under any circumstances. It wasn't until I was on my knees, tears streaming down my face as I begged for our forgiveness, begged for her limp body to move again, that I realized how utterly naive I had been. It wasn't until I watched her corpse be slowly lowered in the ground days later that I realized the consequences weren't just bad—they were deadly.

A hand rubbed my back in a soothing, circular motion.

"It's done. The body is buried." Alice whispered.

"Thank you." I wiped my hand across my mouth and stood. The acidic taste of vomit lingered on my tongue, but it was nothing compared to the heat that spread across my cheeks. How embarrassing. "What do we do now?"

"We keep doing what we've been doing. Nothing changes." Lucille kicked dirt over the puddle of my bodily fluid.

She didn't, nor did Alice or Rebecca, seem phased by anything gory. Working odd jobs their whole lives must have desensitized them to such things.

"We'll make protection-charmed bracelets for each of us. It'll take some time to gather all the materials, though." Then Lucille added, "In the meantime, stay on the lookout for any strange occurrences or anyone who seems to know about witchcraft besides the women in our sorority."

"What if it's someone *in* our sorority?" I asked, even though I hoped it wasn't true.

"It can't be. Not after signing our blood on that pledge. It would be impossible." Lucille walked back to the path.

I gasped. "Are we all cursed?"

Lucille snorted. "No. Just bound to one another."

"What if we're in public when we notice something? How will we communicate it without raising suspicions?" Alice swatted at a mosquito.

"Maybe we could make up some sort of signal?" Rebecca suggested.

"I could teach y'all the hand signals we used at the mill." Victoria raised her hand slightly, as if volunteering for a role. "The powered looms were always so loud we could never hear one another properly enough to speak, and we needed it even more so when our hearing weakened because of them."

"Perfect." Lucille nodded, and the rest chimed in with their own agreements.

"It'll be like learning a different language." I smiled.

My sisters had learned Latin with their tutors. They picked it up so easily. I was never much of a linguist. Not like them. And Mama never let me forget it.

"Who do you think did this?" Susan changed the subject. Her teeth worked away at the already mangled skin of her nail beds.

Branches and limbs crunched under our feet. They snapped into bits and fragments. We each looked around nervously as we scanned for anyone who might see us. Or might be out to get us.

"I predict it's the reverend," Victoria said.

"The reverend," Rebecca grunted. "I second that. He's unsettling."

I let out a shaky breath, thankful to step back onto the path and away from the darkness of the woods and underbrush.

"I don't know. There's more to everyone than meets the eye." Lucille looked behind her at the woods we'd just emerged from before we all turned and walked back to our dormitory together.

I gulped and quickened my pace, more than ready to change out of my blood-stained clothes. And not for the first time.

Chapter Twenty-Five
Victoria

A knotted handkerchief protects whoever carries it from evil spirits.

The bonfire was the largest I'd ever seen. Flames licked the sky. Smoke billowed up and blanketed the stars. Darkness blocked the full moon's light.

The women huddled together on one side of the fire and our male counterparts on the other. We stared through the flames at each other. Shadows played across our faces from the fire casting a bright glow, but deep shadows made our eye sockets sunken and empty—skeletal.

Headmaster Sullivan and Reverend Ward stood between the two sides. They talked to one another, though no one could hear them over the noise of the crowd. Finally, the headmaster and reverend stepped forward and rang a cowbell. Silence spread in an instant.

Headmaster Sullivan yelled over the roar of the fire. "Tonight, in honor of the coming harvest and hunting season, we present our annual bonfire and hunt. Though, this year, it will be a little different thanks to these fine young ladies." He gestured to our side of the fire with his meaty hand. "In previous years, we've started the season with a deer hunt, but since we're in the presence of women now, we'll participate in a different sort of hunt." He smiled.

The mention of a "hunt" had my head filled with the grotesque images of the mutilated hare. A shiver ran like a sharp blade down my spine.

Reverend Ward stepped forward as if they'd rehearsed this talk beforehand. "Yes, tonight will not only be great fun for all y'all but a wonderful spiritual lesson on how to lead." He gestured to the men, then turned to us. "And how to follow. The Bible says, 'Wives, follow the lead of your own husbands as you follow the Lord. The husband is the head of the wife, just as Christ is the head of the church.' And so too does it say, 'As the church submits to Christ, so also wives should submit to their husbands in everything.'"

Lucille leaned over and whispered to me and the other sorority members huddled close to us, "Great, we're getting another sermon from the esteemed reverend. What an honor." Her words dripped with sarcasm and southern twang.

The group of men cheered on the reverend. Headmaster Sullivan held up his hand, settling them down. "Tonight, we will pair each woman with a man to go on a hunt. We have hidden different attributes of a deer in the woods. A tail, antlers, and furs are tied to posts. You and your partner will race against the other teams to find a deer appendage and return to the bonfire. The first pair back with a deer part in hand, will be crowned as this year's Mr. and Mrs. Bama Bonnet."

The men cheered. We stayed silent.

Reverend Ward interrupted the cheering as he clutched his crucifix in one hand and his long beard in the other. He yanked it out of the path of stray embers. "For y'all to learn the lesson of subservience, as is God's word, you ladies will be blindfolded, and each paired with a male companion to lead you in the hunt. For your part, ladies, you must be submissive to your partner's leadership and trust them to guide you along the way, just as you trust God to do the same. Headmaster

Sullivan and I will gladly act as chaperones and walk through the woods to monitor your progress."

The roaring flames and darkness made it nearly impossible for me to hear or read his lips. Lucille had to repeat his words to me.

A few of the men whispered to one another, grins spreading across their faces. I caught the tail end of a crude joke about the women being submissive to them. My stomach twisted. Were the headmaster and reverend so blind that they really thought this would go well?

"Well, this is going to be a disaster," Lucille said.

Alice lifted her chin. "I would rather be partnered with a bear."

Catherine laughed, though it sounded more like a sob.

"They can't think this is a good idea, can they?" Susan's fingertips were already bloody with her anxious gnawing.

I watched the headmaster hand out handkerchiefs to be used as blindfolds. "Apparently so."

"I wish we'd made those damn charmed protection bracelets before this," Lucille grunted and grasped our hands in hers "Fight if you need to. Don't be afraid to use what we've been practicing."

We nodded.

"Just stay safe." Lucille wrapped her long arms around as many of us as she could. The others followed suit and hugged one another for a moment before dispersing.

"We will." Catherine's voice wavered. "You too."

"Hell, you don't have to worry about me. Worry about the poor bastard I get paired with." Lucille pulled away with a smirk. It didn't meet her eyes.

We separated as men paired with women and tied their blindfolds with the glee of children about to have their first bicycle rides.

Christopher paired with me. He smiled as he approached, his hands held slightly before him as if letting me know he intended no harm. Though, after spending several hours discussing books at the library, I already knew that to be the case. But I still couldn't force myself to smile back as he gently placed the handkerchief over my eyes. His breath tickled my ear. "Let's try to get through this as quickly as possible so we can both get back to what we really want to be doing—reading." He tried to say it with light amusement in his voice, no doubt to ease the tension.

"Yes. Let's." My voice wasn't nearly as light.

He tied a knot in the handkerchief at the back of my head and lingered close behind me. "You have nothing to be afraid of. It's just me and you, just like when we're at the library."

I grunted. It wasn't that I didn't trust Christopher. We had become close, friends even, but that didn't negate the fact that we were still going into the woods alone. With several other men. Blindfolded. Vulnerable. Unable to see danger coming until it was already here. Unable to protect ourselves.

"You know I mean you no harm." He whispered close enough to my ear that I had no trouble hearing him. "If . . ."

Oh, no. 'If' was never good. What if I had been fooled, and he wasn't the person I thought he was?

He swallowed, then continued, "If you don't mean *me* any harm."

What? We'd spent many hours together. His words didn't make any sense. "Why would I—"

"My birth name is Christopher, as you well know. However, there's something I've been wanting to tell you . . ." His breaths were heavy and fast in my ear. "I prefer to go by Chrissy." He'd finished tying the knot by now and gently guided me forward, his hands shaking. "I prefer to be referred to as a . . . woman."

I sucked in a breath. My steps halted. A coughing fit racked my body. I'd heard of men and even women wanting to be what they weren't. Dressing and acting as such. I hadn't met anyone like that or hadn't known if I had. It was always too dangerous for them to admit to such feelings publicly or even confidentially with someone. Yet here we were, in a delicate dance with one another. I could turn around and shout Chrissy's confession to the world—sign her death warrant.

But so could she sign mine out here in the dark woods, all alone, surrounded by men.

Chrissy's grip tightened on my shoulders, not with harm, but with anticipation, her fingers twitching as she waited for my response. Waited to see who would damn whom first. But I was in no position to condemn anyone, not with all that I had done. And I'd enjoyed our discussions on literature, man or woman.

"You're safe with me," I whispered.

Chrissy exhaled. Her breath sent shivers down my back like ice. She continued to nudge me forward, but her grip loosened. "As are you with me."

I relaxed slightly. I *wasn't* paired with a man.

"There's strength in numbers." Chrissy squeezed my shoulders with a silent thanks. "We literary women have to stick together, right?"

We certainly did.

We continued into the woods. I listened to Chrissy's gentle directions and only hoped the others had gotten as lucky with their partnerships as I had.

Though, I doubted it.

Chapter Twenty-Six

Lucille

To hear an owl screech is to link oneself with wisdom and justice.

Pitch-black greeted my eyes like an abyss of darkness. Only when I tilted my head toward the sky did a brief blur of light from the moon peek through the coarse fabric that scratched against my face. Though I couldn't see, I could certainly hear. I heard everything. The crunch of leaves and branches under my feet. The chatter and whispers of the other partners who slowly made their way through the woods. Owls screeched at our intrusion into their homes. Creatures scurried, frightened by our presence. Henry's smooth voice guided me.

My sense of touch became heightened, too. Henry's warm hand heated the small of my back, but it did not move any lower. His other hand wrapped around my own as he helped to steady me and himself. His breath on my cheek. The tree limbs that crunched and broke under my weight like bones.

"There's a large branch on the ground ahead of us. You'll have to step over it," Henry said. "Or I could lift you and carry you over it."

"After all our letters and exchanges, what makes you think I would ever choose the latter?" I scoffed.

"Just dumb hope, I suppose." I could hear the grin in his voice and picture the way the right corner of his lips tugged upward and exposed a dimple just above it.

"This is ridiculous. Do they really expect us to learn a lesson from this?"

"Are their expectations something you really want to discuss?" Henry chuckled.

"No, I suppose not. Their low expectations of women would only agitate me more." I huffed and wanted to cross my arms, but I didn't want to risk losing my balance.

"They're fools if that's what they really believe, but I don't think so." Henry's uneven steps halted. "The branch I told you about is before us. Are you sure you don't want a lift?"

"Positive." I raised my foot to feel in front of me and tried to gauge how big the branch was and how high I needed to step. Henry continued to talk me through it and hold most of my weight when I almost stumbled, but he respected my wishes not to be carried. He used my shoulder to lean on as he stepped over the branch with his only leg and then dragged his wooden prosthetic across.

Once we were both back on solid ground and back to our slow, wobbly pace, I asked, "If you don't think their expectations are low, what do you think?"

"Why, Miss Lucille, are you asking for my opinion?" His hand lifted from my back, and I could only assume he splayed it on his chest dramatically as he said, "I'm honored."

"Don't get your knickers in a twist, Henry. I only wish to be entertained on such a long, arduous walk." Though my words were harsh, I couldn't stop a small smile from crossing my lips.

"Well, if you really want to know . . ."

I elbowed him where I thought his ribs would be.

"Alright, alright," he said. "I think their expectations for women are actually high. So high, in fact, that they are afraid."

"Afraid?" I hadn't expected that.

"Yes. Afraid of what could happen if y'all reached your full potential. Afraid of the power they would lose. They surely must recognize y'all are more resilient. How could they not be afraid of such things?"

I stayed quiet and let that sink in.

"They think if they reduce you to be something submissive, they can make themselves feel as if they have the upper hand."

"Are you afraid of us?" I whispered, though my voice seemed to echo in the depths of the dark woods.

"Never. Not because I doubt your strength but because I believe in it. I am in awe of you." My cheeks grew hot. Henry cleared his throat. "Of women, I mean."

"I must say, I am quite surprised."

"Surely, after all our letters, you don't think I'm as ignorant as the headmaster or the reverend?" His voice feigned hurt. "You've wounded me."

My eyes rolled under the blindfold. "I don't think you are *quite* as ignorant as them. That is a rather progressive way of thinking you have. Especially down here in the South. Doesn't that make you unpopular with others around here? Say, for example, Thomas?"

"Well, I should hope I think progressively compared to them. I can't bring myself to care much about my popularity. Besides, one can't care for others' opinions of them before they must first face their own. When surrounded and taught by strong women, my mother and sisters, respect for them comes easily and naturally. It baffles me how any man who was created, birthed, and raised by a woman can have anything less than respect for the gender. It's not just ignorance. It's blatant stupidity."

For once, my mind went blank except for his words. I would've gladly kept it that way for the rest of my life. Swam in those words, drunk them up, let them fill me to the brim.

"Looks like we've made it." Henry's steps halted.

"We're already in the middle of the woods?" I asked, shocked.

"Time flies when you're having fun, doesn't it?" Henry untied my blindfold.

"Don't flatter yourself too much." I slid the scratchy fabric from my eyes.

A gasp escaped my lips. Henry stood mere inches from me. We were the same height, and though his stance was uneven, I could stare into his hazel eyes, almost brown in the dark.

"I wouldn't dare." Henry smirked and turned toward a wooden post stuck in the ground with a furry tail hanging from it.

I hated the disappointment that arose in my chest when he was no longer close.

"Shall we get back to the bonfire?" He extended the crook of his elbow for me to take hold of. The animal tail dangled from his hand.

"If we must."

I wrapped my hand around his bicep, content to take our time getting back.

Chapter Twenty-Seven
Catherine

Sleeping in moonlight will invite evil spirits to take over the mind.

We'd stumbled through the woods for what seemed like an eternity. I couldn't see anything. My hair stuck to the sweat on my forehead, and my feet hurt from the uneven ground. Yet, all of that combined was more tolerable than who I'd been paired with. Percy's nonstop talking made my head hurt more than my flute tutor had back at home. At least his terrible flute playing was only an intolerable noise and not words.

"Have you considered ingesting opium? I've heard it helps with weight loss." Percy's words were only slightly worse than his whining, nasal voice. Between that and his constant talk of how valuable a lesson in submission this blindfold exercise was, I was about ready to take on the rest of the hike in the woods alone, regardless of the darkness or the creatures that roamed about.

"Are you listening to me, Miss Stanley?" His high-pitched voice rose even higher.

I didn't bother to respond.

"Has your corpulence disrupted your ability to hear?"

"That's it!" I spun around and yanked the blindfold from my eyes. "I can't endure your idiocy another moment!"

Percy's mouth fell open. Even with one less arm, he was, by every standard, a handsome man. Strong jawline. Thick brown hair. Crystal blue eyes that penetrated, even in the darkness of night. Tall and broad-shouldered that took up space in a world that only accepts such from men. Everything a woman might dream of. But I was not that woman.

"Excuse me?" he huffed, his muscular shoulders shrugging with the movement. "This is supposed to be a lesson on being submissive and taking orders. You *have* to obey."

"Like heck I do." I stomped away from him and didn't care which direction I was going or how dark my surroundings were.

Percy reached for me with his one hand, grasped my arm, and yanked me toward him. I stumbled, and we collided. We both crashed to the ground. Sticks, stones, and branches stabbed my skin through my corset. They no doubt drew blood. Percy pinned me to the ground. I couldn't get a scream out before he slapped his sweaty hand over my mouth. It smelled of smoke and something tangy, like onions.

"You *will* listen to me, and you *will* do as I say, like a good, little, submissive woman should!"

Memories of Cousin Frederick's body pressing me against the wall resurfaced. His words, "*Because claiming you will be a victory. Because breaking you will be a conquest.*" echoed through my mind. I wouldn't let a man control me like that again. Wouldn't let him frighten me.

I bit Percy's hand as hard as I could until I tasted salt and copper. He screamed as he yanked it away. His blood remained in my mouth. I spat it in his face. He jerked to the side. As soon as his weight shifted, I jumped up.

"How about this for a submissive woman?" I yelled. My fingers already tingled with the hot urge of witchcraft.

I grabbed a nearby sharp stone and ripped it across the meaty flesh of my palm. The searing pain was only an afterthought as the blood spilled over, and I whispered the words of The Superstition.

Sleeping in moonlight will invite evil spirits to take over the mind.

The Spirit. The Sacrifice. The Superstition.

The tingle in my fingers spread as a burning pool of molten lead in my stomach. An unnatural wind ripped through the woods and ruffled the leaves. A group of midnight birds flew into the sky with a resounding echo of unsettled chirps.

Percy let out a piercing shriek and hugged himself. He rolled around on the ground until he went limp altogether. Dirt and leaves stuck to his still body.

Oh, God. I killed him.

Not again.

His hand twitched, and a small moan came from his lips. I sucked in a breath. I may not like the man, but I certainly didn't want his death on my hands.

I stared at his limp form a moment longer and waited for him to twitch again to be certain I wasn't leaving him for dead. My heart raced and my stomach twisted into knots. With a gulp, I took off and tried to put as much distance between us as possible before he gained consciousness again. I didn't pay attention to the direction I went.

His groans as he woke up and began to yell echoed through the trees. I ran faster.

A safe distance from Percy, I stopped and bent over with my hands on my knees and gulped in the thick air. Despite the humidity, my throat was dry, and the tang of blood still lingered in my mouth, along with the salt of my sweat.

After my heart slowed, I straightened and took in my surroundings. The full moon's light barely shone through the layers of branches and their leaves. Dark lattice shadows draped over the woods. Stars glimpsed through gaps in the tall silhouettes stretched from the ground to the sky like hands ready to claw the heavens.

My heart raced again, but not from physical exertion. Twigs snapped in the distance. I jerked from side to side and looked for any creatures who lurked among the clumps of bushes. A howl echoed through the woods close by. From the many complaints of our estate's gardeners, I knew coyotes were prevalent in this area. I'd never concerned myself with it, hadn't felt like I needed to. But now, things were much more dire.

I had to get out of here.

My legs moved slowly at first. Then faster. Soon, I was running. Branches raked across my skin and tangled in my hair. My feet labored to hit solid ground. I tried to avoid the stray branches and odd holes. A twisted ankle could very well be the death of me.

A spider web wrapped around me as I ran between two trees. A scream ripped through my throat. My nails clawed at my face. As much as I wanted to sink down onto the ground and cry, I urged myself to keep going. The shadows of the trees followed me. Reached for me. Tried to drag me back into the depths of the woods.

Scrapes, cuts, and dirt caked my skin. Panic crept into my chest, making it hard to breathe. Just as I lost all sense of sanity and logic, a glow peaked through the leaves. It looked small, far off in the distance, but I could see the dance of the flames that made the shadows around me move and sway.

I pushed my legs to move as fast as my muscles would allow. In my rush, my foot caught on something, and brought me down to the hard ground. Sprawled out, I felt around me. My hands connected with something warm. Something wet and furry.

My eyes took a moment to adjust, to see what my hands were feeling.

Red. Sticky. Blood.

Lots of blood.

The mutilated doe's body was almost identical to the hare we'd found in the woods a few days ago, except bigger. Much bigger. And so, too, were the slashes and gashes covering it. They opened up its flesh and exposed its insides to the dark world. Its fur was caked and matted. Organs bulged through skin. Intestines spilled over. Bodily fluids seeped out.

I swallowed back bile that burned my throat. I crawled away on my elbows and knees as quickly as I could. Sticky, thick blood covered my hands like sick gloves. It acted as a glue. Leaves and twigs adhered to me. I jumped up and sprinted the remaining distance to the opening of the woods. As I burst through the tree line, I fell to the ground in front of the fire.

At first, I was so thankful to have escaped the woods and be back where this atrocious night had begun, I didn't notice how unnaturally quiet it was around the bonfire despite the crowd.

Then, I saw it. Everyone stared in stunned silence, and they didn't stare at my blood and dirt-covered self.

Above the enormous pile of burning wood, the flames had turned into something else, as if someone had sculpted them into a human-like figure. It had fiery limbs, a flaming torso, and hair made of black smoke that rose into the sky.

Lucille and Victoria raced over to me, helping me up from the ground.

"Are you okay?" Lucille eyed the blood caked on my hands.

I ignored her question, unable to take my eyes off the flaming beast.

"What is that thing?" I shouted over the fire's roar.

Oh, God. Did I do this?

"I don't know!" Lucille and Victoria yelled on either side of me. "It just appeared!"

Phantom words floated in the mysterious wind. "You," the figure pointed to us, the women crowded to the side, "are not meant to be here."

Gasps sounded from all around the bonfire, men and women alike. Everyone stood, stunned. Mouths hung agape in silent screams. A figure stood in the shadow of the trees. When I blinked, it was gone.

"You must leave now, or you will not leave with your life," the eerie words echoed off our trembling bodies. "Get out. Get out! GET OUT!"

I gulped. A shiver shimmied down my spine like the slow drip of thick blood down a corpse.

With one last screech, it vanished. The unnatural wind went with it. The fire's roar resumed as if it had never stopped.

Chapter Twenty-Eight
Victoria

Tie a knot and you won't be forgot.

The screams from around the bonfire rang in my ears even hours later. Even after Headmaster Sullivan and Reverend Ward tried to calm everyone down and maintain some semblance of control and civility. After Reverend Ward tried to console us and convince everyone that what we had seen was a vision from the Lord and nothing to be afraid of so they could maintain control and uphold the university's reputation. Even with their efforts, mass hysteria continued to ensue. Mary Ann packed up her things and left before the sun had a chance to rise and reveal what was hiding in the darkness.

Lucille, Catherine, and I stayed up and tried to do a better job of calming down the rest of the women than Headmaster Sullivan and Reverend Ward had. Catherine was most frantic of all.

"I did it. I made the monster. I used the craft in the woods and must've done it wrong. It's all my fault. It's all because of me." She rambled those same words over and over again. Ruby blood drenched the front of her dress and her arms. Dirt clung to her like vultures to a corpse.

Once upstairs in our meeting space, Lucille took hold of Catherine's trembling shoulders and looked down into her eyes. "You didn't do this."

My own heart still beat like a drum in my ears.

"But, but, I cut my hand and I said the—"

"No." Lucille's voice was one of finality, not to be argued with further. "You didn't do this. You couldn't have. Besides, you said you found another mutilated animal, didn't you?"

Catherine's eyes, the size of serving dishes, looked down at herself. She gasped at the gore that covered her. "The animal! I nearly forgot! Oh, it was horrible! Horribly mangled. And there was so much blood."

"Blood," Rebecca grunted. Black dirt and ash also covered her attire. She'd been shoved down and nearly trampled during the chaos that ensued after the fire's threat. "Did it have the same markings as the hare?"

Catherine's gaze flitted around the room aimlessly and her eyebrows scrunched together. "I . . . I . . . I think so. I don't know. It was so dark. And there was a spider web around me and then the thing in the fire and the blood and dirt and—"

Alice stepped forward. She took Lucille's place in front of Catherine. "Sh. Sh. It's okay. Breath."

She embraced Catherine and rubbed soothing circles on her back. The smell of smoke lingered on all of us. It burned our lungs with each inhale and stung our eyes with each exhale.

"Either way, it had to have been something dark making that fire come to life like that." Susan mumbled shakily. Her fingernails already brought to her mouth to be nervously chewed on. "Maybe we should all leave, too. Didn't you hear what it said? We're going to die if we don't."

"No!" Lucille, Alice, and I all said in unison.

"The program has already lost one woman tonight," I said.

"If we leave, the person doing all of this will win." Alice held her chin up. She continued to rub circles on Catherine's back, who seemed to be taking full advantage of the position she was in.

Candles melted wax onto the floor. Small puddles formed underneath them. Their light gyrated wickedly across the walls and against our skin.

"We can't lose anyone else." I looked at each of the scared women. "In fact, I think it might not be a bad idea to try and invite more people into our coven."

Lucille narrowed her eyes as if she already knew what I was thinking. "What people?"

"Well, I was thinking . . ." I mumbled as I broke eye contact and looked around the old meeting room.

Maybe I shouldn't have mentioned it. Wasn't I the one who was so hesitant to form such a group with so many people in the first place? Too many to care for. To grow attached to.

To lose.

"People." Rebecca considered this. "You didn't say women."

"Men?" Susan shrieked. "You want to invite men into our sorority?" She threw her arms up and crossed them over her chest. Her chewed nail beds all but forgotten.

"Well not exactly." I sighed and told them about my walk through the woods with Chrissy just as Chrissy and I had discussed me doing after I had told her of our coven. She wanted to be just as much a part of this fight as we were. Once I finished telling the sorority everything about my and Chrissy's time at the library and our discussion in the woods, I turned to Lucille and added, "You could invite Henry, too."

"I don't know if we're that desperate for more members." Catherine finally came out of her stupor and stepped away from Alice as if getting singed by a fire poker. As if adding space between them could stop the obvious attraction growing there.

"I second that." Susan raised her hand with bleeding fingertips.

I eyed Lucille. She hadn't said anything during this short debate, which was unusual for her.

"What do *you* think?" I asked her.

She stayed silent for a moment longer. I could practically see her weighing the options in her mind. The dance of the candle flames made shadows crawl their way across her face. Darkened her eyes.

"You're right." She stated finally.

Susan gasped. "What?"

Out of anyone, I'm sure she expected Lucille to be on her side. I was a little surprised as well.

Lucille held up a shaking hand to silence any protests. "She's right. We need the numbers. The more of us there are, the stronger we are. The stronger our witchcraft is. Plus, Chrissy and Henry could be good for intel. They're with the other men more than we are. They'll hear more."

"But what if *they're* doing the dark witchcraft? What if they're the ones wanting us gone?" Susan argued, her arms still crossed defiantly over her chest.

"Chrissy isn't doing it." I was pretty certain. Wasn't I? She had seemed genuine. But what if it were a ruse? What if I was wrong, and I was setting us up for certain destruction?

"And neither is Henry." Lucille waved off the concerns as if they were merely an annoying gnat swarming around her. The pit of doubt that had begun to form in my stomach lightened, if only a little. "Besides, once they sign the pledge, they can't do us harm anyway."

Susan dropped her arms and let out a small huff, but otherwise subdued. She brought her fingers back to her teeth.

"What about everyone else who hasn't signed the pledge? We seem to have a target—an even bigger one now—on our backs. Someone's bound to get hurt again, or worse, if we stay." Alice slumped to the floor and spread her long legs out over the stained patterned carpet.

"My bet is still on the reverend." I slid down the wall behind me and brought my knees to my chest, wrapping my arms around them. My muscles stayed tense. They refused to loosen the tightness brought on by the night's wicked events.

Everyone else followed suit. They collapsed on the floor in their own heaps of exhaustion and worry.

"I agree." Catherine rested her head on a bundled-up sheet she'd grabbed off the old furniture nearby.

"Agree," Rebecca repeated. Worry wrinkled her dark forehead. "What if they come for one of us?"

She was right to worry. We all were. Maggie and I had participated in equal, if not less, risky behavior to help women in certain situations and they had come for us. Come for her. Her screams mixed with the ones from tonight's bonfire in my head. They formed a symphony of masochistic torture.

Lucille shot up from her sprawled position on the floor. "The protection bracelets!" she all but yelled.

I jumped. Some of the others did, too. Our senses were on high alert.

Lucille got to her feet faster than a needle swiped across a loom and sprinted out of the room. We all stared after her, not bothering to say anything, either out of shock or just sheer fatigue.

When she returned, she carried a basket of vines, herbs, and string. She lay the basket in the middle of our imperfect circle and sat back down in the spot she'd left.

We all continued to stare.

"They're not going to come for us, because of these." Lucille gestured to the basket.

"Some dried weeds?" Catherine wrinkled her nose.

Lucille rolled her eyes. It was almost comical—if we weren't all facing death threats. "No. It's the ingredients for a protection charm. We'll make them into bracelets and wear them—"

"We're making friendship bracelets?" Catherine gushed, clearly delighted with such an idea. The expression seemed far removed from her still-gore-soaked clothes and dirt-matted hair.

Lucille gritted her teeth, but her eyes shone with amusement. "No. We're making protection bracelets. As long as you wear it, it'll keep you from harm."

"How do we make them?" Alice scooted closer to the basket.

"Here, take these." Lucille passed around the bundle of dried flowers, vines, and string. "And you'll need a couple of strands of hair."

"Our own hair?" Catherine gasped, not nearly as amused with that idea.

"Yes, just a couple of strands. It's The Sacrifice for this type of witchcraft." Lucille demonstrated as she plucked two of her hay-like, blonde strands from her head without a flinch. "And you braid them all together like this." She demonstrated how to do it. Her fingers intertwined and knotted each of the items until they formed a makeshift chain. As she did, she repeated the superstition.

Tie a knot and you won't be forgot.

The Spirit. The Sacrifice. The Superstition.

We each mimicked her motions. As we did, we talked and speculated about who was behind the fire and who walked with whom in the woods. On request, I shared some more hand motions that the mill girls and I used, modeling them between braiding the materials together.

Once everyone seemed less ready to take off, we spent the rest of the night and early morning hours drawing the symbols we each had witnessed, both on the hare and the doe. Just like with the rest of the witchcraft we'd been practicing, Lucille said these needed all three parts: The Spirit, The Sacrifice, and The Superstition. Drawing them in plain ink or graphite wouldn't evoke any harm.

The symbols on both animals had to be connected. So did the vision in the fire. Someone was clearly eager to get rid of us, and they had succeeded, only eight of us were left. We couldn't lose anymore.

Mr. Edmonton studied the sketches I spread across the mahogany table at the back of the library. If anyone could point us to more information on such symbols, it was the librarian. His frail sweater-clad arms crossed over his chest, and his graying hair fell in his eyes as he leaned forward.

He pushed his glasses over the crook of his nose and asked, "These were cut into the animals, or just smeared on them with blood?"

I gulped and shook my head. A silky black strand fell from my updo. "They were cut *into* them. Deep." I swallowed down the bile that rose in my throat.

Mr. Edmonton nodded solemnly. "I believe there may be some books here on runes, Egyptian markings, voodoo markings, and other such things. They might not be the perfect fit, but we could try to make some connections between them and figure something out. I'll go look for them."

"Thank you, Mr. Edmonton. And thank you again for letting me take the day off. I promise I will make up for it."

"Of course, dear. It's the least I could do after last night's horrifying events." His smile was weary. He walked off into the maze of bookshelves.

I turned away from the markers, unable to stare at them any longer, and leaned back against the table. My head ached. Sleep burned behind my eyes.

Things had been getting better. Our use of witchcraft was helping. Thomas and his gang had been messing with us less and less, but now, we were on the verge of the whole program being in jeopardy.

"What are you daydreaming about?" Lucille's voice broke through my thoughts and snapped me back to reality.

Sweat glazed Catherine and Lucille's faces, and their hair was a wild mess of frizz from their walk here, even with the time Catherine must have put in fixing it like always.

"Just the weight of the world on our shoulders."

Lucille snorted, "So, just the same ol', same ol', then?"

"Hey, we'll get through this," Catherine said, always the optimist. Then frowned at the drawings strewn across the table. "Once we figure this all out."

"Who do y'all think is doing it now that we've seen more evidence and the outcome of such?" Lucille asked. She took an apple from her satchel and bit a chunk out of it, undeterred by one of the library's few rules.

"My bet is still on Reverend Ward," Catherine offered. "He was so quick to dismiss the fire as a sign from God."

"Or the headmaster. He obviously isn't too fond of us being here, either," I stated. "But why wouldn't he use this as his perfect excuse to see us go? Why would he go along with Reverend Ward's crazy evangelical ramblings?"

"Or Thomas and his gang." Catherine counted the possibilities on her plump fingers. "They seemed thrilled with what the fire thing said last night."

"So, everyone is trying to get rid of us, and it could be any of them?" Lucille asked. She finished her apple and stuck the core back in her satchel.

"Why don't you just throw that in the wastebasket instead of getting it all over the inside of your purse?" Catherine wrinkled her nose.

"Why throw it away when I can replant it? It'll grow into a mighty fine apple tree."

An obnoxious laugh sounded from around the corner. I knew who it belonged to immediately. I snatched up all the drawings from the table and shoved them in my bag before Josephine came into view. She was the last person who needed to see them. She'd probably report us to her father as devil worshippers. Though if a talking fire hadn't disturbed the man, I wasn't entirely sure what would.

"Well, hello, ladies," Josephine said upon seeing us.

Penelope, the one who remained after last night, stood at her side like a sheep blindly following an even blinder shepherd. Her dress's neckline was so high it almost touched her chin. Tight ringlets peaked out from under her bonnet.

"I'm glad to find y'all here." Josephine stated. "We just wanted to come and say goodbye before we left. I couldn't find you after the bonfire last night."

My eyebrows scrunched together as Lucille asked, "Goodbye? You're leaving?"

"*We're* leaving." Josephine motioned between her and Penelope.

Penelope glanced at us through her eyelashes, her face sullen.

Josephine looked over at her when she didn't say anything and nudged Penelope's shoulder with her elbow. "Isn't that right?"

"Yes." Penelope said just above a whisper.

That would leave only six of us. If one more left, the program would be over. This opportunity for every woman in the state would vanish. Gone. Just like that.

"And why the hell would you do that?" Lucille spat out. "You complained through this whole thing and now you leave right when we need you to stay the most?"

I figured that was exactly why she was leaving now. It had the most detrimental impact now.

She sighed. "We aren't meant for this lifestyle. It's not what God intended for us. I don't plan on continuing this silly parade of indecency for a single second longer, and neither does Penelope."

Penelope didn't say anything to agree, but Josephine went on anyway.

"Don't you see why I was picked to be here? Why *y'all* were picked?" She waited, as if realization would hit us at any moment. "Because we were the least likely to make it to the end of the program. Everyone knows I don't support such things, obviously. But why else would they pick a dumb farm girl," she nodded at Lucille, "or a mill girl who would undoubtedly skip town before the end of term anyway?" she nodded to me. "And you," she turned to Catherine, "you're just here because your daddy donated money to the university." She smiled, but her cold gaze looked at us as if we were nothing more than trash left on the side of the street.

How *godly* of her.

"That's ridiculous," I said with a newfound sense of confidence, "we have just as much chance of making it as anyone. Don't you know how much having a higher education could help women? Help them get out of poverty and live better lives?" Maggie flashed before my eyes. Prim, Danielle, Beth, my mother. All the women this would affect.

Josephine looked at me for a moment before replying, her eyes narrowing. The corners of her lips twitched, but she wouldn't allow them to turn down into a frown. "Maybe if they weren't living in sin and were closer to God, they wouldn't be in poverty in the first place." She paused and then added with a menacing grin, "The pleasures of this world blind you. And, from what I've heard, the pleasures of everyone in this town. The apple doesn't fall far from the tree, does it?"

Penelope's lips pressed into a firm line. She looked down at the floor, as if not wanting to meet our eyes.

Before I could muster up the words to respond, never one to have fast and witty comebacks, Lucille spoke up. "Oh, please, Josephine, you wouldn't know pleasure if it were a copperhead snake that bit you on that prude ass of yours."

Josephine's mouth dropped open.

"Maybe," Catherine stood at my side, "a little pleasure could do you some good, might help knock that stick from where it's stuck so far up inside you."

Living with Lucille had rubbed off on her, though her cheeks still tinted red after she said it.

Josephine gasped. The corners of her lips won the battle. She frowned, deep and disconsolate. "You three are of the devil. And you're going to get what's coming to you. " She spun around on her heels and practically sprinted from the library.

Penelope didn't move until Josephine hissed her name in command.

"Well, that was the highlight of my day," Lucille laughed from where she stood by my side. She towered over Catherine and me by at least a foot.

"I concur." Catherine laughed. "Maybe she's really the one behind all of this. She's zealous enough."

"Nah, she's not nearly resourceful enough," Lucille snorted.

I laughed, too, and for the first time in several months, since losing Maggie, I felt glad to be around people instead of alone.

Not just people.

Friends.

Maybe this place wasn't giving me what I needed to leave; maybe it was giving me what I needed to stay.

Chapter Twenty-Nine

Lucille

Mimicking the call of wild animals will attract wild spirits upon you.

We continued to laugh as we left the library in the dim light, our troubles from the night before forgotten—even if just for a moment. The sun went down earlier and earlier each day. The world shrouded itself in darkness for its season of death.

Once a little farther down the path, I stepped off and pulled my obnoxious skirts out of the way to kneel to the ground.

"What are you doing?" Catherine asked.

"What does it look like I'm doing?" I dug a small hole in the ground with my fingers. I tried not to think about the hole I'd dug and buried that poor mutilated animal in a few days ago. Or the chaos that ensued afterward.

"Defacing university property?" Catherine laughed nervously.

"The university will thank me in a few years when they have an apple tree growing and providing them with shade and sustenance." I placed the apple core I'd eaten from into the hole and covered it with the pile of dirt I'd tossed to the side.

I stood, wiped my hands on my skirt, and started back on the path.

"I wish I could be as free as you are sometimes," Catherine looked down at her hands as we walked. She picked at her cuticles.

"Freedom is everything," I agreed.

"You didn't grow up with my mama. To her, beauty is everything. Well, only second to marriage." Catherine's voice dripped with misery.

"Well, isn't beauty subjective, anyway? Just something society created for advertising and monetary purposes?" I asked though it was meant to be rhetorical.

"Try telling that to Mama. She knows what beauty is, and she knows I'm not it." Catherine mumbled.

"Hating one's own body would make for a long and miserable life. You shouldn't let society's—or your mother's—cruel ways dictate that." Victoria held eye contact with Catherine for a moment longer before continuing her stride forward.

She didn't speak often, but when she did, she always left me speechless. What went on inside her head? Did she watch everyone around her and take in observations? Collect them like a magpie collects shiny trinkets?

We came upon a group of men huddled together and blocking the path. The men gathered around something. My stomach dropped. I hoped it wasn't another mutilated animal.

We pushed through their sweaty bodies. They barely noticed as they each held a large piece of parchment in their hands. Of course, Thomas was in the middle, as he always was. He stood beside a basket of papers with his arms crossed and arrogance splayed across his features.

Inked at the top of the parchment, in big, bold letters, it read *The Brimham Tribune*. From all the excitement, it must've been the first printing since the new lowerclassmen writers had been picked.

I snatched one from the basket and scanned it. Catherine and Victoria peeked over my shoulder. For a moment, I imagined what it would feel like to pick up a paper with something I had written published in it. My dream come true. But this wasn't the case. My imagination evaporated as I read the pages in front of me. Everything was about the men's program, their accomplishments, and their next academic events and ceremonies. It didn't mention anything about us, about the women's program.

"Hey," I yelled at Thomas over the surrounding commotion. The smirk on his face grew. "Why doesn't this mention our program? Isn't that important?"

"Well, we writers," he gestured to himself, "didn't feel it necessary to write about something that is only *temporary*."

"You call yourself a writer? This is trash!" I shoved the parchment into his chest.

"You think you could do better?" He took a step back to steady himself. "Oh, wait, it doesn't matter, does it? You're not *allowed* to write for this paper. Headmaster's orders." His sinister smirk grew to an unnatural smile.

"What about *our* freedom of speech? Doesn't that mean anything?" I replied, though I already knew what his answer would be. Just a handful of weeks ago, I had laughed at Catherine for asking the same thing.

Thomas laughed, and so did his friends, who eyed us. "You think what you have to say matters?" he laughed. "The Constitution was written by men, for men." He spat a thick wad of mucus onto the ground.

I growled. My fingers itched to be torn open, to spill my blood. The craft begged to be used. Before I could unleash it, Catherine pulled on my arm.

"Come on, Lucille. He's not worth it."

I allowed myself to be pulled away from him with one last growl.

"Looks like one of your daddy's farm animals got lost from the farm," Thomas called as we walked away. He and his friends made oinking and mooing noises, laughing at their own jokes.

"I swear, I'm going to make him pay," I spat.

"We will. But if we do something to them in the middle of campus, for all to see, *we'll* be the ones to pay the price for that," Victoria said, always the voice of reason.

I nodded. The fire still burned hot and molten in my chest. "We're going to start our own paper." I had nearly forgotten about the notion with everything that had happened. A renewed sense of determination hit me with each resounding cackle from Thomas behind us.

"We are?" Victoria asked.

"Yes, we are." I looked at the two women beside me, afternoon shadows hollowed their eyes into skeletons.

I already had enough of those in my closet.

Chapter Thirty

Catherine

Itchy palms mean good luck and good news are heading your way.

Lucille brought her pinky fingers up to her mouth. A loud, high-pitched whistle captured the attention of everyone in the large, empty attic. All the sorority members were there, including Henry and Chrissy.

We took a few moments to recite our pledge and let Henry and Chrissy prick their fingers to sign their blood at the bottom of the rust-stained parchment. We eyed the russet-red smear they left behind. We knew it would bring to light any untoward intentions they may be harboring.

I held my breath and waited for something to happen.

Everyone else seemed to hold their breath, too.

Chrissy and Henry looked from the parchment to each of us.

After a moment, Lucille let out a sigh and clapped her hand on Henry's and Chrissy's shoulders. "Welcome to the sorority."

We all let out a relieved breath and we each said our own welcoming words to the pair. Though Susan still seemed less than pleased with their presence, she didn't bother protesting again.

I couldn't help but watch Chrissy as she shook hands with everyone. I understood her desire to be something different from what society deemed acceptable, to want something different from what was considered normal. After spending most of my life pushing my desires down deep, I envied Chrissy's courage to be what felt right to her, no matter how dangerous.

As those thoughts ran through my mind, I looked up. My gaze landed on Alice. She gave me a wink that made butterflies erupt in my stomach.

After a moment of being lost in her dark eyes, maybe more than a moment, Lucille and the others talked. Their words were only a rumble in the background until I drew my eyes away from Alice's.

"We need our own newspaper." Lucille declared.

"Newspaper?" Rebecca grunted. "What for?"

"To spread the good word around this town."

I snorted. "You sound like my mama and her church league ladies."

"What kind of word are we spreading? We can't exactly write that we're a coven disguised as a sorority and we're using witchcraft against men. They'd have our heads before the rooster's crow in the morning." Susan crossed an arm over her chest, but her other hand was already too occupied with being chewed on.

"Well, of course we're not putting that." Lucille rolled her eyes. "But the notion still stands that there is power in numbers. The more of us there are, the stronger we'll be, and a newspaper would be a great way to invite people in. Even with Henry and Chrissy, it still wouldn't hurt to get more members, especially since we still don't know who or what is after us."

Alice nodded. "It could also show others that they aren't alone. There are people like them, people willing to fight for them and with them. Not to mention, it would just be nice to have something out there that talks about us."

"The sorority?" I asked.

"Women." Alice's eyes made me want to melt to the floor along with the candles around us.

"And the university newspaper sure as hell isn't talking about us. Did you read that load of cow manure? It didn't even mention what happened at the bonfire." Lucille's face turned as red as Mama's favorite pair of Sunday jewels.

Henry scooted closer to her and placed his arm gently on her back to rub small, slow circles. Lucille acted unfazed by his actions, but her shoulders relaxed into him ever so slightly.

"They act like the women's program doesn't even exist." Chrissy gave an apologetic look as she spoke.

"Women always get left out or erased from history," Alice stated.

"If we created our own newspaper, what would be in it?" I tried and failed to take my eyes off of Alice.

"What would it be called?"

"How would we print it?"

The others chimed in with questions.

Victoria stepped forward and sat down on the old carpeted floor. She dug a pen and parchment from her satchel, spread it out in front of her, and then looked up at us.

We circled around the parchment and moved the candles closer. Their light cast a warm glow across the paper. I eyed the flickering flame and half expected it to grow arms and a head at any moment. I only took my eyes off it to watch Alice as she hiked up her skirts to kneel. Her tawny skin showed from underneath the lace fabric. It looked radiant despite the dingy, stained carpet around her.

"Let's start with what to call it." Victoria hovered the pen over the top of the parchment.

"Maybe something with sisterhood? Like *The Sisterhood Times* or *Stories of the Sisterhood.*"

Henry cleared his throat from where he sat by Lucille. "Perhaps I could suggest going with something a bit more inclusive, as there may be more men out there who aren't complete pigs."

Lucille snorted.

"He has a point." Alice gestured to Henry. "This isn't a fight for women alone. It's a plea for humanity. A rebellion for what is right. A revolution for the next generation."

"That's it!" Lucile jumped. "*The Revolution.*"

"That's spectacular." Chrissy smiled.

"Okay. *The Revolution* it is." Victoria scrawled the title in neat cursive letters. "What about a motto or a mission statement?"

"We should have our own poems and stories in there, so people know we are more than just our reproductive organs and a pair of breasts." Rebecca suggested. "I know a woman on the west side of town who could make the prints. May not exactly be . . . legal but printed is printed." She shrugged.

"Right. And we could advertise women-made and women-sold goods and services, too, to benefit women who are trying to make their own way in the world." said Alice.

Lucille nodded. "And propose amendments to the student code of conduct, like the dress code."

We all threw out more ideas. They grew more enthusiastic with each one, but as their voices rose in excitement, I couldn't help getting lost in Alice's mouth as she spoke or her eyes as they narrowed when she smiled. She mesmerized me, and I couldn't seem to push my feelings down anymore, not when they screamed and demanded such attention.

Consequences be damned.

THE REVOLUTION (an excerpt)

Vol. 1—No. 1

For women's rights and nothing less. For men's rights and nothing more. In spite of color or class, for rich or poor.

The Revolution Will Advocate:

1. *For the rights of all to have equal opportunity to: proper education, respectable work, substantial pay, and ownership of land and accounts.*
2. *For the freedom and liberty: freedom of thought and mind, body and reproduction, and spirituality or religion.*
3. *For the set standard in society: no double standards in regard to the moral choices made by men and women. The ability to show love and be loved by whomever the heart and mind desire by both men and women.*

The Revolution is for anyone who sees these are not only needed for individually well-lived lives, but also necessary for the growth of humanity. This new paper is the promise of new thought; of something better than what has gone before. If you are like-minded, join our cause and fight for what is right.

Chapter Thirty-One Victoria

Leaving an empty chair at a table invites unwanted spirits.

I crept through campus under the veil of darkness. Only the crescent moon and gas lamps lit my path. We'd already distributed *The Revolution* to the women in our dormitory, those of us left. Henry and Chrissy would distribute it to any men in the other cohorts and classes who supported us. With my bag full of rolled-up newspapers, I walked around the library. I knew no matter how late it was, Mr. Edmonton would still be there. He practically never left the building. The university had provided him with small living quarters in the library's basement.

I went around to the back of the building. The moon splayed my shadow across the large brick walls like a monster made of darkness. It grew smaller the closer I crept. Down a small slope at the library's basement level was a weathered wooden door with metal latches surrounded by faded brick.

I grasped the metal knocker and rapped on the door three times. The knocks disturbed the night's silence. No sounds came from inside, or at least none that my damaged ears could hear. Was he asleep? Minutes later, rusted metal latches screeched unlocked.

The door swung open. Mr. Edmonton regarded me with his kind eyes, though his brows creased with worry.

"Miss Woodhall, is everything okay?" He gestured for me to enter.

I nodded and stepped into the cozy space. It was small but homey, consisting of just one room, like those in the women's dormitory. On one side, against a wall, sat a twin bed covered in hand-sewn quilts, undoubtedly his late wife's handiwork. Dresser drawers, with an intricately carved wooden chest sat atop them, stood by the bed, and a table filled the space in the middle. A small, fire-lit stove with copper pots and pans hanging from it was on the other side of the room. How wonderful it must feel to call such a place home.

"I didn't mean to disturb you. I only wanted to give you this." I pulled a rolled-up copy of *The Revolution* from my bag and handed it to him.

He pulled his robe tighter around himself and pushed his glasses over the hump on his nose as he grabbed the newspaper. He unraveled it and skimmed over the words. His hand absentmindedly drifted to the top of a wooden chair and pulled it out. He took a seat, then gestured for me to do the same.

I watched in patient silence as he read the paper from front to back. After a while, he looked up at me. Tears sparkled in the corners of his eyes.

"This is . . ."

I held my breath.

"Marvelous," he smiled.

"You think so?" I smiled back and my chest warmed. I'd grown to respect and maybe even care for Mr. Edmonton over the past several months, as much as I'd tried not to.

"Yes. This is truly . . . well, exactly what it's named: a revolution. This is groundbreaking." He looked from me to the newspaper and wiped his eyes with his free hand. "I wish my wife could see this. She would be delighted. You know, she'd dreamed of a day when something like this would exist. Dreamed of a time when women could do all the same things as men." He sniffled. A stray tear ran down his wrinkled cheek. "Thank you for bringing this to me."

After a half hour of talking with Mr. Edmonton, he yawned and his eyelids drooped. I said my goodnights and farewells and headed out into the night again.

The walk to my next destination would be long, but I'd done it many times and memorized the safest shortcuts and knew which alleys to avoid. And I certainly didn't aim to take any chances with some unknown dark-witchcraft user after us.

Most of the roads were dirt. They didn't bother with gravel or cobblestones in a small country town like this. The bottom of my skirts would be covered with orange-red dust by the time I was done. Most of my dresses and skirts were, though.

As I reached the heart of the small town's industrial park, the crescent moon tipped over the middle of the black sky and started its downward descent. I crept through the back alley that led to the cotton mill. Some of the bigger cities up north had four, five, or even six cotton mills, not to mention all the other factories and sweatshops. In Brimham, though, this was the only mill, which is why many women who worked here put up with such poor conditions. Where else would they get a job if they didn't?

As I walked through the alley between the mill and another factory, I forced myself not to look at the pavement, the only place they could afford to pave. They'd likely used what was left over from the foundation of the buildings to pave between them. I knew the bloodstains were washed away long ago, but if I looked at it, I would still see the blood, regardless of whether it was actually there or not.

My stomach turned sour at the thought and familiarity of my surroundings. I could still see every detail from that night. Maggie's screams and the men yelling their accusations were loud enough to be heard from inside the mill. The black, claw-like shadows of the men attacking her and, afterward, her crumpled body.

While the men were distracted by someone else, I'd taken the opportunity to go to her. My only concern was Maggie's too-small and too-fragile body. By the time I'd carried her from the scene, she was bleeding at a deadly rate. She was only a child, but the men who attacked her didn't care.

Mother always said men liked their victims to be young, vulnerable, and easy to control.

I swallowed the bile in my throat. I was here on a mission that would help girls like her. The whole reason I had agreed to be in the sorority and remain in town in the first place.

The back door was locked, but it wasn't a problem. I'd long ago learned how to pick it with nothing but a hairpin. Once the lock clicked, the large metal door swung open easily. I knew exactly where to go, even in the dark. The lockers were at the front of the mill, so all the girls could put their things away before starting their work.

I couldn't help but look at the looms as I snuck past the foreman's office, from which light still poured. Even in the empty darkness of the rest of the mill, I could see the face of each woman who sat at the machines during work hours, hear their voices. I'd once been close with each of them, but after the incident with Maggie, I couldn't let myself indulge in such luxuries as friendship anymore.

I shoved a newspaper in the back of each locker and covered them with the other items in case the foreman looked over their shoulders.

"What are you doing?"

My heart stopped. I sucked in a breath as I turned.

Prim, who I had worked with at the mill for years, stood behind me. Her arms crossed over her chest. Her face showed nothing but curiosity. She must hide her hatred for me well.

"I'll leave. I just wanted to bring y'all these." I handed her a newspaper.

Prim took it and unrolled it. Her eyes scanned from one side of the paper to the other. I began to walk away. She wouldn't want my presence around any longer than necessary, not after all of the pain and suffering I had caused all of the mill girls.

"Wait," Prim called. My limbs went rigid, like a taxidermic corpse. "You don't have to go."

I didn't turn around to face her. I couldn't. Couldn't bring myself to look in her eyes as I said, "I know you hate me. And you have every right to. It was my fault. It's my fault Maggie is dead."

Silence.

I took another step to get out of this memory-infested mill.

"No."

I froze again; this time, my foot still lifted midstep. "What?"

"No, it's not. We wish you hadn't left, hadn't run away from us every time we tried to talk, because if you hadn't, you would know that we don't hate you. Or blame you. None of us do."

I turned and finally came face to face with the woman I had once been close to. Once would have considered her a sister. But I had avoided her, and all the others, for so long because of my own fear. Shame. Guilt. Hatred.

Tears burned behind my eyes. "You don't?"

"No." Prim stepped closer, her own eyes glassy and wet. As she spoke, she emphasized her words with the signed language that I had once been so familiar with. "We cared about Maggie and we are all grieving her loss, but we cared about you, too. And the past few months, it has felt like we've been grieving for both of you."

The tears spilled over my cheeks and mixed with the sweat and dirt that coated my skin like a second layer. Prim rushed forward. She wrapped her long arms around me and pulled my head into her bony shoulder. Her collarbone protruded from her thin figure, sharp as a knife against my cheek. The tears came harder, faster. Sobs racked through my body, an earthquake in an already ravaged land. And then, relief. Sweet and calm. Quiet.

"We don't want to lose you, too." Prim petted my head.

I nodded into her.

"Come back to us."

I pulled away, though my body fought against the movement. I wanted to stay wrapped up in the home made of her stick-thin arms and bone-sharp edges. My cheeks were still wet and salty, and my nose dripped snot. I sucked it back in.

"I can't come back. I'm at the university now. We're making a change, making a difference."

We. The word felt odd on my tongue. To talk about the women at the university, the sorority, as if we were a unit, one whole. I was a part of something. Something more than just myself.

"I understand." Prim nodded and looked down at the newspaper still hanging limp from her hand. "And I'm proud of you, truly. Maggie would be proud of you, too."

I knew those words should make me happy, make me feel a sense of pride, but a shard of ice splintered my heart instead. It never melted. How could it when Maggie would never come back, never have another chance at life?

"If we hadn't made those tinctures, Maggie would still be here to tell me so—

"If you hadn't made those tinctures, more women would be living half-lives, cast out, left to starve and fend for themselves. Or they would be dead." Prim's own moss green eyes stared holes into mine. Stared into my heart. Into my soul. "Actually . . . another tincture would be of great help right now."

My eyebrows shot together. I immediately shook my head. Midnight hair scattered over my shoulders. "No, I can't—"

"It's Beth," Prim fired off. "Our new foreman is . . . a vile creature." Her face contorted. Disgust was written in her scrunched eyebrows and pinched lips.

I sucked in a breath. "The new foreman impreg—"

"He threatened to fire her, to spread word to all the other mills that she was unmanageable. He was going to ruin her if she didn't do what he wanted. And now she is stuck with the consequences of his seed . . . Unless you make—"

"No, I can't." I shook my head harder. "I can't do that again. You saw the results of that." My voice broke, snapped like a thread pulled too hard, too tight. Severed. Never one piece again, never whole.

Prim must have seen the anguish in my eyes, the finality in my posture. "Think about it, at least."

I nodded without much effort in the motion, without meaning.

"There's something else." Prim looked around.

"What is it?" I asked, voice full of hope. Even if they weren't mad at me, I still felt the need to get in their good graces, make up for running away, avoiding them, not making the tincture for Beth.

"We need to get into the foreman's office. He keeps all the documents in there of doctor's notes, reports about the air, the lint, and the fevers. Even records of girls who have died from it. We've seen him lock them away. He almost never leaves that office. When he does, he has someone guard it." Her eyebrows furrowed as she frowned. "He'll never show the documents to the authorities or anyone who could do anything about it. Not unless someone forces him to."

Of course no one would listen until a man's files were released. Even though girls, the actual victims, have been talking about them—and dying from them—for years.

"And you're going to force him."

"He forces much worse fates on us."

Those words hung in the air, heavier than the humidity.

"We need a tincture. Something to knock him unconscious. Just for a bit." Her eyes widened as they looked at me, begging in the same way Maggie had when she'd asked me to help her make the abortive tinctures.

I held her gaze. It had been months since I'd mixed anything stronger than a headache draught. Months since I'd tried not to remember other mixtures, other consequences. But this was simpler. Plants. Proportions. Something I could measure, something I *could* do for them.

"Okay," I said.

Prim's face lit up.

We worked in the small storage room where the girls kept their shawls and pails. I crushed dried roots between stones, added laudanum sparingly from a bottle Prim had and diluted it carefully. Enough to drop a man where he stood, but not enough to stop his breathing.

When I handed it to her, Prim studied the small vial with awe, then looked at me through her lashes. "There's one more thing."

I raised a brow but waited for her to go on.

"You were always the fastest with locks."

The foreman remained in his office at the back of the mill floor, easier to watch the girls from, moving ledgers around, muttering to himself. If he were anything like the last, he preferred to work late when no one could question him, when he could drink bourbon, tempt the occasional mill girl in, and close the door behind them.

I stayed back in the shadow of the looms as Prim approached his open office door. She feigned uncertainty.

"Sir," she said sweetly, "One of the girls has taken ill. We gave her this medicine you provided us with, but she says it tastes wrong, like it's expired."

"Expired? I *just* purchased that for you ungrateful lot."

"It doesn't taste right. You must've gotten a bad batch." Prim said innocently.

"Bad batch?" He got up from where he'd been sitting behind his desk, his overgrown stomach nearly knocking papers off the counter. "Give me that!"

He snatched the vial from her, without hesitating to even smell it, he swallowed a mouthful. After his loud gulp echoed through the mill, he eyed Prim, raising his eyebrows in a way that said, "See? Didn't I tell you it's not bad?"

I counted silently. He made it three seconds before his hand gripped the doorframe. By five, he was slumping toward Prim. By seven, she eased him down by the shoulder. By ten, his breathing slowed into snores.

"Good?" she whispered.

I got up from my hiding spot and bent forward to check his pulse, my own hammered in my ears. It came in even, strong beats. I sighed in relief. "Good," I confirmed. "We need to hurry. It'll only take a few minutes for the draft to wear off."

Prim spun. I followed her into the office. Inside, the air smelled of ink and stale tobacco. Shelves lined the walls, ledgers stacked with false neatness. We circled the large oak desk. Either side of the desk housed two large drawers, each one with its own keyhole. Each one locked.

"Which one are the documents in?" I asked, already planning the best way to get them unlocked.

"I think it's. . . ." Prim's eyebrows scrunched. "I'm not sure. Let's try that one first." She pointed to the top drawer on the right.

I kneeled in front of it and withdrew the small hairpin I'd used earlier. My fingers shook as I started working the contraption in front of me. The lock mechanism was old and stubborn. I listened more than I looked, feeling for the subtle resistance of the tumblers. My hands remembered the rhythm even if I'd tried to forget it.

Click.

The drawer's lock gave way.

Prim moved immediately to the drawer and started rifling through it. Halfway through its contents, she hissed, "I'm not seeing anything. Start opening the next drawer."

With more confidence, and less shaking, I repeated the process. By the time Prim finished looking through the first drawer, I had the second unlocked. She repeated her frantic search.

A groan sounded from where the foreman lay.

"We need to hurry." I urged and unlocked the next drawer.

After what seemed like far too long, and another grunt sounded from the foreman, Prim finally exclaimed, "Here!"

Inside the drawer lay correspondence. Letters were stamped with a physician's seal. Reports detailed "*persistent respiratory decline among operatives*" and recommended improved ventilation. Pages noted increased sick days. Reduced output blamed on "*female fragility*" and signed by the foreman. Even death certificates, signed by the coroner, noting the causes as brown lung.

Prim's jaw tightened. "They knew."

"They did," I wasn't surprised, but the sight of them still caused a lump to form in my throat. All of those girls, and no justice.

Both of our heads jerked up at the sound of shuffling coming from the floor. We looked at each other, slammed the drawers shut, and sprinted without another word.

Only when we were clear and out of sight of the office, our chests heaving and rattling with excitement, did I finally ask, "What will you do with them?"

Prim slowed, the papers clutched tight against her ribs. "Show them," she said. "To someone who can't ignore it."

"I can add it to our next newspaper print," I told her. I didn't think anyone in the sorority would object to that idea. "Nothing grand. But we choose what goes in there. We could use this. Publish excerpts. Names."

"I like that idea." She smiled a jagged smile. "I think that might just be what we do with them as well. Submit them anonymously to all of the press around town."

"You think they'll actually print it?"

Her eyes hardened with resolve. "If one refuses, another won't. And if they all print it, if everyone sees—"

"They can't bury our deaths under *female fragility*?" I asked, knowing.

For a moment, we stood there in the dark street, the mill behind us like some enormous sleeping beast. I felt the old fear stir, of consequences, of retaliation, but it didn't root as deeply as it once had.

Prim smiled at me then, fierce and grateful all at once.

"Exactly," she said. "Let them try to hide *this* away."

THE REVOLUTION (an excerpt)

Vol. 1—No. 2

For women's rights and nothing less. For men's rights and nothing more. In spite of color or class, for rich or poor.

BREAKING—DEADLY CONDITIONS AT RIVER STREET COTTON MILL REVEALED

It is with grave concern that we lay before our readers certain facts recently brought to light regarding the conditions endured by the young women employed at the cotton mill on River Street. The information herein is drawn from internal correspondence and medical reports authored by individuals in positions of authority, and thus cannot be dismissed as rumor or exaggeration.

For some time, operatives have complained of persistent cough, shortness of breath, dizziness, and fainting spells while at their posts. These symptoms, long attributed to "female fragility," are in truth consistent with prolonged exposure to airborne cotton fiber and inadequate ventilation.

Medical memoranda addressed to management describe "a marked decline in respiratory strength among female operatives," as well as "increasing incidence of fever and chest inflammation." One physician explicitly recommended the installation of improved ventilation systems and periodic cessation of work to allow the air to clear of lint and dust. This recommendation was dismissed in writing as "cost-prohibitive" and "unnecessary to the maintenance of production."

Most alarming of all are the reports concerning fatalities. Several girls formerly employed at the mill have succumbed to prolonged respiratory illness, and in more than one case, death followed. The documents contain acknowledgment of the correlation between the work environment and the deterioration of health, yet no substantive action was undertaken to alter conditions.

We ask our readers: at what cost is cloth produced? How many weakened lungs must be counted as incidental to profit? How many daughters must be buried before reform is deemed affordable?

Let this be the beginning, not the end, of inquiry. Let those in positions of authority answer plainly why nothing was done.

Silence in matters such as these is not neutrality. It is complicity.

Chapter Thirty-Two
Lucille

Turning a horseshoe upside down will make all the good luck fall out and cause bad luck to the owner.

The air had finally cooled, though the humidity never ceased to make matters worse. Instead of everything feeling like a hot, sticky swamp, it now made the morning air feel as frigid as ice. Then, by the late afternoon, we were often sweating again.

Even with the chill, Henry and I continued what had become our morning routine. We walked the entire path around campus until it brought us back to my dormitory.

Henry laughed as we walked. "When my younger sister was born, the doctor handed her to me instead of my mother, since I was supposedly the head of the household and all. Though anyone who really knew us could've told the poor chap that my mother was more than capable of being the head, and if not her, then my older sister."

His laugh always made me want to join in.

Then his smile slipped. "As he placed her small body in my own small arms, he said, 'Oh dear, I'm so sorry it's a girl. A woman's lot is hard.' And even though my mother and older sister were present and heard him, they didn't rebuke his comment. I didn't understand why he made those comments at the time, and I was much too young to know how to respond, but it always stuck with me." Henry looked at me. "I wish I could go back and argue. Tell the chap off."

I wrapped my arm around his coat-clad bicep and bore the brunt of his weight when he stepped on his prosthetic leg. He wrapped his other hand around mine and gently rubbed it to keep it warm.

"I wouldn't have argued with him, either," I said.

"No? The most outspoken woman I know wouldn't have argued? I'm shocked." He smiled jokingly.

I snorted a laugh. "The man wasn't wrong about what he said. He was just daft for saying it in a room full of women, including a woman who had just spent hours laboring to birth a girl."

"I suppose you're right." He looked at me. His top hat cast a shadow over our faces.

"What do your sisters do now?" I asked.

Henry turned his face toward the rising sun and away from me. Dissatisfaction bubbled up in me when I could no longer see his hazel eyes or dimple.

"My mother is too old to do much of anything anymore. My older sister still works at an iron manufacturer and takes care of Mother. That's why I'm here. If I can get a degree, I can help pay for them and hopefully get my sister out of factory work."

"What about your little sister?" I asked, and then immediately regretted it when Henry's head dropped and his posture slumped.

"She passed away."

"I'm so sorry, Henry." I gave his arm a reassuring squeeze.

"It happened several months ago while she was working at a mill." His head continued to hang. "I don't want to lose my older sister to the same fate. I must get her out."

"You will," I assured him, then added insistently, "*we* will."

He looked back at me. My dissatisfaction washed away as our eyes met again.

"Thank you." A ghost of a smile spread across his face, though it didn't reach his eyes. Sadness still filled them. At that moment, I would do anything to make that sadness disappear. How did I let myself get this attached to a man? I never thought I would let that happen again after Reece's betrayal. Even if he were just trying to please Pa. He still ruined my plan. Still caused my mother's death.

And then, I caused his.

"Have you heard anything in the men's dormitory that might be of interest to the sorority?" I asked to change the subject.

"No, I have—"

A cacophony of sounds in the middle of the campus interrupted him. A large group had gathered. Smoke billowed into the air from the center of the crowd. Thomas's voice was louder than everyone else's, and I knew there must be trouble.

Closer to the group, a fire in a tin barrel heated our cheeks. Everyone around it laughed and hollered profanities. Where was Reverend Ward or Headmaster Sullivan now? How were they never around when their male students participated in incriminating activities?

"Serves those whores right!"

"Might as well be a pile of ash. Was a pile of shit, anyway!"

"Fire is gonna be their fate, too, if they keep on!"

Their screams echoed in the air as the sun rose to heat the landscape. Their words bounced off the old buildings and dying trees and echoed back at us.

"What are they raving about now?" Henry's eyebrows furrowed.

"I'm not sure . . ." A pit formed in my stomach.

We were close enough to see the fire burning something other than wood. Stacks of something white . . . with black ink . . . beginning to melt . . .

"Our papers!" I let go of Henry's arm and sprinted forward. I didn't care if my skirts ripped. How did they get their hands on copies of *our* newspapers?

I pushed through the crowd of men. "Hey, get away from those!" My yells fell on deaf ears. They laughed and hurled their insults more loudly.

"As leaders, we must rid the world of these unnatural and disgraceful things!" someone shouted.

More people gathered, attracted by the commotion, like vultures to a rotting carcass.

"You want the fire out so badly, little lady? Why don't I help you with that?" asked an older man.

In stunned shock, I watched as he unzipped his pants and pulled out his small, shriveled penis. Henry jerked me out of the way just as the man pissed on the fire and our newspapers. The yellow stream wafted the scent of alcohol and ammonia into the air.

The men laughed harder and hollered their support for the man urinating. They smiled at me as if to say this was exactly what I deserved, to be in the middle of a shower of yellow piss.

My vision turned red. Everything blurred around me. I shoved the pissing man, his penis still in his hand. He stumbled and sprayed his stream onto his own shoe.

"You little bitch," he growled. He lifted his fist in the air and swung.

Before it could land true, Henry jumped in front of me. He took the hit to his jaw. I caught him before he hit the ground or landed in the simmering flames of the fire.

I laid him safely out of the way and turned back to the man. "Don't touch him!"

I reared back and, with all my might, punched the man square in the nose. Blood sprayed out as soon as my fist connected. It coated the front of my dress and my face. I smiled and licked the blood from my lips.

The man howled. His hands flew up to his nose as he yelled. The crowd around me erupted at the same time. Many joined the fight. I saw two other familiar faces: Catherine's red curls and Victoria's raven silk were easy to spot through the commotion.

Both fighting with me. For me.

Like true sisters.

I made a mental note to teach Catherine how to properly throw a punch so she didn't end up with a broken thumb.

The man, whose nose still dripped blood, lunged forward again. Clearly, he hadn't learned his lesson. This time, I went for his manhood. My kick landed true. His face strained in agony.

I looked around. We might have been in more of a predicament than I'd bargained for. Well over a dozen men fought and only a handful of women, all from our sorority. Susan grunted as she tried to get away from a man who had grabbed her and Rebecca fought to pull her arm free of her assailant. Her charmed bracelet broke in the process. Its remains scattered across the ground around her.

But we're not *just* a sorority.

We're a coven.

I quickly used the hand signals Victoria had taught us to sign The Superstition to the others.

Turning a horseshoe upside down will make all the good luck fall out of it and cause bad luck to the owner.

I used a sharp rock from the ground to slice open my palm and spread the blood across it to draw the shape of an upside-down horseshoe. Just as another man approached, about to grab me around the waist, I whipped around and pressed the bloody horseshoe to his chest. The color instantly drained from his face, and his body fell limp to the ground.

Panic clenched in my chest and squeezed. Air evaded me.

The sight looked nearly identical to that of Reece and the others who I had . . . who had died, but the man's chest before me rose and fell with deep breaths.

I breathed. In through my nostrils, out through my mouth. They're not dead. Just unconscious. The panic dissipated.

Victoria, Catherine, and the others followed suit. They repeated The Superstition and their own bloody drawings. Their assailants fell to the ground just as mine had.

I sighed, but our victory was short-lived. At the sound of approaching footsteps, I urged the women to run, not wanting them to stick around for the aftermath. Catherine, Victoria, and I were the only women left around the men's unconscious bodies, including Henry's. Smoke, piss, and sweat lingered in the air as four tall men dressed in campus security uniforms approached. Batons slapped against their palms as their gazes roamed over us. Taking in our ash- and dirt-clad attire and the men limp on the ground around us. Their eyes darkened with judgment. Without them having to say anything, I knew who they'd come to help.

And who they had come to condemn.

Chapter Thirty-Three

Catherine

Spit on the ground around you to ward off evil spirits.

We entered Headmaster Sullivan's office more like criminals than high-cotton women. He insisted we sit on the too-low-to-the-ground velvet sofa he'd moved in front of his desk since the last time I was here. He and Reverend Ward looked down on us from where they stood.

Their act of discontent didn't hold up against the excitement in their eyes. Hauling us in here on an occasion like this was exactly what they'd been waiting for. My stomach dropped at the possibility of them writing my parents. Daddy would be furious I'd made such a fool of our family—his reputation.

"As much as we're glad you . . . ladies are unharmed, we're more concerned about the circumstances that led to this unfortunate event to begin with." The headmaster choked on the word *ladies*. He made a face as if it left a bad taste.

"You three could very well be on grounds for expulsion or even arrest. Especially *you*." Headmaster Sullivan pointed to Lucille. "You always seem to be the leader of such untoward behavior."

My stomach sank. If we were expelled, even just one of us, the program would end. This would be all for nothing. The feeling of Cousin Fredrick's hot breath against my ear haunted me.

Lucille bristled. She opened her mouth, no doubt to argue her defense.

"It's not her fault!" Victoria beat her to it. "We were only trying to—"

The headmaster held up his hand to stop her.

"*However*, the board is determined to make this work and has insisted we give y'all a second chance." The headmaster had a pained expression. His plump, oily cheeks wrinkled as his mouth turned down in a frown. He at least had the decency to try to hide it with his handkerchief as he wiped the sweat from his upper lip. "Instead, we agreed to put y'all on academic probation and enact curfew from now until the end of the term. If y'all make it to then."

"What about the *men* involved in this? They started it, and you and Reverend Ward always turn a blind eye to everything they do!" Lucille burst out.

I patted her hand to calm her down before we got into more trouble.

"Young girl, you're lucky you're not being thrown into one of the university's jail cells. There have been many accusations of you three starting fights around campus and causing one mishap after another." The headmaster spat. Hot liquid sprayed from his mouth and hit my cheek and forehead. I might've been appalled if I weren't already covered in blood and dirt.

Lucille sprang up from beside me. "I'm sure those accusations came from the same men who have been behind everything else. They just want us gone, and you know it!"

"Those are very serious allegations coming from you, young lady. The consequences of such actions would be—"

"We couldn't possibly be participating in such crimes. Our minds are far too *feeble*, isn't that right, headmaster?" Victoria looked at him with raised eyebrows, using his own words against him.

"Now, now." Reverend Ward spoke up for the first time. One long, scrawny hand grasped his Bible and the other held up to halt the conversation. "We should all just thank the Lord no one had been hurt in this little incident of yours. The men you somehow managed to incapacitate, have since awoken and seem to be fine. The headmaster is right. Things could've ended a lot worse, but our Lord and Savior has other plans."

"Oh, really? And does He speak to you directly?" Lucille's words dripped with venom.

"Well, if you must know, He's been gracing me with visions, not unlike what we all saw at the bonfire a few weeks ago."

Lucille, Victoria, and I looked at each other. The bonfire hadn't been a vision from God. If he was receiving them personally, either he was a liar, the person behind them, or someone else was doing this to persuade him.

I tried to picture the reverend traversing the woods, slaughtering one of those poor animals, and carving those symbols into them. The very thought made my stomach curdle, but it wasn't impossible to imagine.

He was more suspicious by the minute, and from the way Lucille and Victoria stared at him with squinted eyes, I could tell they thought the same.

"We have a real prophet on our hands here at Brimham." Headmaster Sullivan beamed with pride.

"Do these visions entail the same message that was given at the bonfire? That *God* is condemning our presence here?" Victoria asked.

Headmaster Sullivan and Reverend Ward exchanged glances.

"That is not for you to worry about. His will shall be done, and His plan shall be executed." Reverend Ward smiled.

I took that as a yes. A chill ran cold and deadly down my spine.

"Now, you three must head back to your dormitory and get cleaned up. With the new curfew, we'll have one of our officers come around to ensure you are all safely in your rooms." The headmaster gestured for us to be on our way.

I knew what he really meant. Security would watch us, lock us in. This campus was our prison instead of our freedom.

Gravel crunched, sharp beneath our boots, as we made our way back into the open air, the headmaster's office looming over our backs. The late afternoon sun hung low over the trees. The air smelled of dust and something faintly sweet from the magnolias lining the path. I kept my gloves clenched tight in my fists so Victoria and Lucille wouldn't see the way my hands trembled.

Behind us, the tall windows of the administration building glowed with the last light. I could still imagine the two accusing men as we had left them: Headmaster Sullivan rigid behind his mahogany desk, and Reverend Ward standing beside him, hands folded, eyes bright with that peculiar fervor.

"They had no right," Lucille muttered, her voice quivering more with fury than fear. "Academic probation? As though we had been the ones to instigate the whole thing."

"And a curfew," Victoria added bitterly. "They're going to lock us in our own rooms like we're criminals."

I swallowed. "It was never our fault."

The Reverend's voice echoed in my memory.

He's been gracing me with visions, not unlike what we all saw at the bonfire a few weeks ago.

He had said it as though it were a blessing. As though we ought to be comforted.

Lucille eyed the thick woods that lined the path, the same woods where we'd found those poor, slaughtered animals. "You think he did it?"

"I think," I said carefully, "that a man claiming divine visions might conceal darker ones behind them."

I thought of Mama and the ladies' church league, indifference and hate hidden behind devout words of God. Thought of Daddy. Cousin Frederick. Self-proclaimed god-fearing men, high-cotton men, held higher than most in the community, making dishonest deals behind closed doors.

Victoria glanced back toward the office we'd just come from as if the two men might still be listening. "There's something else."

She reached into her satchel and withdrew the small leather-bound book Mr. Edmonton had found for her the morning after the bonfire. Its cover was cracked, the title long since faded.

"Mr. Edmonton said it was a curiosity," she murmured. "An old text on ancient hieroglyphics and folklore."

Lucille and I leaned close as Victoria opened it. The pages were filled with inked symbols and cramped notes in a hand too old-fashioned to be recent.

"I didn't see the exact symbols we'd found carved into the animals," Victoria continued, turning pages carefully. "Not precisely the same. But there were similar forms. Some circles and intersecting lines. Invocations, I believe."

My throat dried. "Invocations of what?"

"I'm not sure," Victoria admitted. "Some pages are torn out. See?" She showed us the stubs where sheets had once been bound. "I didn't notice them at first because of how neatly they were cut. Like someone didn't want anyone to notice their absence."

I drew back. "Why would someone do that?"

"That's what troubles me," Victoria replied. "The sections missing came just after a passage speaking of 'drawing power from the vessel.'"

Cicadas screeched and a wind stirred the trees, carrying with it the scent of damp earth from the creek behind one side of the campus. A phantom weight of something unseen watched from the undergrowth.

"Whoever cut those pages out is the same person working against us. The same person using dark witchcraft to do so." Lucille stated. "And with what the reverend just said in there, I would bet my last penny it's him."

"Or someone close to him," Victoria countered.

"The Headmaster?" Lucille asked sharply. "He certainly didn't seem surprised."

It was true. In fact, the headmaster had almost seemed excited, boastful . . . *proud*. Just as proud as Mama when she bought new jewels or Daddy while he smoked his pipe.

The thought settled heavy between us. We resumed walking, slower now. The bell tolled in the distance. Our new curfew would soon be enacted.

"And Josephine?" Victoria asked quietly.

She had access to the woods, probably more access to the university than the rest of us. More access to the library late at night when no one was there.

"But she left?" Lucille questioned.

I shrugged. "She would know more about her father's habits. His wanderings. His . . . visions. And it's not like she went far."

Victoria closed the book and hugged it to her corseted chest. "What if she has seen the missing pages? What if she knows what he's doing?"

Lucille nodded. "We should confront her."

"What if she tells her father and gets us in more trouble, though?" Victoria nearly whispered. "We can't afford any more trouble. None of us can now."

The light was fading quickly, the sky turning bruised purple over the horizon. Soon the new curfew would demand we be in our rooms, our doors locked from the outside like prisoners, isolated and alone.

Lucille squared her shoulders. "Then, we'll watch. Carefully."

"And speak to Josephine," Victoria added. "*Gently.*"

A distant crow cawed from the treetops, harsh and solitary.

As we approached the dormitory steps once more, I could not shake the feeling that the Reverend's eyes were still watching us somewhere behind lace curtains and shadowed glass.

He claimed God's will was being executed.

But as the sun hid behind the horizon, our doors shut behind us, and a key turned heavy in the locks, I began to wonder whether we were the ones on the executioner's block.

THE REVOLUTION (an excerpt)
Vol. 1—No. 1

For women's rights and nothing less. For men's rights and nothing more. In spite of color or class, for rich or poor.
CALL TO ACTION
(This section has been charmed, and will be revealed only to those who mean no harm.)
If you have The Spirit to fight for the cause, to do the right thing regardless of one's race, gender, or social standings. If you are willing to Sacrifice to gain the retribution for women of the past and make a better tomorrow for the women of the future. If you are ready to let the words of The Superstitions roll off your tongue and craft a new way. JOIN US. Our next meeting will be held under the full moon in the highest room of the women's dormitory at Brimham University.
Come. Say the Pledge. Join our sorority.
Join our coven.
For the revolution!

Chapter Thirty-Four
Victoria

If your right foot itches, a visitor is coming your way.

The university parsonage where Reverend Ward and Josephine lived sat a little apart from the main campus, modest and whitewashed, with climbing ivy encasing the narrow porch. The evening air lay thick as syrup, scented with jasmine and the faint smoke of dinner cooking wafting across the grounds.

After some debate, we decided it was best for only Catherine and me to go. Josephine had never taken kindly to Lucille's sharp tongue. This required a gentler hand.

Catherine squeezed my wrist once before I lifted it to knock. It was our silent agreement: I would occupy Josephine. She would search.

Catherine stood beside me on the steps, gloved and straight-backed, every inch her father's daughter. Even when visiting the Reverend's house, she carried herself as if she were entering a ballroom. My own hands were worn in comparison, not ruined by the mill exactly, but shaped by it all the same.

Josephine answered, as we knew she would. We'd waited until we saw Reverend Ward leave. Pale blue dress, collar pinned high despite the heat. Her little silver crucifix rested against her throat like she'd never known doubt a day in her life. Her eyes flicked to Catherine first, cool and measured, then softened some for me.

"Well." Her lips tilted up in a sly grin. "Isn't this a surprise?"

Her tone wasn't unkind, just careful. Like she was already bracing for impropriety.

"We thought we might see how life outside of the lecture hall is treating you," Catherine said, smiling as easily as summer. "Besides, the dormitories feel quite stuffy now that we're getting locked into them each night."

Josephine hesitated a beat too long, then stepped aside. "Father is at the chapel, rehearsing for his sermon. He says twilight helps him hear the Lord more clearly."

Her words settled in my stomach like lead.

Hear the Lord. Or see visions in bonfires.

Inside, the parsonage smelled of lamp oil and old paper, the kind that holds secrets. A Bible lay open on the small table, margins crowded with Josephine's neat handwriting. A hallway led into an open door, where a desk sat just inside—the reverend's office.

She motioned for us to follow her into the cramped parlor. Catherine and I squished ourselves together on the snug couch. Josephine sat across from us in a high-back chair, her hands folded in her lap.

"You both look tired." She eyed us and lifted her chin. "University life does not suit you. Or any woman, for that matter."

There it was. That was exactly why Lucille couldn't come. That statement alone would've set her off, and this whole plan would've gone up in flames without ever having the chance to really begin.

I took a deep breath and forced a smile. "We're managing. Some days feel like standing in front of a loom that won't quit throwing thread, but you learn to keep your fingers quick." I shrugged, trying to come off light and casual.

She blinked at that, like she'd never pictured me anywhere but here. Never pictured a woman working.

The couch creaked as Catherine leaned back, exuding an air of confidence only someone who had been raised in high society could. "You know, Headmaster Sullivan has quite a friendship with my Daddy. They talked plenty before I came here. Even told Daddy there were . . . concerns before we arrived. Is your father that close? Or had he not been privy to such information?"

Josephine's grin fell as she wrinkled her nose. "Of course he was. Headmaster Sullivan told him all about the letters."

Letters? That didn't sound good. My pulse quickened, the way it used to when a belt started slipping overhead in the mill. It had the potential to be dangerous but hadn't yet snapped. I knew to proceed with caution.

"Letters?" I asked while straightening my skirts, feigning disinterest.

"Anonymous." The corners of her mouth lifted once more. She knew more than we did, and she liked it that way. "Some gentlemen felt the program was improper. I can't blame him."

"And your father?" Catherine asked gently.

Josephine's eyes flashed. "He believes the Lord grants intellect where He wills it."

That was certainly a surprise. He never seemed much like he cared for our intellect at all.

"But he still punishes us," I said, then silently cursed myself for being so quick to respond. Either Lucille had rubbed off on me more than I realized, or the stress of it all was getting the better of me. Neither could erase the words that now hung in the air.

Josephine's gaze cooled, her expression neutral—locked. "Order must be kept. But enough of that, the Lord doesn't reward those who gossip."

We wouldn't be getting any more information from her. I'd said too much, too quickly.

But that word she'd used echoed in my head. *Order.*

In the mill, order meant noise so loud you couldn't hear your own thoughts. It meant keeping pace or getting swallowed by the machinery. Order was whatever the foreman said it was. Not stopping or slowing even for those whose lungs ached, who coughed and coughed without relief.

Catherine rose smooth as silk. "I've always thought parsonages were only second in holiness to the chapel itself. I'd love to have a moment to connect with the Lord in such a holy place. If you'll excuse me."

Josephine hesitated.

But Catherine knew her audience. "It's best to speak to the Lord in solitude, isn't it? I won't be but a minute," Catherine said sweetly.

Josephine nodded, clutching her crucifix. "I suppose so. Help yourself."

Catherine slipped down the hallway, shifting from banker's daughter to the fierce activist she'd become.

I leaned forward a little, wanting Josephine's attention back on me, and away from Catherine. "Josephine, how has your father been lately? I imagine taking on such a role here at the university can be quite stressful."

She stiffened. "Father handles his duties with grace. The Lord doesn't give his followers more than they can handle."

"How *does* he handle all of his tasks?" I asked carefully, trying to come off light and curious, as if making small talk. "Does he take walks in the woods often? Write in journals?"

"He does both, I suppose. Walks when he needs to clear his head and writes correspondences and sermons when time allows." She tilted her head. "Why?"

I shrugged. "Just curious, is all."

In the hallway, a drawer slid open as soft as a sigh. I coughed to cover the sound.

Josephine studied me like I was a problem set before her. "You know," she said, "he and the headmaster are only doing the best they can. Many here believe women at the university invite disruption, and they have to deal with that. It's a heavy load to bear."

"In the mill," I said slowly, "when new machinery came in, the older hands swore it would ruin everything. Truth was, they were just scared it'd replace them."

Josephine didn't dignify that with a response.

Catherine appeared in the doorway then. Her face was composed, but her eyes were bright the way cotton flashes white when a spindle catches it wrong. Footsteps creaked on the porch. She stepped back into the parlor just as the front door opened.

Reverend Ward entered, hat in hand, twilight clinging to his shoulders. His expression was tired, but not fever-bright. Josephine rose at once, ever the dutiful daughter.

We hadn't expected him back so soon. We'd hoped to be gone before his return. His gaze passed over us as his eyebrows rose, lingering a fraction longer on me than on Catherine.

"Well now," he said. "This is a surprise."

Like father, like daughter.

"We wanted to check on Josephine since she left us so quickly after the bonfire. We're just leaving now. Good evening." Catherine bowed her head slightly, smooth as cream, before passing him to make for the front door.

I followed on her heels, not making eye contact with the man as he continued to stare at us.

Outside, the evening air felt thicker than before, the bugs louder. Our feet scuffed against the path as we made our way back to campus. A red cloud of dirt trailed us.

When we were far enough from the parsonage and any wandering eyes or listening ears, I leaned into Catherine. "Did you find anything?"

"I didn't find the torn pages from the book," Catherine whispered.

My stomach dropped. *This had been for nothing?*

"But look." She reached into her bodice and produced a clump of folded papers. She flattened them across her skirts and handed them to me.

I scanned over the first one quickly, taking in as much of the information printed on it as I could. A list of professors. Beside each name: *for* or *against* the women's program.

Another sheet showed student placements.

My stomach knotted. Anger heated my chest.

"They put us almost entirely with the professors who voted *against* us," I murmured.

Catherine nodded. "They doomed us from the start."

The same emotions I'd felt when reading over the documents Prim and I had stolen from the foreman flooded through me again. Disgust. Outrage.

"They set the odds against us on purpose," I said under my breath. "Thread pulled too tight. Waiting for us to snap."

"But look," Catherine said, pointing lower. "There are more in favor than we thought."

She was right. Several names were marked *for*, rather than *against*. Quiet allies, hidden among the rest. Purposefully kept from us.

Hope flickered, small but steady. Then I looked at the other papers. They had no name, no signature, but their words were sharp and angry enough to cut skin.

"This corruption must be halted. Women in lecture halls invite moral decay. They are not meant to be here."

My jaw tightened. The paper shook between my trembling fingers.

Not meant to be here. That was the same thing the figure in the bonfire had said.

The next letter was a copy, written with a different hand. Reverend Ward's. No doubt kept for his and the headmaster's documents.

"The board insists this program is necessary and lawful. We will listen to them and guide these young women while they are here. They are the Lord's children just as us. We mustn't interfere."

I read it twice, then said, "The reverend argued against whoever wrote these."

Catherine nodded.

"That doesn't sound like a man carving symbols into deer to do witchcraft against us," I murmured.

"No, it doesn't." She said, "It isn't him."

"No, it isn't," I agreed.

In the mill, when the thread kept breaking, the foreman could waste days blaming the girl at the frame. But sometimes the fault lay in the bale itself. We'd been just as blind as the foreman, blaming the wrong thing this whole time.

"At least now we know where to look. We have a list of all the professors who didn't agree with us being here."

Other employees of the university hadn't been included in the records. I supposed it was because they weren't the ones in direct contact with us quite like the professors.

For the first time since the bonfire visions began, the fear inside me shifted shape. It wasn't wild anymore.

It had edges now.

And edges, I knew, could be worked with.

"We have to do something!" Lucille's voice echoed off the vaulted ceilings. She was always the first to speak, always the first to get angry. Her passion etched into her features. It was unmistakable, like she didn't have a thing in the world to hide.

We'd spent several days scoping out the professors on the list who hadn't approved of our program with nothing to show for it. Between that, getting locked in our rooms each night, and Thomas and his gang's constant terrorizing ramped up since what had happened in the courtyard, everyone's patience was hanging on by a thread.

"We will." Alice tried to calm her.

"But how?" Catherine asked.

"I can't believe they're locking us in our rooms at night," said Catherine. "I feel like a caged animal."

"I hate it." Lucille winced.

The first night they came to lock our doors, she nearly rioted. Catherine had held her back and reminded her that they'd kick her out if she did, and the whole program would come to an end.

"They're trying to rile y'all up," Henry suggested, "to get a reaction out of you." His hand rested on Lucille's back.

"Have y'all noticed the extra security around campus watching us all the time?" Chrissy asked.

"Yeah. They were even in the library when I went to study the other day," Susan chimed in.

"Thomas and his gang have remained unaffected. If anything, they've been worse," Catherine said.

"This dormitory is starting to feel like a prison." Lucille persisted. "I can't stand another night getting locked into these measly rooms."

"We should throw snakes into *their* dorm." Susan suggested.

"Yeah, rabid ones." Catherine grinned and nudged Lucille with her elbow. Lucille smiled, but only slightly.

Everyone in the room threw out different ideas and suggestions. I leaned against the wall in the back of the room and listened.

Chrissy leaned beside me and whispered, "Isn't this group remarkable? You have a room full of strong, intelligent women, apart from Henry, debating with one another and giving their opinions without biting each other's heads off. I've never been in a debate room full of men without such aggression."

She was right. This *was* remarkable. As much as I'd tried to keep my distance from people, I enjoyed being a part of this group, this sorority.

This coven.

Without them, I wouldn't have made it at the university this long, and would've been far away from here and this town by now. It felt nice being a part of something again, to care about something again.

"Why do they get to live in their glossy new buildings, while we're stuck here in this rotting hole?" Catherine asked. "At least if we had better, safer, more comfortable housing we could even the playing field a little. Better resources and better living conditions would mean we can put up a better fight."

I nodded and thought through her words. *Rotting hole?*

"I think I have an idea," I announced to the room as a smile spread across my face.

We spent several hours planning our big act of revenge. As the night took root in the sky, darkness spreading just as fast as cotton in the mill air, some women left, succumbed to the call of sleep, and others came in their place.

Familiar faces peeked through the meeting room door. Hesitated.

I gasped. "Prim?"

I leapt from where I sat on the floor and went to the door. She and the other mill girls huddled around it, unsure if they should come in or not. Danielle, with her curved posture and wrinkled forehead, despite her being only a few years my senior, and Beth, with her girlish grin and wide child-like eyes. The sight of them here at the university was like seeing my two worlds suddenly collide.

"We decided to accept your invitation." Prim waved the newspaper I'd given her the last time we'd seen each other.

"I'm glad. We could always use the numbers." I tried to smile. It still felt odd smiling at the people I'd thought hated me for so long. It was a hard notion to let go of, even if I had helped Prim break into the foreman's office.

Lucille hurried over, her chest puffed out. "Everything okay over here?"

She eyed the unfamiliar women and then looked at me, waiting for my signal, ready to protect me if need be.

I nodded. "Everything is okay."

Lucille's chest and shoulders relaxed, but only slightly.

"These are the women I worked with at the mill. I gave them a newspaper and they're here to join us." I gestured to them and the paper.

Beth stepped forward. "Well, actually . . . we also hoped we could persuade you." She looked at me and then down at her stomach. Her face contorted as if she were looking at her own tombstone.

And she might as well have been.

I'd helped make the tincture to knock out the foreman, but this . . . this was a whole different thing entirely. It was too close to what I'd helped Maggie with. "I'm not sure I've changed my mi—"

"Please." Beth looked up at me again. Her eyes pleaded.

I didn't want to be the one she was begging. If I helped her, she could have negative effects from the tincture or backlash just as Maggie had. But, if I didn't help her, I was condemning her to a life on the outskirts. A life cast out of society.

Damned if I do. Damned if I don't.

"We're preparing for something really big, I can't leave the sorority right now." As I said this, Beth's face fell. "But, after this I'll—"

"Thank you! Thank you! Thank you!" Beth threw her arms around me.

I nodded and tried to match her enthusiasm as I introduced them to Lucille and everyone else, then led them in signing the pledge. I hoped I was the savior she looked upon me as.

And not the condemner.

Chapter Thirty-Five Lucille

Breaking a mirror shatters what you see
and brings seven years of bad luck.

The office they'd turned into our dormitory had been nearly unlivable from the start. Low ceiling. One narrow window that stuck in damp weather. Two beds crammed into each room so tight together you had to turn sideways to pass between them. The plaster already cracked in the corners like a dry creek bed in August.

I'd slept in barn stalls more spacious than those rooms.

The sorority members, except for Susan, who had gone to fetch Headmaster Sullivan and Reverend Ward, stood shoulder to shoulder in the middle of the hallway. We looked around like farmers surveying a field that had given all it meant to give.

"We need it to look as shitty as it feels." I said.

Rebecca shut the door and slid the bolt. "You're certain this witchcraft won't spread into other parts of the campus?"

Victoria gave a small smile. "It's an illusion only. Not true rot."

"Just the look of it," Catherine added. "And the smell."

I grinned. "Exactly. If we're going to show blight, let's show blight properly."

On a farm, you learn the difference between a fence post that's weathered and one that's rotted clean through. One'll hold a season longer. The other crumbles if you lean on it. We needed crumble.

We formed a loose circle, hands brushing. The air in the cramped space already felt thin, waiting. My fingertips tingled, then burned. My blood was ready to be spilled. Only the briefest hint of panic flared in my chest until I looked around at my friends, my sisters. We were in this together. As we sliced our palms with shards from a broken mirror and rubbed our blood on the handful of poppy we'd spent the morning assembling, my anxiety disappeared completely. Excitement took root in its place.

Breaking a mirror shatters what you see and brings seven years of bad luck.

Draw blood with a piece of a broken mirror and rub it on one petal of poppy for every minute of illusion you want to curse your intended victim with.

We did as the witchcraft instructed.

A strange wind blew. Hairline cracks spread wide and jagged on the walls, crawling across the plaster like frost splitting soil. The faint water stain above Susan's bed darkened, bled outward, then sagged as if the ceiling itself were surrendering.

Alice wrinkled her nose. "Can we make it smell?"

I thought of wet hay left too long in the loft. Of potatoes gone soft and fermented in the cellar.

The air shifted, with a hint of decay following it. A sour dampness settled in, thick and wrong.

"Make it smell, indeed we did." Rebecca coughed, waving her hand in front of her nose. "Lord a-mercy."

The floorboards darkened next, warping and bowing like they'd soaked through a dozen hard rains. One near the door split with a sharp crack that made us all jump, though we knew it was only sound, not truth.

Cobwebs thickened in the corners, draping down in silver veils like the bride of death herself. The single windowpane filmed over, as if mildew had claimed it inch by inch.

Catherine looked around, eyes wide despite herself. "Lucille . . . it looks condemned."

"Good," I said. "That's the word I want them thinking."

By the time we finished, the room looked like an abandoned smokehouse after a flood. The walls buckling, the ceiling sagging, the boards soft as compost.

Just in time, the doors opened at the end of the hall, and light flooded into the now grotesque space. The Headmaster poked his head in, peering around, before he stepped fully inside. The Reverend followed behind him, brow furrowed.

"What is the meaning of this?" the Headmaster demanded as he retrieved a handkerchief from his pocket, using it to cover his nose.

"You need to see this. It seems the building is succumbing to its age." I insisted. "Never meant to be lived in, I suppose."

Headmaster Sullivan's face drained nearly white as he looked around. Reverend Ward stepped forward slowly, eyes tracing the warped floorboards, the sagging ceiling, the creeping black along the walls.

"This is—" the Headmaster sputtered. "This is impossible."

"Sir," Victoria said, steady as a fence line, "this is where you've housed us."

"These rooms were inspected before the term began," he snapped.

Victoria moved toward them, university handbook in hand. "Section four," she said, sweet as pie. "Student accommodations must be maintained in livable condition, fit to code, and free of hazard." She held it out for them to read.

The Headmaster barely glanced at it, his eyes still scrutinizing the damage before him.

Rebecca nudged a warped board with her toe. It gave in with a sickening creak.

"If this were a corn crib," I said plainly, "I wouldn't even trust it to hold spoiled corn."

The Reverend turned slowly in place, studying the illusion with narrowed eyes. For a heartbeat, I worried he might see through the witchcraft entirely. I squeezed my palm harder from where I held it behind my back, making sure plenty of blood still dripped, and still held the illusion firmly in place.

Reverend Ward hesitantly said, "The structure does appear a bit . . . compromised."

"Appears?" I echoed.

"A bit?" Alice mimicked.

The Headmaster pinched the bridge of his nose. "Very well. You cannot remain here tonight."

"We surely can't," Susan agreed.

"You may return to the auditorium," he said briskly. "As you did during the . . . snake incident."

At the mention of Thomas's prank, my jaw tightened. But we'd planned for this.

"The auditorium is in use," Alice said quickly. "Winter play rehearsals."

"That is correct," Catherine added. "They already have the sets built."

The Headmaster grunted. "Then we'll find some other temporary arrangement."

Victoria spoke up, gentle but firm. "Sir, the male students have *two* new dormitories."

Silence fell heavy as a storm about to break.

The Headmaster's eyes sharpened. "Those are assigned."

"Yes, sir," I said. "Assigned among how many?"

He did not answer.

Rebecca stepped forward. "The male students could double up."

"Just for the term," Catherine added. "Besides, I'm sure my Daddy would be very interested to learn that all the money he'd donated to the campus hadn't been put to good use, such as keeping up the building his very own daughter stayed in."

Headmaster Sullivan looked from us to the ruined room and back again. Seeming to make up his mind, he exhaled sharply. "I suppose it wouldn't be impossible," he said slowly, "for adjustments to be made in light of these . . . circumstances. One of the new dormitories will be vacated and reassigned."

A thrill ran through us, quick and bright.

"However," he continued sharply, "your curfew remains. Your doors will continue to be locked at night."

After months of having to put up with such unequal and inhumane living, we'd finally won this battle, gotten ourselves a better living arrangement, leveled the playing field in a small but impactful way, but we hadn't won the war.

Catherine inclined her head. "We understand."

"You are not to mistake this concession for leniency." Headmaster Sullivan eyed us, one eyebrow quirked higher than the other, before turning on his heels and hurrying from the building. Reverend Ward followed, pinching his nose and coughing on his way out.

Within the hour, we stood outside our so-called rotted room as trunks were fetched and assignments rearranged. The illusion still held, sagging and foul, but was beginning to fade as our blood dried and crusted.

When at last we gathered our things and stepped into the new dormitory, we admired the taller ceilings, real windows, and space enough to breathe. Something inside me eased. It wasn't freedom. The locks would still turn at night. Curfew would still fall like frost.

But we would not be packed like feed sacks in a damp storeroom. It was a small but needed win.

As we spent the day settling into our new home, Thomas and many of the other male students were not subtle in their displeasure. Complaints rolled off of them like thunder. Shouts of favoritism and refusals flashed like lightning. Several said they would be taking it up with their fathers, rich with money and esteem. But in the end, they went.

Thomas was angrier than anyone. He sneered, his face red, all but his scar. "You're going to pay for this," he growled, lugging his luggage out the door.

Lucille flashed him a filthy gesture in farewell as he made his reluctant leave.

By dark, once all of them were gone, unhappily rehomed, we celebrated our small victory. In the open space of our new common room, a room much like a large and spacious parlor, a room I hadn't even known could exist in a dormitory, everyone celebrated. I took in the smiles and congratulatory hugs. Catherine and Alice embraced.

About damn time.

Victoria danced and laughed with the others. I was glad she'd made friends, including me. The mill girls who had shown up at our last meeting were back. They talked with Victoria for a while before she seemed to agree to do something and left with them. I watched as she went and as the others celebrated our victory.

"Hey, there." Henry weaved through the maze of dancing bodies. His smile revealed my favorite dimple of his. Once he reached me, he slid his warm hands around my waist and pulled me in. His cedar smell enveloped me. I wanted to stay there, inhaling it forever. Tingles shot through my body, but not the sinister tingle of witchcraft. Instead, it felt like freshly brewed tea on a breezy summer day.

It felt like home.

"For a man who just had to move out of his own dormitory, you sure are supportive." I grinned and tilted my chin to the side. His eyes were only inches from mine.

"I never much cared which dormitory we were in. Anyhow, I heard one woman who was responsible has a distrust and distaste for men, and I just can't seem to stay away from that, can I?" He laughed and inched closer. His breath fluttered across my face.

"Well, maybe there is one man I don't entirely distrust," I said, centimeters from his lips. My heart pounded. Every nerve in my body lit on fire.

I could almost taste him.

"Is that so?" His lips brushed mine. Our lips slammed together in a tight, perfect mold. My arms raised and circled around his neck involuntarily. My fingers slid into his hair. His hands caressed my hips and pulled me closer. The warmth of his soft lips sent a current of electricity down my body. It heated me to my core. Then they opened. It was as if lightning had struck. My every nerve lit up. Our tongues mingled and tasted before we devoured each other. So intertwined with one another, I didn't know where I ended and Henry started.

Whooping and hollering from the crowd brought us back to reality. We reluctantly pulled apart, but not completely. Our foreheads remained pressed together, and our arms around each other. "You are truly remarkable, Lucille Rockwell." Henry grinned, and then quickly pecked my lips once more.

"You're not so bad yourself, Henry Lockhart."

A sigh escaped my tingling lips.

Chapter Thirty-Six

Catherine

Dream of flames out of season, you will be angry for a reason.

Alice and I had been dancing, even daring to hold hands. The way she'd looked at me all night made me want nothing more than to be alone with her. Alice pulled me by the hand toward our new, and much more spacious, rooms. We said our quick farewells and practically sprinted down the stairs and into my new room. I shut and bolted the door behind us, though I knew it wouldn't be long before campus security came and locked it, anyway.

Darkness enveloped us as I faced Alice. My eyes needed to adjust as they leveled with her chest. This was the first time we'd been completely alone together. Not out in public, not with other people, but completely alone. Able to express ourselves however we liked.

I swallowed the hot lump that formed in my throat and blurted, "You're beautiful."

"As are you." Alice smiled. "Do you want me to kiss you?"

I sucked in a breath. "I . . . but what if someone finds out?"

"So?"

"It's dangerous."

"You didn't answer the question."

My mouth was suddenly very dry. "Yes." I tried to swallow again. An embarrassingly loud gulp echoed through the small, quiet space. "Yes, I want you to kiss me. I've wanted it since I first saw you. I've wanted to feel your lips and your skin and—"

Her lips fervently pressed into mine. A sound of surprise escaped my throat, but it was soon replaced with pleasure. Her lips were even softer and more supple than I had imagined. I lifted my hands to her face. Her skin felt like silk under my fingers.

Her body pressed against mine and then pushed me backward until we landed on my bed. Our legs tangled in our skirts until we pulled them up and out of the way. Our lips separated from each other just long enough to yank out our hatpins and throw our hats onto the floor. Hair fell around our faces, and the smell of lavender filled the air from Alice's tightly coiled curls. Then our lips met again. Sounds of soft moans and panting echoed through the room.

Alice's mouth opened, and her tongue caressed my bottom lip as she asked for access, which I quickly granted. Our tongues did the same dance that Alice and I'd been doing with our bodies an hour before. She tasted sweet, like remnants of the cookies and sweet tea. There was another flavor, something more luscious and salty. It was how *she* tasted, and I loved it. I wanted this taste for the rest of my life. I was hooked and would never get enough. After minutes or maybe hours of passionate kissing, our lips parted. Both red and swollen. Mine tingled as if phantom spiders ran over them. Our foreheads remained pressed together, both of us still catching our breath. For a moment, neither of us moved.

We had crossed something, a line maybe, or maybe we were teetering perfectly on its edge. I wondered if she, too, worried we would fall over it if we shifted, even an inch. But I knew, without a doubt, I could never go back to before. Before this. Before *her*.

Eventually, though, our breathing slowed. The fog from our passionate embrace dissipated ever so slowly. We rearranged ourselves on the narrow bed and pulled the blankets over our bodies. I tucked my head into the crook of Alice's neck, breathing her in. Our arms wrapped around each other, cautious at first, then certain. I held on tight, fear suddenly clenching my heart. Fear of losing her. Fear of being caught. Fear for what this meant.

"Does it frighten you?" I asked, unable to hold in my worries any longer. "These feelings?"

"It did when I was younger. But not now. How long have you known," Alice asked quietly, "that you were different?"

The question settled between us. Outside the window, night insects hummed. The world beyond these walls seemed so close and so far away at the same time. As if the small bubble of space we occupied together could break open at any moment, exposing us—exposing what we had done.

"Ever since I can remember," I said, swallowing the lump that had begun to form in my throat. "My sisters talked about boys. They staged weddings with their dolls, practiced signing their married names." I let out a shaky breath. Chill bumps scattered across Alice's skin in response. "I never understood why I was supposed to want that."

"Mmm." Her fingers traced idle lines along my sleeve. "I never felt the same pull toward boys, either. I only ever noticed girls."

Her lips brushed my forehead. The touch sent warmth through me. Then a sharp thought jolted my awareness. Awareness of how different this moment could be judged, depending on who was seen and who was believed. My chest tightened. What was a risk for me was ruin for her. My fingers curled tighter into her sleeve.

"Have you been with another woman before, Catherine?"

Alice's hand was at my waist, thumb moving in small, absent circles, as if she hadn't realized she was doing it, as I gathered my thoughts. The lamplight caught the gold in her skin. She could move through certain spaces unquestioned if she chose to, but not safely. Never safely. Passing was not protection. It was performance.

I swallowed. "I've never told anyone this."

She continued to rub circles on my waist, but didn't rush me or try to fill the silence.

"When I was younger, one of Mama's church league members had a daughter my age. Sarah." Even now, her name pressed like a bruise. I squeezed my eyes shut, unable to look up at Alice while I laid my transgressions before her. "Mama didn't approve. Said her family came from the wrong side of town. Not landowners. Not . . . our kind of people."

High-cotton. Wealthy. *Privileged.*

"But I couldn't stay away from her. When we got older, I started feeling things I didn't have words for. Things I had been taught were unnatural. Sinful."

Alice's hand moved slowly along my back. Chills shot down my spine. I shivered.

"One night, Mama walked in on us kissing." My voice thinned. "She called for Daddy. I panicked. I pushed Sarah away from me. Harder than I meant to." My fingers tightened in the blanket, no longer on Alice. I couldn't let them touch her, the same fingers that had delivered the fatal blow.

The memories shot through my mind in quick succession. The hearth. The sound of the crack. The blood pouring too fast, too steady. My hands held out in front of me, frozen and trembling.

"She fell backward. Hit her head. And then there was just . . ." My throat closed. The next word was barely audible. "Silence."

Alice's body went still beneath mine. My eyes shot open to search her face. My breath caught in my throat. That was it, that was where the line had been crossed, and I couldn't return. But my words continued to spew out anyway.

"I thought they would hate me," I whispered. "I thought I had ruined everything. But Mama told the sheriff it was an accident. They believed her. So easily."

Of course, they had.

"A white family," I said, bitter words still pouring out of me. "A respected name. They didn't question it. Not when they carried Sarah out. Not when they buried her." Tears slid down my face. "This . . .

What we're doing . . . Doesn't have the same risk for me as it does for you. If it had been . . ."

Alice's hand stopped moving. I felt it immediately, but there was no stopping my words from coming now, no stopping this final guilt-ridden admission.

"If it had been you," I finished, quieter, barely a whisper. "If a black girl had stood where I stood—"

"She wouldn't have been standing for long," Alice said. Her voice wasn't angry, but flat and certain.

The truth of it settled heavily in the small room, with just a door and some walls keeping us safe from the outside. Me more than her. The thought of it, of the world, discovering us, putting her—Alice, with the softest skin, the strongest will, and the fiercest love—in danger, made my stomach curdle. Made me want to burn the whole system down.

"I know," I whispered instead.

She shifted slightly so I could see her face. "Do you?" she asked, not cruelly, but not gently either. Her eyes were lit with a fire I had seen before, when she talked of the injustices of this world, and our fight within it.

I nodded. "I don't want to cause you more harm. If this . . ." I struggled to find the right words. "If safety isn't a possibility when we are together . . ." I couldn't finish.

Heat crawled up my neck. I was all too aware of what she saw and suddenly felt foolish for thinking my affection was enough. She must look at me and see the privilege. Comfort. Safety. Things she hadn't been afforded as a child. Things that a war had to be fought over to gain for her, and even then, it wasn't equal. Wasn't the same as it was for me.

Alice's gaze didn't waver, though. Her hands didn't drop from my waist or let go of my sleeve. "Safety is not an abstract thing for me, Catherine. It's not guaranteed or even expected. But I get to choose what, and who, I risk it for. That's *my* choice."

Relief washed over me. I nodded against her skin, damp from my tears. Silence stretched between us for a moment, but it did not break us.

"They don't want Rebecca and me here even more than the rest of the women." Alice's thumb swept under my dress collar and brushed my shoulder. "If we ever made a big enough mistake, we wouldn't be quietly sent home. It wouldn't be brushed under the rug as an accident."

The implication lingered.

My chest tightened. "Will we ever get to live a life that is truly ours?" I asked. *In the open. Not hidden behind closed doors and thin walls.*

Alice drew a slow breath. "I don't know," she said honestly. "Reconstruction could collapse tomorrow. Men like your father are already trying to make sure it does. But knowledge," she continued, "is harder to chain than a body. If we learn. If we teach others. If we succeed in this program." Her fingers threaded through mine. "That is not nothing."

It was hope, fragile but edged.

I pressed my forehead to hers. It was not a fairy tale promise. It was real.

We lay there long after the lamp burned low, the world outside still dangerous, still unequal. But in that narrow bed, we were not pretending the world was kind. We were choosing each other anyway.

And that felt stronger than pretending everything would be okay.

Dreams of Sarah floated through my unconscious mind. Then her smile and her laugh turned into Alice's. I smiled, feeling her velvet skin under my fingers, taking in her smoky smell.

Smoky?

That wasn't right.

I jerked awake. Smoke blanketed the room and obstructed my vision even more than the dark. I looked around frantically and coughed. I covered my mouth with my undergarments. Light and more smoke poured in from under the door.

The building was on fire.

Alice wasn't there. She must've gone back to her room before campus security locked the doors for the night. I grabbed the door handle. Blinding hot pain raced through me. I yanked my hand back, cradling it against my chest.

Panic constricted my throat just as much as the smoke did. I had to escape, but I needed to ensure everyone else was out, too. The moonlight reflected off the windows' dusty glass.

The windows.

I snatched my pillow from my bed and held it to the window. With all my might, I reared back and rammed my elbow into the glass. One time. Two times. Finally, on the third time, when I was sure my elbow would break, the glass cracked and shattered on the ground. The hole wasn't quite big enough for my curvy body to fit through comfortably. I squeezed through anyway and clenched my teeth as sharp shards of glass cut into my sides.

Safely on the ground, I took a moment to breathe in fresh air, but I needed to make sure the others had escaped, too. The flames illuminated the endless black sky. The crackle and snap of burning wood sounded through the heated wind.

How did this happen? How did the fire start?

I rushed to the window beside mine and charged toward it. Pain shot through my arm. I couldn't keep doing this for every window. I squinted and tried to make out what was on the ground. I grabbed the largest stone I could find and hurled it at the window. It shattered. I poked my head through the hole. Susan was frantically clawing at her door to the hallway.

"This way!" I yelled.

She rushed to the broken window and climbed out without too much difficulty. I hurriedly pointed to the rocks on the ground. "Use these to break the windows and get the others out!"

Wide-eyed, she nodded and wiped soot from her face.

Another window close to us burst out. Lucille and Henry hoisted themselves through the opening. A sigh of relief escaped through my dry lips at the sight of familiar faces.

"Have you seen Alice?" I called to Lucille.

"No! Have you seen Victoria?"

"I think she went somewhere with the women from the mill earlier. She's probably still there." I sprinted to the other side of the building before I could hear her response. I grabbed more stones and threw them at every window on that side of the building. Glass littered the ground. With all the windows broken, I ran to the back of the building, helping anyone who needed it before moving on to the next window. After two windows, only one was left. I poked my head in and nearly wanted to cry.

Alice.

She and Rebecca hadn't noticed me or their busted window yet. Their hands were wrapped with towels as they tried to yank open their door, but the handle was too hot and melted.

"Alice!" My voice was hoarse from yelling and from the smoke I had inhaled.

Alice turned her soot-and-tear-streaked face to mine. She blinked several times and then jumped up. She grabbed Rebecca and pushed her toward the window. We helped her up and through the broken shards of glass and then Alice climbed through. I gripped her hands until she made it out and onto the ground. We collapsed into a heap. Tears streamed down our faces, making rivulets in the ash on skin.

A scream cut through the smoke-filled air.

"She's not breathing!"

Chapter Thirty-Seven

Victoria

Lightning will never strike a house with a burning fire.

My hands ached from grinding and mixing the necessary herbs for Beth's tincture. I rubbed and stretched them on my slow walk back to the university until the stench of smoke wafted up my nose. That's when I saw the flames lapping at the underbelly of the night. The smoke smothered the sky and choked out the stars' light. It came from the campus, the dormitory where my friends were. My sorority sisters—women I had grown to care so much for.

My stomach dropped so low it would surely be splayed across the ground.

No. This couldn't be happening again.

I wrenched my skirts up to my thighs and sprinted toward the black smoke. My muscles burned by the time I arrived at the site of the fire. Flames engulfed the dormitory. Fire raged from windows and chimneys. It was a good sign that people had made it out. But I needed to see my friends. As I got closer, Lucille's gangly frame came into view, then Catherine's curvier one on the ground, with Alice beside her.

Lucille was . . . What was she doing? Was she kissing the woman laying before her? Kissing her and then pushing on her chest? That didn't make sense.

"What are you doing? What happened?" I shouted over the roar of the flames.

Lucille spun, her eyes wild, as she continued to rapidly push on the woman's chest.

"I'm trying to get her heart going! She's not breathing!" She sucked in a large gulp of air and bent forward. She spread her mouth over the woman's and blew the air into it.

Up close, I could see who it was . . .

No. No. No! I couldn't lose someone else!

"Rebecca!" I shrieked and scrambled to the ground beside Lucille. I didn't know what to do or how to help. I swept a single singed curl from Rebecca's soot-covered forehead. "How did this happen?" Though there should've been a million other things to ask or do, I didn't know a single one. I sat there, useless, and watched Lucille doing what she no doubt learned to do with animals on the farm.

That's what we might as well be—merely animals—for someone to do this to us. To do something so horrible that could—did—kill an innocent life.

The life of our friend.

Our sister.

My heart quaked and broke apart all together. How could this happen again? How could I go through the loss of someone I cared for, someone I had become close to, again? How would I survive it another time?

"No one knows! Henry and I were in the common room when we smelled smoke, but everyone else was already locked in their rooms!" The flames reflected in Lucille's eyes. She continued to push against Rebecca's chest. "We had to break windows to help the others! But she collapsed when she got out! Must've inhaled too much smoke . . ."

A loud quake echoed through the air. All at once, the building heaved a final groan and collapsed in on itself. We jumped back.

Lucille dragged Rebecca's limp body and narrowly avoided the falling rubble and debris.

Soot and ash blanketed the air, raining down like blackened snowfall. Of course the weather would choose tonight to have the coldest temperatures so far this year. The humidity gave the cold a bite. It nipped at our skin while the flames diminished. Most of the women wore only nightgowns or undergarments. They shivered and stared at the remains of the building we'd only just moved into and the ash-covered body Lucille still worked on.

She would've no doubt kept her efforts going, kept pushing, until her own body gave out from exhaustion, but a deep voice from behind us interrupted.

"Lucille Rockwell?"

We all turned. Lucille continued to pump.

"You are hereby under arrest for arson, murder, and the use of Satan's craft." The campus officer stepped forward. Handcuffs hung from his grasp.

Headmaster Sullivan and Reverend Ward stared in horror at the scene before them. They looked from the building's remains to the body Lucille hunched over and tried to breathe life into. Thomas stood behind the officer. He held the crumpled remains of Lucille's handwritten pages on witchcraft. He didn't even look sorry. Not for the building or the life. His usual pack flanked his sides and sneered.

Lucille continued her lifesaving efforts as she shouted, "I didn't do this! I helped everyone get out of the fire! I'm trying to save her!" Her face was as red-hot as the flames had been.

Thomas stepped forward. Darkness spread across his features. He mouthed something to us, after years of reading lips I knew exactly what he was saying, "If I couldn't live there, neither could you."

He had done this out of spite. Taken a life out of petty spite.

Then he said, his voice plenty loud for everyone to hear, "I told you, Officer, this woman is insane. I heard her using the dark craft, planning wicked deeds, to set the dorms on fire. She was going to come for ours next, not caring who was inside it."

The officer grabbed Lucille's arms and yanked her up and away from Rebbeca's too-still body. She kicked and clawed. Every word of profanity known to man came from her mouth.

"No, I have to save her! I have to keep going!" Lucille cried out. Then she turned on Thomas. Only the guard's grip on her arms kept her from pouncing on him. "*You* did this!"

He feigned fear and pretended to back away from her.

Henry, Catherine, and I stepped forward to protest.

Thomas gave us an evil, mischievous look while the other men wrestled Lucille to the ground and handcuffed her. He added, "These women were helping her! I saw them! They've all been using the craft together like some satanic coven of the Devil!"

The officer looked at us and then back at the headmaster.

Reverend Ward spoke up. Tears ran over the dark circles that rimmed his eyes and down his hollowed cheeks. "I saw a vision from God of these women doing horrendously sinful things. And to think, my sweet Josephine had to endure living with these vile monsters this entire time. These *murderers*. You should all pray to the Lord your soul to take." He shook his head.

I jerked back. He was calling *us* the monsters?

Headmaster Sullivan ordered, "Arrest them all!"

My mouth dropped open. How could they think we did this? Yet the gleam in the headmaster's eyes showed he didn't really have to believe we did it, he just had to convince the council to doubt us so we would get expelled. He wanted this just as much as Thomas did.

Though with an alleged murder on our hands, we would be much more than expelled now.

Lucille's hands frantically moved from their pinned position. I could hardly see them from behind her back, even with her efforts to make them visible to us. But I didn't need to. I knew what she was signing to us, over and over.

Run. Run. RUN.

I looked to Catherine, seeing Alice urging her to run. I nodded and signed the same thing. She looked at me and then at Lucille, who fought against the officer as he handed her off to the headmaster and started toward us. At that moment, Catherine seemed to make up her mind. She turned, grabbing Alice's hand, and ran.

Suddenly, everyone ran this way and that. Some ran from the officers; some ran toward them. I looked at Rebecca's body and at Lucille one last time. I would be of better help to her outside jail than in jail beside her. So I ran from the scene of the crime, not for the first time in my life, and certainly not the last. At least this time I knew exactly where to go.

I sprinted through the campus and weaved in and out of the thick woods that lined it. Far enough from the dormitory that the chaotic roar of the fire no longer echoed in my ears. Footsteps pounded against the ground behind me. I glanced back between strides. Thomas, George, and some of the others chased after me. They laughed, as if this were a friendly game of tag.

A hunt between predator and prey.

I was smaller—faster than them. I continued to weave in and out of the tree line, behind bushes, and around sharp corners of buildings. My heartbeat thrummed in my ears. The taste of sweat was on my tongue. It made my mouth feel more parched as I sucked in air. My muscles burned and ached, but I forced them to keep moving, to keep going.

Eventually, I slipped behind a rock wall, and squatted. I listened as my pursuers' footsteps rumbled past me. As soon as the coast was clear I sprinted close to the ground and in the shadows until I made it all the way to my destination.

I rapped my knuckles against the small wooden door and hoped the sound wouldn't attract attention. Hoped he wasn't asleep and would hear me.

Finally, after what seemed like an eternity, Mr. Edmonton opened the door. I didn't wait for him to invite me in. I rushed into his small room and slammed the door closed, then locked and bolted it

"My dear. What has happened? Are you okay?"

My back hit the closed door. I breathed heavily as I tried to tell Mr. Edmonton what had happened.

His brow furrowed. He tugged his dressing robe tighter around himself. "Oh, dear . . . that is awful!"

"Would it be okay if I hide out here?" I asked, and then added, "just for a little while? Until I figure out what to do next?"

"Of course," he said without hesitation. "Stay as long as you need."

He gestured for me to come further into his living quarters as a smile spread across his face.

Chapter Thirty-Eight

Lucille

Bad luck comes in threes.

The metal bars slammed shut, and the key clicked in the lock. My head pounded where the officer had struck me earlier. I hoped fighting and causing such a disturbance gave the others time to escape.

The cell crept dark with shadows. I shook the rusted iron bars. They didn't budge. Wet, mildew-covered stone walls formed the other sides of the cell. Damp straw lay stacked in one corner to serve as a makeshift bed, if you could even call it that. In the other corner sat a wooden bucket. From the odor wafting from it, I hoped I wouldn't have to use it.

My body throbbed, sore from the night's events. Gravel stuck out from my bloodied hands and knees. I spit the copper taste from my mouth. It stained the uneven ground with red. Iron chains clanked and pulled around my ankles. I was almost flattered they thought iron bars weren't enough to hold me, but my stomach soured at just how little freedom I still had, if any.

Torches flickered from the sconces on the wall opposite to my cell. Their light reflected off the puddles on the ground. The cells beside me looked very similar to my own through the reflection, but they were empty. Catherine and Victoria escaped. They're safe.

At least I had that to be thankful for.

Just to be sure, I shook the bars and called out, "Is anyone here?" My voice was raspy, no doubt from screaming and inhaling so much smoke. "Let me out!"

After I shouted a few more times, I trudged slowly over to the pile of hay. The chains scraped across the floor as I moved, and sat down. The hay wasn't thick enough to be a mattress. I'd made better hay bales for the horses on the farm. Even the pigs were provided more comfort than this.

I thought coming to receive a higher education would grant me, as well as other women, freedom. But where did it get me?

Here.

If they truly intended to convict me for arson, murder, and witchcraft, I'd be dead before the next full moon graced the sky. All of this would be for nothing.

I tried not to feel sorry for myself. But as a rat's claws scratched against the ground and echoed through my empty cell, it was a losing battle.

Wait.

A rat.

We had used witchcraft to turn wine into *rat's* blood. We had used it to help us do a lot of things.

I bolted upright. Quickly reaching out to grab hold of the long chain connecting me to the stone floor, I held it at an angle, cinching it to make a sharp edge. I jabbed it into the meaty flesh of my palm until it drew blood.

"Come on, come on," I chanted to myself. "Please work."

I thought of The Spirit, The Sacrifice, The Superstition.

And waited.

And waited.

Nothing.

Nothing happened.

I let go of the chain, it dropped to the ground with a thud. I slumped back onto the meager stack of hay for only a moment before footsteps slapped against stone and water. I bolted back up. I didn't want to seem any more vulnerable than I already was.

Three silhouetted figures darkened my cell. The light from the sconces behind them made their shadows claw at the ground, making it hard to identify who they were. Though, from their height and build, two of them had to be men, and I didn't have to think very hard to guess which two men would be here to see me locked in a cell and condemned.

One of my visitors reached for a sconce, removed it from its wall mount, and held it so that the light illuminated the three faces. Headmaster Sullivan, Reverend Ward, and Josephine Ward stood outside the door to my cell.

The headmaster cleared his throat, a smug grin wrinkled his cheeks. "As I suppose you've already guessed, Miss Rockwell, you are hereby expelled from Brimham University. And because of tonight's events, as well as previous incidents, the women's program at Brimham has ended, for good. Women will no longer be allowed on this campus, or any other campus in Alabama for that matter."

The flame from the torch made shadows dance unnaturally on his face, and his unabashed grin seemed to stretch up to his hollowed eye sockets.

"Have a good night, Miss. Rockwell." He handed the torch to Reverend Ward and walked off without another glance back. He whistled a cheery tune that lingered like a ghost and haunted the cells with its echo.

He hadn't even mentioned Rebecca. If she were alive. Or dead.

Reverend Ward and Josephine stared at me through the bars of the cell as if they were at the zoo, gawking at a wild animal. Josephine fidgeted and carried a look of disgust on her face. That wasn't too out of the ordinary for her, though.

"Father, why did you bring me here?" she asked, her voice high-pitched and whiny like a child's.

"I wanted you to see what it looks like when one allows themselves to be persuaded by the Devil toward worldly temptations." His voice echoed off the damp walls. It ricocheted and created a nightmarish effect. "And I thought you might be able to talk your friend into repenting so she can be saved from eternal damnation in case the verdict in these accusations against her results in the death penalty."

I snarled and wished I could fit my hands through the bars to choke some sense into Reverend Ward and his daughter. "I will never apologize for anything, but especially not something I was falsely accused of."

Even though my mouth and throat were dry, I produced enough saliva to spit at their feet. Josephine gasped and jumped back as if she'd been struck.

Reverend Ward didn't acknowledge my action, only continued to stare. "We'll see about that after you spend a couple of nights down here." He turned and hung the torch back in the wall sconce. "Come, Josephine, we'll try again in the morning."

They retreated. Their footsteps splashed through dank puddles and echoed down the halls until they faded into silence.

Several hours went by, or so it seemed. There were no windows in the cell to glimpse the sun or moon, only darkness and shadows. As time went on, I shook and banged on the bars, I yelled until my throat felt like I'd swallowed a handful of nails and my body was weak with exhaustion.

Once I could no longer continue, I sat on the pile of hay and stared at the walls of the small, musty cell. Someone had scratched words into them. Prayers, names, messages to loved ones the author thought they might never see again, and tally marks to count their time here. Some had been here for weeks, others no more than a couple of days.

I traced over the markings with my finger and felt the groove of the carved stone against my flesh. Bending down, I searched for a chalky stone, one that could be used to write with. It took several minutes of feeling around to find one with such limited light coming from the sconces.

Eventually, after I'd touched a dead rodent, a torn cloth covered in what felt like dried blood, and a pile of what I hoped was mud and not feces, I found what I'd been searching for. A small, chalky rock. Up against the wall, I carved my own name into it. Then, underneath it, I carved a message I hoped anyone else trapped down here would read.

Let your fear fuel you,
and fight like hell.

Metal scraped against the floor and echoed down the tunnel. I dropped the rock and used the last bit of strength I could muster to push myself off the ground. I hobbled over to the iron bars with a renewed brave front for my visitor.

The dark figure was a man, though I couldn't make out his features. He walked almost all the way to my cell before he grabbed a torch from the wall. The light illuminated his frail fingers first. The glow snaked up his arms and toward his face.

"Mr. Edmonton," I sighed, thankful to see someone who wasn't there to condemn. "What are you doing here? Is Victoria with you?" I looked down the tunnel and hoped to see her midnight hair and fair skin.

"No, I'm afraid not. It's only me." He looked at me. Then around the cell and stone walls. His gray hair seemed black in the darkness and his cheeks looked sunken by shadows. "I'm sure you know that these cells were once used to hold slaves as they awaited to be bid on and sold. But what I'm sure you don't know is that these cells were reinforced with purified alkaline metal. That prevented the inmates from being able to use any sort of witchcraft or voodoo while imprisoned in them."

If my stomach didn't already feel sick, it sure did then. The thought alone was horrendous. I couldn't imagine having my freedom stripped so completely. So inhumanely.

I gulped. "No, I didn't know that." Even with the terror this information brought, I still wasn't sure why he was telling me that right now. "Can you help me get out?"

Mr. Edmonton smiled and he reached into his pocket. My chest filled with a warm excitement.

He was going to get me out. I would be free again.

His hand pulled out a folded piece of paper.

"Victoria came to me about y'all's little sorority," he began in a low voice that whispered like a ghost floating in the stale air.

He unfolded the piece of paper. At the top, in bold printed letters it read *The Revolution*.

Our newspaper.

"At first, I thought I should just stick to my original plan and report y'all for using the witchcraft I had planted for Victoria to find, but then what would stop the university from trying this women's program again in the future? I needed to make sure when this ended, it ended for good."

I stared at the man before me, the man Victoria had trusted and, even though she was hard-pressed to admit it, cared for. His voice no longer sounded feeble. It sounded deeper and darker. His words trudged through my muddled mind, but I couldn't comprehend them.

"No, instead, I needed to plant small seeds in others that would lead them to see the truth." He paused to roll up his sleeves and bare his arms under the light of the torch.

I gasped. The words he said finally made sense. Scars littered his arms. Evidence of deep cuts and gashes, now mounded over with fresh, pink skin.

"The Sacrifice needed for the witchcraft to make those *visions from God*." He laughed, emphasizing the last words, "was more than I could give on my own."

"Those animals," I stammered, "you . . . you were the one mutilating those animals? Carving marks into them?" My brain tried to attach the man in front of me to the gory memories of those mutilated corpses.

"They were sacrifices that needed to be made." He slid his sleeves back down.

"But why?" I asked as I tried to connect the dots. My heart wouldn't let my brain believe it. How could it have been him? Victoria trusted him. *We* trusted him. "I thought you said your wife—"

"My wife," he growled, "was just like y'all. Hungry for freedom and rights that could never be hers. So daft and stupid it got her killed. She died in an accident while protesting for women's rights, or so the police said." He spat at the ground. "Freedom and rights, what a stupid thing to die for, stupid thing to take my unborn heir away from me for."

"But don't you want to continue fighting for the cause that she died for? Give her death, and your child's, a purpose?" My voice broke.

"No! What I want is to save all of y'all from yourselves. Save society from becoming unbalanced. Make the people in this town and the whole state see the truth. See what those *rights* you women claim you want will really do to the world. See how ridiculous the whole notion is."

"What about Victoria?" I whimpered in a last-ditch effort to get the man back who she'd grown close to, who we all had.

"Victoria will know soon enough. In fact, she's sleeping in my living quarters right now. Shall I go wake her?" An evil grin spread over his face.

"No! Don't touch her! Don't you dare!" I yelled as he turned and walked away from me with the torch still in hand. My only source of light disappeared with him.

The darkness overtook me, covering me in a blanket of despair. It nipped me with fangs of gloom. I slumped to the floor and continued to scream until my voice left me, too.

Then I cried.

THE BRIMHAM TRIBUNE (an excerpt)
Vol. 23—No. 6

BREAKING—WOMAN ARRESTED FOR ARSON, WITCHCRAFT, AND MURDER
Lucille Rockwell, a FORMER Brimham pupil, has been arrested on the charges of arson, murder, and witchcraft. Late last night, the women's dormitory on campus went up in flames. Headmaster Sullivan, Reverend Ward, and the campus officers were able to arrive just in time to see the accused brutalizing a corpse, no doubt performing the craft of the devil on the body. With the help of the brave and trusted, Thomas Black, they were able to apprehend the woman. She will be brought to a swift trial and justice. Her consorts are still at large.

Please be on the lookout for these persons of interest:

Victoria Woodhall
Catherine Stanley
Alice Paul
Susan St. Clair

Chapter Thirty-Nine
Catherine

Haint blue ceilings repel bad spirits, tricking them into thinking the ceiling is part of the sky.

Under a dark sky, I ran through icy rain. It drenched me to my core. Anger burned like lightning in my chest. I wasn't angry at Alice, just myself for how I'd acted and what I'd said after we had gotten away.

We'd narrowly escaped campus security, then ran from Thomas's crew. We sprinted toward town as we darted between buildings and eventually hid behind trash barrels until we no longer heard footsteps or voices calling giddily to one another.

Still crouched down, I'd whispered, "Where should we go now? The campus isn't safe anymore."

Alice had looked around. Her forehead wrinkled with worried lines. "We should go to your family's estate. Your father holds sway with the headmaster and the university board members. Maybe he can convince them to let Lucille go."

Her answer was immediate. Practical. She was thinking about Lucille. Not herself, certainly not her own safety.

With my heart still racing, blood pounding in my ears, I was only thinking about myself. I should've said yes. Agreed to that proposal happily. But panic had overtaken my senses, still shaken up from the night's events. Images flashed before me, Alice standing in Daddy's entry hall. The portraits. All white men, wealth passed down from one to the next. The servants who still cleaned for wages that looked too much like chains.

Daddy's face. Mama's. The neighbors'.

"I . . . I don't think you should come," I'd panted.

Alice gulped down air as if it were in short supply. "Why not?"

Because they would assume. Because they would question. Because they would look at her and see everything they had been taught to fear. Because they would look at me and see betrayal.

"They can't see you with me. You're . . ."

"I'm what? A woman? Black? Say it." Her voice rose and her eyes glazed, not with tears, but with fire.

I couldn't bring myself to answer her questions. Instead, I said, "They . . . they won't take kindly to you. Not in the house."

Even as I said them, the words broke me. Broke me because I said them. Broke me because they were true.

A crack of thunder split the sky, close enough to rattle the ground beneath us. The silence that followed was colder and harder than the rain. It ran down Alice's face in thin, shining lines, but she didn't wipe it away. She just looked at me, like she was waiting to see if I would take it back.

"Not in the house," she repeated.

I flinched. It sounded even worse coming from her lips.

"I'm trying to protect you," I insisted, hating how weak I sounded. "You don't know them like I do."

Lightning flashed, illuminating her face, not tearful. Furious.

"No," she said quietly. "I know men like them very well. You think I don't understand what your father's house represents?" she asked. "You think I haven't spent my entire life calculating which doors are safe to knock on and which ones will close with a rifle behind them?"

"That's not what I meant."

"Then what did you mean?" Her eyes glistened, but her voice steadied with a sharp edge to it. "You're not protecting me, Catherine. You're protecting yourself."

The truth of it struck harder than if she had slapped me. I stepped toward her without thinking, reaching for her.

She pulled back before I could touch her.

"They would see me walk through that door and remember exactly how their wealth was built," she continued. "And you would have to choose."

"I . . ." The truth hovered there, ugly and undeniable. *I'm afraid of what they'll think, of what they'll say, what they'll do.* The thought alone filled me with shame. "I am choosing!" I burst out instead.

"Are you?" she asked.

The storm roared around us. Thunder shook the ground.

"If Lucille were here," Alice said, "would you hesitate to take her to your family's home? To your mother and father?"

I shook my head, unable to say my answer out loud.

Her jaw tightened.

"I thought so," she nodded slowly, her lips pressed into a thin line.

I stepped toward her. "What happened with Sarah, can't happen with you. I know how quickly things can turn inside that house. I don't want that for you."

Something in her expression flickered, recognition, perhaps, but it didn't soften. "What happened with Sarah," she said, "was an accident born of fear." She stepped closer, rain streaming down her face. "What you're doing now is a choice."

Her hands trembled, but her spine did not bend. "I was willing to walk into that house knowing the danger," she said, "for Rebecca, for Lucille, the other women, they all matter more than my pride. But don't pretend this is about *my* safety. You are afraid of being seen standing beside me."

The rain blurred my vision. Lightning flashed across the sky.

For a moment, neither of us spoke. I opened my mouth, trying to figure out what to say, how to fix this. The storm filled the silence for us. Rain hammered the ground and wind tugged at our skirts. I hoped—stupidly—that she might step back toward me.

She didn't.

"I'll find my own way," she said before I could speak.

Alice rose from her crouch and wiped her hands on her soaked skirts, as if brushing off more than mud.

"Alice—" I tried.

She looked at me once more. Not pleading. Not begging.

Measuring.

"If you want to fight for women," she said, "you must decide which women you mean."

Alice turned and ran into the storm. She didn't look back at me even as I called her name.

I took a step toward her. Then another. My body knew what to do even if my mind was still catching up. But the distance between us was already widening, her figure blurring into rain and shadow.

The storm plastered my clothes to my skin, cold and heavy. I should've followed her—run to her. I should've chosen differently at that moment. I should've begged her to come back and pleaded for her to forgive me.

Instead, I stood there too long, long enough for the decision to make itself. The path to Daddy's house wide and familiar behind me, and the cost of walking it suddenly, unbearably clear.

Even as those thoughts raced through my mind, beat against my cranium like a sledgehammer, I couldn't help the relief that came from the glow of gas lanterns that lit my parent's large white home. The pillars that held up the front porch looked even bigger now than they had before. I climbed the steps and looked up at the haint blue porch ceiling, the size of the house, and the yard around me. I'd been around them my whole life, but they made me feel insignificant in comparison, even with the weight of our predicament on my shoulders and the worry about my friends.

I didn't knock. It was the middle of the night and my parents were asleep. I planned to sneak up to my old bedchamber, slip into bed, and talk to my parents in the morning when everything would be brighter and the shroud of doubt and doom had been lifted from the world for another day.

I yanked open one of the two large double doors and tried not to let the hinges squeak. When I shut the door and turned around, I froze, like a thief caught in the act.

Mama stood in her curlers and a night robe. Daddy stood beside her in his business suit. He'd tossed his coat over the stair railing. His hair went in all directions, as though he'd run his hand through it several times. Their expressions were identical. The kind that would've forewarned me of the deep trouble I was in as a kid.

And now.

"What . . . what are y'all doing up?" My voice squeaked.

Our maid, Natalie, came from the cigar room, a glass of gold liquid in her hand. She gave it to Daddy without making eye contact. He knocked it back in one big gulp and coughed. The glass wasn't filled with sweet tea, but something much stronger.

He shoved the glass back at Natalie. She stumbled. Daddy stomped toward me. I didn't know what to expect. Some sort of welcome back? I surely hadn't expected him to raise the back of his hand and swing it, but he did. Pain exploded in my cheek. Pounded through my head. I yelped and fell to the floor.

"Richard!" Mama rushed forward.

But Daddy held up his hand to halt her.

I cupped my stinging cheek, not sure what to do as I propped myself up with my other hand. I was just as naive as others had warned me. I'd waltzed in here and thought my parents would help me, help the others. Of course not. Not after everything I'd learned about the true monsters of this world and the real worries and fears that haunted people. Not just worries about the newest fashion or getting married to the richest bachelor, as Mama always fussed about, but *real* worries, of rights, freedoms, and even death.

Daddy shook his hand out. "Another glass. Now," he barked at Natalie to fetch. He looked me up and down as if he were truly seeing me for the first time.

"You've disgraced this family." His voice was deep, roughened with age and cigar smoke. "The university's headmaster came by here earlier. Imagine our surprise when he told us our very own daughter had been an accomplice to vulgar crimes on campus. And that she'd been seen in the *company* of a woman—a *black* woman." He spat the last part out as if that were the worst crime of all.

I recoiled, as if I'd been struck again, not because I was surprised, but because I wasn't. If I could just tell him what had happened, get him to listen, maybe he would change his mind.

"Daddy, I can explain—"

"No, you've done enough. You've dishonored this family's reputation." He growled. "My reputation."

I knew, despite everything, that was what truly upset him. His reputation. And even though I wasn't happy with how Alice and I had parted, I was glad she wasn't here to witness this.

"I . . . I . . ." I didn't know what to say or if there *was* anything to say.

Then, as if to add kindling to the fire, a man rounded the corner from the cigar room.

Cousin Frederick.

His greasy skin wrinkled around his grotesque smile, eyes full of humor and something else. Something I couldn't quite put my finger on. Something close to lust but slimier, more indecent.

"You will marry Frederick by the end of the week," Daddy stated in finality. "That will keep you from being in any more trouble and tarnishing this family's reputation."

I gasped. "No." It came out weak, in a broken sob. I wanted to yell, to scream at the top of my lungs at the injustice around me.

Daddy's eyes narrowed. "You *will* marry him or you will not set foot on this land again. You'll have nothing."

Mama remained silent. She looked from her crumpled daughter on the floor to her unyielding husband. But I knew who she would choose. She was ever the subservient wife.

Frederick sneered, his peeling lips upturned in a sly grin. He scanned over me as if surveying his livestock. I tried to picture a life under that stare—under his crooked fingers and scaly lips. No. I couldn't—wouldn't—do this.

"No," I said again, this time louder, stronger. "I won't marry him."

"Then get out," Daddy said quietly, then louder when I didn't move. "Get out!"

Mama stepped forward and put her hand on Daddy's shoulder. "Richard, don't you think you're being too harsh?"

Daddy shook her hand off his shoulder as Natalie brought him another glass of bourbon. He gulped it down without coughing, and yelled again, "Get out!"

I jumped to my feet and pushed through the large wooden door. I continued to run even as my feet stumbled down the steps and onto the ground outside. I ran from the people I'd thought of as my family. But family didn't turn on you in a time of need. Family didn't strive to change who you are, they helped to make you a better person.

My real family was the women I'd spent the last several months with, the women who would risk their lives to help me. The women I had just left behind out of my own naivete.

As I ran, I passed a slowly decaying corn field that had already been harvested, leaving behind remains of branches and limbs.

The field matched the feeling in my chest, sorrowful and wilting. Part of me had died. Left me forever. I was no longer the girl I'd once been. No longer a girl at all, but rather a woman. A woman who now knew the cruelties of this world.

Chapter Forty

Victoria

Never talk ill of the dead lest you bring their misfortunes upon yourself.

There was one window in Mr. Edmonton's living space. It was barely a foot long and a foot wide, but it let in enough light to wake me from my fitful sleep. I jerked up. At first, I didn't recognize where I was. The smell of smoke wafted from my hair, and memories of the night flooded back.

The fire. The arrest. Arriving at Mr. Edmonton's.

I sprung up from his small bed where he'd insisted I sleep while he slept on the floor. Even with the warmth and comfort, I hadn't been able to get much rest. I'd tossed and turned as I thought about Lucille and Catherine and all the other women in our sorority. How would I help them?

"Mr. Edmonton?" I called, though I knew he wasn't there. There was nowhere he could be that I wouldn't have seen him in this cramped space. He must've gone to open up the library.

I searched for my cloak as I tried to devise a plan, absentmindedly moving things around. A cup clattered to the floor and shattered into tiny pieces.

I cursed my clumsiness and bent down to scrape together a few pieces. A couple of them skittered out of reach underneath the bed. I crouched on the floor and searched for the missing pieces under the dark, shadowy bed.

My stomach lurched at what I found instead.

There, on the floor, lay a pile of blood-soaked cloth wrapped around something. I told myself it was none of my business. These weren't my things. I shouldn't look. But my hands didn't obey those screams of warning from my brain. They reached forward as if they had a mind of their own and grabbed the rust-colored pile. They dragged it across the floor until it was free from the shadows.

I hesitated to unwrap the bloody bundle. Almost changed my mind completely and pushed it all back under the bed, but something in me screamed for me to open it. I needed to see what it was.

I held my breath as I unwrapped it with trembling hands. Ever so slowly, I lifted one side of the cloth and revealed a blood-soaked dagger.

Maybe Mr. Edmonton hunted for sport. Though I couldn't imagine the old man out in the woods participating in such activities, it wasn't uncommon around these parts.

I took another deep breath and lifted the other side of the cloth. And kept holding that breath.

Choking.

Under that side of the red-stained fabric were the ripped-out pages we'd been searching for from the old book. Ripped-out pages of witchcraft. *Dark* witchcraft. It detailed The Sacrifice needed to make dark visions appear to others. Sketches showed the markings required to make the craft succeed. The same markings we'd found carved into the bloody, dead animals in the woods.

I scanned the pages. The dagger. The blood-soaked cloth. My brain struggled to comprehend their connection. Why would Mr. Edmonton have these things under his bed?

The answer was in my head, but I refused to let it drift into my consciousness. I couldn't.

The door creaked. I jerked around. There stood Mr. Edmonton. He eyed the incriminating evidence I held. I gaped at him, watching as his face distorted and changed to someone I didn't recognize, someone worn down by hatred and vengeance.

He stayed silent as he turned and shut the door behind him. The dead bolt clicked into place.

"I really wished you hadn't seen that." His voice sounded unfamiliar, no longer filled with kindness. It was the voice of a stranger, deep and guttural.

"I don't . . . I don't understand." Though I understood perfectly, I just didn't want to believe it.

"I'm afraid you do," he said. "You're a smart girl, Victoria."

"But . . . I trusted you." My brain finally wrapped around the dark thoughts I'd been struggling with. "I trusted you. How could you?"

"How could I do what? Help keep order? Balance?" he growled. "Don't you see? A woman who fills her head with philosophy and law begins to believe she should shape the world rather than serve within it. And if enough women believe this, the balance tips. Men lose their rightful authority. Professions grow crowded, and the order that has governed us for centuries begins to fracture."

His words seemed contrary in my mind.

"But I thought you were helping us. I thought your wife was like us."

"Oh, she was. She *was* like you. Strong-willed, determined, seeking to win over the world. And that stupidity is exactly what killed her." He inched closer to me. "Foolish woman. I only wished she would've pushed out my heir before her demise."

Shock and the deep pain of betrayal paralyzed me.

Mr. Edmonton took another step toward me. I forced my body to my feet and brought the dagger with me, thrusting it out in front of me.

"Now, now," Mr. Edmonton tsked, "there's no need to get violent. I was merely trying to help y'all, just in a different way than you thought you needed."

"Help us?" I spat and stepped around the small table as he slowly continued to approach me. I tried to keep as much distance between us as I could in such a small space. "How can you read so many books and not believe in human rights? Human decency? Empathy?"

"You mean the works of *fiction* that I've read? That's all they are, fiction. Not real. Make believe. Fairy tale. Nothing more."

Those words did me in. Hit me with realization and horror so hard I felt as if I might fall over. He had missed the point of the books entirely. He was not the man I thought I knew.

"But I don't want to merely stop this program, this whole thing has made me realize my purpose. And now I have bigger plans. In a few days, at the winter solstice, I'll show the whole town another *vision from God*. The same visions I've been showing to the headmaster, the reverend, and to Thomas, planting seeds of doubt and distrust." He snickered.

I gasped. "Thomas?"

"You think someone like him is smart enough to frame y'all the way he did? I merely needed to water the seed of distrust his former beloved had sowed in him. Nourish it. Let it grow and fester." Mr. Edmonton's laugh grew darker. "After the winter solstice, everyone will know once and for all what a woman's place should be in this world. Once this town knows it, then we'll convince the entire state, and then maybe even the entire country."

"You're insane." I inched further around the table.

I made my last leap to the door. Mr. Edmonton lunged for me. He caught me just before I could wrench open the old wooden door.

A scream ripped from me, throaty and wild. I swung at him with all my might, hitting him with the blunt edge of the dagger handle. He fell to one side, but his hand remained wrapped around my wrist. He pulled me back into the room. I raised the dagger in the air, about to bring the sharp edge down onto him, the man I'd trusted and adored. His eyes searched mine. He questioned if I could do it just as much as I did. I brought the dagger down, but not on his torso, on his hand that still gripped me. The dagger pierced his wafer-thin skin and struck bone with a wet thud.

His scream cut, sharp and piercing, through the air as I yanked the door open, and sprinted out into the icy humid air.

I ran from campus and into town. There was only one place I could think of to go.

Despite the icy chill in the air and the fog created by my heavy breathing, I made it to the cotton mill as sweat soaked through my bodice. I never thought I would feel so relieved to see the rusty old metal building that looked like nothing more than an eyesore on the edge of a growing town.

I searched frantically for something to pick the lock on the door to the building with but came up empty-handed. Heavy footsteps beat against the ground around the corner. Desperate to gain access to the building I'd run away from not too many months ago, I pulled at the door handle and shook it. Mr. Edmonton followed me. I had to get in. I shook harder. My whole body convulsed with my frantic movements.

The footsteps grew louder and echoed through the dim alley. I pulled with all my might. He rounded the corner. I jerked around and threw the dagger up in front of me, still covered with Mr. Edmonton's blood. I was prepared to do whatever I had to.

"Victoria?" It was Henry, not Mr. Edmonton. His voice was high-pitched and startled. His wide eyes traveled from my face to the shaking dagger in my hand.

I slumped to the ground, my back against the rusty old metal door. My chest heaved, tight and rattled. A coughing fit I could no longer ignore made its way up my throat and out my mouth.

"Are you okay?" Henry asked tentatively. He eyed the dagger.

"What are *you* doing here?" I asked between coughs.

He looked from the dagger to my face one more time before he came to sit beside me. He slid down the rusty metal wall a foot away.

"My little sister used to work here, but I never visited the place. Even when she passed away here, I still couldn't bring myself to come, not even when her possessions needed to be collected. I sent my older sister to do that." He shook his head and then leaned it back against the cold metal. His breath clouded in front of him as he rested his arms across his bent knees. "I needed to prove to myself I could do it, come here, be brave enough to do this and then be brave enough to save Lucille."

"What was your little sister's name? I might've known her." I didn't know any other words of consolation, especially not while my heart still pounded in my chest.

"Maggie," Henry said hesitantly, as if he hadn't spoken her name in a long time. "Her name was Maggie."

I shot up, my back ramrod straight. Everything blurred as I whipped my head around to look at him. "Maggie was your *sister*?"

Henry lifted his head and looked at me with raised eyebrows. "You knew her?"

I stared at him and tried to put the pieces together. His pointy nose and hazel eyes were the same as hers. How did I not see it before?

"Yes. We were . . ." I tried to stop my chin from quivering, ". . . very close."

Henry stared at me a moment longer before he laid his head back on the wall again. I relaxed against the door as I turned this new information over.

We sat in silence until Henry's lips formed his question. "Was she . . . was she alone when she . . ."

"No." I sniffed. "I was with her."

Henry nodded but didn't speak.

I went on. "We'd been helping women in the town when they . . . got in a predicament. At first, I'd told her it was a bad idea, that we shouldn't get ourselves involved in such messes." I didn't say the thought of my mother, the thought of how different her life could've been if she'd been given a choice, had changed my mind. "Eventually, though, I agreed. We made the herbal tinctures and delivered them together. I had come to really care about her . . . love her." I couldn't swallow it down anymore. A sob escaped me. Tears traced a cold wet trail down my cheeks.

Henry laid a hand on my shoulder but didn't say anything. He let me continue at my own pace.

"She was like a little sister to me. I should've been there with her that night, but I was helping take care of another factory girl who had gotten sick with Brown Lung. Maggie had insisted on making the deliveries by herself. She was so strong-willed, so independent even at such a young age." I sobbed harder. "I should've been the one they attacked. It should've been me," I said finally. The words exploded out of me, words that had been poisoning me and making me sick with sorrow and guilt for the past year. They were just as deadly as the cotton particles we mill girls inhaled daily. They couldn't stay buried anymore. They couldn't fester, stew, and slowly kill me from the inside out.

The warmth from Henry's hand enveloped my shoulder as his thumb rubbed back and forth on my sleeve while I cried. He sat with me until the sobs faded and the wet trails on my cheeks turned to a cold frost. I wiped them away with the back of my hands.

"Knowing Maggie, no one could've talked her out of anything once she'd set her mind to it," Henry looked up at the hazy sky. "Thank you for being with her when she . . ."

"Of course."

Henry cleared his throat. "So, what's with the dagger covered in blood? Should I be concerned? Or finding a shovel so we can bury some poor lad?"

A dry laugh escaped my lips. I stared at the dagger that lay on the ground beside me and summarized the morning's events for him. I started with what I'd found under Mr. Edmonton's bed and went through everything that had happened up until Henry rounded the corner.

After I finished, he stared at me with his mouth slightly agape.

"Wow," he said finally.

"Yeah." I tilted my head up toward the sky then over at him before asking, "Your sister also died fighting for what she believed in, like Mr. Edmonton's wife had, for a woman's right to choose. Would you have stopped her from doing that if you knew it would have kept her alive?"

"No," he answered without hesitation. "No, I wouldn't."

"Why?"

"You don't keep a bird in a cage because you love it and *you* want to be happy. You let it fly free because you love it and want *it* to be happy."

I nodded again. "I'm glad Lucille has you."

Henry let out a dull laugh before he hoisted himself up from the ground. "Speaking of, how do you feel about breaking a few more laws?"

He held his hand out to me. I stared at it for a moment and wondered how it would feel to run away instead, get far, far away from here and from these problems. But that was just it, there was no getting away from them, not the ones I was truly fighting.

I reached out and took Henry's hand. "Let's go break some laws."

Chapter Forty-One

Lucille

Cutting your hair after the death of a loved one cuts away their memory.

My stomach growled loud enough to echo through the cement walls, though that could've been malnourishment and exhaustion getting the best of me. I'd lost count of how long I'd been down here, how many sunrises and sunsets I'd missed. I only had the constant drip of water off the molded walls and the pitter-patter of mice to count the minutes as they turned into hours.

Time escaped me through bouts of unconsciousness when my body couldn't hold on to the world around me any longer. Visions and memories floated through my mind. They blurred with my current reality: policemen coming to question my pa about Reece's death, Pa claiming he and I had been at the farm all night, lying to save himself from having to find another farmhand; my hair—the long hair Reece had adored—falling to the ground in clumps as I chopped it off, overtaken by rage and anguish after my ma died; tears falling onto parchment as I readied myself to rip pages out of the leather-bound notebook

Reece had bought for me many moons before, but words for my ma spilled out onto the pages instead.

Footsteps sloshed against the wet pavement and brought me out of my memory-filled stupor. Were the steps real or merely my imagination? I used as much of my strength that remained to lift my head and look at the person, or maybe the figments of my imagination.

Headmaster Sullivan's plump silhouette darkened the entry to my cell. He slid a metal tray covered with stale bread, old dry cheese, and a cup of water between the bars.

"Eat, girl."

I struggled to push myself up from the floor and only managed to get to my knees. With a quick and shaky swipe, I knocked the tray out of his grasp. The metal clattered against the hard floor and the water splashed against the already damp ground. I'd decided after my first night here they couldn't take everything from me. Not my will. I would control what I still could until they either released me or until my freedom came in another manner.

"Foolish girl," the headmaster spat. He wiped his hand on his waistcoat as if I were infectious.

"I won't eat. Not until you free me," I said, though it came out raspy and weak rather than determined.

"I cannot let you starve yourself to death. We already have one murder investigation ensuing. We don't need another girl dying on our property. It would be bad for our reputation, even if she is a criminal."

My stomach dropped. So Rebecca had died.

He snapped his fingers. "Security!"

My mind was far too muddled with dehydration and lack of food to track the movements of the three guards. They yanked me up and slung me down onto a hard wooden chair. Where did the chair come from? One guard tied a rope around my torso to bind me to the chair and keep me upright. The others tied both my arms to the chair.

I looked at each guard. My vision blurred with their movements. The torches' light danced behind them. Shadows filled their eyes with deep darkness and made them look like ghosts.

Or demons.

I opened my mouth to scream, and all too late realized that was exactly what they wanted. They lunged at me. One took hold of my chin. The other pulled back the top of my head. My jaw stretched open to an uncomfortable width. They produced a long metal tube and a pitcher filled with a thick, gooey substance. They aimed the metal tube at my throat. I shook my head violently. Screams wracked through my body. I knew what they were about to do. I'd watched my pa force-feed cattle to fatten them up faster for slaughter.

The cold metal set fire to my throat. Scratched and sliced. Forced down. Down. Down.

I gagged and convulsed, unable to suck air in or push screams out. Bile threatened to come up if not for the tube in its way. They poured the sludge down the tube. It pooled in my stomach like lead.

Hot. Heavy. Unnatural.

By the time black spots darkened my vision, they yanked the metal tube out of me just as forcefully as it had invaded. The filthy hands of my violators vanished. The guards untied me and threw me down onto the pile of hay. Then they were gone, just like that. I may have thought I'd dreamed up the whole thing if not for the unbearable burn in my throat, like molten lava.

I coughed, sputtered, and gagged, but somehow kept down the sludge that had trespassed into my stomach. My vision returned slowly. In spurts. Empty space surrounded me. The headmaster hadn't even stayed long enough to see if my forced feeding was successful.

I spat bright red blood, then slumped into the soggy hay and watched the bloody saliva float on the surface of the wet ground. It dispersed. The water around it turned red until it blended with the mud and slosh. My will slowly dispersed along with it until it, too, disappeared. Tears poured from my eyes.

What little freedom I had and all of my control were gone. Stolen from me.

I had nothing left.

It may have been minutes or hours later when the splash of footsteps echoed down the corridor again. They quickly grew louder as if someone were running.

I didn't want to admit how effective the sludge had been. Though my throat still burned as if I'd swallowed acid, my consciousness was much more intact with the nutrients it'd provided. I pushed myself into a sitting position and backed further into the corner. Even if it was effective, I still wasn't willing to undergo another metal tube tearing its way down my esophagus.

"Lucille!" two voices shouted. The light from a torch brought Henry and Victoria's faces into view.

I blinked as they somehow got my cell door open and approached. "Are you really here?" I asked weakly.

"What have they done to you?" Henry growled as he picked me up from the ground.

"How . . . how did y'all get in here?" I lifted my hand to Henry's face and caressed his cheek. I had to make sure he wasn't a figment of my imagination.

"I knocked the guards out with the craft and stole these," Victoria held up two large, rusted keys.

A commotion sounded from somewhere down the corridor near the entrance.

"Uh-oh, the spell must be wearing off. I'll go knock them out again. You—" Victoria ordered Henry, "get her out of here."

"Yes, ma'am," Henry said. Without a moment's hesitation, he took me, still cradled in his arms, out of the cell and into the hallway. His steps were wobbly, from one foot to his prosthetic leg, and his breathing labored, but he didn't put me down. Didn't give up. He was going to get me out of here.

We went through a maze of dark cells, damp stone walls, and rat-infested corridors before we ended up in an underground cellar.

"Can you walk?" Henry came to a halt. His chest heaved.

"I can try." My words sounded just as weak as I felt.

He lowered me gently to the ground and held his arm under me until I was steady enough to stand.

Henry caught his breath as he looked around. Crates were stacked against the walls. Only the torches' light from the tunnels relieved us from total darkness.

"I think we're in the clear now." Henry looked down the tunnel we'd come from.

I watched him closely. Mr. Edmonton had seemed caring and trustworthy until he showed his true self. So had Reece. Henry could be the same.

All men could.

I searched for something, anything, that could be used as a weapon. A broken bottle on the ground would have to do. I snatched it up and spun around. I held the neck of the bottle. The sharp edge jutted out toward Henry.

When he turned back to me, the broken glass grazed his neck. He didn't gasp as one would expect. Instead, he slowly lifted his hands, palms out, in a gesture of surrender.

"Lucille, it's me . . . Henry," he said, as if I were confused.

"I know." I held my chin up and acted stronger and more confident than I felt. "Mr. Edmonton turned on us. He did this. All of this. If he can do this, risk everything for me and the rest of us, then so can you."

"You would kill me for them?" Henry's questioning eyes looked straight into mine.

"To gain the freedom and rights of these women—my sisters? I would do anything." I meant it with every fiber of my being, too.

"I have never loved you more." Henry's eyes were wide, full of admiration.

Not a single hint of fear darkened them. No hints of doubt. No deception.

Footsteps pounded from the tunnel we'd come from. I moved and shoved Henry behind me as I held the glass bottle toward our newcomer.

"It's me!" Victoria came into view.

I sighed. There was no way I could've fought anyone.

"Let's get the hell out of here!" Victoria pushed a pile of crates away to reveal a door. She wrenched it open. A cry escaped my lips as the first rays of sunlight I'd seen in days poured over me.

I was free.

Chapter Forty-Two
Catherine

If a candle sputters out on its own, the presence of an evil spirit is nearby.

Our new dormitory–the place we had finally been so proud to call ours but barely gotten to enjoy—was gone, turned into nothing more than a pile of rubble and ash. I looked upon it while wearing an illusion, as long as the blood continued to drip from my finger, anyone looking at me would see nothing but an ordinary man. Certainly not a wanted woman.

The campus had the life drained out of it. The trees were no longer full of greenery, and the ground was colorless and barren. Even the sky had been painted with a pallet of dull grays and monotone whites.

I stopped ogling the remains of the dormitory and scurried along the path as fast as I could without drawing attention to myself. My finger would only keep bleeding for so long. I needed to find the others and get Lucille out of her cell, though I still wasn't exactly sure how I'd accomplish that.

Around the corner that led down to the old cellars, I stopped midstep. A security guard lay in front of the door to the dark, damp cells.

His body, limp on the ground, unconscious or maybe dead. I bent forward and pressed my fingers on his neck for a pulse. The blood from my finger had dried up and crusted over. I was no longer disguised.

Just as I felt the man's blood pump through his veins, the door nearby burst open. I jumped back with a scream and froze in place. My heart hammered in my chest. Three people burst from the door. Each one looked wildly around. Their hands were thrown up, ready to fight.

I took in their forms and their faces. I lunged forward to throw my arms around them. "How did you get her out?" I squeezed Victoria, Lucille, and Henry before I pulled back and assessed them.

Victoria let her arms fall to her sides. Henry panted. Lucille collapsed altogether, completely limp in our arms.

"We'll fill you in later. Let's get out of here!" Victoria urged. Her body went stiff once again as she supported half of Lucille's weight. I supported the other half.

Considering how Alice and I had left things, coming to her family's home hadn't been my first choice, but it ended up being our only choice. Henry had offered to take us to his mother's home, but Victoria was adamant not to involve or endanger any more of his family, though I wasn't sure what she meant by that.

Alice had mentioned her family home a few times over the past several weeks. It was on the west side of town, which wasn't known for its glamor or prestige. The house was wooden, though many of the panels had large cracks between them that let in the icy humidity. Only one wall separated the bedroom from the combined sitting and dining space. Alice, her younger sister, and their mother must've shared the bedroom, or someone slept on the small sofa.

"Lay her over here." Alice cleared away the books and papers strewn on the sofa.

Victoria and I laid Lucille's limp body across the sofa. We made her as comfortable as we could. A thick mixture of dirt, sweat, blood, and other bodily fluids coated her skin. Her hair remained thoroughly matted.

Victoria asked, "Do you have some water and a cloth we could use to clean her?"

"I'll go down to the well and get a bucket of water. The clothes are hanging on the clothesline out front." Alice nodded toward the front of the house and then turned to go out the back door.

"I'll go with you." The words exploded out of my mouth so quickly I nearly screamed.

Alice gave no response and continued out the back door. Victoria went to the front to gather the cloth and clothes. Henry remained beside Lucille. He wiped her hair from her face and clearly didn't care about the grime that covered her.

There was a small field behind Alice's house. A well stuck out from the center of it, like a stamen from the middle of a flower. Many houses that looked nearly identical to hers surrounded the edge of the field. I dodged clotheslines suspended in the air like ghosts and stepped over dented cans scattered in the grass left out from games of Kick the Can, presumably from kids who lived in the surrounding houses.

As we walked, only the distant calls of vultures who circled an unknown carcass cut through the silence. I opened my mouth several times to speak while Alice drew water from the well, but I couldn't find the right words to say. I was too ashamed. Alice didn't speak either. The air around us grew thick with humidity and words unsaid.

Victoria talked to Henry and a newly conscious Lucille as Alice and I entered the house. "He'll be in the middle of the town square tomorrow to try to convince the entire town to abolish women's rights, to education and beyond. We have to stop him," she insisted.

"Thomas? I don't think he'll be bothering us anymore. He got what he wanted, didn't he?" I placed the water bucket Alice had filled by the sofa, where a pile of cloths now lay.

All three looked at me with blank expressions, like I'd missed something.

"What?" I scrunched my eyebrows.

"Not Thomas," Victoria said, "Mr. Edmonton." Her voice cracked around the librarian's name.

My jaw dropped open. "What?"

They spent the next half hour filling me in on everything I'd missed, and Lucille told us all about her experience in the cell. She revealed in great detail her conversations with the headmaster and the reverend, Mr. Edmonton's visit, and the forced feeding. Everyone in the tiny room looked just as sick to their stomach as I felt by the time she finished.

"I'm so sorry," Henry said first. He wiped her forehead and neck as she spoke, but now he used it to wipe a stray tear that had escaped Lucille's eye. She batted him away and swiped at the tears as if they were nothing more than a nuisance.

"We're all sorry," Alice said next to me. "But how do we stop him? Seems like his witchcraft is an awful lot more powerful than ours, and I'm sure not going to be slaughtering animals either."

Victoria's voice continued to crack as she asked, "We need more women, more witches. The more of us there are, the more powerful we'll be, right?"

Lucille nodded. We all looked around at each other.

"Who else will help us?" I asked. I knew for certain none of my sisters would oblige.

"The mill girls will help," Victoria offered.

"We'll need more than that." Lucille shook her head. "My Mama would've loved to have helped with something like this."

"My sister, too." Henry rubbed slow circles on Lucille's back.

"Well, maybe they can," Victoria said, looking at each of us as if an idea had struck her and she was waiting for it to strike us too.

"We can't raise them from the dead. We'd have to sacrifice a life for that kind of witchcraft. A human life," Lucille croaked.

"We don't have to resurrect them. We just need to summon their spirits!"

Lucille sat up. "I'll be damned. You're a genius."

Everyone nodded, a lightness taking hold of the room, lifting our spirits, even if just a little, as everyone began to plan.

I looked at each woman around me. My friends. My family. They would do anything to protect the ones they cared for. They would do whatever they had to. That's what *real* families did for one another.

Chapter Forty-Three

Victoria

If you spill your tea, it's a sign of stories spread about you.

I knew the plan we had devised. I knew what I needed to do to prepare to stop Mr. Edmonton, but I hadn't been to the flophouse since the day I left in September. Even before then, I had tried to make my presence scarce. I only frequented the slum housing when it was a necessity—when I couldn't sleep at the home of whomever I took pleasures with or when the mosquitoes and gnats were too great in number to sleep out on the streets. I had feared what the other girls would say to me. Feared they hated me for what had happened with Maggie, blamed me for it just as I blamed myself.

Entering the flophouse after not being there for so long was like being doused unexpectedly in freezing water when you'd just begun to warm again. The sheer sight of the landlord's podium at the front made my stomach twist into knots. A reaction ingrained so deeply into my core that even now with no debts to pay, I still was not immune to it.

I stepped into the main boarding room, dingy with years of grime, dozens of small beds, cots, and pallets lay in rows packed tightly together. Light came in through the cracks of the boarded-up windows. The stink of unwashed bodies, sweat, and foul breath mixed in the unventilated chamber. It rose in one revolting concoction of stench. I had expected all the girls from the mill to be there, to turn and see me and either yell in excitement or anger. Truly, I wanted neither.

And neither is what I got.

Instead, they were all gathered around a cot in the back of the room. No one noticed my entrance except for a few of the other residents, though most were mill girls, because of how close the mill was to this particular flophouse.

I neared the cot that everyone surrounded. Prim turned and noticed me first. Her eyes were shiny with tears and her nose red. Snot dripped onto her trembling lips.

My heart raced "What happened?"

I tried to peer around the other girls.

"Beth." Prim's voice trembled.

I sucked in a breath. Was it my tincture?

I pushed through the rest of the girls around the cot. Some grunted in annoyance, others recognized me and asked why I was there, but I didn't acknowledge them. I couldn't.

As my heart hammered in my ears, I looked upon the bed. Took in who lay on it. But she wasn't too cold or still. Her skin wasn't waxy and bloodless. She was alive.

I let out a rattling exhale, but only slightly. Beth was alive, but not well. Her skin was a smorgasbord of blue, black, and yellow around the edges. Some of the coloring was in the shape of fingers or fists.

"What happened?" I repeated.

Beth opened one eye, the other too swollen and puffy. Her cracked lips dripped blood down her chin as she started to speak but one of the others spoke up before she could.

"Mr. Smith, the foreman, found out she'd taken the tincture you made and wasn't too happy about it." Danielle handed a wet rag to

Beth for her to wipe the blood that now trickled down her neck and between her bosoms. It left behind a trail of rust red.

So I *did* cause this. Why did a trail of ruin and pain always follow me? Like a dark stalker, lurking in my shadows and feasting on my sorrows, using my friendships as its preferred prey.

"Why was he angry? Wouldn't he want her to eliminate the problem that he caused in the first place?"

Danielle shrugged. "I suppose he just likes to have a reason to be mad."

"And it doesn't take much to make him so." Prim added. "Beth isn't the first of us that he's beaten and won't be the last. He's begun to set his sights on the younger girls."

Danielle shot up from where she'd been bent over Beth, her face contorted in equal amounts of rage and disgust. "I'll kill him before I let him touch those little girls."

"We can't kill him. They'd have us all strung up before morning." Prim whispered and glanced at the landlord's podium.

Danielle shook her head. "Well, we have to do something. We can't go on getting raped and beaten."

"Actually, that's why I'm here." I said.

They all turned to me.

"The other girls from the university and I have gotten into trouble, but we think we can fix it. Maybe fix all of it." I gestured to everything around us and to Beth, laying limp on the cot.

"What do you need?" Prim asked.

"We just need numbers. More people." I said, then straightened even more and added. "More witches."

Prim, Beth, and Danielle already knew about the witchcraft; they'd come to our last sorority meeting before everything else had gone to shit, and I supposed the others did too from our newspapers I'd distributed to them. In either case, they all seemed too worn and broken to have much of a reaction either way.

Danielle nodded without a moment of thought. "We're in."

Prim nodded too, and so did the others around us without anything else to say.

Seeing all of their determined faces, their instant willingness to help, made my stomach clench in a tight fist meant to strangle. Doubt flooded in between the cracks of broken bits left behind from guilt and blame.

"It's dangerous. Y'all could get hurt. Or worse." I tried to talk them out of their determination, though I had come here to talk them into it.

A weak voice spoke up from below us. "Have our lives ever been anything other than dangerous?" Beth's lips ripped open even more as she moved them around her words, but she continued nonetheless. "Girls are either beaten to death, dying of brown lung, or ending up pregnant with bastard children they're cast out of society for and wish they were dead. We won't ever live a life of freedom or safety if something doesn't change." A tear collected at the edge of her good eye and then spilled over. It made its own path through the dirt and blood caked on her skin.

"It's settled then." Danielle looked at each of the other girls. Everyone's eyes reflected the same fierceness, the same fury. "We're in. But we need help in return."

"Hardly any newspaper printers allowed those documents to get published, and the ones that did weren't seen by many. We need to get them somewhere they can't be missed or denied." Prim stated.

"Okay," I said. "It's a deal."

After spending the day planning with Lucille and the others, I still had my side of the bargain to uphold with Prim and Danielle. We waited until the last lantern went dark in the center of town and slipped into the alley, staying in the shadows with our skirts hitched up just enough to keep from dragging. The air still carried the mill's scent—fiber and oil and something metallic that never quite left our lungs.

The square opened before us. And there it stood exactly where it had been erected only months after the war ended. I scrunched my nose at the sight of it.

A Confederate soldier cast in bronze, chin lifted, rifle at rest, as if guarding something worth preserving. The pedestal beneath him was freshly scrubbed stone with an inscription chiseled deep: "OUR GLORIOUS DEAD—DEFENDERS OF OUR WAY OF LIFE."

"Our way of life," Prim whispered with malice. "They never say whose."

No one lingered. Even the night watchman favored the saloon side of town at this hour.

I drew the documents from beneath my shawl. The pages trembled, but not from the wind.

"Quick," Danielle breathed.

We formed our small triangle at the base of the statue, boots touching the pedestal. I took the vial from my apron pocket, full of river water we'd collected at the old crossing earlier today, where, years ago, striking workers had been dragged back by force. I pricked my thumb with a sewing needle and let three drops of blood fall into the vial.

"For the lives they stole, and the bodies they hid," I said softly and sprinkled the contents of the vial around the base of the statue, as my heart sped in anticipation of the craft.

The two other women repeated my actions as I instructed them. Once they finished, I unfolded the first document and held it up to the statue, then began chanting the words of The Superstition.

If you spill your tea, it's a sign of stories spread about you.

The Spirit. The Sacrifice. The Superstition.

A strange wind blew. I gripped the papers tighter, pressing them firmly against the statue. Prim and Danielle did the same with more of the papers, each documenting bad conditions, sick girls, and even deaths. I wondered if they felt the burning tingle of the craft rising in their fingers, spreading through their hands, and down their arms as I did. I wondered if it excited them, too.

The water-and-blood mixture hissed as it was absorbed into the base of the statue. Not loud. Just enough. The bronze above us shuddered. For a terrible second, I thought the rifle might come crashing down, drawing attention to us. Instead, the ink from the pages seemed to dissolve until they disappeared completely.

Danielle yanked her paper away, turning it over in her hands, and then she looked at the statue. She gasped. Where she'd held the pages, where the words had been touching the statue, they were now carved into the bronze itself. Prim and I yanked our papers away, too. They had done the same. Words etched directly into the statue in every place the papers had been.

RENAE HARPER—AGE 16
ELIZA MAY—AGE 14
PATRICIA CARTER—AGE 19
SHANEA BETH COLLINS—AGE 22

The girls who had died of brown lung, who had been forgotten and overlooked by all but us. They wouldn't be anymore. Tears burned my eyes.

We held up more of the pages that we'd stolen from the foreman's office, more evidence. The inscriptions on the statue grew with each one, faster and faster. Names pulled from the pages in my hands, rising like steam and branding themselves into the monument. The bronze soldier's polished boots dulled, dark streaks climbing his legs like creeping soot.

Prim began to cry, though she did not stop chanting. Tears streamed down her cheeks. The drops landed and mixed with the words on the statue. Its bronze face changed. The proud set of its jaw slackened. The eyes hollowed. Cotton dust, fine, pale, and relentless, spilled from the bronze mouth and scattered across the pedestal.

I slapped the final page against the stone, the signature from the foreman, claiming it was all due to "female fragility."

"Let them see!" I shouted, my voice breaking around my words, filled with emotion and excitement. "Make them unable to ignore our suffering any longer!"

The wind answered. It tore through the square, sudden and fierce, snatching the papers from my grip. But instead of scattering, they struck the statue and dissolved into it.

When the gust died, the transformation was complete.

The Confederate soldier no longer stood alone in noble silence. His bronze body was now crowded with dozens of words, names, evidence, carved deep and impossible to ignore. Beneath the final name, new words etched themselves on the pedestal with deliberate force:

KILLED IN THE MILL
PROFITED BY THE FOREMAN
MOURNED BY US

We had only a moment to admire it, tears streaming from each of our eyes, before footsteps echoed faintly from the far end of the square. Though we could've stood there admiring our work for hours, we couldn't hesitate. There was more work to be done. Prim grabbed my hand. Danielle snatched the empty vials from the ground. We ran down side streets, through alleys, and across the narrow footbridge. My lungs burned with more than cotton particles and infection now. I welcomed the pain.

It reminded me I was still alive.

Chapter Forty-Four
Lucille

Never leave a house through a different door from which you came lest you take the owner's luck with you.

I would be a lying fool if I said I hadn't missed the farm these months of being gone. Missed the rooster's crow to wake me and the cicadas' deep hum to lull me to sleep. Missed the red dirt that coated my skin by the end of the day or the soft fur that greeted my touch when guiding the animals around the farm.

Even with the dread that burned in my stomach and weighed in my limbs, I couldn't ignore how my heart fluttered at the sight of it as Henry and I trudged up the dirt path. Though I still replied with an annoyed "let's just get this over with" when Henry asked me to repeat our plan for the dozenth time.

We weren't here to reminisce over the farm's luscious greenery and fresh air. We were here on a mission: find more of Ma's witchcraft. If there was more.

The only catch was that I couldn't simply just go in and ask my dear ol' Pa if Ma had any more witchcraft lying around that he'd be willing to part with. I wasn't exactly excited to see Pa and knew he surely wasn't in any rush to see me either. And Pa, as far as I knew, had no knowledge of Ma's dabble in the craft. In the same way as if a friend confided in you about a crime they just committed, you would pretty well know not to blab about it to anyone and everyone.

We made our way onto the farm from the back of the property. Winter had begun in the south. The fields were far too bare to hide us from plain sight. Instead, we stayed behind the tree line around the edge of the property for as long as we could. Then we transitioned to a sprint between hay bales. We ducked behind cows and horses and squatted behind stray wheelbarrows. The farm animals had plenty to say about that. They squealed and bucked at the sight of us.

"Sh. It's just me." I rubbed my callused hands over the stomach of Pa's oldest mares. The horse neighed as if to let me know she wasn't pleased with being startled and went back to eating her pile of hay.

"Remind me again why we can't go knock on the door like civilized visitors." Henry kicked his shoes against the red dirt around us to get off the dung he'd stepped in while sprinting from one hiding spot to the next.

"Pa and I didn't exactly leave off on good terms." I gestured for him to follow me as I darted closer to the house and then ducked behind the wagon out front.

Henry followed closely behind me. "Surely, you can talk to him—"

"No. Trust me, I cannot."

As I peeked around the edge of the wagon, I tried to get a clear look at the house. There was no movement inside, but I knew he had to be in there. His wagon was out front and his boots rested by the front door.

Henry crouched behind me. He looked around as if here to take in the scenery instead of breaking and entering.

"I don't see any movement inside. Come on." Henry followed as I dashed across the yard and to the side of the house. We crouched under a small window. The same window where I had listened to my parents argue. The same window I'd heard Pa tell my ma that she would have the baby in her stomach whether it would kill her or not. The same window under which I had decided to take matters into my own hands.

"Are you okay?" Henry's voice pulled me from the past.

"I'm fine." I shook the thoughts from my head. "Still feeling the effects of captivity, I suppose."

"You should've stayed at Alice's and rested."

I snorted. "Let's just get this over with."

I poked my head over the ledge of the window and peered inside. The bedchamber was empty. I slowly lifted the window, careful not to push it too hard or too fast lest it creak and give us away.

"I'll go in and search through my ma's things. You stay here and watch for any sign of movement," I instructed Henry as the window slid to its highest point.

I climbed into the opening without giving him time to respond or protest.

With my feet planted firmly on the floor in my folk's bedchamber, I looked around. This used to be theirs, now it only housed Pa and the haunting memories of what could have been.

Ma and Pa's bed was plain. Iron bed posts surrounded a lumpy mattress. At the end of the bed lay a large wooden trunk. A chest of drawers sat beside it. Surely Pa kept her things. Or, at least, I hoped he had felt some semblance of sentimentality.

I sprinted to the chest of drawers first and yanked open the top drawer, cringing at the sight of men's undergarments and held my breath as I sifted through them. The second drawer down was the same. Men's clothing, nothing more.

Surely Pa had *something* left of Ma.

I jerked open the third and final drawer. *Thank the Lord.* Ma's clothes. I dug through the delicate fabrics that Ma had tirelessly sewn by hand. All that time and sweat only to be shoved in a drawer to collect dust.

Even with the sentimentality of the clothes, nothing else was there. Though, I couldn't stop myself from pausing my frantic search to lift a lace-edged dress to my nose. I breathed in the scent.

Honey. Lavender. Rose.

Ma's perfume.

Tears stung the back of my eyes. It had been so long since I'd smelled the scent. It took all of my willpower to tuck the dress back into the drawer and close it. As if closing the door to the things that could have been.

But I wasn't here to reminisce. I was here on a mission.

I spun around and raced over to the trunk. The old hinges let out a loud squeal.

My heart skipped a beat.

Footsteps approached the room.

I spun. "He heard me!"

Henry's eyes widened. He jumped up. "I'll distract him."

Before I could respond, he'd disappeared from the square of light. I rolled under the bed and held my breath as the footsteps pounded louder the closer they got to the bedchamber. They were a few feet from the room. I waited for it to open, for Pa to find me here and beat me senseless, maybe even enough to make me wish I was back in that horrible cell.

Suddenly, a knock sounded through the house from the front door and the footsteps retreated away from the bedchamber.

Pa grumbled all the way to the door.

"Hello there, sir!" Henry's voice was nonchalant but loud.

"Can I help you?" Pa asked, clearly not enthused to have company.

Henry talked cheerily. I smiled at how quickly and brilliantly he made up such complete horse manure. A true man of the south no doubt. I scrambled out from underneath the bed and off the dust-covered floor. My foot caught on a rip in the fabric of the underbelly of the mattress.

"Crumby old thing," I started to curse, but as I pulled my foot from the hole, something else came out with it.

"Well I'll be damned." I muttered to myself as I swept up the contents that fell from the secret spot. "Well. I'll. Be. Damned." I said again, this time out of complete and utter amazement.

I had somehow managed to stumble right into Ma's treasure trove of journals. Dozens and dozens of handwritten pages.

I was so enamored with what I had found, I hadn't even bothered to dust myself off as I got up from the floor. I wasn't paying attention to how close I was to the open trunk. Hadn't noticed that my elbow was about to bump the lid until—BANG! The lid slammed down on the trunk so hard the sound reverberated through the floor and sent vibrations into my feet and up my legs.

"What the hell?" Pa's voice echoed. His footsteps pounded through the house faster than before.

Henry came behind him and tried to keep his attention, with no luck. Pa yanked open the door before I could swing one leg over the ledge of the window, corset stuffed with Ma's journals and papers. This corset did have some perks.

"Why you little bitch!" Pa raged. He stormed into the room and grabbed my ankle just as I dove head first to the ground below.

"Unhand her, sir!" Henry yelled from behind him. He made a grab for Pa.

Pa spun, letting go of me, and punched Henry. I ran toward the fields, then I turned back and yelled, "Henry, run!"

Henry sprinted, or the best he could with a prosthetic leg, from the front door moments later. Blood dripped from his nose. A ring of red and deep purple started to bloom around his eye. Pa tried to chase after him but was at just as much of a disadvantage with his limp and stopped at the porch.

Henry took my hand. We ran—or hobbled.

Pa yelled behind us, "You'll regret being with her! She'll kill ya! She'll kill ya just like she did the last one!"

His words rang through the farm even as we made it to the edge of the fields and back into the woods. Far enough away that we no longer worried Pa would follow us, we stopped, slumping against tree trunks.

"Thank you," I panted between ragged breaths, "for saving me."

"Of course. Always." Henry slumped over. His hands rested on his knees and his head bowed. Then he looked up at me. "What your father said back there, about the last one—"

"I didn't mean to." I blurted out.

Henry straightened. "I never said you did. You don't have to tell—"

"I was Ma's only successful pregnancy. Each one she had after me was a miscarriage and they only got worse. But Pa wanted a son, wanted a son so bad he didn't care what it cost him. Or her. When she got pregnant the last time, it wasn't looking too good, but Pa was going to make her go through with it anyway. I'd heard of a mill girl that made tinctures to . . . take care of such situations."

Henry remained silent. He listened intently as he slid down a tree trunk and sat on the moss-covered ground.

"I snuck off to where I had arranged a secret meeting. I traded Ma's brooch for a tincture. "I hid it inside my bodice and managed to get back just as Reece had. I didn't notice the tincture had started to come out, or that Reece had seen it.

"When we returned to the farm, I went to find Ma and I thought Reece went to work on his chores. I didn't know Reece was off telling my pa what I'd done. I didn't hear Pa's heavy footsteps until it was too late. I should've gotten Ma to drink it right away, as soon as I'd seen her. I should've hidden my correspondence with the girl who made the remedy. Burned all of it."

Tears stung my eyes. I wiped them away with the back of my hand.

"You were so brave for helping your mother like that." Henry said.

I held up my hand to stop him. "I didn't help anyone. Pa threw the tincture into the fire. Reece claimed he'd done it all because he loved me and wanted to protect me. He said he would keep doing what needed to be done to protect me.

"I followed him that night. I trailed him until he met up with other men, until they went like a mob to the same dark alley I'd been at only a couple of hours prior. They were after the girl who had made the tincture, wanted to stop her from *playing God*.

"By the time I gathered up The Spirit, The Sacrifice, and The Superstition, they had already begun attacking her. So much rage filled my spirit and strengthened my craft, that when it took effect, it did more than I intended. I only meant to knock them out, even Reece, but instead, I sent them into a much deeper slumber."

Henry stayed silent. A flock of buzzards cawed overhead and dove somewhere into the mass of woods around us. They no doubt approached their next decomposing meal.

"I killed them. Just like that." I snapped my fingers. "Pa threw me in the cellar after that, locked me in there for days. I thought I would die there, and maybe I should've for what I had done."

"No. You tried to save your mother and that girl . . ." Henry's voice was all hard edges and cracked surfaces. "That girl was . . . is . . . my sister."

I sucked in a breath so hard I nearly choked on it. "What?"

My brain struggled to process this new information, maybe it was still muddled from food deprivation or maybe it was just too shocking.

"That mill girl you met with, the one that you tried to save. That was my little sister. Maggie."

"I . . . I'm so . . ." I couldn't take this. Not only had I failed my mother and that little girl, I had failed Henry, too. Sobs racked my body as I went limp and fell to the ground.

Henry sprang to my side. "You did the right thing, Lucille. You tried to help when no one else would have."

"But I failed. What if I fail again? What if we can't stop Mr. Edmonton? What if I fail all of the women?" Tears burned in my eyes and bile rose like lava in my throat, like the searing pain of the medal being shoved down it only a few days prior. The memory of it nearly made me gag.

"You won't." Henry said, then added with finality. "*We* won't."

Chapter Forty-Five

Catherine

Never leave a rocking chair rocking while empty lest you invite ghosts of the past to linger.

The worn pages scattered across the table as Lucille dumped them from her pockets and her corset. She'd arrived moments before and read through the handwritten pages from her daddy's farm.

"From what I've read of my ma's writing, we need a mirror that belongs to the person whom we're trying to summon, a hefty sacrifice, some candles, and something to make the spirit stick to this realm long enough for them to help us stop Mr. Edmonton." Lucille sifted through the pages.

"We have plenty of candles to use." Alice offered from her seat at the table.

"Surely we each have a mirror of someone we'd summon." Victoria said.

Lucille glanced at me. "You got any more of that hair goop you tried to put on my head?"

I started to nod, but stopped, and frowned. "Well I don't, but my mama does."

"Can you get more from her?"

"I suppose so." I didn't bother explaining that mama and I hadn't exactly left off on the best foot. "Alice, will you come with me?"

I held my breath, hoped she would see this for the change of heart that it was. The choice I should've made from the start.

Alice nodded.

Surprise rolled through me in equal parts excitement and guilt. We hadn't talked since we'd arrived at her doorstep. She'd avoided my gaze, hadn't looked at me once.

As we left Alice's neighborhood, I searched for something to say, something large enough to hold the apology I owed her.

Alice beat me to it. "Taking me to your family's estate was unthinkable, but coming to my family's home isn't?"

"It wasn't my choice to come." I winced at how that had come out, and sidestepped a pair of trousers that hung from a clothesline, momentarily losing sight of Alice.

"Oh, I see. Coming here to my family home is just as unthinkable?"

I could tell by the high pitch of her voice she was upset. "It's not like that," I said.

Alice spun as we reached the outskirts of the neighborhood and the road into town. "Not like that? It seems to me that is exactly what it's like. Please do tell me what it's like then." Her eyes were glassy with tears despite her voice being steady and strong.

"I . . ." I struggled to come up with the right words to express myself, to express the feelings I had for her and the deep fear that clutched my chest at the thought of losing her. "I'm scared."

Alice let out a dry laugh. "We're all scared. My sister is scared every time she walks alone at dusk. My mother is scared when a white man lingers too long at her stall. Fear is not rare, Catherine. You're not the first to be scared, or the last, but you know what matters most about being scared?"

I shook my head, though I wasn't quite sure she really needed a response.

"It's what you do with that fear that matters." Alice took a step toward me and lifted my chin, not gently, firmly. "Do it scared. Do it frightened. Do it worried. But do it anyway, no matter how you're feeling. That's what bravery is."

She looked into my eyes a moment longer and then spun and kept walking.

I followed.

I couldn't believe I was going back to the place that I had gotten chastised, hit, and cast out. Like a sinner exiled from the church. How fitting it was for me to go crawling back, a beggar brought to my knees.

The sight of the house on its sprawling land, a porch wrapped around its sides, and rocking chairs at its entrance, only days ago would've brought me great comfort. Solace even. But now—now they meant ownership. They meant labor I had never performed. They meant names I did not know.

My heart ached and burned in my chest. The familiar creak of each porch step under my feet brought a feverish heat upon my skin. My fingers and toes tingled.

I shouldn't be here. We shouldn't have come.

I sucked in a breath and spun around. I nearly ran into Alice's chest. She caught my shoulders, not to soothe, but to steady.

"I can't do this." My breath came out in short, sporadic spurts.

Alice's thumb rubbed circles against my shoulders as she looked into my eyes. "Yes. You can." She turned me back toward the door. "Now knock." *Do it scared. Do it anyway. Do it scared. Do it anyway.*

I repeated the words over in my head as I traversed the rest of the porch steps and the entryway. I continued to repeat the words as I raised my hand to the door. It hung there in the dead space. One decision, one move away from not being able to go back. Not being able to hide.

Do it scared. Do it anyway.

As if it made the decision on its own, I watched in horror as my hand rapped three times against the large wooden door. The knock rang out around us and echoed through the house—too loud, too final.

My hand hung there, frozen. Behind it, the house held its breath. And so did I.

For a moment, nothing happened, only silence. The next, I wished for the silence back. Footsteps descended the stairwell and crossed the foyer. Latches unlocked on the other side of the door. It swung open.

Mama.

At first, she didn't look like my mother. Just a woman in a doorway. Then her eyes found mine, and I was a child all over again. I was simultaneously relieved and terrified it was her and not Daddy.

She sucked in a sharp breath at the sight of me. And my guest.

"Mama. I . . ." My words stalled. What was I supposed to say to her? Did I need to apologize? Should I demand she apologize to me?

Her lips pursed. "You look terrible." She said finally.

The words landed harder than they should've. Not because of their cruelty. But because of their familiarity.

I stared at her. A laugh escaped my lips. Of course, that would be the first thing she said.

"Nice to see you too, Mama." My words had a bitter edge. An edge I had never had the courage to have when talking to Mama before. But everything was different now. Including me.

Mama's gaze flicked again to Alice. Calculating, not welcoming. She finally jerked her head back. "Get inside." She gestured us in with an annoyed wave. "You should be happy your father isn't home. He has been in a particularly bad . . . state since you left."

"I didn't leave. Y'all kicked me out." I held my chin up. I knew the hint of a bruise still lingered on my cheek.

"Well, if you came here for an apology, you'll be disappointed." Mama scanned over me, and then Alice, again, but didn't bother to introduce herself or ask for an introduction.

The foyer looked different. This house had always run like clockwork. Now it sagged in on itself. At first, I couldn't quite put my finger on why, other than maybe my feeling for it, but then it came to me. The space was unkept. Dust had begun to collect on the stair banisters, the carpets weren't scrubbed, the potted plants were dead, candle wax dripped on the floors and down the walls.

"What happened to Natalie?" My heart leapt in my throat.

Mama huffed and waved a hand in the air. "That daft girl quit the day after you . . ." She looked at my cheek and down at the floor. ". . . left."

Alice's posture shifted beside me. She noticed it too.

"I didn't leave," I repeated, my teeth grinding together. "You kicked me out."

"And you deserved it," Mama snapped.

My fingers curled at my sides. For a moment, I was back to that night, standing there vulnerable. Heat still on my cheek, and the crack of Daddy's hand still echoing through the halls. The world narrowed to survival and realization that family didn't mean loyalty.

"Parading radical ideas. Bringing shame." Mama continued. Her gaze flicked again to Alice. "And guests."

Alice did not lower her eyes. I stepped between them, protecting her. My heart pounded. "Mama, I need—"

"I knew it!" Mama snapped. "You only came back to get something from us. Your father was right—"

"Oh, please, Mama! Don't you ever get tired of living under his shadow? Letting him control—"

"You think I *like* living this way?" Her voice was so loud and shrill it echoed through the large, empty house.

I stared at her. She looked older than I remembered her being a few days ago. Strands of graying hair were out of place and she still had her night robe tied around her small waist though it was already midday.

"Then why?" I whispered.

"Why do you think?" Mama laughed. "Do you think you and your sisters would've had the life you had if I hadn't stayed with your father? Do you think y'all would have gotten the best education, the finest clothes, the freshest food? The safety?"

Safety.

The word rang differently now with Alice standing beside me.

Mama continued to laugh the saddest laugh I'd ever heard. "You think that bruise on your cheek is the only one your father has ever left on a woman?"

The room tilted. I searched her face for something, anything to make it less true. I didn't find it.

Mama looked away. "It was all for you and your sisters. It always has been."

"Come with us." The words escaped past my lips before I could stop them.

Alice's hand tightened on my sleeve, not stopping me, but grounding me.

"I can't." Mama's lip quivered, but she kept her chin held high.

"But—"

Mama raised her feeble hand to stop my protests. "Someone has to stay here. Someone has to keep him from going after y'all. Men like your father don't go quietly."

Men like your father. The words were deliberate.

Alice's gaze shifted toward the hallway, toward the unseen rooms. The portrait of Daddy, and all the wealthy white men who had come before him.

A sharp stinging pain shot through my heart and sunk like lead to the bottom of my stomach. Tears stung the backs of my eyes. Bile rose in my throat.

"Mama, I'm . . . I'm so—"

Her thin arms wrapped around me before I could finish my apology. She squeezed, tight. And then dropped her arms and turned away with a sniff. "If I give you what you need, promise me you'll never come back here."

Alice spoke before I could. "She shouldn't have to trade herself for safety."

Mama stiffened. "No," she replied. "But that is how this world works."

"For now," Alice said.

The two women held each other's gaze. Not enemies. Not allies. Just women who understood the cost of men like my father.

"Promise me." Mama repeated.

I sniffled and wiped a tear from my cheek. I looked at Alice. She didn't instruct me. She stood there, present, equal, waiting for me to make my own choice, because she knew the cost of not having one.

The house loomed behind her, heavy and watching. I could feel it, the old version of me that lived here, the version that obeyed, pulling me back in.

Beside me, Alice waited. Not pulling or pushing. Letting me make this choice.

Do it scared. Do it anyway.

"I . . . I promise." My voice broke around the words. It echoed the feeling of my heart breaking apart in my chest.

After Mama gave us what we needed, we stepped back out onto the porch. The air felt different. Not lighter. Just clearer.

I grew up in that house. But I had never truly seen it. Beside me, Alice descended the steps without hesitation. She did not look back.

Neither did I.

Chapter Forty-Six

Victoria

Gazing into a mirror by candlelight will show you ghosts.

The sun came up late, the latest it would come up all year. It seemed fitting that we could die today.

Though exhaustion weighed my limbs down, I was glad we kept busy. Even in my thoughts, Mr. Edmonton's name made my stomach churn and my chest tighten. The all-too-familiar hole left behind from losing someone you cared for was enough on its own, but when paired with betrayal, it turned into a chasm so wide one could easily lose themself in it.

We traveled through tunnels, the ones left over from when enslaved people made a run for freedom before Alabama surrendered to the Union. The tunnels were endless caves. They enveloped us in dark, deep earth. Only our lanterns lit our paths, but even that seemed to get swallowed into the black nothingness that lay before us. So much dirt around us left little air to breathe, and even that was thick and heady, the scent wild and untamed, less oxygen and more musk. This must've been what it's like to be buried. Surrounded by darkness and ground. No sunlight. No fresh air.

By the time we reached the surface again, my skin was damp with sweat despite the chill in the air and my heartbeat drummed in my ears. I greeted the sun like an old lover—with yearning and desire, ready to grovel at their knees and plant kisses on their feet.

Our breath mingled with the fog as we crept closer to the center of town just as Prim, Danielle, and I had the night before. The sun crawled higher in the morning sky toward a blanket of clouds. The shortest day of the year would also be the coldest thus far, especially with the unrelenting humidity making the air damp with icicles. However, one could never tell when the heat would show back up again in the late recesses of the day, like an unwelcome visitor who never knew when to say goodbye.

A latch clicked, and a shop door creaked open to our left. The shopkeeper stepped out onto his front porch and gasped. I readied myself to run. The small, gangly man must have recognized one of us despite the witchcraft that disguised us. We were wanted, after all. It wasn't unlikely that wanted posters hung all around town with our faces sketched on them. Henry pointed to the sky before I could warn the others.

"What is that?" His breath clouded in front of him.

Above the tall buildings, a stream of dark, almost black, smoke rose into the sky.

"It's coming from the town square," Alice said.

The acrid smell of smoke and something burnt hit my nose. I hoped it didn't have anything to do with what we had done to the statue.

"We should hurry," Catherine advised.

Even with the mirage of disguises crafted onto us, we blended in with the crowd of distracted workers, market goers, and businessmen as they began their morning routines. They were all too busy staring at the same thing we were.

The sky filled with black smoke by the time we reached the town square. Its odor burned my eyes and scorched my throat. I blinked away tears and tried to see what was on fire. It wasn't the statue, though plenty of people gathered around it, some with anger written on their faces, some with sorrow. No, the pile that burned was to the far left of the statue, on the other side of the clearing, in middle of all the stores and businesses. They looked almost like bricks at first, stacked one on top of the other, but as my vision cleared, white bits fluttering through the air caught my attention.

Newspapers.

Books.

Papers. Hundreds of them.

Even the bold title, *The Revolution,* stood out among the rest. There were books discussing women's rights and freedoms. I recognized the spines of *Little Women, On the Subjection of Women,* and even copies of Emily Dickinson's poetry floating in the debris.

Why would anyone burn these books?

As quickly as I thought it, my answer came.

Thomas shouted to the crowd that gathered around the square, in part because of the statue we'd covered in words, and because of the scene he was creating. His eyes were bloodshot and his clothes were disheveled as if he, too, hadn't slept since the last time we saw him.

"Gentlemen, take back your households! Take back your families! Take back your *pride*!" Spit flew from his mouth and drooled down his chin. "Don't let the Devil enter your home and take what is yours! You, and only you, are the head of your household! If you let your wives read this . . ." he gestured to the disintegrating pile, ". . . this trash, the Devil will trick them into the sins of this world just as he once tricked Eve!"

The crowd murmured.

"Come, my brothers, and throw away the works of the Devil!" Thomas continued his manic chant.

"Surely, no one is stupid enough to—"

Before Lucille could finish saying the words, a man stepped forward from the crowd and threw a handful of books into the fire.

And then another man.

And another.

On the Equality of the Sexes flew through the air along with *The Scarlet Letter, The Responsibilities of Women, The Destructive Male,* and many other titles I recognized. All books I'd read. All books I'd adored.

"Do you see him?" Catherine asked.

Among the crowd, two other familiar faces watched. Headmaster Sullivan and Reverend Ward didn't participate or jeer, but they watched with upturned grins.

Then I saw Mr. Edmonton. My throat constricted with a cry I wouldn't let escape.

"There." I pointed to the corner of the square where Mr. Edmonton crouched. No one seemed to notice his odd behavior. They were too distracted by the commotion Thomas made, and by the statue covered in our own handiwork. I wondered if the two of them had planned this or if it was just a happy coincidence.

"What's he doing?" Lucille squinted.

It looked as if Mr. Edmonton was merely bent over to tie his shoe, but as I looked closer, he drew symbols on the ground with dark red ink. No. Not ink. Blood. He painted with blood he poured from a canister. My stomach soured at the thought of the poor animals he must've killed to get it.

After he drew a symbol on the ground, he stepped to the side and repeated his action. I looked around the rest of the large fire's perimeter and saw he'd already painted around half of it.

"He's making a circle around the fire," I said. "We'd better get moving before he completes it."

Everyone around me nodded and moved. Just like we'd planned, we all spread out and stood in nearly a complete circle around the town square, though we left a few feet between each other so as not to look too suspicious.

The two other women I now called friends and the others we'd gathered throughout the night were all there: Lucille, Catherine, Alice, Henry, Chrissy, Susan, Natalie, Prim, Danielle, Beth, all the other women from the mills. We all looked at one another. Lucille signed and we all repeated it, down the line.

It was time. We had one shot. We could not make any mistakes.

Underneath my petticoats, I grasped the kitchen knife, one of several Alice had passed out to everyone. I touched the metal blade to the flesh of my palm. I stretched my fingers wide and dug the sharp tip into the taut skin, then dragged it across. My breath caught at the burning trail of pain it left behind. My comrades winced and then nodded their confirmation that they, too, had made The Sacrifice.

Lucille and Catherine passed out small candles until we all held one in our bloody palms. I held Annie's mirror. The others had mirrors of their own, ones from their mothers, sisters, or grandmothers. Lucille lit her candle using a small match and then used her flame to spark Catherine's candle, who used hers to start mine. We each turned to the women nearest us and lit their candles until all our faces glowed in the light. Then we chanted the words of an old Southern superstition:

Gazing into a mirror by candlelight will show you ghosts.

Draw a large portion of blood while gazing into a loved one's mirror by candlelight to summon a ghost. Mix blood with a sticky substance to make the spirit stick in this realm.

The Spirit. The Sacrifice. The Superstition.

We chanted over and over again. We willed the craft to work. Willed them to show up.

A strange wind battered the square. Loose hats flew into the air and the flames of the fire whipped furiously. It danced a wicked dance. Embers and small remnants of printed pages flew toward the clouds and further darkened the sky. Our candle flames burned bright blue.

"I think it's working!" Lucille's voice carried on the wind.

Even with the change in the atmosphere, everyone in the square, so distracted by the riot, didn't notice their missing hats or hair whipping around. Almost as if the ferocity of the wind and the darkened sky fueled them more, people began to yell. Profanities flew through the air just as often as books.

The flames suddenly grew to an alarming height when Mr. Edmonton finished his circle of blood-soaked symbols. Fire ripped into the air and grew taller and wider in every direction. I didn't let that stop me, and continued to chant the words of The Superstition as I watched Mr. Edmonton stare up at the growing flames with a cruel smile.

The flames accelerated their dancing and gyrating. The movement became more pronounced. It seemed to reach a peak in its wild frolic and took on another form. It was still flames and fire, yes, but the flames formed a torso, and the torso sprouted arms, and the body grew a head. It was a flaming *being* that would seem almost angelic if it weren't utterly terrifying. Eyes like two small infernos looked around the square. Smoke rose from its blazing head like black hair. A gape in its burning face opened and formed a raging mouth. Whatever Mr. Edmonton had summoned the fire creature to say sputtered out on its flaming tongue as the beast watched the angry, jeering crowd around it, as if captivated by the chaos.

The figure in the flames closed its mouth. And Mr. Edmonton's jaw dropped. He yanked tattered papers from his pockets and frantically flipped through them.

Gasps sounded from others who finally came out of their hate-fueled trance long enough to notice what had become of the fire. Mr. Edmonton's face fell, and his eyes grew wide.

"What's happening?" Catherine yelled over the chaos that broke out across the town square.

"Mr. Edmonton lost control!" I yelled, putting together his shocked look and frantic page flipping.

"We have to stop it!" Lucille yelled.

"How?" Catherine asked.

The others' voices drowned out in my ringing ears. The sounds of disarray around us made my hearing even more inadequate.

There was no time for an answer anyway. Thomas, no longer playing the part of a righteous prophet, ran from the flame. Its fiery arms reached out and dragged him back.

"Father! Help me!" He yelled out to an older man who stood to the edge of the square and had been jeering along with Thomas earlier.

The man didn't move. Only watched as Thomas continued to be dragged backward until he disappeared into the fire entirely. His sickening, high-pitched screams could be heard long after the flames engulfed his body.

Everyone watched, transfixed, and then, as his body was engulfed, they ran. The square became more chaotic than ever. In their panic and desire to escape, many from the crowd ran into us. They broke any chants of the craft that we hadn't been able to finish.

The fire monster lashed out again and caught awnings of shops and people on fire. More black smoke filled the air than oxygen. It made it hard to see and even harder to breathe. At this rate, it would burn the whole town to the ground.

I fought the urge to run as I tried to find everyone in the commotion. Henry had Lucille in his arms. He kept her from getting hit by flying debris or panicked people. Alice helped Catherine up off the ground. Blood dripped not only from Catherine's palm but from a new cut on her forehead. They weren't alone. They had people to take care of them.

Mr. Edmonton's blood-curdling scream pierced the air. A flaming hand wrapped around his ankle and dragged him along the ground. His fate looked to be the same as Thomas's.

The flaming creature lifted him into the air and whipped his body around as if he weighed nothing. His hand was frail and wet with sweat, still wrapped with a bloody gauze for the wound I had inflicted only a couple of days prior, but as he came whizzing past me, he latched on to me. I tried to pull away, tried to get loose, before I could so much as scream, my breath whooshed out of me as he and the fire beast yanked me forward, dragging me across the ground, playing a gruesome game of tug-of-war. I anchored my feet into the ground and pulled with all my might. A guttural scream escaped from deep within me.

But the flaming hands returned with a vengeance. Two hands of fire wrapped around Mr. Edmonton's ankles this time. They pulled with more force than I could handle. We both screamed. My hands turned white around his. The fire dragged us toward its molten core.

At least my friends are safe.

I accepted what was to come as the flames scorched my skin.

Chapter Forty-Seven
Lucille

Evil spirits cannot harm a person standing within the barrier of a tightly wound circle.

"I've got you!" Henry wrapped his arms around me and shielded me from stampeding bodies.

He always protected me. Warmth spread in me despite our situation. But he was a man. Just like Pa. Just like Reece. Just like Thomas, and Headmaster Sullivan, and Mr. Edmonton. He would turn on me, too. I couldn't rely on him or anyone else.

With blood pounding in my ears, I shoved his arms away. "I don't need you to get me. I am perfectly capable of defending myself!"

"I don't doubt your capabilities." A tinge of humor coated his voice despite everything.

"Then why do you keep acting like it?" I yelled.

"Why can't you accept that I care about you? Why can't you trust me?" All humor gone.

"I—" A sharp, piercing scream cut me off. A scream that I could distinguish over all the others.

My gaze snapped to the center of the town square.

I gasped. "Victoria!"

Henry's eyes followed mine and his jaw dropped. In the middle of the town square, the wild flames dragged Mr. Edmonton and Victoria toward them. Flames engulfed his ankle, and his hands held her. He pulled her along with him into the fiery pit.

My breath caught in my throat and my stomach dropped so low I thought it might fall to the ground completely.

No!

I sprinted forward as I pushed through the crowd.

"Keep holding on!" I screamed. "Don't let go! I'm coming!"

I leaped forward and landed only a few feet from her outstretched hand. She grasped around her for anything to hold on to. Gravel dug into my elbows as I crawled forward. Though it only took seconds, it seemed like an eternity by the time I grabbed her hand and pulled with all my might. Her sweaty palm made it even harder to keep my grip locked around hers. I moved my hands up to her forearms.

"I've got you!" I yelled, though my feet continued to slide forward under the powerful pull of Mr. Edmonton. "Try to push him off of you!"

A grunt and another yell escaped my lips. I pulled harder. My muscles strained and cramped. Beads of sweat collected on my ash-covered forehead. They dripped down my face and burned my eyes, leaving an aftertaste of salt and soot in my mouth.

Victoria looked from me to the flames, now only mere feet from us, and then back at me with desperation. I expected her to beg me to pull harder, but instead, she cried, "Let go, or you'll die too!"

"No! I'm not letting you die!" I released her forearm with one hand and shoveled gravel underneath me, anything to try and stop us from reaching the fire.

"Grab my hand!" Henry's voice called from behind me. His hand appeared in my peripheral vision. "Let me help you!"

I looked at the fire, Victoria's desperate face, and Henry's outstretched hand. I reached out and grabbed him, grateful for the dirt and ash on my own hand to soak up the sweat.

Henry pulled one arm and Victoria pulled the other. I felt like my body would tear in half by the time Henry's efforts started to pay off. He pulled us backward with our conjoined efforts. The fire monster roared and added another arm of fire around Mr. Edmonton, who had gone pale, but still held on tightly to Victoria.

"We need more help!" Henry cried, his voice strained.

"I'm here!" Catherine responded from behind Henry.

"Me too!" Alice chimed in behind her.

"We all are!" chorused Susan and the others.

They all joined their outstretched hands together to form a human chain. One bloody palm to another.

Screams and sounds of struggle came from the chain as we all worked together to pull against the inhuman strength of the flaming beast. The sky was dark, almost black, when a strange wind returned, stronger than before. Suddenly, as if our connected hands and mixed blood had been the key we'd been missing all along, glowing figures appeared around the town square.

"The witchcraft! It worked!" I eyed the ghostly figures in awe.

"It did more than work! There are hundreds!" Catherine's voice was a mix of awe and exhaustion.

Those who were still in the town square, whether on the ground, hidden under benches, or behind trees, gaped at the scene before them.

The ghosts were women from the past. They all moved toward us as they glided over the ground. They joined hands, just as we had, and united our human chain.

I recognized Annie's ghost from a picture Mr. Edmonton had shown to us. I saw her fly directly to her husband and Victoria, but she didn't grab hold of her husband, instead she grabbed Victoria.

Henry gasped from behind me. The spirit of a girl, the same girl I'd gotten the tincture for Mama from—Henry's sister—came forward and stood beside Victoria. As did Rebecca's ghost and many others.

A little girl—human, not ghost—stepped forward from where she'd hidden with her mother, who urged her to get back, but the girl seemed mesmerized.

"That's Grandma!" She pointed to a ghostly woman. "We have to help Grandma, Mama!"

She ran to her grandmother's side and held the ghostly hand before her mother could stop her. Then her mother stepped forward as well. She stood beside the little girl. Many others followed suit. They joined with their ghostly loved ones around the square.

A nearly translucent hand slid onto my shoulder. I sucked in a breath. "Ma?" I asked in both awe and shock. My hand slipped, but I quickly regained my grip and pulled again.

"My Lulu. You've worked so hard." Ma said in a gentle voice, full of pride. "Let us help from here. You don't have to do it alone anymore. You never had to do it alone."

Ma wrapped her hands around mine and pulled.

Along with my ma and the other women from the past, people of all colors, shapes, and sizes joined together to stop the menacing fire-created monster. Our efforts were working. We pulled Victoria away from its grip of rage, hatred, and anger, away from the fire that tried to consume our hearts.

Mr. Edmonton escaped the fire beast's grip, too, and tipped over backward. His fall nearly caused a domino effect that knocked us all over. However, there was still the issue of the flaming beast. It only became more outraged by our escape.

"Chant with me," Ma yelled, her voice like a song on the wind. Not belonging to this Earth, but not meant to scare. "*Evil spirits cannot harm a person standing within the barrier of a tightly wound circle.*"

Annie and Ma chanted into the air. Their palms connected with Victoria's. They linked to each of us. Blood intermingled with blood. The chanting slowly spread and grew louder until it filled the entire town square and echoed into the sky.

The flaming beast raged, though it sounded as if its screams were in pain. It eyed each of us and threw a ball of fire straight for me. The heat came so fast I didn't have time to so much as blink. The thought of death barely entered my mind before the fireball stopped inches from my face and bounced away as if it hit an invisible wall right in front of me.

"It's working!" Victoria tried to shout. Her voice came out in a croak, damaged from screaming for so long.

The creature hissed and yelled and gurgled. We chanted louder. The earth shook from our words. Finally, the creature of fire imploded. Ash and remnants of burnt pages flew into the air.

Everyone stared, stunned. We watched the pages rain down from the sky. Then, our victory finally registering, we cheered. Emotion-filled cheers erupted in cries of happiness and sadness alike. That's the way with emotions—rarely ever only one thing or another.

We dropped hands and unlinked ourselves physically, though our souls would forever be linked. The actions of the past, present, and future were permanently interconnected.

People around the square gathered with their ghostly loved ones.

And then there was my ma. She drifted in front of me, solid enough that I could see the wrinkles beside her eyes and dimples on her cheeks. I could make out the small scar on her forearms from an accident on the farm, and crease lines in her forehead from years of worrying about me as I climbed up the tallest trees or caught snakes whose bites could kill. My ma. But she was translucent enough that I could see through her, see the crowd of people I had come to love. The people who were my family now, too.

"My Lulu." Ma's voice was a melody that hung in the air.

"Ma, I'm so sorry—"

Ma held up her ghostly hand and then rested it on one shoulder. Her other hand caressed my cheek.

"You have nothing to be sorry for." She smiled.

"But what happened with Pa and Reece. I didn't—"

Ma shook her head. "Lulu, it was not your fault then, and it is not your fault or burden to carry now. It was my life and my death. My burdens to carry, not yours. You have been holding on to them for far too long."

She moved her hands to either side of my cheeks. Her eyes shimmered. I had always thought my eyes were a dull gray like Pa's, but now, standing before Ma, they were her eyes. Her vibrant pools of sapphire.

"Let the burdens go, honey. Let them all go with me and live *your* life. Live your life full. Full of happiness." She looked over to where Henry talked to the ghost of his sister. "And full of love. Stop letting my burdens hold you back from all that life has to offer. All that is ahead of you."

Ma rubbed the pad of her thumb over my cheek, wet with tears I hadn't realized I had cried. "I will, Ma. I love you."

"I love you, my wild child. My Lulu." She leaned forward and kissed my cheek. "Now, go, and live your life."

Ma's words floated in the chilled air and then dispersed just as her spirit did. Her figure, as lanky and tall as mine, faded. I yanked my palm up, ready to slash into my flesh to make the spell last longer, but Ma shook her head.

"Let go, Lulu. Let go."

My hands fell to my sides. I watched Ma's spirit disperse into the frigid, humid air. The people who I'd grown close with these past several months slowly came into clearer view around me. One last phantom squeeze of my shoulders, and Ma was gone. But in her place were the people who had filled my life and my heart, who had patched up what remained of it, sewn up my broken trust, and stitched up my fear of betrayal. The people who saw all those broken bits and misplaced views, saw my darkest sides and my lowest moment, and didn't run. They didn't turn away. They saw it and they loved me anyway.

A smile spread across my face, making my cheeks lift into my eyes. I would live fully. Completely. With my friends. My family. My sisters. My love.

My joy quickly evaporated as Headmaster Sullivan and Reverend Ward approached. Victoria and Catherine must've seen them, too. They scurried over to my side, ready to stand with me no matter the consequences. I couldn't help but smile again even if these men were about to hurdle accusations at us or arrest us. They couldn't take what we had, not really.

Officers flanked them and stepped closer, producing handcuffs from their pockets.

"You can punish me if you want," I said, "but first . . ." I turned slightly toward the crowd, raising my voice for them to hear. "You'll have to explain why your laws protected no one. Why the university ignored harassment and even harm toward minority students. Why the mill girls worked until their lungs failed. Why women were silenced at every turn. And why the law has only ever served those already in power!"

Everyone was silent while I spoke. Now, whispers rippled through the square. Even Headmaster Sullivan's face paled as his eyebrows rose to his receding hairline. The remnants of the fire monster still smoldered behind us, smoke curling upward, a reminder of what happens when the system fails to protect the people it's supposed to serve.

Before the officers could respond, a sudden commotion erupted from the edge of the square. Papers fluttered like wild birds, and a familiar voice shouted, "Wait! Wait! I have something everyone should see!"

Penelope barreled forward, a bundle of yellowed documents clutched to her chest. I barely recognized her without Josephine's shadow falling over her. The last time I had seen her flashed in my mind: Her reluctance to leave the program and her resignation as she followed Josephine away. But here she was now.

She'd come back.

"I retrieved this from the Town Hall archives! Look!" She dumped them onto a nearby barrel, and everyone scrambled to inspect them. "It outlines a 'Disaster and Crisis Provision,' enacted decades ago, meant to allow temporary, extraordinary measures in cases where public safety, industry, or health were at risk. Conditions so severe that usual legal boundaries could be suspended temporarily."

My heart hammered in my chest as I scanned the documents. "This . . . this means," I whispered, my mind processing and voice trembling, "what we did to contain the fire, or expose the mill conditions, or defend the women's program, were legally justifiable, regardless of the means. We weren't breaking the law, we were responding to a crisis no one else would acknowledge or prevent."

Victoria stepped forward, addressing the crowd. "We didn't start the fire in the dormitory, nor did we start the fire here. That was Mr. Edmonton's doing. We only acted to prevent it, to protect the women and the girls of this town and beyond. And now, the law can recognize it as a crisis response, not a crime."

The crowd began to murmur. Heads began to nod as understanding dawned on them.

Headmaster Sullivan sputtered, "Well, crisis or not, the women's program has been canceled and will remain so under the council's guidelines. And the charges against you will—"

"Actually," Alice spoke as she scanned through the stack of pages Penelope had brought. "The Disaster and Crisis Provision isn't all that's here. There's the fourteenth amendment of 1868."

George and Derek, who'd been in the crowd jeering and cheering Thomas on, scoffed.

"How does *that* damn thing pertain to women at the university?" asked George, his nose scrunched.

"Well, if you look closely." Alice pointed at the paper for all to see. "It states that no state shall deny any person within its jurisdiction—"

"That amendment was ratified after the war to address freed *men*, not to dictate who educational institutions allow in!" Headmaster Sulliven exclaimed.

My heart sank.

George and Derek agreed, though I was certain they had never taken the time to read through these records, or any other, for that matter. Mr. Edmonton cheered in agreement, too, from where he still sat on the ground, too torn up from the fire beast he'd brought to life to get up.

Alice held up her hand to silence them, then kept reading. "The amendment does not say 'men.' It does not say 'certain' persons. It says *persons*. If women are subject to the law, then we are entitled to its protections. You cannot narrow its meaning simply because equality is *inconvenient* for you. " She looked up at the Headmaster, but said loudly enough for all to hear as she held the documents above her head. "You say the courts do not support this. The courts have been wrong before. They have upheld injustice before. That is not proof of righteousness, only of delay!"

She turned away from the headmaster, facing the people gathered around us, faces still covered in soot and shock.

"For decades, since Seneca Falls, women have demanded recognition as equal citizens. Not as a favor. Not as a temporary allowance, but as a right. If we're capable of studying elsewhere, then we are capable here. And if there is no difference in ability, then what remains is not law—" Her voice lowered an octave, the entire square went dead silent. "—It is exclusion."

One person from the crowd cheered in agreement. Then another. And another. Soon they erupted, no doubt still reeling and shocked from the events that'd occurred there that day. But more importantly, they could see that the system had failed, and we had filled that gap with what we had and did what we needed to in order to survive, just as they had when they'd run from the flaming beast minutes before.

Alice turned back to Headmaster Sullivan and lifted an eyebrow. "With these statutes," she said, "the charges against Lucille will be dropped as long as we no longer continue to use witchcraft unless wholly necessary for survival and the women's program made legally sanctioned and continued, not as a trial, but with *permanence*."

"Well, I would have to discuss all of this with the board . . ." Headmaster Sullivan rested his hands on his hips, his boisterous chest thrust forward.

The crowd, not just me, or the other sorority members, but everyone who had gathered, who had witnessed all that had happened there that day, who looked upon the burnt books and the word-covered statue, saw what could happen when tradition took precedence over growth, and could no longer deny seeing its affects just because they didn't affect *them*, started to protest, raising their fists to the sky, screaming out and chanting, not words of witchcraft, but words of demand.

"SAVE THE PROGRAM!" they chanted, over and over.

"SAVE THE PROGRAM!"

"SAVE THE PROGRAM!"

"SAVE THE PROGRAM!"

Reverend Ward leaned over and said something into the headmaster's ear. Headmaster Sullivan held up his hands.

"Alright! Alright!" He cleared his throat. The chants died down to whispers, but didn't stop. "I suppose I could convince the board to make the program a more . . . permanent endeavor."

A scream of bliss erupted from me just as it did from everyone else, loud and proud around the square.

We had only a moment to celebrate before a tall man stepped forward from the crowd holding up his hands to silence us, a notebook tucked under his arm and a look of sober authority in his eyes. His uniform marked him as a government official.

"I need to speak," he said, voice carrying over the murmurs. "I'm a safety inspector. I requested reports from the cotton mills months ago. They never arrived. I never saw the conditions for myself because the foreman never allowed a visit." He paused, glancing over to the bronze statue still etched with doctors' notes, firsthand accounts, incident reports, injuries, and even deaths, all meticulously crafted by Victoria, Prim, and Danielle.

He exhaled slowly, eyes glistening. "But now I see it. I've seen the wages, the hours, the brown lung statistics, the injuries, the negligence, the deaths. This . . . this cannot continue."

Victoria stepped forward, her fellow mill girls flanking her. "We tried to make them see it before, through reports and petitions, but no one listened. The system ignored us." Victoria's voice barely carried over it all, but the emotion could not be ignored, "How will *you* change anything?" The hope was so clearly evident, marked on her face like a lipstick print from a mother's kiss.

"With the evidence you've provided, I have the authority and the obligation to act. The workers' rights, their health, their safety, will be enforced." The inspector nodded, a tear rolling from his eyes, and pointed firmly toward the statue. "I will personally ensure the completion of immediate inspections. Safety regulations *will* be enforced. Any mill found in violation will be held accountable, and families affected by loss or injury will be compensated. No more hiding behind silence or bureaucracy. This stops *now.*"

The crowd erupted again, not for spectacle, but for justice finally catching up. For once, the system couldn't hide behind apathy or authority. I exhaled, letting the weight of months of struggle lift from my shoulders. Feeling freer than I had in years, maybe ever.

The fire monster, Mr. Edmonton, the corruption, the silencing, they hadn't won. We had. I felt something swell in my chest. It wasn't witchcraft that fixed this, not really. It was courage, persistence, and the willingness to expose injustice for everyone to see.

We did it. We were going to be okay.

Mr. Edmonton's face twisted in fury as the officers who had been posed to arrest me only moments before, now turned their attention to him. "What is this treachery? You can't—"

The lead officer raised his voice. "You've incited harm and threatened the townspeople with reckless intent. We're taking you." Chains rattled as his wrists were secured in handcuffs.

His blue eyes blazed with disbelief and rage. "You'll pay for this! I . . . I—"

"Not them," A ghostly voice emerged from the rest. The woman I recognized as Mr. Edmonton's wife, floated forward. She was almost entirely faded away, barely able to be seen as she said to her husband. "This is justice. You used fear and suppression to keep these women powerless. They acted to protect lives. You acted to destroy them. The universe sides with those who uphold empathy for humanity."

Mr. Edmonton's shoulders slumped as his wife's spirit faded away entirely, but he didn't argue. Chains rattled as he was led away, his protests echoing, meaningless now in the face of evidence, witnesses, and the collective action of the women he'd tried to oppress.

Henry came to my side. His eyes red-rimmed and glassy. He looked at Victoria. "I believe my sister would like to speak with you."

He smiled and nodded his head toward the spirit of the curly-headed girl. Victoria gasped and took off in a sprint. She nearly tackled the spirit in a hug if such a thing were possible.

Catherine took off too, running to Alice and embracing her.

"And then there were two." Henry wiped his hands on his already-filthy pants. He seemed to look anywhere but at me. I had been so unfair to him, taking anger from someone else's betrayals out on him when he had shown me nothing but love and kindness. And empowerment.

"I love you, too," I blurted. My cheeks heated. I had never said such a thing to a man, not even Reece.

Henry straightened. His wide eyes finally met mine. "What?"

"I love you, too, and I trust you. I want to keep loving you and trusting you, and . . ." Before I could blather out more words, his lips found mine. We tasted our salty tears of anguish and joy.

After a minute, Henry pulled back, his hands firmly planted on both sides of my face. "I love you. I love you, Lucille Rockwell." He kissed me again and then sprinkled kisses along my cheeks and forehead, not caring that I was covered in ash and dirt. "Please be mine, forever," he begged between kisses.

I pulled back and gazed into his eyes. "Is that a proposal?"

"Would you accept it if it were?" he asked, breathless. His eyes filled with hope.

I looked from one hazel eye to the other and took in the man before me. Ma's words echoed in my ears. I smiled. My cheeks ached from the repetitive movement, but it was a good ache. "Only if I can keep my last name."

"It's a deal!" Henry's face lit up. His smile matched mine. He enveloped my waist in his arms and picked me up. He spun me around in a wobbly circle. I laughed. Joy flooded through me. I leaned forward and planted another long kiss on his lips.

My heart was full.

Chapter Forty-Eight

Catherine

Yule logs ward off bad luck and prevent lightning from striking

Our dormitory lay in a skeletal, bone-like pile of broken bits and pieces. I'd looked upon its shattered bones with sadness and despair weeks before, but now, I saw it as it really was. The ashes of a phoenix. Its remains prepared themselves to birth a new generation.

A stronger generation.

"Now, that section over there," Headmaster Sullivan glanced over the architectural sketches and gestured to a portion of the ruins. "Will be the common room. And all the women's bedchambers will branch off from there."

"How large will each of the bedchambers be? And how many women will be housed in each one?" I got on my toes to try and peak over the headmaster's shoulders at the sketch.

"They will be quite large and will only house one woman each." The headmaster said. "Though they are large enough to fit two or three women; that would make more money for the uni—."

"No, one woman per room is perfect." I smiled and rested back on my heels.

"Wonderful. I'm so very glad it measures up to your standards, Miss Stanley." Headmaster Sullivan grumbled sarcastically and then walked around to the other side of the building to stop Lucille from digging through the rubble with her bare hands. Of course, he was only met with snarky comments and witty banter.

I turned to Alice, who had been listening as the headmaster and I went over the plans for the new building.

"What do you think?" I asked.

She looked from the ruins to the sky overhead. "It's a start," she said.

Not perfect. Not triumphant. A start.

I slipped my arms around her without thinking, pressing my face against her shoulder. She laughed softly and wrapped her arms around me. Her lavender scent enveloped me. I breathed in deeper, wanting it to fill me and envelop me like a cocoon.

Someone cleared their throat behind us. Alice gasped. I pulled away and turned to see my parents staring at us.

My parents. Here. At the university.

Nothing made sense for a moment. It was like two different versions of my life colliding. Their fine attire looked out of place beside the rubble- and dirt-covered remains of the collapsed building.

My arms dropped from Alice, but I didn't move from her side. Instead, my fingers tightened around Alice's hand.

"Daddy. Mama. What are you doing here?"

The memory of the last time I saw them together was still fresh in my mind, and the sting of my daddy's blow haunted my cheek.

Daddy stepped forward. He cleared his throat again. "We read in the paper and heard from others in town of what you did. The . . . heroics."

Heroics. As though courage were palatable only when it made good headlines.

He glanced at Alice, and then back at me. "And it seems," he continued carefully, "that your . . . friend was instrumental in saving lives."

I stared. Had I heard him correctly?

"We came," Mama said, stepping forward, "because the town is talking. And because we have had time to consider our conduct."

"We're not here to debate the past, though."

Not here to apologize, is what he meant. *Of course.*

"We're just here to . . ." Daddy's voice lacked its usual iron as he searched for what to say.

I spoke for him. "You're here because public opinion has shifted." And they want to stay on the right side of that opinion.

His jaw tightened, but he didn't deny it. "You're admired now," he said. "Respected. The paper spoke highly of you."

There it was. *Reputation*. That's what it had always been about.

Not transformation. Not remorse. Not acceptance.

Mama stepped forward. "We can't undo what's been done. But we won't oppose you again, or force you into a marriage . . . however respectable it may have been."

"And," Daddy added, clearly forcing himself, "your portion of the estate remains yours, should you wish to claim it."

The estate. Their land. Money drawn from generations of forced labor.

I felt Alice's fingers still in mine. "I won't take money earned from the suffering of others," I said.

"It's not so simple," Daddy muttered.

"It never was," Alice replied.

He studied her again, longer this time. As if trying to understand something he had never allowed himself to see clearly before.

"I'm staying," I said. "With her. With this work. Without your help or money."

A long silence stretched between us. Finally, Daddy nodded once. "We won't interfere."

It wasn't a blessing, or a celebration, but a withdrawal of force. Mama stepped closer and brushed soot from my sleeve. The gesture was automatic, almost maternal. For a second, I leaned into it.

"You look thinner," she murmured.

I jerked back, quickly remembering what that same hand had allowed. *Better,* I knew that's what she meant to say. Once, those words would have crushed me.

Now—"I'm freer," I replied.

For a brief, startling second, Mama's mouth twitched. My father cleared his throat. "If circumstances change," he said, "you may send word."

"I won't," I answered, remembering my promise to Mama.

He gave a single, tight nod.

They said their farewells and walked back to their carriage, arm-in-arm, as they swatted stray soot off of their coats and avoided stepping too close to any rubble that might dirty their attire.

Alice turned to me. "That wasn't approval, you know?" she said gently, squeezing my hand.

"I know."

"Are you disappointed?"

I considered it. "No," I said at last. "Because I didn't bend or break. I didn't back down."

She searched my face, ensuring I meant it. Then she smiled, dimples appearing like jewels on her cheeks. "You are becoming who you say you are," she said.

My chest warmed, pride swelling with each heartbeat. "Only because you refused to let me become comfortable instead."

She squeezed my hand.

The ruins stood around us. All splintered beams, shattered glass, exposed foundation. A start. Not a phoenix yet. But the fire had revealed what was rotten. And what might be rebuilt differently. Better.

"Come," Alice said, wrapping an arm around my waist. "We still have work to do."

And this time, when I followed her, it was not toward approval. It was toward transformation. It was forward.

Epilogue

Victoria

Rainbows are a sign of good luck and good fortune to all who see them.

Two Years Later

"Alright, ladies, time to pick your rooms!" I called, as I led the large group of women, some from mills and factories, others from high-cotton life, into the newly built dormitories, the largest building on campus, second only to the library.

I watched them rush forward, excitement in their voices as they ducked their heads into each room. They squealed about how spacious each one was and argued over which would be whose.

"Now, don't get too feisty. There's plenty of space for everyone. You know, when I first came here, we lived in rooms made of tiny offices." Catherine said for what must've been the hundredth time since the women arrived this morning. Alice's laugh sounded along with it.

I turned to look out the open door and into the university courtyard, where a rainbow peaked through dissipating clouds. A small sapling grew at the edge, right off the path. Not yet big enough to produce apples, but I knew one day it would. Just as I knew Lucille and Henry weren't here for a good reason, it didn't stop me from missing Lucille. I imagined all the things she would tell this group of women about our own adventures here. I could only imagine the mischief she was causing as she and Henry made their way around the state and helped open women's programs at other universities. At least he was by her side to keep her out of too much trouble, or to bail her out of the trouble she did get into.

I hadn't settled down with someone as Lucille and Catherine had, but I felt more loved and connected to people than ever. I'd built more friendships and sisterhoods in the past several semesters as the Women's Program Coordinator, and now in the medical program where I could put my tincture-mixing skills to good use, than I had my whole life.

I looked back on the decisions I made to get me here, and though there were plenty of heartaches and disappointments, I couldn't bring myself to regret a single one. Without them, I wouldn't have the family I had now—the people I knew would stick by my side through thick and thin, for better or worse.

"Miss Woodhall?" one of the new recruits asked. She came to stand beside me at the doorway.

"Please, call me Victoria." I smiled.

She nodded, her dark hair pinned underneath a velvet violet hat. She leaned close to me, her voice a whisper. "I heard there's a sorority. A *secret* sorority."

The smile on my face grew.

She went on, "Will we get to join?"

"Of course. It's for anyone willing to fight for what is rightfully ours."

She squealed and jumped up and down, then ran off to tell her friends.

I smiled down at the remnants of scars on my palm. I traced my finger over the deepest one that stood out from the rest and remembered the battle we had won and the pledge I'd made to my sorority. My coven.

We, the Southern Sorority of Superstitious Witches,
will use the craft to help pave the path
for the women of the future,
And the retribution of women past.

A Note to the Reader

When the idea of *The Southern Sorority of Superstitious Witches* first began to take root in the summer of 2023, the United States had just had the one-year anniversary of overturning *Roe v. Wade.* Researchers estimated that maternal mortality rates were 62% higher in states with abortion restrictions than in states with access to abortion. As I write this note now, it is July 2025. The United States just saw steep cuts to Medicaid, estimating that nearly twelve million Americans will lose their health care coverage, rollbacks and removals of Diversity, Equity, and Inclusion initiatives leading to fewer opportunities for people with disabilities and those in minority groups, funding withheld for K–12 education decreasing the available resources and supports for low-income families, and double the amount of ICE raids and detentions leaving families torn apart and invoking a climate of fear.

When I sat down to write this novel, I knew making an "issue" book would be controversial, and it wouldn't be for everyone. However, I firmly believed in our freedom of speech and our right to have a voice. I also believed that there are lessons to be learned from history, as well as hope in those who fought for their rights and ultimately won.

Although *The Southern Sorority of Superstitious Witches* is set in a fictional town and focuses on fictional characters, Lucille, Catherine, Victoria, and the other members of their sorority represent thousands of women who have fought for their rights and freedoms during the 1800s and beyond. Although they may have been slightly altered or dramatized to fit into the narrative, many of the most unbelievable and stomach-churning scenes are based on actual, real-life events experienced by women's rights activists.

One woman of note, who had a significant impact on the conception of this novel, was Lucy Stone. In the summer of 2023, I listened to the podcast *Stuff You Missed in History Class,* and the episode aptly titled "Lucy Stone." Lucy Stone's story immediately enthralled me, especially the first coeducational university in the United States (and the only one at the time) inviting Lucy to be one of only seven women enrolled along with the thirty-four male students. I had known before then that I wanted to write a book that exemplified the many obstacles women faced, both in the past and in the world as it is today. Upon listening to the episode, I knew this inspiring tale would be the premise of my novel.

The episode also discussed Lucy Stone and Henry Blackwell's relationship, the letters they exchanged, and Lucy's insistence on retaining her maiden name after marriage (which challenged tradition and laid the groundwork for future name-change movements). After finishing the episode, I discovered a book titled *Loving Warriors: Selected Letters of Lucy Stone and Henry B. Blackwell, 1853–1893,* edited and introduced by Leslie Wheeler. This book encompasses over 300 pages of letters between the two historical figures, detailing their courtship and marriage. Awed, I immediately knew I had to include an epistolary element. Because of this, many of the letters between my fictional characters, Lucille and Henry, in *The Southern Sorority of Superstitious Witches* include direct quotes inspired by their real-life counterparts, adhering to the same themes and conversations that Lucy Stone and Henry Blackwell wrote in their letters during their courtship.

In another podcast, *American History Tellers: The Fight For Women's Suffrage,* I learned about Christabel Pankhurst, who was spat on, mocked, and even had dead mice thrown at her during a lecture in

Birmingham, England, in the early 1900s, inspiring the scene in *The Southern Sorority of Superstitious Witches* in which Catherine is pelted with dead rats during her speech. The speech is also heavily inspired by Elizabeth Cady Stanton's speech at Seneca Falls on July 19, 1848, which advocated for women's rights and equality.

Alice Paul was another notable inspiration. Alice was arrested while she and several other activists disguised themselves as men and snuck into a government banquet. In jail, she protested by going on a hunger strike. Displeased with her actions, guards strapped her to a chair, wrapped a towel around her neck, and shoved a long glass tube down her nose to force-feed her a mixture of eggs and milk. This inspired the stomach-churning scene in *The Southern Sorority of Superstitious Witches* of Lucille being force-fed while imprisoned.

Victoria Woodhull and Susan B. Anthony also inspired several aspects of this story. Victoria Woodhull gave a speech on the theory of free love in New York. Her beliefs in free love greatly inspired the fictional character of Victoria in *The Southern Sorority of Superstitious Witches.* Susan B. Anthony's and Elizabeth Cady Stanton's newspaper, *The Revolution,* is the namesake and inspiration for the newspaper excerpts in this novel. I collected and read several prints of the real-life newspaper *The Revolution* to accurately imitate its themes, information, and quotes.

Though these certainly aren't all of the women and events that inspired *The Southern Sorority of Superstitious Witches*, and these were certainly not all of the women who have or will fight for our rights, I am proud to have written a book that brings awareness to their stories and sends my readers a message of hope and inspiration to continue to fight for what is right.

Or as Lucille Rockwell once said,

"Let your fear fuel you,
and fight like hell."
—Katie Ortiz

Acknowledgments

Like all good things, this book took the long way here. There were years of querying, waiting, hoping, revising, and trusting the process, but I wouldn't go back and do it any other way.

To my agent, Alexandra D'Amico, thank you for seeing the potential in this story and, just as importantly, the potential in me, and thank you for welcoming me into your coven. Your belief changed everything. To my editors, Melissa Rechter and Katie McGuire, thank you for your guidance, insight, and care for this book at every stage. And to Alcove Press, thank you for giving this story a home and for championing it so wholeheartedly.

To my husband—there are not enough words. Thank you for supporting me through every high and low, being my steady rock when everything else felt far from steady, for believing in me when I doubted myself, picking me back up after every rejection, celebrating every success, no matter how small, and for being my biggest cheerleader from day one. You're my everything.

To my mom, thank you for raising me to be a woman who knows my worth and when to fight for it. To my dad, thank you for showing me how a man should treat his family. To both of you, thank you for raising me to believe I could achieve anything I put my mind to and for being the examples of how to do it.

To Leigh, thank you for saving my purse in the rain and continuing to do so for the past twenty-five years. To Molly, thank you for swapping fortunes with me. To Haley, thank you for letting me run all my ideas by you and helping me refine them to their full potential. To Natalie, thank you for the hours of "homework" sessions at The Coffee Bar that inevitably turned into the best chats. To Laura, thank you for our thrift shopping trips that got me away from my desk long enough to restore my creative energy. To Samantha, thank you for being there for me, always, and being my biggest hype-person. To The Coffee Bar, thank you for providing me with copious amounts of coffee, matcha, and good vibes. To all of you, thank you for forming the most incredible support system I could ask for. You will never know how much it meant to me.

To my writing community, especially Michelle, my query twin, thank you for helping me through the trenches. To Demi, thank you for helping me bring my story to life before anyone else saw its potential. To Ann, thank you for sharing your historian's expertise and insight. And finally, to everyone who read, reviewed, discussed, or touched this book in any way, thank you for helping bring it into the world.

This book exists because of you.